THE
FORTUNES
OF
JADED
WOMEN

THE
FORTUNES
OF
JADED
WOMEN

a novel

CAROLYN HUYNH

ATRIA BOOKS

New York   London   Toronto   Sydney   New Delhi

ATRIA
BOOKS

An Imprint of Simon & Schuster, Inc.
1230 Avenue of the Americas
New York, NY 10020

First Atria Books hardcover edition September 2022

ATRIA BOOKS and colophon are trademarks of Simon & Schuster, Inc.

For information about special discounts for bulk purchases, please contact Simon & Schuster Special Sales at 1-866-506-1949 or business@simonandschuster.com.

The Simon & Schuster Speakers Bureau can bring authors to your live event. For more information or to book an event, contact the Simon & Schuster Speakers Bureau at 1-866-248-3049 or visit our website at www.simonspeakers.com.

Interior design by Hope Herr-Cardillo

Manufactured in China

1   3   5   7   9   10   8   6   4   2

Library of Congress Cataloging-in-Publication Data is available.

ISBN 978-1-9821-8873-3
ISBN 978-1-9821-8875-7 (ebook)

For Mẹ, for teaching me how to tell if it's real jade

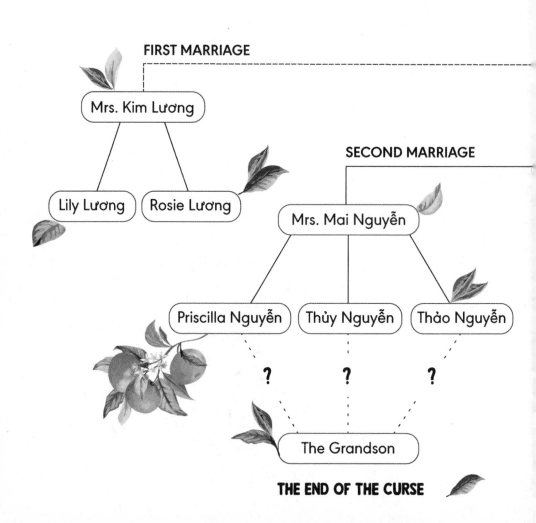

FIRST MARRIAGE

Mrs. Kim Lương

Lily Lương   Rosie Lương

SECOND MARRIAGE

Mrs. Mai Nguyễn

Priscilla Nguyễn   Thủy Nguyễn   Thảo Nguyễn

?   ?   ?

The Grandson

THE END OF THE CURSE

THE CURSE BEGAN

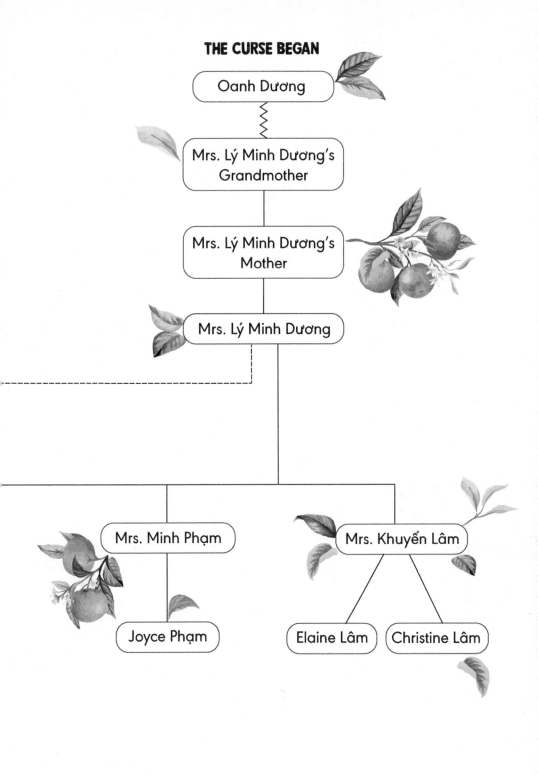

THE
FORTUNES
OF
JADED
WOMEN

1

Oanh Dương

EVERYONE IN ORANGE COUNTY'S Little Saigon knew the Dương sisters were cursed.

They heard that the curse began in Vietnam when Oanh Dương's ex-mother-in-law, Lan Hoàng, had gone north to visit the reclusive witch who lived in Sa Pa, at the foot of the Hoàng Liên Sơn mountains. The trip across the volatile terrain was treacherous; only truly diabolical souls who wanted to inflict generational curses on others would be able to survive. Like all slighted Vietnamese women, Lan Hoàng wished for the type of scarring that would make her wanton daughter-in-law and all her future kin ostracized forever. She just didn't know what that would look like.

The night Lan arrived at the quiet village, she was exhausted. The fickle weather had brought an onslaught of all four seasons within a few days, and she hadn't been as prepared as she thought. The rustling wind had been her enemy one day, and her friend the next. Thankfully, her hired guide had enough shearling to keep her warm for the final leg of her travels. She begged him to take her to see the witch immediately. The more time wasted, the closer Oanh would be to conceiving a child.

The guide dropped Lan off in front of the tiny, all-white stone home at the foot of the mountains, and wished her luck, though he wasn't sure if he meant it. The old man had taken many desperate women—mothers, daughters, and sisters—across the country to visit the witch, but he'd never once stepped foot inside. He knew better than to interrupt the flow of the universe. Only women were brave enough to tempt fate like that.

Like every other French colonial home that lined the dirt road, the house had stone pillars that held up the front, like Atlas holding up the weight of the world. Wild ivy wrapped all the way around them, mirroring hands that held a tight grip on all lost souls who entered. Though the exterior appeared welcoming, the inside looked as if light had never been able to find its way in, no matter how hard it tried.

Lan shivered, suddenly feeling nervous for the first time in her journey. She'd dreamt about this moment for months, and now that she was finally here, she was afraid. Afraid of what she would become if she went through with it. Would she still have a soul after? As she second-guessed her decision, the dilapidated wooden front door squeaked open, expelling a sinful pheromone, tempting Lan inside. The witch's face peeked out from the shadows, and she pushed the door further ajar and beckoned her. The woman was more petite than imagined, and she had a strangeness about her that Lan couldn't place. Though quite angular with her face structure, uncommon for Vietnamese people, the witch's beauty was enhanced by her dark hair that had grown wild every which way. Lan couldn't discern her age; every time she tried to guess, she felt like her eyes were deceiving her.

"You're late." The witch's voice had traces of irritation, but her impish eyes worried Lan the most. She couldn't read the intent behind them, but she could sense the greed, and it exacerbated her nerves. "Hurry up, you're letting the heat out." Lan didn't ask her how she knew she was coming. She didn't want to know more than she should because she was afraid of ghosts and spirits following her home. She was already testing the universe's patience by being there.

Lan timidly entered the house and followed the woman to the back room. Her nose crinkled at the pungent smell that cloaked the room. She spotted a man in the corner, his face hidden behind shadows and a cap. His age was also amorphous. He was busy pounding a gelatinous substance in his mortar. Behind him, stacked glass jars full of questionable liquids and dry herbs teetered back and forth, desperately trying to stay in rhythm with one another to avoid toppling over. He locked eyes with Lan as she passed him by. The bulbous veins on his hands came dangerously close to revealing his real age. She gulped down the bile in her throat, regret once again bubbling up.

"Snake heart," the witch said, as if responding to Lan's thoughts. "Makes men stronger. To produce more sons."

The witch hurried Lan along, past the man, into the windowless back room, and motioned for her to sit on the floor pillows. She took her own place across the circular wooden table, heated up water, and set out some cups. The flimsy table between them was the only thing keeping the gates of hell from opening on Lan, and she prayed that the table would hold the barrier, just a little while longer.

"Why have you come?" the witch asked as she poured tea leaves into a cup, and gently drizzled hot water onto the leaves, allowing the aromatics to open up first.

"My daughter-in-law," Lan said. "She has betrayed her duties. She left my oldest son, her husband, for another man. A *Cambodian* man no less. Claims that she's in *love*. Foolish girl." Lan uttered tut-tuts of heavy disapproval.

"You seek revenge then?"

"Well, no—" Lan stammered, unsure how to say it out loud. "I don't want her *dead*—"

"There are plights worse than death."

"Like what?" she asked nervously.

"Well, malaise can kill you slowly," the witch said. She closed her eyes and allowed the currents to take over her body, so she could see all that was past, present, and what was to come. "Your daughter-in-law is pregnant."

"I *knew* it. That whore. No wonder she left so quickly," Lan seethed through her teeth. Suddenly, her nerves were gone, and she could only see her desire to see Oanh's blood splattered all over this earth. She looked down at her own hands, saw what she was capable of, and it no longer terrified her. "I want her cursed, Auntie. Her and her bastard child."

"It's a boy," the witch said, her eyes still closed. "She carries a son inside of her."

"That should have been *my* grandson," Lan cried out. "That wench doesn't deserve to have love *and* produce a firstborn son. Vietnamese women aren't allowed to have both."

"Then tell me what it is that you want," the witch said slyly, a hint of wicked-ness in her tone. "Believe it or not, I can't read minds."

"I curse Oanh Dương to wander the afterlife alone. Unable to visit her children when she passes. And I curse all her children's children, and all those who follow, to never know love and marry poorly. And as a result, their husbands won't invite Oanh to visit her ancestral altar," Lan said without hesitation.

"I curse her and all the women in her family to never be able to come home."

The witch opened her eyes quickly and stared deep into Lan's as she soaked in her cruel desires. The ivy that wrapped around the outside pillars tightened its grip even further. They both acknowledged the weight of the curse and the significance behind it: Daughters were unable to invite their ancestors into the house without their husbands' permission. And bad husbands only meant that ancestors would be forever blocked from entering.

"Then I curse Oanh Dương to only have daughters," the witch said in a controlled voice. "Those daughters will grow into women, and when those women become mothers, they will only bear daughters. May each daughter carry the weight of their mothers' sins and never escape the cycle."

"Thank you, Auntie," Lan whispered, fearful, yet relieved. She felt powerful in the moment, as if she had transcended the Buddha. Her vindictiveness scared her, but there was no going back now. "What will happen to the son growing inside of her now?"

"Like I said, there are things worse than death."

. . .

A few months later, Oanh Dương suffered a miscarriage. She mourned the loss of what could have been, especially when she realized that she'd been carrying a son. Grief consumed her, but the yearning for motherhood called to her, so the new lovers tried again. This time she was fortunate to carry the baby to term. But when the midwife passed her newborn into Oanh's arms, she had a look of pity on her face.

"You have a beautiful daughter," the midwife said. "She has your eyes."

At first, Oanh tried to mask her disappointment. *Not a son.* But when she looked into the eyes of her daughter, a new emotion surged through her. Her daughter was made entirely in her image. It was the strangest feeling. Staring down at her tiny face, Oanh was reminded of the possibilities and hardships that came with a face like that. Ten little fingers, ten toes, a mop of black hair. And those eyes! So earnest and adventurous, willing to walk barefoot for miles and miles, all for love. Her husband, however, was vocal in his disappointment. His spine stiffened, and there was a hesitation before he finally agreed to hold his daughter in his arms. Oanh told him not to worry. She promised that they'd try again for a son, and that she'd keep going until she produced him an heir.

As the midwife eavesdropped on their conversation, her back turned to them, she knew that Oanh would never conceive a son. But she didn't have the heart to tell her. The midwife had seen curses like this manifest time and time again. Whenever miscarriages for sons happened, followed by the delivery of a firstborn daughter, a witch's work was at play. No shaman, monk, or traveling priest from the Philippines would be able to undo the spell inflicted on Oanh's lineage. All she could do was prepare herself for the type of generational heartbreak that came with daughters because after she passed on, she may never be able to go home.

Because there was nothing wrong with having Vietnamese daughters. It was how the world treated them that turned it into a curse.

THE PREDICTIONS

2

Mrs. Mai Nguyễn

THIRTY YEARS AGO, MAI Nguyễn first heard about the strange, petite Vietnamese woman who lived in the blindingly white, marbled mansion off the Kuhio Highway in Kauai. She heard about her through a friend, and this friend, Mrs. Đào, heard about the woman from Vivi Phạm, the gossip queen of Little Saigon, at one of her infamous karaoke parties. Of course, Vivi had heard from Annie Lau, who heard from *her* mother's best friend's auntie.

Kauai had a secret that only the matriarchs of these families knew about. The word-of-mouth tall tales of this woman had spread faster on the mainland than the whiff of a good discount sale or boasts about whose child got early admission into the college of their choice. Within the small village of the West Coast Asian diasporic scene, from Seattle down to Orange County, gossip was the only true currency that had weight—aside from gold bars, jade with 14-karat gold trimming, and other bits of jewelry that could be easily sewn into linings in times of war.

This woman was known as Auntie Hứa. For over fifty years, the locals would whisper about Auntie Hứa behind her back, too afraid of what she could possibly say to their faces. Could she predict death? Misfortune? Financial ruin? Ever since Auntie Hứa immigrated to Kauai in the seventies, the woman had been going around scaring the crap out of everyone, making off-the-cuff remarks that would send them all into a tailspin. Like that one time she walked into Biên's Bistro in Chinatown and told the owner, Biên, that he would have heart surgery soon. And he did. Though to this day, he's not sure if it was her prediction that kickstarted the heart murmurs. He didn't think to question her. Better safe than sorry when it came to dealing with psychics.

However, to the businessmen who paced in the tallest skyscrapers of Hong Kong, waiting to speak to her before making a final decision, or the aging real estate broker who flew in yearly from South Africa, or the young Instagram-famous backpacker on her spiritual journey, Auntie Hứa was known as Linh Hứa.

The famed Vietnamese psychic of Kauai.

Mrs. Nguyễn sat impatient, twirling her dark jade bracelet on her left wrist, calmed by its coolness. Her mother had taught her that you can tell if jade is real by how cool the stone feels against your skin.

The all-white waiting room that matched the exterior of the mansion had an eeriness to it, making it seem like she was in a psych ward. Mrs. Nguyễn distracted herself by observing the young receptionist, who was also wearing all white, filing her acrylics into a coffin shape. She felt a pang of jealousy at how youthful and pretty the receptionist was, and how her own hair used to be jet black and thick as rope, once upon a time. Mrs. Nguyễn reached up to flatten her thinning gray hair that had wisps of silver peeking out. She shifted her weight and crossed her legs, dangling off her worn penny loafers to allow her sticky feet to breathe a little—a brief respite from the hot Hawaiian sun.

As soon as the clock struck 10:00 a.m., everyone in the waiting room looked up, hopeful that the receptionist would call their name. But the receptionist called out for *Mai Nguyễn*. Mrs. Nguyễn got up rather smugly, putting her shoes back on. She clutched her fake Louis Vuitton bag, along with the two color-coded folders that had been sitting on her lap, and made her way toward the windowless back room.

A chorus of disappointed voices, with accents from all over the world, erupted. Their weary, traveler faces were heavy with jet lag and greasy from the Zippy's breakfast platter they got earlier.

"Blimey, how long are we supposed to wait for this godforsaken woman?"

"How is this woman harder to see than the pope?"

"Kondo wa itsu Auntie San ni aemasuka?"

"I just need five minutes with her! I only have one question! I'll pay extra!"

"Llevo aquí desde las cinco de la mañana!"

Mrs. Nguyễn openly smirked as she walked past them all. Amateurs. *Anyone* who is *anybody* knew that the psychic opened her appointment books only once a year, the day after Lunar New Year. Mrs. Nguyễn had kept the same fixed appointment slot ever since her first visit, those ten some-odd years ago. She had decided to visit the psychic after her sisters and her mother all stopped talking to each other. The silence was bearable at first, but then her three daughters began to leave her, too, scattering to all corners of the world, despite her attempts to keep them close. The more she clawed, the more they pulled away.

Mrs. Nguyễn couldn't help but feel envy, watching her daughters forge their own paths in this world. She had never known what hers was, except what was expected of her: to be a dutiful daughter and mother. But when the ghosts of cackling, gossiping Vietnamese women began haunting her every time she walked past her kitchen, a gnawing pain grew, and she was overcome with a feverish desire to speak with another Vietnamese woman, just to chat about *anything*. That was when she flew in to see Auntie Hứa, a decision fueled by a dangerous mix of loneliness and curiosity to see if the rumors were true about the psychic. Ever since her first visit, she'd never once failed to attend her yearly pilgrimages.

"Chào Cô," Mrs. Nguyễn greeted Auntie Hứa as she entered the white room and quickly closed the door behind her, her smugness evaporating immediately within the woman's presence. Though they'd seen each other once a year for over ten years, they weren't exactly *friends*. Mrs. Nguyễn could never tell if the woman even remembered her. The woman saw so many faces, every day for decades, that it must all seem like a blur to her. Just a sea of heartbroken faces, seeking remedies and answers for things that had no earthly cure.

Auntie Hứa nodded silently in response behind her big, marbled desk, her heavy makeup cracking under the fluorescent bulb. Her face was caked with white powder, as if she were a vintage Hong Kong ad selling face cream. The makeup was done up so badly it seemed intentional, to trick observers, to disguise her real age.

In a show of faith that the woman recognized Mrs. Nguyễn as a repeat client, she took out a box of tissues. She gestured for Mrs. Nguyễn to sit across from her before pulling out a standard fifty-two-card deck of playing cards. Within the spades, hearts, clubs, and diamonds, Auntie Hứa was able to translate the language of the universe out of something so comically ordinary. Her delicate hands swiftly fanned out the cards in a half-moon shape, facing up. Putting on a show to put guests at ease. As if they expected the woman to have some sort of physical object in front of her, a crystal ball, tarot cards, or I Ching sticks. Without looking down, the woman began speaking in Vietnamese.

"You haven't been sleeping well these days," she addressed Mrs. Mai Nguyễn of Garden Grove, Orange County, age sixty-five, the oldest of three sisters, and mother to three daughters. "Your wrinkles are getting worse, and the grays in your hair are multiplying quickly. At your age, you need to sleep more. Enjoy what is left of your life. Maybe try meditating every once in a while."

"Trời ơi, how can I sleep, Auntie? I have demons knocking at my door every night," Mrs. Nguyễn responded in Vietnamese. She felt her body preparing to unload everything that worried her. She *was* going to get her paid hour's worth of information, even if she had to squeeze out every drop from every pore of the woman, shake down the angels, and corner the Devil herself.

"You still haven't spoken to your sisters or your mother. It's been over ten years," the woman said, giving her a raised eyebrow. She seemed exasperated, once again, watching another client of hers not heeding any of her advice. Humans were stubborn, and Vietnamese women were the most stubborn of them all.

Mrs. Nguyễn scoffed. "I'll speak to them *when* I get my apology."

"Tsk, tsk." The woman shook her head. "Careful, Chị, this might be the year you lose everything. Apologies don't mean anything when it's too late."

Mrs. Nguyễn waved off her empty threat. "I've been cursed with three daughters. I suffer enough as it is."

"We are all cursed, Chị, ever since we've been forced to leave our homeland." The woman flipped over a few cards aimlessly. "Why don't you try opening yourself up to love? There is a man willing to come into the role of your life partner. He's a good man. Love *can* happen for you if you allow it."

Mrs. Nguyễn looked confused, not registering what she had just said. *Love?* For *her?* Once Auntie's words sank in, she howled with genuine laughter, and shook off the prediction like it was an annoying fruit fly. "If he's kind, that means he's *poor.* You think I have time for *love?* I'm too old. Besides, I already have an ex-husband who is deep in debt. I don't need to add on another headache. Life is already full of suffering."

Auntie Hứa opened her mouth to protest, but slowly closed it. Her face gave nothing away.

Mrs. Nguyễn then took out the two folders she brought in, and slid the bottom file across the desk. The woman opened the folder, and out fell three photos of women. Each one had a stapled photo of a man paired with it. The photos of the women were crystal clear, while the men's looked like Facebook profile photos that appeared on a web browser, were captured as grainy snapshots through an iPad camera, and *then* printed out.

Classic signs of a tech-illiterate Asian mother with a social media stalking mission.

"My love life is over. It never even began. Focus on my daughters' love lives instead of mine."

Auntie picked up the first photo and focused on the face of a beautiful Vietnamese American woman in her mid-thirties, whose eyes seemed emptier than the usual heartbroken travelers she had been accustomed to seeing stumbling throughout the Hawaiian Islands. It was clear that this woman had been born with sad eyes.

"Your oldest daughter."

"Yes, Priscilla."

"She works with computers. She's done well for herself in this life, and will continue to do so into the next life as well," the woman observed. She felt Priscilla's hands at a keyboard, coding away late at night. She could also feel Priscilla's early-onset arthritis setting in around age fifty, but refrained from saying it. She might be psychic, but she wasn't suicidal.

"Priscilla made her first million at the age of twenty-five," Mrs. Nguyễn said proudly. She raised her voice louder, just in case the woman didn't hear her properly. "A *million* dollars, Auntie!" She never stopped bragging about her children, despite all the stress they caused her over the years. It was innate in her, like a wild beast in the forest stalking their prey. "Priscilla *just* bought a house next to MacKenzie Scott, Jeff Bezos's ex-wife in Seattle. You know Jeff *BEZOS?* The *BALD* one? I paid for all her school in cash—all *CASH!* UCLA! Wharton! She came out debt free, thanks to *me,* but really—"

As Mrs. Nguyễn kept warbling on and on about her oldest daughter's perfect, shiny résumé, the woman paid no attention to her and continued staring at the photo, feeling very sorry for the woman with the empty eyes. Priscilla Nguyễn didn't know who she was. Auntie Hứa was used to all the Asian mothers who came before her, boasting about their children, but the mothers never seemed to learn their lessons, no matter what she told them. The woman closed her eyes and gave permission to the spirits to use her body as their vessel. Mrs. Nguyễn's voice was soon nothing more than a distant haze, and the woman was instantly transported into a memory. She saw a young Mai Nguyễn, pregnant with what seemed to be her third child. They were in a house, a bit dilapidated, each room packed to the brim with babies, and several other Vietnamese families, crammed into a tiny shared space. The woman guessed that the other two young mothers were the younger sisters of Mai Nguyễn, who also seemed to have their own baby girls. Outside the window on the second floor, a towering kumquat tree stood next to a bountiful orange tree, both groaning with the weight of all the plump fruit they had produced. Though the outside looked idyllic, the inside of the house was far from the promise of the American dream.

"Never marry a Vietnamese man!" Mai screamed as she threw an empty glass bottle at her husband, and she turned to her two young daughters, who cowered in fear, unsure of which parent to fear more. One of those crying little girls was a young Priscilla. "You should marry French men. Make half-Asian babies who will grow up to be beautiful. Never marry a man like your father!" She grabbed each of her two girls' hands and pulled them closer, her breath searing their skins with her warning. "Never, *ever* get married to a poor man."

The woman was instantly carried back to the present, leaving behind the memory of a young, pregnant Mai and her two daughters. As the clouds in Auntie's eyes disappeared, Mrs. Nguyễn's voice broke through the fog. She had moved on to boasting about her other two children. "—and Thủy, my second oldest, she's John Cho's dermatologist in Beverly Hills! You know *JOHN CHO*, Auntie? I wonder how much he makes a year. Oh, and my youngest daughter, Thảo, graduated with her MBA from Harvard and already has opened up her own clothing line in Vietnam. I'm worried she's partying too much in Sài Gòn—"

The woman lifted her hand to silence Mrs. Nguyễn, as a headache pierced through her suddenly. She always got migraines when she was transported into memories, especially the kind of memories that reminded her of the lasting hardships of the diaspora. Though this wasn't the darkest memory she had seen in her lifetime, it still made her ill, because in those moments, she was Mai Nguyễn, and Mai Nguyễn was her. Two Vietnamese women who were still enduring, who were battling a different kind of war, despite surviving one. But now she couldn't tell if her headache was caused by Mrs. Nguyễn's shrill voice. She rubbed her left temple gently before beginning.

"The man attached to your oldest daughter"—she flipped to the photo of a redheaded, freckled man stapled to the back of Priscilla's photo and shook her head—"Bad man, bad love. He does not care for what is behind her eyes, only for the way her eyes are shaped. He only desires Asian women. Your daughter lives in sadness; she makes decisions based on her sadness. Like you did, when you were young." Before Mrs. Nguyễn could protest, the woman flipped to the photo of Thủy, the second-oldest daughter, and to the photo of the man next to hers, who was Vietnamese American. "He loves her, maybe too much. I do not know if she loves him back the same. She is the most responsible daughter, out of the three, but the one that lives without joy. This year, she will try to find that joy." Then she flipped to the third photo of the youngest daughter, Thảo, and stapled to the back of her photo was a photo of a young man who was covered in tattoos. They seemed to be partying together on a rooftop in Sài Gòn, and she laughed off this photo. "This man is nothing. He'll always be gone by sunrise. Not serious. She is not serious about life, either, but she wants to be. A man will soon enter her life, and she will want to be serious about life because of him. Be careful, Chị, she is the most selfish daughter, and she keeps to herself. Secrets surround her. But she will grow to be your wealthiest daughter."

Mrs. Nguyễn started tearing up. "Do you think my daughters are all unhappy?" she whispered, scared to hear the answer out loud.

"Yes, Chị," the woman responded firmly. "Your whole family has sad eyes. Your daughters, your sisters, and your mother. Especially your mother. You all have been fighting for too long. Fight over everything. The house, money, who deserves what, who owes what, what to do, what not to do."

"I don't know how to fix them. I've never known."

"That's because you are the unhappiest out of all of them."

Mrs. Nguyễn pushed her feet out of her loafers, digging them into the velvet plush carpet, hoping a black hole would open up so she could disappear into it forever. She suddenly felt very tired. Tired and guilty. Was she a bad mother? She thought about her own marriage in the moment, and how it had been a marriage of convenience between two immigrants who couldn't speak English.

It had always been about survival for Mai. Love and romance were reserved for the privileged.

"They're not going to marry these men, though, right? Right, Auntie?" Mrs. Nguyễn asked, her Asian motherly instincts kicking in. Even if the whole world thought she was a bad mother, she had to keep going. She couldn't allow her daughters to end up like her. Bad husbands would eternally trap them behind their sad eyes. She tapped at the photo of her second-oldest daughter and her boyfriend, Andy. "That man makes sixty thousand dollars a year! Sixty thousand dollars! Do you think *John Cho* makes sixty thousand dollars a year? Why on earth would he choose to go to Stanford then if he was just going to end up helping *children* for *free*? How can he possibly afford to pay California property taxes on that salary!"

The woman sighed heavily, watching Mrs. Nguyễn shift back into meltdown mode, for the tenth year in a row. She continued to rant about how these men in her daughters' lives were a threat to her empire—like a single flick to a domino that would lead to an irreversible cascading effect. Mrs. Nguyễn droned on and on about how she was about to reach retirement, had suffered through menopause silently like the typical south Vietnamese woman that she was, and was in no mood to adjust her will one day to include any of her daughters' unfortunate love interests, all of whom she *affectionately* referred to as chó. (Dogs. She was calling them dogs.)

"Chị, I really don't think this man is as bad as you say—" the woman tried to interject.

"And *look* at Priscilla's boyfriend!" Mrs. Nguyễn hissed back at her, continuing on, as she grabbed the tissue box that had been placed out earlier. "A người da trắng! You know how white men are! Do you know how many Asian women there are on this planet? He's just going to go around, sleeping with all of them! And don't *even* get me started on Thảo. She is probably sleeping with every man in Sài Gòn. White, Black, British, Korean, Australian, German, who knows what scene she hangs out with, always talking about expats and business! She's chowing down on the whole United Nations buffet over there!"

The woman waited patiently for Mrs. Nguyễn to run out of breath. When she finally calmed down, the fear and anxiety exposed themselves through her motherly eyes, and Auntie Hứa was finally able to speak. "What is it that you really want to know, Chị?"

Mrs. Nguyễn sniffled through her tears and dabbed her eyes. "I just want to know that if I were to die tomorrow, would my daughters be okay? Will they be loved for who they are? Will they have children one day? Will they be financially okay? Will I be able to rest peacefully in the next life because *they* are at peace? Will I be able to come visit them at my ancestral altar because they married well?"

The woman, in a moment of tenderness, reached over the table and took Mrs. Nguyễn's fragile hand into hers. "You need to let life unfold as it is meant to."

"So, what? Just *relax*? Allow them to marry these hideous toads?" Mrs. Nguyễn asked, her pitch rising an octave, like a small child asking their parents if they could have something sweet before dinner.

The psychic closed her eyes again, giving permission to allow the currents to flow through her body. She hummed along as best as she could, waiting to see, to receive, and to be. And she saw it all. She saw the lives of all these women unfold before her, for the next year and more. Every thread that linked together, weaving their stories, their heartbreak, their grief, their future husbands, their future children. She saw it all—including Mrs. Nguyễn's future. When she opened her eyes, there was the faintest trace of a smirk.

"Like I said earlier, Chị. This is the year where if you are not careful, you could stand to lose it all. There will be one pregnancy, one funeral, and one marriage. A complete turn around the sun by the next Lunar year. But you must fix your relationship with everyone. And I mean *everyone* in your family. Starting with your daughters."

Mrs. Nguyễn almost fainted out of her chair when she heard this, but the woman quickly jumped up, reached over the table, and steadied her, surprisingly spry despite her untraceable age. "Trời ơi. You're telling me that one of them will get *married*? And one will get *pregnant*? Will the death be mine because I died from heartbreak witnessing this?" Mrs. Nguyễn whispered, her mind spiraling.

The woman patted Mrs. Nguyễn on the back, and gave a soft, sympathetic smile. "I think maybe now is the year you reach out to your sisters and mother again. *All* your sisters."

The color drained from Mrs. Nguyễn's face instantly, and she felt her soul sink, all the way down to her penny loafers. She opened her mouth wide and bawled, accepting the tissue offered to her. Mid-bawl, Mrs. Nguyễn did a quick check to see how she was doing on time. Without even opening the second folder, Auntie Hứa told her that June was the best month to invest in gold and to invest in two Chinese Tesla-competitors for self-driving cars.

She cried even louder in gratitude, "Cảm ơn Cô Hứa."

As a tearful Mrs. Nguyễn gave Auntie Hứa two good-bye kisses on her cheeks, the psychic whispered one final, last-minute prediction into her ear. "Your grandchild will be a boy." And she squeezed her arm in reassurance. Mrs. Nguyễn's eyes widened. There was no need for Auntie Hứa to elaborate. Because it was the type of prediction that she had been waiting to come true her whole life, the type that had always been out of reach for her mother's mother, her mother, for herself, and for her sisters. It was a prediction that could break the type of generational curses that often followed Vietnamese women to their graves and into their next life. A son to a Vietnamese mother meant good fortune, and that ancestral spirits were allowed to come home.

And they'd all been away from their homeland for nearly a century. Mrs. Nguyễn's memories of home had begun to fade as the years had gone on.

She dabbed her eyes, stuffed her two folders into her fake Louis Vuitton handbag, and thanked the woman again. And she walked out of that windowless room without realizing it would be the last time she'd ever lay eyes on Auntie Hứa and visit the island of Kauai.

On her return trip home, Mrs. Nguyễn sat ruminating at the airport lounge, thinking about everything Auntie Hứa said about making amends. She twirled her jade bracelet. Mrs. Nguyễn picked up her phone and waffled over who she was going to call first: The middle or the youngest? She decided to play it safe and go for the middle sister, the forgotten one, the former mediator of the family. She was too scared to call the *other* one. The good thing about the middle child was their reliability. So, she dialed Minh. Known as Minh Dương growing up, but now known as Mrs. Minh Phạm of Garden Grove, Orange County, California, age sixty-three, the middle child out of the three Dương sisters, and a mother to one daughter. Minh picked up almost immediately. *Reliability.* The most important thing you look for in your first commanding officer.

For the first time in ten years, she heard her sister's voice.

3

Priscilla Nguyễn

PRISCILLA NGUYỄN HAD ALWAYS relied on numbers as the source of truth in the universe. While her mother turned to her ancestral altar, psychics, and old Vietnamese tall tales to guide her through life, Priscilla turned to immutable truths like finding comfort in knowing that pi is infinite, and that three points make a data set.

Priscilla stared listlessly out the window in her corner office, facing South Lake Union, when she heard the notification reminder go off on her phone. Dinner reservations tonight with Mark at a Thai restaurant in downtown Bellevue. She hated going across the bridge to the other side of the city, but Mark loved going to the Eastside. "You *know* there's better Asian food over there than in Seattle." Priscilla smiled through her teeth whenever he said that. It was the same disarming smile she'd given in all the VC boardrooms she'd attended the past year to raise money for her start-up. It was a neutral smile. A smile that always played it safe.

There was a knock at the door, and in walked Grace, her executive assistant. "Hey, Pris? Do you have a second?"

"Yeah, what's up?" Priscilla responded, still not tearing her eyes away from her window. She was watching the boats sail by, wondering where they were all heading.

"Two things. First, the new AI research intern started today, Lily. Lily Lương from University of Washington. Aren't you two related somehow? I think that came up as a topic of conversation during her interview rounds."

Priscilla looked up curiously. "Yeah, she's kind of family. A distant cousin, half cousin, or *something*. It's a bit awkward, that whole situation. Just make sure she's settled for the summer, okay? What's the second thing?"

"Don't shoot the messenger, but your mother left ten messages for you."

"My . . . mother?" she asked blankly as if she needed another confirmation. She fully turned her body away from the window and stared at Grace.

Grace nodded. "I don't mean to pry, but when's the last time you two talked? She sounded frantic over the phone."

Priscilla opened her mouth, then quickly closed it as she realized she didn't know the answer. Numbers, dates, events, timelines flew through her mind like a split-flap display.

"I think it may have been a year," she responded softly so that Grace couldn't hear. She was torn between feeling shame, shock, and relief. "What did she want?"

Grace paused and nervously read off several Post-it notes, each message getting increasingly worse. "She kept asking if you were dead. Said that you're an ungrateful daughter for not calling her back this whole time. *Then* she left another message to stop wearing flip-flops because it will cause cancer. *Then* she called again, telling you not to end up with Mark because you're going to regret it for the rest of your life . . . There's quite a few messages left, if you want me to continue reading them all out for you . . ." Grace's voice trailed off as she waved the notes like a white flag, hoping not to get caught between two warring countries.

Priscilla's skin prickled at the last message. She remembered why they hadn't spoken in almost a year. She was sick and tired of hearing about her mother's disapproval of Mark; it only made her want to get married to him even more, to prove her wrong. She sighed, and stared back out at the water, pretending that she was on the beaches of Bali instead. It was always a fight with her mother. Never once did she hear how proud her mother was or that she loved her.

"Did you tell her I've been in meetings all morning?" Priscilla asked in a robotic voice, her oldest-Asian-daughter instincts taking over despite how much she had fought against them her whole life.

"I took a screenshot of your calendar and texted it to her because she wanted proof, but then she'd call back during every gap in between," Grace paused. "She sounded serious. Like it was an emergency?"

"It's *always* an emergency with her," Priscilla muttered, wanting to scream into a pillow. She shuddered, remembering flashbacks from her childhood when her mother would get into verbal fights at the grocery store because they refused to accept her stack of expired coupons, and she wanted Priscilla to explain in English that they had an obligation to take the coupons—because it was an *emergency*.

The last time they had spoken, they had a screaming match at her mother's house down in Orange County. The kitchen island was the only line of defense between the two stubborn women with the same eyes, the same thick hair. Her mother chopped fruit furiously while Priscilla paced back and forth, on her third glass of red wine. Behind them, the sound of a historical romance Chinese soap blared from an old television with foil wrapped around the antennae.

They were arguing over the same subject: Mark. Priscilla's three degrees against her mother, who barely graduated high school. She attempted to fight back with her third-grade-level Vietnamese, feeling reduced to a child again.

"Why are you living with that white man?" her mother yelled at her. "You know he's no good for you."

"You don't know anything about Mark. You don't know what he's like. All my life, you've been dictating my love life. I can't date Vietnamese, I can't date white, I can't date Black, I can't date poor, I can't date old, I can't date anyone according to you, *yet* you still miraculously want me to get married and have children." Priscilla's voice raised to a dangerous octave. "Mark is a *good* man. We support one another. He understands what I do for a living, and I understand what he does for a living. We *love* each other."

"Don't be stupid. There is no such thing as love in a marriage!" her mother snapped back. "Our family is cursed. Cursed for giving me such a stupid daughter."

"I'm not you, Mẹ. Thank god I'm not *you*." Priscilla's words got uglier, but she wasn't able to stop herself. She took another gulp of wine, feeling it dribble down her chin, completing her villain origin story. Her teeth felt stained, her head was woozy, but in her drunken state, she possessed an infallible desire to wound her mother. "The only curse here is being stuck with you for a mother."

There was a loud clattering. Her mother had dropped the fruit plate, but her face remained stoic. She made no move to clean up the fallen fruit. Priscilla waited for her to *say* something, to *do* something. But her mother silently turned toward the stove to blanch the pork belly, and she knew her mother would never apologize. Priscilla slammed her glass down on the counter, accidentally shattering it, red wine spilling over the black-and-white-tiled floor. Priscilla instinctively stepped forward to apologize first, as she always did. She then heard a sickening crunch, and pain jolted through her leg. She looked down. Glass shards. Priscilla saw the rest of the mess in the kitchen. Combined with the fruit stains, her blood and the wine were indistinguishable. An estuary. But unlike the river meeting the sea, she and her mother would never meet in the middle.

She looked up to catch a Chinese couple kissing in the rain on the television, set to the sounds of a guzheng, with her mother's back still turned to her. Feeling numb to the cut in her foot, and in her heart, she swallowed her apology.

Priscilla turned and ran out of the house, feeling a panic attack coming on. As she paced up and down the driveway, she took out her phone and called Mark, who picked up immediately. Her chest tightened, and she felt relief. Mark was her pillar. If only her mother could see these little moments with Mark. She sobbed into the phone, explaining everything that had happened. Being able to talk in English was comforting at that moment. It felt freeing. It felt like herself, and not like her mother's version of her: Priscilla Nguyễn, firstborn daughter, UCLA, Wharton, CEO of her own start-up. Mark didn't interrupt, tell her to calm down, or give poor advice on how to handle the situation. He just silently bought her ticket back to Seattle for the next available flight. To him, she was Priscilla Nguyễn: someone who had to learn to wear different masks depending on the audience, and he still loved her despite witnessing them all.

It'd been a year since that moment between her mother and her.

"Priscilla?" Grace asked gently, jolting her back to the present moment. "Do you want me to pass along a message to your mother?"

Priscilla sighed. She didn't want to engage in another *emergency*. She was too tired to fight. She'd get around to calling her mother back eventually. One day.

"No."

. . .

Mark and Priscilla arrived at the restaurant in separate Teslas. She had left work early to beat traffic to the Eastside. He texted saying that he'd be late; he was stuck at work dealing with a fire drill for some bad code they had released into production.

After thirty minutes, and fending off a stressed-out waiter, Priscilla sent another text asking where he was. When he didn't respond, her mind began to wander to him getting fired by Bezos himself, or perhaps he'd gotten into a horrible accident on the freeway. She checked the app to see if there were any crashes that caused a pileup, and saw that everything was orderly.

Mark arrived an hour late. He breezed in, cheeks flushed from the cold that bombarded his exposed face. He had a boyish smile plastered on. Priscilla hadn't seen this smile in a long time, not since their early years together. He took off his coat, removed his hat, revealing his signature ginger hair, planted a kiss on Priscilla's cheek, and sat down as if everything was *just fine*.

Priscilla tried to refrain from raising her voice. He didn't even apologize. "You're an hour late. Why didn't you respond to my text?"

"You knew I had to stay late for work." His thick British accent coated his excuse like taffy. He barely glanced at the menu, before he turned around to flag down a waitress, not checking to see if Priscilla was ready to order. "When I saw your message, I was driving."

"*Right*. But I've been sitting at this table for over an hour," Priscilla said in an overly saccharine voice, doing that thing with her smile again. She didn't ask why he just didn't do voice text. She held back. She couldn't afford to fight with Mark at this stage in their relationship; they'd been together for well over three years at this point. And ever since Priscilla and her mother stopped speaking to each other, an unfortunate side effect was losing touch with her two younger sisters as well. Mark was all she had left. Somewhere along the way, Priscilla had become desperate for Mark not to abandon her, too.

"You know how bad Seattle traffic is, especially from South Lake Union to the Eastside! Mercer Street is absolutely murder." He laughed it off, and Priscilla forced herself to laugh, too, because she knew he wasn't going to give her the apology she wanted.

A young Thai waitress arrived at their table and asked if they were ready to order.

"How spicy can you make the khao soi?" Mark asked as he looked her up and down casually. Priscilla caught a glint in his eyes and she flinched. She braced for what was about to come next.

"Five stars."

"Make it six," Mark winked at her. "*Olympian* levels of spiciness."

"Are you *sure*?" The waitress raised her eyebrow and eyed Mark's skin, suspicious of any white man who tried to prove their toughness with their spice palate.

"Are you *from* Thailand? Like were you born *there*?" Mark asked her, rerouting her suspicions back to her, as if her authority was suddenly the one that needed to be questioned. "Or were you born *here*?"

Priscilla almost kicked him under the table. But her secondhand embarrassment had a hold on her, and she felt frozen in the moment. Like her legs were trapped between rocks, and the water around her kept rising every time she struggled to break free. The water was at neck level when it came to Mark these days, and she was afraid that if she continued to struggle, she'd have no other option but to allow the ocean to swallow her whole. In the darkest corner of her heart, a part of her was ready to disappear into the black water forever, especially when he did things like this. She felt utterly alone, even when someone was right in front of her.

"I've been living here since I was three," the young waitress said as she put her hand on her hip, staring down at Mark incredulously. "My family is from Ratchaburi."

"Ah! *Ratchaburi!*" Mark exclaimed, his suspicions turning into relief after finding common ground between them, as if he, too, was from Ratchaburi. "I lived in Bangkok after I graduated from uni. Best years of my life. Who'd have thought a young boy from the Sheffield countryside, who lived among the sheep, would wind up in southeast Asia, living among the elephants?"

The waitress's eyes glazed over, tired of all the white men proclaiming their love for southeast Asia, as if it were their little secret. She turned toward Priscilla and asked her what she wanted to eat. Priscilla, feeling self-conscious, simply ordered the pad see ew with tofu, two and a half stars. She could feel Mark's eyes bore into hers.

"I swear, I'm more Asian than my girlfriend sometimes," Mark said jokingly, handing the menu to the waitress.

The waitress gave Priscilla a look before shooting Mark a placating smile, then walked away. Priscilla shivered, and she felt her anxiety unleash and run down her, all the way to her red-bottomed heels. She could have sworn that the waitress had given her a judgmental look. Or a look of pity—the type of pity that screamed, *Why would you settle for such mediocrity?*

Priscilla didn't have an answer. Just like how she didn't have an answer for her mother. These women didn't know what went on behind closed doors. She *needed* Mark.

She had no one else in her life.

"I have to use the loo," Mark said. "I'll be right back." When he got up, he planted another sloppy kiss on Priscilla's head, feeling his lips against her thick, black hair. She flashed him the same neutral smile she'd given him for the past three years of their relationship. She glanced around the restaurant, counting all the Asian women there with their white boyfriends, and felt that same guilty, uncomfortable feeling creep up on her again.

She didn't have an answer for the waitress, her mother, or for herself.

Mark's cell phone *dinged* several times and lit up. She ignored it, but then it kept going off. As she reached over to silence it, she noticed that the notifications were from the same person. She picked it up curiously, and her heart stopped when she saw the Asian last name: Maggie Chen. As she read the clipped messages on the home screen, her hands began to shake, and she felt her family's curse rear its ugly head again at her. Her body turned cold. Here was definitive proof that the numbers Priscilla ran on their relationship were off. Not by a little, but by a lot.

Thx for staying behind and getting that drink with me, Marky.

I swear ur like the only cool person on our team.

U like get me, u know?

Anyways, it was fun getting those drinks.

we should do it again sometime.

Maybe even dinnnnerrr??? ;) xoxo

Mark loved Asian women. Priscilla had always known this; she just never wanted to admit it. When he recounted his dating history when they first met, his body count consisted of Chinese, Japanese, Korean, Vietnamese, Filipina, and Thai women. And she intuitively understood he was lukewarm about Asian women who had a second part to their identity, deeming them a bit more *difficult*. Especially the American ones. But she had overlooked it all because she'd been desperate for a life where she could blend in. She was tired of being someone who made other people uncomfortable whenever they asked about her family or what her plans were for Mother's Day. She just simply wanted to throw dinner parties, order bottomless mimosas at brunch, and have weekend getaways. But the more she pretended to have that life with Mark, the more it became an unreachable narrative.

Because it wasn't in the cards for her to have a normal life.

This was the moment where Priscilla knew she had to find the strength to pivot from this relationship. She was treading on dangerous territory of ending up just like her mother, when she had worked her entire life to avoid that outcome. Priscilla had done everything right, ran every possible simulation, just to make sure she didn't end up in this exact one, sitting here alone in a crowded restaurant, reading flirty messages from a younger Asian woman on her white partner's phone.

Priscilla laughed hollowly, Mark's phone still in her hand. She continued torturing herself, reading Maggie Chen's messages over and over again, imagining what she looked like. Young, supple, optimistic, gorgeous, slender, but most of all . . . *uncomplicated*. The durian really didn't fall far from the tree, did it? Her parents' marriage ruined her mother's life, which ruined her three daughters' lives, and in turn, ruined their ability to attach themselves to the safe kind of love that was hard to see through cursed eyes. Priscilla did some quick calculations, and based on her age, her career growth, and her strong desire to have a biological family soon, she knew that if she left Mark now, the chances for marriage were slim and she'd end up sexless in Seattle once again. She'd become nothing more than a *difficult* woman who was past her prime.

Priscilla put the phone back exactly where it was before. She pasted on that same smile, as if nothing was bothering her. Like when men would creepily stare at her and say "Ni hao?" to her on the street. She didn't flinch, yell, scream, or tell them what she really thought. *"I'm not Chinese, asshole. And also, fuck off."* She didn't say anything. She *never* said anything. Because everything was perfectly fine.

That night, Priscilla slept with Mark. Much to Mark's surprise and delight, she got on top. As soon as Mark finished, he rolled over, and soon his soft snoring was the only thing keeping her company. Priscilla lay there naked, staring at the ceiling. And she quietly began to count as many numbers as she could remember in pi, hoping to reach infinity.

4

Mrs. Nguyễn, Mrs. Phạm, Mrs. Lâm

MRS. MINH PHẠM WAS EITHER early or always on time, depending on who you asked. For their meeting, she chose a table near the exit. She knew the layout of the dim sum restaurant well and was close with the waitstaff, so if any physical altercation happened, she'd be able to have at least *some* backup. When she slipped them a little extra money, she alluded that there could be a small, tiny, *little* shouting match, with a propensity for small, tiny, *little* objects to be thrown through the air. Mrs. Minh Phạm—having grown up as Minh Dương, the second-oldest daughter—had always known her role in the family. She was the middle child. The mediator. Mediators always needed to have a contingency plan in case things went south, as they tend to do when the Dương women gathered. Which is why her car was strategically parked outside the exit door just in case she needed a quick getaway to safety. *Just in case.*

A steaming pot of jasmine tea was placed in front of her with some fried dumplings. Mrs. Phạm poured a cup, and without waiting for it to cool down, she slurped the scalding hot liquid like a zebra at the watering hole, with alert eyes on the lookout for a predator. A predator named Mai Nguyễn. She then wolfed down a dumpling, the hot mochi sticking to her gums, and she savored every bite as she reached for another and then another. Oh Buddha, how she *loved* food. She scanned around for a last-minute inspection, and decided it was best to remove any sharp objects from Mai's place setting. She quickly grabbed the upside-down teacup across from hers and hid it out of view. Mai had a *reputation* for throwing things. Like that time in the eighties, when Mai grabbed an old man's cane at T&K Food Market just to throw it at another old man who tried to take the last bag of rice. Mrs. Phạm also took away the spoon that was next to the teacup. And then the pair of chopsticks. After realizing her efforts still weren't childproof enough, she flagged down a waiter and requested plastic utensils and paper plates to replace everything. Mrs. Phạm suspected that this wouldn't end well, especially since she had a surprise waiting for Mai. And if there was one thing that she knew about her oldest sister, it was that Mai *hated* surprises more than bad husbands.

Mai entered the restaurant, carrying boxes of oranges in her arms. The two sisters locked eyes, nodded in acknowledgment, and Mai shuffled her way over in her signature penny loafers. Her trademark fake Louis Vuitton bag accidentally whacked people on the head along the way. She passed the dark red brocade curtain panels, expertly weaving through the Vietnamese and Chinese women pushing their dim sum carts around, shouting as if they were on the trading floor, calling out to sell steamed plates of siu mai, gai lan, congee, chicken feet, and bean curd skin rolls.

Mrs. Phạm felt shocked by her oldest sister's appearance. Her hair was fully gray, her face was framed by wisps of silver and white, and her back was slightly hunched forward, as all Asian women's bodies tend to curl when they reach a certain age, like flowers that start to wilt when the air begins to drop.

Maybe Mai had become humbler. Maybe she wasn't the same person she had been ten years ago, the person who blamed them all for how miserable her life turned out. Maybe she had called to make amends and spend the golden years of her life with her family again. Mrs. Phạm had hope.

"Minh," Mai greeted her as she reached the round table where Mrs. Phạm sat, and placed the boxes of oranges down. There was an awkward silence where they weren't sure if they should hug it out or not, but both came to the immediate conclusion that that wasn't necessary. It wasn't the Vietnamese way to be awkward. Or to hug. Mai pulled out a chair and sat down, taking in Mrs. Phạm's appearance just like she had done before. She swallowed, likely holding back an insult about Mrs. Phạm's weight gain, and gestured toward the oranges. "A peace offering."

"You look good," Mrs. Phạm said sincerely, as she poured some jasmine tea into a paper cup for Mai. She noticed Mai was twirling the jade bracelet on her wrist, and she knew right away that she was nervous. Mai's strange tick started the day they got on that plane from the refugee camps in Malaysia to America; she hadn't stopped fidgeting with her bracelet since. Even though it'd been ten years since they'd spoken, and Mrs. Phạm's memory had begun to deteriorate, the unspoken language between sisters never needed to be translated. Even if they were always on the brink of war—either with outside forces or with each other.

Mai snorted. "Don't lie to me, Minh. I have a mirror. I know what I look like. I see time hasn't been kind to you, either."

"What do you mean? You've always been jealous of me because you know I was born with taut skin," Mrs. Phạm responded, offended, her hopefulness in their reunion quickly dissipated. She should have known better than to trust that Mai would be altruistic when she reached out. Suddenly, all bets were off for any immediate truce.

"The only taut thing about you are your purse strings," Mai said roughly, her bullying instincts kicking in. She just *couldn't* help herself, even after all these years.

"Here we go! It's always *money, money, money* with you, isn't it? Some things always remain steadfast in history. Like arrogant men who start wars—and your attitude," Mrs. Phạm snapped back. Barely three minutes into their meeting, and they were ready to enter the ring.

"Ten years, Minh! Trời ơi Minh ơi, it's been ten years!" Mai said, wagging her finger at her. "That house belongs to *me*."

Mrs. Phạm threw her hands in the air in defeat. She was never able to handle a fight with Mai. She could hold her ground in these fights, but eventually she was always the first to succumb. "That was Mẹ's final decision on the house. That house didn't belong to you, it belonged to—"

"Don't you *dare* say her name in front of me! I can't believe you're still defending our mother *and* that *other* woman."

"She's our *mother*, and that *other* woman happens to be family by blood, even if you refuse to acknowledge it. What's wrong with you? She's suffered enough—"

Mai's face quickly lost oxygen. One fat vein began throbbing on the side of her neck; it was Mai's lighthouse warning in a storm. Mrs. Phạm immediately recognized these signs, and stopped talking. She braced herself against the table, readying herself to hide underneath it, in case the San Andreas Fault, otherwise known as Mrs. Mai Nguyễn, would erupt on the scene. Mrs. Phạm immediately reached over the table to remove the paper cup full of hot tea.

"*Don't* you *dare* lecture me on suffering—" Mai began, her eyes almost bulging out of her sockets.

Mrs. Phạm suddenly winced, spilling the hot tea all over the table. It cascaded all the way down its lining and onto the carpet, like blood that had been forced from its host. A sharp pain had come over Mrs. Phạm's chest. Like a knife went through her heart. She tried her best to hide her contorted face from her older sister, but she wasn't strong enough to hide this kind of pain. Her unsteady hands tried to clean up the mess she made, but it only made it worse.

"Minh!" Mai's voice cried out, her anger quickly subsiding, the vein releasing itself. She ran over to her side, throwing her arm around her. "What's wrong? Are you okay?"

"I'm fine," Mrs. Phạm lied as she tried to straighten back up. "Just a little gassy from last night is all." But she wasn't fine. She'd been having these chest pains for a long time. She had planned on going to the same old Vietnamese herbalist she'd been going to for the last twenty years, but she just couldn't do it. She didn't want to know the truth. What if what was inside of her wasn't curable? But she locked the fear deep inside her mind. She was alive and breathing; that was all that mattered, no need to involve any type of paper trail like health insurance or western medicine.

Mrs. Phạm noticed that Mai's arms were still wrapped around her. Mai hadn't shown that kind of physical affection since they were kids. "What *are* you doing? It's not like I'm dying or anything." She wiggled out of her sister's embrace.

Mai quickly dropped her arms, straightened up, and smoothed out her linen pants before stiffly sitting down in her chair. "I know you're not *dying*. I haven't seen you in ten years, I don't know what you've been up to! For all I know you could be recovering from cancer!" Mai said gruffly, then eyed her up and down. "Though from the looks of your weight, you probably ate that cancer."

Mrs. Phạm got up quickly, despite her chest pain, and grabbed her own fake Louis Vuitton bag off the table. "I'm leaving. I didn't come here to be *insulted*. It's clear you're still miserable, ten years later, and still an insufferable person. No wonder you're all alone. I'm probably the only person who picked up for you when you called."

Mai's face turned a deep red. Mrs. Phạm wasn't the type of woman to ever talk back. Especially not to her.

"Just sit down, Minh," she said. Her voice was commanding, but her eyes appeared shifty. "I didn't come here to argue. I came to . . . *catch up*."

Before Mrs. Phạm could leave, Mai flagged down the woman manning the congee cart, pointing to a bowl of steaming hot rice porridge with specks of dried pork on top. She then signaled to another woman for some gai lan, its garlic-sautéed green leaves glistening under the cheap lights. She almost did a defensive tackle, equivalent to a professional NFL player, to stop the next woman in charge of the chicken feet cart.

Mrs. Phạm eyed her sister suspiciously as she slowly sat back down. "*What* are you doing?" Mai was assembling all the small, tin metal steamers in the middle of the table. She spooned some congee into a bowl, drizzling chili oil on top, layering it with gai lan and one chicken foot. She placed it down in front of Mrs. Phạm with the accompanying dark hoisin sauce.

"I'm taking care of you. Am I not allowed to take care of you?" Mai snapped at her.

"I know how to order food."

"I know you do."

Still suspicious of her sister, Mrs. Phạm ate quietly, observing how strangely Mai was behaving. She must want something. Was she here to take back that house in Santa Ana? Did she need a favor for one of her daughters? Was *she* dying, and here to make amends?

After a moment of silence, Mai asked quietly. "It's not cancer, right?"

Mrs. Phạm laughed hoarsely, sputtering congee from her mouth. "Of course it's not cancer. I've had my back cupped three times a week for twenty years, don't be stupid. I'm invincible. Healthier than I ever have been." But deep down, Mrs. Phạm's worry about what was plaguing her body was growing out of control. Perhaps it was a message from the Buddha that it was finally her time to leave this world. Her mind immediately went to her one daughter, Joyce, and her fear grew. She decided today was the day to get her affairs in order. Finalize her will. Write instructions on what photo to use for the funeral. She had to figure out where she had hidden all her jewelry, jade, gold bars, and twenty thousand dollars in cash. Probably in the nooks and crannies of her house. They were all purposely kept out of sight from her husband, in case there was ever a divorce. The problem was, she had hidden so much over the years, like a squirrel in winter, she hadn't been able to keep track of it all. But her first priority was her daughter, and making sure that she would be taken care of, in this life and in the next.

"How is your daughter? How is Joyce? Trời ơi, your one and only daughter is so far away from you. Tell Joyce to come back home to Orange County, to take care of you. You're clearly not in good shape," Mai said as she slurped off the skin on a braised chicken foot. "New York is cold and dangerous. She's probably been mugged a hundred times by now. I don't know how Joyce has survived so far, with her *liberal arts* degrees. She should be dead on the street by now."

Mrs. Phạm narrowed her eyes. If she was somehow already on the brink of death, maybe it wouldn't be so bad in comparison to this torture chamber right here.

"I tell Joyce there are plenty of curator jobs in Los Angeles, but she won't come back. She's too important in New York City." Mrs. Phạm sat up a bit straighter and cleared her throat, coughing out any rogue rice grain stuck between her teeth. She knew what was about to happen, and she braced herself. She was ready to ram her daughter's accomplishments down Mai's throat. She had to get ahead of her on this one. Though she'd never admit it out loud, she *hated* how successful her three nieces were in comparison to her daughter. She took out her sword from her mind palace, and began sharpening it. "Her work is so specialized you know, not *anyone* can do her job. Joyce graduated top of her class in her master's program. Got a job immediately in New York, while the rest of her classmates are still struggling to find work."

"I mean, what can you do with an *anthropology* degree? Not a lot of jobs out there for that," Mai said with a bit of a smirk on her face. She proceeded to take out her sniper rifle from *her* mind palace, already loaded for this moment. She'd been waiting ten years for this fight, and she knew never to bring a knife to a gunfight. "Tell her to go into tech or start her own business. Being an engineer is the new doctor, you know. My Priscilla has lots of connections in tech, or my youngest, Thảo, can hire Joyce to help her business. Her business is doing so well, she needs all the help she can get! But too late now to go into the medical field, she needs years of training, like my Thủy. Went to the best, USC. You know Thủy is *JOHN CHO'S* dermatologist? That's why he's so handsome. He has Thủy to thank for his award-winning career. Anyways, tell Joyce to call up her cousins. Anything for the family. Let's not let *our* squabbling affect *their* relationship."

Mrs. Phạm calmly poured herself another tea. Though she was wounded in the first round, she always knew how to throw steady punches to stay in the fight. "My Joyce has handled the rarest art from around the world. Oldest, most expensive. Her job is important, archiving all these important things, making sure they are categorized and preserved for all of history. *For all of humanity.* Not just anyone can do what she does. She's practically *God*, preserving history for all our future children to see. People need years of training to do her job. Just because it doesn't pay as much as being an engineer, doctor, or businesswoman, doesn't mean it's not important!"

Mai scoffed and dismissed Mrs. Phạm's points with an eye roll. "Joyce labels objects with a Sharpie, how hard can it—" Mai quickly stood up, hitting her knee on the table along the way.

Mrs. Phạm turned, instantly knowing the cause. Another woman stood across the room. Her thick, gray hair was tightly pulled back into a neat bun, piled high up on top of her small frame. Her fake Louis Vuitton bag hung off her arm so casually, it looked like she could have been standing in line at the bank.

As Mai tried to steady her shaky legs, Mrs. Phạm watched her oldest sister's face turn from ghost white to blood red.

Their youngest sister, Khuyến, stood before them. Now known as Mrs. Khuyến Lâm. The youngest of the Dương sisters, and mother to two daughters, Elaine and Christine Lâm.

Mrs. Phạm felt Mai's dagger eyes. Inviting Khuyến to show up unannounced without giving her any warning, she may as well have sided with the North Vietnamese army. Still, she maintained a steady smirk, though on the inside, she was shaking from fear, like a dog's knees right before a thunderstorm. Because as a sword and a sniper rifle, neither of them was a match against a military tank.

• • •

The restaurant had kicked the three sisters out. The last thing patrons witnessed before the Dương sisters were thrown out—and after a dim sum cart had been overturned—was Mrs. Mai Nguyễn being restrained by the elderly waitstaff as she attempted to throw a bowl of congee into her youngest sister's face. As she was being carried out, her voice trailed behind her, and she managed to sputter out: "You got some nerve showing up here after not siding with me! You practically left me for dead!"

So, the three sisters had no choice but to migrate over to the Bánh Mì Chè Cali Bakery on Brookhurst Street. They sat outside under the umbrella tables, drinking cà phê sữa đá. Mrs. Nguyễn scowled, her boxes of oranges on her lap, while Mrs. Lâm angrily jammed her straw in and out of her iced coffee. Though Mrs. Nguyễn's reputation for her temper was infamous all over Little Saigon,

Mrs. Lâm's reputation as the de facto person to consult if anything needed to be done in a *discretionary* manner was more notorious. She knew how to escape the watchful eyes of the IRS and immigration and, along with her two daughters, was in the "import/export" trade. Especially with smuggling things in and out of Vietnam, under TSA's watchful eye. The staff at Ché Cali Bakery feared Mrs. Lâm's wrath, and had given them all extra sữa chua. Just in case.

"Can we try to be nice? At least for today?" Mrs. Phạm, the middle sister, pleaded. "It's been ten years."

"I can if *she* can," Mrs. Lâm said icily, avoiding her oldest sister's gaze.

"I'll start if *she* starts," Mrs. Nguyễn shot back, also skirting eye contact.

"Can we hurry this up? I have things to tend to with my businesses." Mrs. Lâm sniffed. "My coffee business is *exploding*, you know. I don't have much time for this second little *reunion*. Or whatever we are calling this."

Mrs. Nguyễn scoffed. "Your *coffee* business? Come now, Khuyến, unfortunately, we're *family*. You can be honest with me; you don't need to cover up what it is you *actually* do."

"Trời ơi. We *serve* coffee, believe it or not," Mrs. Lâm hissed, lowering her voice so no one around them could eavesdrop. "It just so *happens* that the uniforms the women wear are *different* from your regular coffee shops. We're not Starbucks, you know. In fact, we're better. We provide *entertainment*."

"You don't actually have your daughters work as one of the girls inside, do you?" Mrs. Phạm asked, genuinely curious. "I'd imagine it's not the most glamorous work, wearing a bikini all day."

"Of course not, they are in charge of *operations*. They take care of the women inside, make sure they're safe," Mrs. Lâm snapped. "Elaine is basically the mini CEO of the coffee business, and Christine runs the nail salons."

"You always had an entrepreneurial spirit! You're willing to take risks no other woman will," Mrs. Phạm said, admiringly. "All that cash, untaxed."

Mrs. Nguyễn scoffed. "*Sure*. If you want to earn your money as a criminal."

"Don't you pretend you're above it all. I remember when you used to butcher pigs out in the San Fernando Valley!" Mrs. Lâm sniped.

"At least I'm not a pimp!"

"*What* did you *call* me?" Mrs. Lâm said, her voice rising.

"Keep your voice down!" Mrs. Nguyễn shouted as she grabbed oranges out from a box and began throwing them at Khuyến to silence her. "Don't tell all of Little Saigon that we're related to a *pimp*!"

"I *knew* you always thought you were better than me!" Mrs. Lâm shouted, catching the oranges, then lobbing them back.

"Can we all please just calm down!" Mrs. Phạm was hysterical as she watched oranges flying past her. As the calm one, the mediator, the middle child, this was out of her comfort level.

"Oh, shut up! Just focus on your own daughter and less on us! She makes less than my daughters!" Mrs. Nguyễn screamed at Mrs. Phạm. "What kind of mother allows their daughter to major in anthropology?!"

"Yes, you babied her too much!" Mrs. Lâm chimed in as she ducked behind a chair. "Joyce *is* a bit strange, isn't she?"

Mrs. Phạm suddenly saw red in a sea of orange. There was no way she couldn't defend her only daughter. If she was already on death's door, she wasn't going to leave this earth without smacking these two around first. She cracked open another orange box and began to throw them at her sisters. "She's *just* a late bloomer! And I told you, her work is *important*. She's preserving *art*! *For the world!*"

"I AM NOT A PIMP!" Mrs. Lâm screamed into the void, haphazardly throwing oranges in any direction, not caring which sister they hit, as long as they hit any sister. "I am a *businesswoman!*"

"Don't waste all this fruit!" Mrs. Nguyễn shrieked, now trying to catch all the oranges in the air before they hit the ground. "They were on *sale*!!"

"Don't *lie* to us! You got them from the *white* grocery store!" Mrs. Phạm yelled back in her face. With the spirit of Jackie Robinson taking over her right arm, she threw her final orange into the side of Mrs. Nguyễn's face and watched as her oldest sister hurled herself into the side of the deli to try to avoid the impact. Soon came a flurry of Vietnamese slurs, accusations, oranges, and ten years of pent-up sisterly rage and repression from all three women. But not one single apology was uttered.

• • •

To the outside, it did look troublesome to see three sexagenarian Vietnamese women shout and throw perfectly good oranges at each other. The visiting elderly white bystanders from Arizona watched with their mouths agape. They had come to try one of the oldest Vietnamese delis in Orange County, based on a "Best of" foodie list, and they turned their noses up at the Dương sisters, as they clutched their fresh bánh mì close to their chest. They all had a similar thought that President Ford should *never* have granted asylum to the south Vietnamese, and this was a prime example of why. But the actual Vietnamese residents who had sought refuge in the small village of Little Saigon—who had been aware of the decades-long Dương family drama, its origins stemming from before the war—knew better than to interrupt. In fact, they saw it as rather therapeutic, cathartic even, and a long time coming. It wasn't the Vietnamese way to talk rationally. Better to get it all out like this.

The old men and women, who dreamt about seeing the beaches of Đà Nẵng again one day, watched from the sidelines, smoking their cigarettes and drinking their iced coffees with sweetened condensed milk. They watched the three sisters with the same bemusement as they watched episodes of *Paris by Night*. Their Go board game lay stagnant as they diverted their attention to the live action in front of them, and began taking bets on which sister would emerge victorious. A majority gambled in favor of Mrs. Lâm based on her dodgy reputation alone, while some surprisingly picked Mrs. Phạm. It was always the quiet ones you watch out for. For the next hour, they continued to sit on their little red plastic stools, unperturbed by the whole scene, as if everything were perfectly normal. Because they had seen worse things in their lifetime, caused by men whose skin was lighter than theirs.

• • •

After being ushered away from Bánh Mì Chè Cali Bakery, Mrs. Nguyễn, Mrs. Phạm, and Mrs. Lâm moved to a third location. They sat side by side, slightly out of breath, on a bench at the edge of Mile Square Park, far away from other humans. The women's clothes were stained with circles of lightly colored orange blobs. Their sun visors sat askew on their thick, gray hair, and sunglasses were crooked on their noses, while a graveyard of fake Louis Vuitton handbags littered the ground. The Vietnamese deli workers had handed them towels to clean themselves up after their orange fight, then given them ice packs to nurse their wounds and cups of cold chè to nurse their egos. They gently told the sisters to *please* find somewhere else to fight, before they called in their sons to escort them out of the complex. First sons were the only trusted law enforcement around Little Saigon. The sisters thanked them, apologized for their behavior, and began chewing on their complimentary sweet lychee jellies as they limped their way to the neighboring park.

Despite kicking them out, the old deli workers were sympathetic to the Dương women, also having been privy to gossip about their family. It was a very known fact that everyone in Little Saigon knew the Dương women were cursed. The proof was in the family tree, trời ơi—*so* many daughters and not *one* son!

Black crows had descended on bits of orange carcasses that the women picked off their clothes. Mrs. Phạm watched the crows, wishing that they'd divert their focus to come pick at her instead. Maybe then death would come for her faster.

"Someone in our family will die this year. The famous psychic in Kauai told me," Mrs. Nguyễn revealed at last, breaking the silence, her mouth full of jelly. "She said that it's time for me to reach out and try to reconcile before it's too late."

"Which psychic—?" Both Mrs. Phạm and Mrs. Lâm asked at the same time, curious about who their oldest sister saw, since they each had their own woman, on other Hawaiian Islands, they frequented.

"Linh Hứa," Mrs. Nguyễn said solemnly, and closed her eyes dramatically, waiting for her sisters to react in shock. When her formal name didn't elicit the kind of urgency she was hoping for, she said, "*Auntie* Hứa."

"Trời ơi," Mrs. Lâm muttered. "Then someone will *definitely* die. Also, doesn't Auntie Hứa charge more than the rest? She's quite expensive, isn't she?"

"I'm *sorry*, did you think I'd go to some low-rent psychic, Khuyến?" Mrs. Nguyễn scoffed.

"I'm *just* saying, you can see my woman, much cheaper, located near Waikiki," Mrs. Lâm raised her hands placatingly. "*And* she'll give you a discount."

"Seems like a tourist trap for white people," Mrs. Nguyễn muttered.

Mrs. Phạm could feel beads of sweat forming on her brow, and she considered telling her sisters about her recent health issues that had been ravaging her chest, but thought better of it. Why worry them when they have enough to worry about? She couldn't help but wonder if the person who would pass this year would be her . . .

"You don't think the person that will pass is—" Mrs. Phạm started, hoping to throw them off her scent.

"—I *told* you to never say her name in my presence—" Mrs. Nguyễn said, gritting her teeth.

"—but—"

"Mai ơi là Mai," Mrs. Lâm said, frustrated. "It's been over twenty years since you've said her name! Just say her name! And ten years since you've made your point and broken up this family. Yes, Kim Lương. You can say our half sister's name! You don't think it's her that's going to pass, right?"

Mrs. Nguyễn turned her nose up in the air. "I don't consider *her* family, so no, it isn't her."

"Oh god," Mrs. Lâm whispered. "You don't think it's—?"

All three of them had the same thought. They knew that it was finally time they contacted the matriarch of the family, their mother, Mrs. Lý Minh Dương. They had all managed to avoid their mother for a whole decade, and all the temples she frequented, her favorite restaurants, and even her favorite park where she did her tai chi exercise classes with her friend group. Now the time had come to kneel before her and beg for her forgiveness. Finally, for the first time all day, the sisters felt united on this front. They shared a commonality now. The enemy of their enemy is . . . well, a *much* bigger dragon.

"W-what else did Auntie Hứa say?" Mrs. Phạm asked.

Mrs. Nguyễn groaned, icing the sore spot where a rogue orange had pummeled the side of her face following Mrs. Phạm's perfect pitch. Mrs. Nguyễn told her sisters all of Auntie Hứa's predictions for the year. *A pregnancy, a death, a wedding.* She paused before telling them about the *grandson*, still afraid that it might not come to fruition. She talked about how Auntie Hứa told her that this would be the year she could lose everything, if she wasn't careful. As if a stone had been lifted off her, she began unleashing a waterfall of memories from the past twenty years to her two sisters. Everything about her fears about growing older, her daughters' romantic relationships, how strained their own relationships were, and how none of her daughters would call her back. The sisters were all able to relate to her fears. Because none of their daughters would call them back, either. And finally, she told them the final prediction that Auntie Hứa had whispered in her ear right before she left Kauai.

"A *boy*?" Mrs. Phạm gasped. "You think the curse is finally broken?"

"I don't know," Mrs. Nguyễn whispered. "I don't want to get my hopes up."

Mrs. Lâm rubbed her chin with her fingers, mulling over everything. She looked at Mai, and leaned in. "I know how to help the fortune come true. You mentioned you were worried about Thủy ending up with a broke man and procreating with him? I know the *perfect* man to set her up with. He's healthy *and* wealthy *and* buys everything in cash. *And* you can bet his sperm is *full* of sons."

"I don't know, Khuyến," Mrs. Nguyễn said hesitantly. "Your line of work isn't exactly *comforting* to me . . ."

"Just trust me," Mrs. Lâm said confidently. "We're *family* after all."

5

Thủy Nguyễn

THỦY NGUYỄN WAS UP at 6:00 a.m., drinking coffee on the bathroom floor.

The bathroom had always been her safe space, a slice of privacy, especially after her tumultuous childhood where she'd seek refuge on the cold tiles when everyone else was asleep at night. Six little Vietnamese girls and three other families all crammed under one roof in that little house in Santa Ana. The bathroom was the only space where she was able to be herself and remember who she was. She would bring her books, reading about magical worlds and white princesses with their white Prince Charmings. She'd sit in the bathtub and try to learn French, because she was ashamed of speaking Vietnamese. And at night, she would paint her nails in the colors she wanted, and not the wild colors that her Auntie Lâm would practice on her with for her nail salon business.

There was a soft knock on the door, and Andy peeked in. She saw his thick black hair, an angular mess, and the most gigantic pair of thin, wire-framed glasses on his low-bridged nose. "Good morning, sorry for interrupting. I know how much your morning bathroom ritual means to you, but your mother called. She needs you to do a favor for her today."

Thủy sighed and gestured for Andy to enter. "It's okay. My mother has an instinct for knowing when I'm in a peaceful mood. That's when she usually swoops in."

Andy opened the door wider and brought Thủy another cup of fresh coffee, and he slid down next to her on the ground. The sun had just cracked the horizon and was streaming through the skylight, littering the bathroom with specks of yellow dust. Thủy loved mornings like this in her little home in east Los Angeles, and she leaned her head over Andy's shoulder, until she found the perfect spot:

that little crevice above his collarbone that turned into a hammock for her head. Andy had always been so comforting to her, like a big bowl of fresh phở. Safe, warm, sweet. A golden retriever. That was Andy Trần.

"So, what's the errand of the day for the infamous Mrs. Nguyễn?" Thủy asked.

"She wants you to head to Pasadena to pick up a package for her temple."

Thủy groaned. "*Again?* The last time she made me go pick up something for her, it was a life-size golden statue of Buddha. I nearly threw out my back."

"You mean *I* nearly threw out my back," Andy teased as he playfully pinched her nose. "She also weirdly requested that you dress up. Or in her words: Đừng ăn mặc như ma lem."

Thủy tried hard not to roll her eyes. "Why is her go-to insult to always say I look like a ghost?" She buried her face deeper into his neck and let out a muffled scream. Andy didn't say anything. He just patiently waited for her to let it out. Like he always did.

"All better?" he asked.

"Yes." Thủy was now smiling, even though her face was still hidden. It was these little moments that bound them after two years together, reminding her of the comfort of stability, something she never experienced growing up. Because as the second-oldest daughter of Mai Nguyễn, she knew she was anything but normal.

"Want some company going to Pasadena?" Andy asked.

Thủy paused and her body stiffened. Though it was such a simple question in theory, she couldn't help but instinctively withdraw. Her mother's words from the past were like a branding iron, echoing through her, reminding her to never rely on a man—that in the end, marriage would ruin her, like it had ruined every woman in their family.

"No, I'll handle it," she said, pretending to laugh it off. "It's my fault for never escaping California like my sisters did. I'm my mother's personal secretary, body guard, and therapist. All in one. I just don't get any of the credit. Middle child problems, you know?"

"Come on, let me help. You've had a long work week." He went in to pinch her nose again, but it was as if her evil alter ego took control of her motor functions, and she watched in horror as she slapped his hand away and slid across the bathroom floor from him. Her heart dropped when she saw his face contort in confusion, and she wondered why she just couldn't be *normal*.

"I said don't worry about it. I got it," she said, her voice instantly cold, but her eyes remained apologetic. She had ruined yet another nondescript morning, and made a mental scratch in her head, tallying all the times she screwed up.

Andy stared at her; his big brown eyes, full of endless questions, went from puzzlement to sadness. "When are you ever going to let me in, Thủy?"

Thủy pretended to look confused. "What do you mean? You basically live here now."

He sighed. "I want to be there for you. You know I do. You *just* need to let me in. Please, I'm begging you. I *want* to be the perfect son-in-law one day, the perfect husband, but every time I mention or do anything that proves I'm ready for the next step, you freeze up and shut me out."

Thủy broke off eye contact. "Sorry. I'm not trying to shut down the conversation, you know I have a hard time talking about marriage. Or the 'next step.'"

Andy didn't say anything. He just rubbed her knee in a circular pattern. Over and over again, as if he were desperately making his final wish with a lamp. His eyes felt heavy on her. As they sat in silence, basking in the sun now fully streaming in through the windows, they both wondered if there was anything left in this relationship that they could salvage—especially when one wanted to move on to big moments, and the other wanted to stay forever in the little moments.

"I'm not your father you know," Andy said lowly. "We won't have a marriage like your parents. I won't treat you like that."

"I know."

"Why do I have a feeling that you don't believe me?"

Thủy closed her eyes, and flashbacks of the little house in Santa Ana ran through her mind. All six little girls were forced to huddle outside under the orange tree because all the adults were yelling inside in Vietnamese, telling each other how much they hated each other. Meanwhile, their neighbors to the right and left would yell in Spanish inside their own homes. Though Thủy didn't speak Spanish, she knew that regret was universal and transcended language barriers. Regret was the only thing every family on that block had in common. Though they were the only Buddhists on a block full of, well, *Catholics*, they all shared the same pain of being trapped somewhere they weren't meant to be.

Thủy refused to be trapped like they had been. Under that tree, a young Thủy had promised herself that things would be different next time around, with her generation. But she didn't say any of this to Andy. She never did because she knew Andy wouldn't understand. Andy had grown up in a stable, educated Vietnamese family in a nice part of town. His parents weren't hoarders or in constant survival mode. His assimilation was easier than hers, and it brewed resentment in her.

Thủy did what she did best: shut down. She bit her lip and hoped he would move on to another topic.

"Will you ever marry me one day?" Andy asked, breaking the silence.

"C'mon, Andy," she protested softly.

He paused, and Thủy watched with reluctance as hope slowly returned to his big, brown eyes. Her realism magnified as she felt his steadfast romanticism try to be big enough for the two of them, like it always did. She kept waiting for him to break up with her, waiting for him to finally realize that he deserved better. But Andy only looked more determined.

"All I need is possibility."

Thủy didn't respond, and turned her head, catching her reflection in the bathroom mirror. All she could see staring back at her was a young Thủy under the orange tree in Santa Ana.

· · ·

As soon as Thủy pulled into the parking lot of the long-running Vietnamese restaurant, tucked away in a corner in old Pasadena, she immediately knew what the "package" was. She slammed on the brakes, gripped the steering wheel, and loudly cursed her mother. The meditation audio she had been listening to suddenly lost all meaning. The mantras dissipated into gibberish compared to the backdrop of dealing with a Vietnamese mother who just *couldn't ever let anything go.*

Because there was *no* package. There was never a package.

Instead, a man with slicked-back black hair, wearing sunglasses and a crisp white button-down, began waving at her. The sharp Southern California sun reflected off his gold Rolex and nearly blinded Thủy. As she adjusted her eyes, she kicked herself for falling for her mother's trickery. *Again.*

This was another one of her mother's setups. Thủy still had residual PTSD from the last time her mother had tried setting her up. Her mother had made a match tail her from behind during one of her night jogs, trying to "accidentally" bump into her. When she tried explaining to her mother that she shouldn't have strange men follow her at night when she's jogging, her mother had put the blame on her. Because exercising at night is bad for digestion. Thủy never jogged again.

Thủy was about to turn the car around and not get out at all, when the man slowly lowered his sunglasses to reveal his full face. He sent her a smile that exposed his dimples, sharp jaw, and amber brown eyes, and accentuated his golden skin tone. Thủy went temporarily blind, punishing her for being a mere mortal woman. She did more than go blind; she forgot her social security number.

Her brain shut off. Thủy found herself suddenly parking the car, putting on the parking brake, as if once again, her evil alter ego had taken control of her body. She got out of the car and began walking toward him, her curiosity getting the better of her. *Why was she so drawn to this man?* He was like a shiny object on the sidewalk that she couldn't help but pick up. She knew the right thing to have done was to do a massive U-turn and head back home, straight into Andy's arms. They had plans to make banana bread and binge Korean dramas. Routine. Stability. Comfort. The opposite of her father in every way. These were things that she had gravitated toward her whole adult life. Andy represented all of this. She felt another scratch go on her tally wall of screwups as she heard her car lock go off behind her.

"Thủy, right? Thủy Nguyễn?" the man asked her as she approached him. "Recognized you from the photo that my mother sent me."

Thủy could barely nod her head, feeling unprepared for this moment and guilty for *feeling* unprepared for this moment. Standing there in yoga pants, with a messy bun, looking like a cartoon caricature of a white Angeleno female, she felt like a bridge troll in comparison to him. She quickly unfurled her bun and adjusted her gait. She knew her goopy, thick sunscreen wasn't properly applied on her face, and recognized the irony that she probably really did look like a ghost. This was the one time she wished she had listened to her mother and gotten dressed up.

She eyed him up and down, unsure if the man before her was real. He seemed almost *too* perfect. Out of all the men her mother had tried to set her up with throughout the years—to break her and Andy up—this was her most bullish attempt. Her mother had removed the pin from an atomic bomb, and played her final hand. All in the name of stopping Andy from potentially becoming her son-in-law one day. Her mother never approved of how little Andy made in comparison to Thủy. This man in front of her signaled that her mother still didn't approve of Andy's salary. He was the opposite of Andy in every way. He possessed an ostentatious suaveness that could only stem from Asian men who grew up in Los Angeles. This was the type of Asian man Thủy had avoided her whole life. They unnerved her. Because they came equipped with a staggering kind of confidence that could only belong to the firstborn son of a wealthy, highly educated, Asian family. Whereas Thủy had spent her entire life being told that she was cursed for being born a girl. And she carried that stain like a scarlet "A" carved into her breastbone.

"Oh god, sorry about all of this. My mother, I mean," Thủy managed to finally croak out. "I assume your mother is within the Vietnamese-meddling-mother-network from the same temple . . . ?"

He laughed. "You guessed correctly. Shall we go inside? Get some food? We can exchange war stories."

"Look, we don't have to do this. I don't know what my mother told your mother, but I have a boyfriend," Thủy said, even though Andy's name escaped her at the moment. "Just tell your mother we met, that you're not interested, and we can both go on with our lives."

"Hey, I also have a girlfriend. But my mother doesn't want me to marry her. Let's just say she's not exactly 'wifey' material," he said, flashing a set of perfect teeth at her. "This isn't the first 'setup' she's forced me to go on. But she also knows when I lie, and I'm pretty sure she has someone that follows me around to make sure I actually go through with these setups."

Thủy quickly turned around and scanned the parking lot, expecting a private investigator to pop out. Or both their mothers in trench coats, watching from a car with binoculars.

"I'm joking. No one is following me. Or you, I hope," he laughed at her as she turned back around, red-faced. "My mother is not that crazy. Though I wouldn't put it past her. By the way, I'm Daniel." He extended his hand, and Thủy took it cautiously. Even his handshake was perfect. She could feel the calluses on his hands, and something awakened in her. His hand in hers didn't feel comforting or stable, and yet here she was, unable to move away from the flame.

"I still have a boyfriend, you know."

"And I still have a girlfriend," he said. "But you just got here, and I just got here. We can still talk over some noodles? Might as well satisfy both our mothers *and* our stomachs. What do you say?" He flashed her a mysterious and mischievous smile, and the walls crumbled around her in a way they hadn't before around Andy. "You *know* they'd chastise us for not eating the đặc biệt at least."

That smoothness. He might as well have been one of those Asian guys wearing a gold chain necklace and track pants, walking around Koreatown, holding a bubble tea. It was that type of smoothness she actively avoided because she never thought she could handle it, deserved it, or was the type of *cool* Asian girl to receive it.

She mentally scratched another tally in her screwup count, as she found herself following him inside the restaurant, trying to hide a small smile.

· · ·

It was a strange sensation, being around someone who wasn't sensible. Thủy didn't know what to make of it. Even the waitress had given them free dessert because she was so charmed by Daniel. Thủy had never been the type of woman to ever get free *anything* anywhere she went. Andy and she were the type to always wait for their turn in a queue, and they'd allow anyone to cut in front of them, even if that person didn't deserve to.

As they walked out of the restaurant, a toothpick hung loosely from Daniel's lips. He put his sunglasses back on, and much to Thủy's surprise, wrapped his arm over her lower waist and steered her toward his car. "Want to head to the beach?"

Thủy's body immediately froze, and guilt washed over her. *Go home to Andy,* she was screaming inside her head. The more she repeated it, the less she became sentient. "Nobody in California actually goes to the beach," she said awkwardly. She felt sixteen and insecure all over again. He opened the passenger-side door of an old convertible for her.

"Well, it's a good thing we're not like everybody else then, isn't it?" he said as he grinned at her, the toothpick still hanging on for dear life off his supple lips.

Thủy, still not in control of her own body, slowly crawled into the passenger seat. "What about my car?" she asked numbly.

"Give me your keys," he replied. "I'll have someone come pick up the keys at the restaurant and drive it to your house for you." How could *anyone* be so smooth? Daniel laughed at her shocked expression, and leaned over her until their faces were an inch apart. Thủy closed her eyes, and clenched her hands, afraid he was going to kiss her, but he simply reached over into her coat pocket and pulled out her keys. "Don't worry. I won't do anything you're not ready for."

Thủy didn't respond, and Daniel turned around to head inside the restaurant to drop the keys off. She didn't know what to say, her fists still tightly wound. Her fingernails dug into her palms, almost bloodying them. But she was too afraid to unwind them; she needed the pain as a distraction. Because the minute she uncurled her fist, she knew she wasn't ready to face anything real.

· · ·

At the end of the night, Daniel had pulled his car up toward a park bench on the hillside that overlooked Echo Park Lake. Thủy's alter ego had fully taken over by now. She felt like a woman who *belonged* in the passenger seat of a convertible. The morning with Andy sitting next to her on the bathroom tile felt light-years ago. Vignettes of their relationship had flashed through her as long-forgotten memories, far removed from the reality she was experiencing now.

When Daniel opened up her door for her, he held out his hand, and she blushed as she accepted it. He held on as they walked around the lake.

"Favorite color?" he asked her.

"I prefer neutrals. I'm not adventurous enough for color."

"Coffee order?"

"Iced Americanos. But with tonic water."

"Whoa, you're bougie."

"Says the guy with the Rolex."

"Okay, favorite childhood memory?"

Thủy was caught off guard. But for some reason, she felt it was easier to talk to Daniel than it was to open up to Andy. Maybe because Daniel was still a stranger, and he could possibly still remain a stranger forever. If she opened up to Andy, she knew that Andy would hug her and tell her to cry and let it all out, when that was the last thing she wanted to do. Andy always claimed that he understood what she was going through, but she never believed him. Because how could he possibly?

"I don't have one," she said quietly. "I had a shitty childhood. I prefer to lock those memories away, far in the back of my mind."

Daniel didn't respond right away. He squeezed her hand tighter. "It's okay, I also didn't have the best. Probably why I turned out the way I did. We don't have to talk about it."

They kept walking and Daniel stopped pelting her with questions. But Thủy recognized the kind of silence coming from him because she went into those shutdown modes, too. She knew they had a similar childhood and it made them abnormal to others, and she was oddly comforted by this.

"What happens now?" Thủy whispered.

"I think that's up to you, not me."

Long after the sun had disappeared behind the rolling desert hills, Daniel finally took her home and dropped her off around the corner, since she knew that Andy would be home. She paced up and down her dark driveway for another hour, too afraid to go in. The bathroom was no longer her safe space because she couldn't face her reflection. She looked up and saw that their bedroom light was off. She already knew how she was going to find Andy. His glasses would sit askew on his face, his fantasy book would be folded on his chest, the humidifier would be running, and he'd have set out a glass of iced water for Thủy on her side of the bed. Not too much ice, not too little. *Just* enough.

Routine. Stability. Comfort. And Thủy was about to blow it all up.

· · ·

Thủy slept in for the first time in years. She woke up to ten missed calls from her curious mother, wondering about her first meeting with Daniel. She immediately felt lonely when she saw her mother's missed calls because she realized she had no one to go to about this. Her older sister, Priscilla, was in Seattle and had cut off the family last year, and her younger sister, Thảo, was living in Sài Gòn.

What the hell was she doing? How could she do this to sweet, golden retriever Andy? *Her Andy?* Andy made his own kimchi from scratch. He learned how to read all seven Harry Potter books in French. He had sex with his socks on. The kids he took care of as a social worker called him *Mr. Andy.* Andy couldn't even handle more than one cup of coffee, and even then, he had to be conservative about it, or else he'd have stomach issues all day.

She felt nauseated. Daniel had texted her as soon as she got home, asking to meet again, saying that he couldn't stop thinking about her, their conversation, and their impromptu day at the beach and late-night walk around Echo Park Lake. He then sent another text soon after, saying that *maybe,* just *maybe,* for the first time in his life, his mother had gotten it right. That there could be something here, and he said that he felt it coming from her, too. When she didn't respond for a while, he sent a follow-up text saying it was okay if they started slow. There was no point in rushing anything. They could be friends. *Friends*. That wasn't *cheating*. Thủy justified it in her mind, but she hadn't responded back yet.

Thủy ran to the bathroom, turned on the water to the highest pressure point until it sounded like Niagara Falls, and slinked down onto the cold, stony tiles. Her safe space was now a place of guilt. She was hiding. Andy was in the kitchen, laughing along to a podcast, making her favorite gluten-free waffles. Thủy took out her phone, her eyes kept running over Daniel's texts, poring over every curve of his messages, imagining his hands around her, going over every curve on her body. She couldn't stop herself; even when she threw her phone across the room, she ran after it like an addict. She picked it up and immediately responded: when and where

Thủy had become her worst nightmare. She had grown up and become like her father. A cheat, liar, and gambler. The thing is, she knew she turned out worse than her father, because her father, despite his flaws, did it all in the name of family and survival. Thủy had no tangible excuse for what she was about to do. All she knew was that she had always been good at running.

6

Mrs. Lý Minh Dương

MRS. LÝ MINH DƯƠNG REALLY only had one regret in her lifetime. She had forgiven herself for the rest of her mistakes, because she knew she was not like her mother, or her mother's mother, *or* her mother's *mother's* mother. She accepted the burden of having daughters. Vietnamese women lived with enough grief, and she would not allow this narrative to dictate her daughters' lives. After the loss of her first husband, Mrs. Dương thought she knew pain, but it wasn't until she lost her first daughter, Kim, that she knew what it was like to want to die.

Then, Kim had come back from the dead. Twenty-five years ago, she showed up to their Santa Ana home with two daughters. Her appearance brought on a chasm within her family, like lightning striking a tree, rotting it from the inside out. Once the trunk had been hit, the branches had little to no chance of survival.

It had been ten years since Mrs. Dương had spoken to her daughters Mai, Minh, and Khuyến. Mai had painted her as practically immoral, a devil of a mother who had kicked her and her three young children out of the house in Santa Ana five years after Kim's return. So her oldest was the first to cut ties; she couldn't let go of her resentment. Her second oldest, Minh, who often sought peace, decided to side with Mai because she didn't want to see Mai be alone. Meanwhile, her youngest daughter, Khuyến, who had originally sided with her, eventually went her own separate way, not picking any side, because she was tired of the fighting and wanted to see more of the world on her own terms.

Now she was surprised to come outside today and, from her front porch, see Mai, Minh, and Khuyến standing in the distance, bickering loudly with each other about who should ring the doorbell first. It had been too long since they all stood within the same vicinity of each other, and as she watched them argue, she realized that time had passed through them like the Santa Ana winds. Her three daughters' thick, black hair had gotten grayer with age while hers had turned ghost white. Though they had all woken up a decade older, and lines had deepened around their eyes, they'd all lived a thousand lifetimes already. Because life had gone on, as it always does for survivors. Mrs. Dương envisioned her life flashing before her like a movie reel, recounting the greatest hits that lead to ten years of silence, and reminding her of her one true regret . . .

. . .

After surviving the refugee camps in Malaysia and landing in America, Mrs. Dương and her three daughters, Mai, Minh, and Khuyến, settled in a small one-bedroom off Bolsa and Ward. It had a stench they couldn't get rid of, no matter how many times they put bleach on the carpet. They were living off blocks of government cheese and flipping food stamps for profit. And they were all terribly homesick. Homesick for the South China sea, the old tamarind trees that lined their streets, the floating markets that ran along the Mekong Delta, where they would bargain for fresh fruit, and where they would lay on their backs and float as far as the river would take them. Young Mai, Minh, and Khuyến were uncharacteristically hopeful and worked day and night, saving what money they could, flipping bánh xèo at the night market. On weekends, they would clean the homes of rich, white Christians, because they were the only ones who took pity on the newly settled Vietnamese. Or the *Veet-mayon-naise*. Mrs. Dương squirreled away any bit of cash that came their way, and even took a few liberties with Little Saigon's underground gambling schemes to double, even triple, what she could. Or how it was pitched to her, *their* version of the "stock market."

The night Mrs. Dương saw a cockroach crawl over Mai's arm when she was sleeping, she knew it was time. They didn't live like sewer rats back in their hometown of Cần Thơ. This was insulting to their dignity. Mrs. Dương had been ready for this moment; she had been scraping an escape plan together to get her and her daughters out of their current living situation.

Mrs. Dương hired a young man from the local temple to drive her around Orange County. Thanh Nguyễn was one of the few refugees who had been brave enough to get his driver's license, and would borrow cars to drive anyone in Little

Saigon around to help run errands for free. He was young and amiable enough, and desperately needed the cash. Which only meant he would be perfect to boss around.

"Where to, Cô?" Thanh asked her, after he helped her climb into the car.

"Drive me around the neighborhoods where you can buy a house for less than seventy thousand dollars in cash and some gold bars."

"In *Orange County*?" Thanh asked incredulously, staring at her in the rearview mirror, as if she forgot where they were and *who* they were. Nothing more than two Vietnamese immigrants in a beat-up sedan with a mismatched-colored hood. There was a difference between dreaming about owning land in this country and actually owning land, and that difference was based on the shape of their eyes.

"I don't pay you to question me," she snapped at him. "Just drive. America is a big place, plenty of space for everyone. Now hurry up, we're losing light."

"It's seven a.m.," he grumbled as he started the ignition.

They drove for a whole week straight, from morning till night, looking at ads in newspapers and driving through neighborhoods in search of any *For Sale* signs. They stuck to the Eastside, because they knew better than to look in the white neighborhoods. There was already a lot of disdain and criticism for the large influx of the southern Vietnamese who had come into Orange County, and Mrs. Dương was doing her best to avoid any violence or altercation again. She'd just lived through a war; she wasn't about to fight some white woman who kept going on and on about some bearded white guy named Jesus to save her soul. She saw what the white men did to her country, and saving souls was the last thing they did.

But one day, Thanh accidentally drove into one of those neighborhoods. He had gotten lost along the I-5 South, and because he was embarrassed by his English, he was too proud to ask Mrs. Dương for help reading the highway signs. He exited the highway, turned a corner, and another corner, *and* another corner, hoping to find a way back east before she noticed.

"Where are we?" she asked from the back seat.

"Sorry, Cô," he replied. "I'll get us back on track, the lanes are just so wide here. Everything really is bigger in America, isn't it?" He gave a fake chuckle, hoping she wouldn't notice how lost he really was, and sat up a bit straighter.

Mrs. Dương didn't say anything. She just observed how pristine the streets were in comparison to Little Saigon. She watched men carrying surfboards heading down the street and women, their hair wrapped in expensive silk, driving past them in convertibles. One of the women waved at someone on the sidewalk, and Mrs. Dương saw how smooth her palms were. The woman didn't have working-class hands, unlike Mrs. Dương. She was able to identify every one of her scars. Battle wounds from flashing hot oil after making batches of egg rolls for the night market. The blatant wealth wasn't what stuck out to Mrs. Dương, though. It was that everyone seemed so *relaxed*. Not a worry or a wrinkle in sight. The sound of seagulls made her look up, and she noticed everyone was heading west, inadvertently following them. It was an auspicious sign because she knew immediately what was nearby, and her heart skipped. Ever since arriving in California, Mrs. Dương craved to be near a body of water again. The ghost sounds of the Mekong Delta kept her awake at night ever since she left Vietnam. Meanwhile, the Pacific Ocean had been calling out to her, extending an olive branch, hoping she'd take it.

"Follow them," she commanded Thanh, though she wasn't sure if she meant the birds or where all the beautiful women were going.

"Cô, we're heading deep into a *different* area," he said nervously. "I don't feel comfortable being in this neighborhood."

"What are they going to do? *Shoot* us? In *this* neighborhood? These people have no calluses on their hands. They're the ones that fund wars, not fight in them! Have some courage! We belong here just as much as they do!" she barked at him. "Follow the road!"

Terrified of the matriarch in his back seat, Thanh took them down the winding road, and Mrs. Dương rolled down the window, taking in the salt-encrusted air. She inhaled greedily, as much as her lungs could hold. Because who knows when she'd be able to breathe air on this side of town ever again.

Mrs. Dương's eyes followed the houses, her irises growing bigger and bigger. She drank in the white picket fences, the fresh-cut lawns, and the large windows that gave her a glimpse of how the other half lived. Out of the corner of her eyes, she spotted a *For Sale* sign at the end of the block, and screeched for Thanh to stop in front of it. He managed to discreetly pull off to the side, and parked under a looming sycamore tree that shielded them from the nosy neighbors.

They sat in silence and stared at the littlest house on the block, both lost in thought. Thanh thought about his mother back in Vietnam and how she would have loved to live in this house that overlooked the beach. Absentmindedly, Mrs. Dương gently tugged on her jade Buddha necklace, the stone felt familiar and comforting between her thumbs. It was a rather unusual jade color because it had elements of both purple and green that faded into each other. Despite being centered by the jade, she was still swept up in a dream about her three daughters and imagined coming home with the keys to this house. The littlest house on the block wasn't ostentatious like the surrounding houses. Or particularly eye-catching. There was nothing that stood out, aside from the faded green door that had been weathered by the ocean. But it called out to her because it was the kind of home you keep in your family for generations. It was a home with four walls and a roof that you passed down to your children and their children's children to keep them warm. Mrs. Dương had nothing to pass down because she'd been forced to start over from scratch. And at her age, she didn't know if she could pull it off.

"Let's go," Mrs. Dương said quietly as reality crept back in. Maybe, one day, she could live in a neighborhood like this. But that reality was so far away from where she was now, that it physically hurt her. The longer they stayed in this neighborhood, the harder it would be for her to return to the life that was waiting for her. Thanh turned the car on and took off without saying anything. Mrs. Dương willed herself not to look back at that house, unable to accept the olive branch.

After a quiet drive back to the Eastside, Thanh turned into a different neighborhood they hadn't explored yet. And as they slowly drove through, Mrs. Dương heard the strangest, most raucous music blaring from the car stereos, and her ears strained trying to figure out what language it was in. Children were dancing, playing soccer, and running in the streets. The adults were sitting on stoops, drinking iced tea, gossiping loudly, and peeling fruit. It reminded her of Vietnam. There was so much commotion and chaos that Mrs. Dương wasn't sure where to look. She felt nervous, being so far away from her own segregated hub of Orange County, because she wasn't white, she wasn't brown, and she felt uncomfortable in her own skin in this country.

"What on *earth* is that music?" Mrs. Dương asked.

"I think the Mexicans call it mari-*a*-chi, Cô!" he said, grinning. "It's pretty fun, isn't it?"

"Where *are* we?" Mrs. Dương asked, staring as if they'd been teleported into a different country.

"We're in Santa Ana," he replied, as he pulled up to the end of the cul-de-sac, to a crooked blue house. "Here we go! I found this ad the other day. Sixty-seven thousand five hundred dollars I think it was listed at."

Mrs. Dương stared at the house that looked like it was built by blind pigs and could easily crumble if the winds blew the wrong way. "It looks like dog shit," she told the young man. "Do I look like a dog to you?"

He shrugged. "You didn't say anything about the *condition* of the house, just the price tag." He helped Mrs. Dương get out of the car. She felt all the neighbors' eyes on them, watching two Vietnamese people walk around in *their* segregated hub of Orange County.

"We're a long way away from Little Saigon," Mrs. Dương muttered to him.

"Cô, we're a long way away from Sài Gòn," he reminded her gently as he helped her up the stairs. "So? What do you think?" He stood proudly in front of the house, as if he'd accomplished the impossible. His only life's ambition since arriving in America had been to please elderly Vietnamese women—a replacement for his family. During their car ride, he had talked at length about his mother who was still in the fallen city of Sài Gòn and how, one day, he'll be back with bags of American money to give to her.

Mrs. Dương stared at the dilapidated house with the blue awning; dying rose bushes lined the hedges. She stared and stared, trying to imagine the possibilities that could come with it. Suddenly she felt even *more* eyes on her, and as she turned around, she saw that all the neighbors had gathered to stare at the two Buddhists on a block full of Catholics. She began to hyperventilate, fearing an altercation. She wanted to apologize immediately for invading their space, their territory, their *home*. Her PTSD still hadn't gone fully away, and she'd done her best to find herbal remedies to cure bad memories, but sometimes, she could still see the fire. But then people began to slowly wave at her curiously. There was no "go back to China" or "Commie cunt" being thrown her way. They were just as curious of her as she was of them. And she weirdly felt safe. She felt much safer here than she did at the other house by the beach. As she looked around the neighborhood more, she realized it didn't get any more American than this.

"I'll take it," Mrs. Dương said to no one in particular.

As the young man drove Mrs. Dương back home, they began to talk more. Mrs. Dương began to grill him about which part of Vietnam he was from, his education level, and his plans for the future. He didn't have much going for him, Mrs. Dương would admit, but he was better than nothing. They came to an agreement at the end of the car ride, which was no more than twenty minutes long. When they arrived back at Mrs. Dương's one-bedroom apartment in Bolsa, she instructed him to wait outside. She went in and pulled her oldest daughter, Mai, out. In order for them to survive, her daughters needed husbands, even if they didn't want them. Husbands were useful; they gave societal protection, and every home needed one. Even if she didn't agree with the reasoning in private.

Mrs. Dương put her arm over Mai, introduced her to the young driver, and gave her a small push forward. "Don't be rude. Mai, meet your new husband," she told her. "This is Thanh. Thanh Nguyễn."

"*What!?*" Mai burst out screaming, staring at Thanh like he was vermin. She backed all the way up, accidentally shoving her mother out of the way. "I'm not marrying him! I don't even *know* him." Minh and Khuyến both came running out when they heard their oldest sister yell, thinking she was in trouble.

"You *will* marry him. The time has come for you to settle down. I've bought you a home in Santa Ana. The house will be under Thanh's name—and yours. You can use it to build equity and your new life here in America. This is for your future children, to build generational wealth."

Mai began crying hysterically. "What kind of mother are you? What if I don't even *want* children?"

Mrs. Dương slapped her across the cheek. "Pull yourself together, Mai. It's your duty as a Vietnamese woman to have children." Mrs. Dương felt a twinge of regret, slapping her, but she needed Mai to get in line with her reasoning, for her to see that this was her only way out.

Shocked, Mai touched her cheek and stopped crying, and her eyes became steely as she stared at her mother with venom. "I'll *never* be like you if I ever become a mother."

Mrs. Dương fought back her tears, as she looked at her daughter's eyes full of hatred for her. Every night she dreamt that Mai's life would turn out differently than hers. Maybe she'd get a well-paying job one day, get into a position of power in society, and be well respected in the community. But she knew the truth, and the truth was that none of the Dương women on that lawn would have those opportunities.

But maybe their children would one day, and that's what Mrs. Dương held out for. "You *will* become a mother. One day, Mai, your child will look at you exactly how you are looking at me now. And maybe you'll understand what sacrifice means then."

"I will *never* understand how anyone can be so cruel. I don't *love* him. How can I get married to him? Look at him, he looks like a garbage can!"

"Hey!" Thanh protested from behind. "I'm not *that* bad!"

"It's not about love, Mai, it's about survival," Mrs. Dương said, her principles steadfast. "You're a refugee in America with no college education. What chances and opportunities do you think you will have here without a husband and a family of your own?"

Everyone on that front lawn knew that Mrs. Dương wasn't going to change her mind. Not today, not ever. She was of a different generation, who preferred living within the social constructs of society, even if they were archaic. Mai Dương made a promise to herself right then and there, that she'd never force her daughters to do anything they didn't want to. She promised herself that she'd never turn out like her mother. Because next time around, it would be different, with her generation.

The following week, a small ceremony was held at the Buddhist temple near Fountain Valley. Mrs. Dương grieved watching her oldest daughter go from a Mai Dương to a Mrs. Mai Nguyễn. It was a different type of grief. Though the person was still physically there, their old life was long gone. Mrs. Dương had felt that kind of aching sorrow before; it was always after giving birth because the moment the baby had exited her, she felt a cavernous space in her womb. Mrs. Dương was forever stuck in the past, despite pushing her daughters forward. Mrs. Dương experienced that pain two more times, as she watched Minh become Mrs. Phạm, and then Khuyến become Mrs. Lâm.

But she never said a word. Because it just wasn't the Vietnamese way to talk about it. That day, as she watched Mai walk down the aisle wearing an ill-fitting áo dài that she had sewn together in a week, Mrs. Dương felt her first and only regret as a mother.

7

Mrs. Nguyễn, Mrs. Phạm, Mrs. Lâm

MRS. NGUYỄN, MRS. PHẠM, AND MRS. LÂM all stood outside the gated white house in Anaheim. Two towering, stone Foo dogs guarded the front, their teeth bared, threatening any harmful spirits who dared cross the threshold. The three sisters knew their mother's house would have several layers of superstitious protection that they had to bypass. After all, who knew what other curses had been inflicted on the Dương women throughout their reincarnations. They weren't *exactly* the most well liked or well behaved.

The Foo dogs were the first trap. The second was a hexagonal talisman, a bagua mirror, that hung above the iron door. The mirror warded off evil spirits by showing their reflection, and once the spirits saw their image, they wouldn't be able to enter the home. Mrs. Dương had seen enough evil spirits in her lifetime, both in flesh and celestial forms, and she always warned her daughters to be more afraid of the ones that came in human form than anything else. The mirror was noticeably turned toward the noisy Chinese neighbors across the street so that the evil spirits would head in their direction.

The shade was subtle but loud enough.

The three sisters must have stood there for what felt like an eternity, each of them arguing, barely above a whisper, about who was responsible for making the first move and ringing the doorbell. Minh and Khuyến posed the argument that Mai should do it, since she was *technically* responsible for causing the family estrangement for all these years. She did *make* them pick sides, after all. Mai argued that Khuyến should do it, since she's the youngest and nobody ever blames the youngest. Khuyến turned it around and pointed fingers at Minh, saying that the middle child was the mediator of the family, and that their mother wouldn't get mad at *her*.

As the arguing escalated, the iron door creaked open, and out stepped an old man. He meandered to the garden, carrying a metal basket and a pair of gardening shears, humming a tune. His bifocals glistened in the sun. The three sisters shushed each other and watched suspiciously as the old man began to cut Thai basil, mint, parsley, and green onions, and plucked fresh lemons into the basket.

"Who the *hell* is that?" Mrs. Nguyễn whispered.

"Maybe her caretaker?" Mrs. Lâm responded back. "Or a friend checking in?"

"Maybe she got the son she finally wanted," Mrs. Nguyễn said jokingly, though there was an edge of bitterness.

"*What* old person, especially an *old, Vietnamese man,* would willingly *take care* of another elderly Vietnamese *woman*?" Mrs. Phạm snapped. "Nobody has *friends* anymore. I can't even get my own daughter to call me back, my bones are about to give out any minute now. I could be in the gutter and she'd call me back in three months after my funeral has passed, *when she has time—*"

"Maybe if you hadn't babied her, her entire life—" Mrs. Nguyễn interrupted.

"Oh, like *you're* the best mother? You haven't talked to Priscilla in a year! *A year!* She's probably done being molded into your perfect daughter. Titles aren't everything you know," Mrs. Phạm hissed at her. "Believe it or not, people *can* be happy without money—"

"—Joyce *is* a bit strange, isn't she—" Mrs. Lâm murmured.

"—only poor people say that," Mrs. Nguyễn said, turning her nose in the air. "And those who went to a *public* university. Would you rather have your daughters crying in a Lexus or a Toyota?"

"Joyce went to one of the *top* public universities in the world—" Mrs. Phạm started to respond, as she prepared to take out her sword hidden in her mind palace.

"Would you two shut the hell up?" Mrs. Lâm snarled, irritated at her sisters for botching their attempt to reunite with their mother. "Someone needs to go up there and ring the bell."

They all looked up and watched in fascination as the old man shuffled back into the home and quietly closed the door behind him.

"Do you think . . . they're . . . *together*? That's impossible, right? Isn't it too soon for her to move on?" Mrs. Phạm whispered. Suddenly she bowled over, grabbed her knee to steady herself, and winced in pain.

Mrs. Nguyễn eyed Mrs. Phạm suspiciously. "What's wrong with you? You winced in pain, just like you did at the dim sum restaurant—"

"—the woman has been widowed for almost fifty years, maybe she *did* remarry," Mrs. Lâm whispered back, not realizing what was going on between Mai and Minh. "Exactly how long did you expect her to wait? Till she's six feet under? Though I bet there are better options in the afterlife to date—"

Too lost in their bickering—again—they didn't notice that the door had opened and this time, their mother, the matriarch Mrs. Dương, a lioness, stood looking out. She leaned against her cane and watched her three cubs fight among themselves. Her white hair was pulled back into a neat bun that sat on top of her head. Her signature mole on the right side of her cheek became more prominent in the sun, as if it were a third eye who had seen it all.

. . .

Once inside, Mrs. Mai Nguyễn, Mrs. Minh Phạm, and Mrs. Khuyến Lâm sat lined up on the couch, looking guilty, as if they had been caught stealing candy. Mai observed her mother, and how much she had allowed time to capture her the past few decades. She quickly recognized the antique dark jade Buddha necklace below her mother's collarbone. It was the most unusual jade necklace, going from dark purple to dark green. She'd never once seen her mother take it off her neck. It had been passed down from Dương woman to Dương woman throughout the years, and nobody knew where it originated from.

The old man from before came out with a gongfu set and a pot of boiling hot water. He set the tray down, fanned out the mini cups, and poured hot water all over it, making sure it was pure enough to host the tea leaves. The wooden slats in the tray caught the water underneath, like catching rainwater. The sisters watched with respect, their heads bowed, as he put dry tea leaves into the pot, poured hot water into it, rinsed out the leaves, and repeated himself until the water ran clear. He then offered a cup to each sister and their mother. As everyone gingerly picked up a teacup, he smiled and raised his own glass toward them. When he smiled, he revealed missing teeth, and Mai couldn't help but think of her father, who had been deceased for as long as she could remember. All she had were clipped memories of him, but she could vividly see him smiling at her, also with missing teeth. She wondered if their father had been alive, if the estrangement could have been avoided.

"Cảm ơn, Chú," Mai said. She sipped her tea.

"Save it," Mrs. Dương said. "He doesn't speak Vietnamese. He's Chinese."

"Oh!" Khuyến said, confused. "Why is he here—?"

"Bao is my boyfriend," Mrs. Dương said calmly. "Companionship is important in our old age. You'll soon all understand. *Especially* since all our ingrate children abandoned us. We play Chinese checkers and watch TV together. That's all we need." Exposing his missing teeth even more, the old man waved at the three sisters whose mouths hung from shock.

"But . . . how do you speak to each other?" Mai asked suspiciously, staring back and forth between Bao and her mother.

"There's no need for us to communicate with each other beyond indicating when to flip the channel and say when we are hungry."

"So, how'd you meet Bao?" Minh asked hesitantly, as if she didn't really want to know the answer.

"We met at the temple. Mutual friends." Mrs. Dương sipped her tea calmly, though there was a dangerous tone in her voice, warning her daughters not to ask too many questions.

"And . . . is it serious?" Khuyến asked, genuinely curious. She put her teacup down and stared at Bao as if he were a zoo animal that was playing dress-up in a white, sleeveless shirt, silk pajama bottoms, and slip-ons.

"More serious than the fact that you've all descended upon my body like a pack of vultures? Picking whatever is left for your inheritance?" Mrs. Dương said as her gaze drilled into each of their faces.

The sisters shifted in their seats. Though they were well beyond their adolescence, they couldn't help but feel small in their mother's presence. It felt like they were back in their tiny home in south Vietnam, when they were all kids, arguing about whose turn it was to ride the bike into town.

"We didn't come here to seek money, Mẹ," Mai said, coughing nervously. "We came to make amends with you. To spend your golden years with you while we can. You know, before it's . . . too late."

Mrs. Dương sighed and stared back at them, barely recognizing them. Mai, the dramatic one. Minh, the quiet one. Khuyến, the headstrong one. "I'm healthy, just in case you're wondering."

"Have you been to the doctor? When was your last checkup?" Minh asked urgently, as she tried to cover up another oncoming sharp pain in her chest. She swallowed and suppressed the pain.

"I'm not paying for a doctor. Don't be stupid. I'm fine."

"Mẹ, I went to see a woman in Hawaii, Auntie Hứa. Linh Hứa," Mai said, her voice shaking. "She . . . she mentioned that there would be a death this year, a death in this family. And she advised me that this is the year I reach back out to my sisters and my mother, before it's too late."

Silence fell over the group as all eyes stared at Mrs. Dương, as if they were waiting for her to be struck by lightning at that very moment. All eyes except for Bao, who had fallen asleep in his chair and was lightly snoring, head tilted back, mouth ajar. Mrs. Dương did not blink at the prediction. In fact, she didn't seem surprised at all.

"Well, are you *sure* it's not one of you three?" she asked nonchalantly. Mai and Khuyến burst out protesting, saying that it surely had to be *her*. After all, it made the *most* sense. The *age* difference and all. Minh simply shifted her eyes down and stayed quiet.

"And what about your other sister? Kim? Did the woman in Hawaii say to make up with her as well? She is your sister, is she not?" Mrs. Dương said, still acting as if they were having a regular conversation in line at the grocery store, and not deciding who would bite the dust, like a macabre parlor game. Mrs. Dương had the memory of an elephant, and she was never one to let go of grudges easily. She could never forget that day when her oldest daughter, Kim Lương, came back into her life from the dead, and how her other daughters treated her, like she was an infestation that needed to be taken care of. "Have you also come to make amends with her and her two daughters as well? They *are* your nieces."

"*Technically,* half nieces—" Minh started, but stopped when she saw Khuyến shoot her a death glare.

Khuyến quickly got off the couch, sank to her knees, and bowed before their mother. "Mẹ, we came to make things right with you, if that means making things right with Kim and her daughters, we will."

Mai guffawed and threw her hands in the air. "Are you kidding, Khuyến? Stand up! We all got kicked out of the Santa Ana house because of that woman! That house was under *my* name, and it went to Kim and her daughters. I suffered through that marriage with Thanh for that home! My daughters were *homeless—*"

"ENOUGH!" Mrs. Dương shouted, banging her cane down. "I will not rehash the same arguments anymore. I gave my reasons back then, and those reasons still hold true to this day. I didn't know Kim was alive this whole time, and in return, I vowed to spend the rest of my life making it up to her, for abandoning her like that. I am not my mother; I will not abandon my daughters. How can *you* all call yourself mothers?" She began to feel faint and teetered on her feet. Bao immediately snapped out of his sleep and ran toward her, helping her get back on her feet. Nothing else needed to be said between them, because their need for each other was the only language that they spoke fluently.

"Mẹ! Are you okay?" Khuyến cried out and ran toward her mother. Minh shot up and grabbed a pillow to put behind her mother's back. Everyone began scrambling and fussing around Mrs. Dương, making sure that she was comfortable, hydrated, and stable. Minh glanced behind her to see where Mai was, and saw that she was still quietly sitting on the couch. The look on her face was indecipherable, but the one fat vein on the side of her neck was back, and Minh's face went ghost pale when she saw it begin to pulse.

"Trời ơi," Minh whispered. "Not the *vein*."

Mrs. Dương quickly recovered from her faint spell and pushed Bao's hand away. He was furiously fanning her with a palm leaf. She looked up and stared at her oldest daughter, who sat immobile, her stubbornness radiating from her like the remnants of a bombed war zone. "Did you come all this way to make sure that that psychic was correct?" she spat out. "You wanted to see for yourself if I was the one who would pass away this year, didn't you?"

Mai folded her hands in her lap and stared at her mother, a mother who had turned into a stranger. Their eyes met each other, and they both had the same question cross their minds. *Who really was the woman before her?* Did they ever really know each other? Or were they put on this earth, forced to orbit each other? "You always loved Kim more than you loved me, didn't you, Mẹ? She's technically your firstborn, not me," Mai asked quietly.

Khuyến and Minh both fell quiet, avoiding contact with their mother and Mai. Just like the day when their mother forced Mai into marriage, they stayed silent. And just like the day when their mother forced Mai out of the house so she could give it to Kim, they stayed silent.

"Don't be so sensitive and dramatic, Mai," Mrs. Dương said. "What's love have to do with any of this? I taught you better than this. I taught *all* my daughters how to survive. I didn't abandon any of you. I am not my mother. It's all of *you* who abandoned me."

"How can we get back to how we were before, Mẹ?" Minh asked quietly.

Mai got up, draped her fake Louis bag over her arm, and wrapped her silk scarf around her head again. "Forget it, Minh. There's nothing to go back to. I don't even know why I bothered trying. Nothing ever changes with our mother. Stone never bends, and neither will she." Despite her two sisters protesting for Mai to stop talking nonsense and to sit back down, Mai walked past her mother without another word. She knew that her mother wouldn't stop her.

"Don't do this," Minh pleaded to Mai. "Let's stay and work it out. Just like you said before, *before* it's too late."

"Come back!" Khuyến begged as well. "I want all of us to be a family again."

"Let her go," Mrs. Dương said, emotionless. "She's always done what she's wanted to do. She was born a stubborn, foolish girl and she will die stubborn."

"Mẹ!" Minh cried out, frustrated. "Why are you two always like this!"

Mai didn't say anything; she just kept walking. She walked past the family's ancestral altar, which was crowded with black-and-white photos of their ancestors— all women, *so* many women. Women who had the same thick, black rope hair they all once had. Women whose blood flowed through Mai and her own three daughters, cursed blood that carried the sins of their mothers, and their mother's mother. All because one woman, an epoch ago, fell in love with a man, and ran away to Cambodia, because she wanted to live for herself for once.

For the second time in her life, Mrs. Dương watched Mai turn her back on her, not knowing if she'd come back. And just like last time, Mrs. Dương didn't chase or beg, because she knew that it wouldn't matter. Mai had inherited her stubbornness from her after all. She heard Mai slam the front door, and then she heard it slam a second time as Minh and Khuyến ran after her.

• • •

The house grew still once again, just like it had been before her daughters stopped by. Silence was all Mrs. Dương had known the past decade; in fact, it had been her primary companion.

As the sun set behind the house, and Bao shuffled off to his separate bedroom to get ready for bed, Mrs. Dương sat alone in the dim living room. She sat until the darkness engulfed her surroundings completely. She reflected on everything that transpired earlier during the mini-reunion with her daughters, wondering if she had unnecessarily lost her temper again. Ultimately she decided that it had unfolded exactly as it was meant to. Everything always does. She felt confident in this, because her *own* psychic was never wrong.

The last burning remnants of incense on the ancestral altar began to die out, and she allowed the familiar musty smell to linger in the cracks of her home. She reached up toward her neck, and instinctively thumbed her jade Buddha necklace, looking for a sign, but instead of the usual coolness, the stone felt lukewarm between her fingers, and she knew that it was almost time. Not yet, but almost.

8

Mrs. Minh Phạm

MRS. MINH PHẠM TUGGED ON her jade necklace pendant as she waited in the entryway of the apothecary. Trying to distract herself, she counted the many different mason jars and burlap sacks containing herbs and questionable fermented liquids precariously stacked on top of one another. Then she quickly lost count. The repetitive humming of Buddhist chants played softly from an old boom box sitting in the corner on top of a pile of yellowed Vietnamese newspapers. The familiar smell of sandalwood incense wafted in and out from under her nose, depending on where the wind blew through the open window.

Mrs. Phạm was no stranger to this particular shop, tucked away from a bustling outdoor complex in Garden Grove. The storefront was a forgotten relic of Little Saigon, only remembered by the first wave of refugees. Now, it was overshadowed by its new neighbors: trendy boba tea shops and modern Vietnamese fare with neon signs that catered to Orange County influencers. Mrs. Phạm turned to this shop for all her needs; she abhorred modern medicine. She hated everything to do with it—the *smell* of hospitals, the *look* of hospitals, the *idea* of hospitals. It always made her want to gag, especially when she gave in to the memories of her father being wheeled into the hospital after being shot in the war. He never came back out.

For the past two decades the shop had grown wary of Mrs. Phạm's erratic presence. The staff lived in constant fear of Mrs. Phạm, who would burst through the front door on any given day and hour of the week, demanding herbs and remedies to cure her daughter, Joyce. And don't even speak of the day before Lunar New Year—she'd come banging on their window the moment they flipped the sign to Open. Despite whatever herbs they gave her or their assurances that Joyce was *just fine*, Mrs. Phạm was insistent that her daughter was . . . đặc biệt. That Joyce was *special*. But Mrs. Phạm was looking for a very *particular* cure because she knew that being different came with its own set of grievances and hardships. She didn't want her daughter to suffer from loneliness. To Mrs. Phạm, loneliness was the real curse. She gave birth to a distant daughter and was legally tied to a distant husband; nothing was worse than living under a roof full of people with no one to talk to.

On this particular day, however, Mrs. Phạm came to the shop for herself, to get some thuốc nam to cure her of whatever was causing her chest pain. It had gotten particularly worse the past month, since their disastrous wreck of a family reunion at her mother's house.

After that day, neither her sisters nor her mother had reached out. They were all back to resuming the same schedule they had during the estrangement: avoiding the T&K Food Market on Sunday, praying at separate temples, and going to different vendors for fake designer bags at the Golden West swap meet.

Mrs. Phạm's stress levels were affecting her sleep, forcing her awake every three hours throughout the night. She'd jolt up, decompressing from the strangest dreams about her ancestor, Oanh Dương. All she could see in her nightmares was a faceless witch, cursing their family over and over again, plaguing them for generations. Mrs. Phạm would shuffle past her snoring husband to the kitchen in her silk pajamas and grab any cold leftovers from the fridge. Or fry up an egg with Maggi seasoning drizzled on top, or haphazardly cut up some lạp xưởng to put in her rice with fatty bì crumbles on top. In those lost hours, deep in thought—and carbs—she allowed herself to cry.

The store assistant came out from behind the beaded curtains and told her the herbalist was ready to see her. Her legs were wobbly when she got up, but she squared her shoulders and marched toward the back room like she was getting a beer with the grim reaper himself.

"Chị! How are you!" The old man got on his creaky knees from behind his workstation. He put down the ladle he had been using to scoop out a black, tarlike liquid into smaller vials, and extended his arms out to Mrs. Phạm. His newsboy cap covered what was left of his white hair and his eyes crinkled warmly. "It has been a long time."

"Clearly I'm not doing well," she responded, giving him a side eye as she embraced his hand. "If I find myself back in your store."

He laughed. "Come now, Chị, you know that everyone comes in for different needs, not all of it is bad. Even good things need a bit of prodding along, otherwise there would be people out there who still wouldn't have the courage to ask someone to dance with them. Sit, sit. How is Joyce? Is she still in New York?" He gestured toward the oak rocking chair that she'd sat in for over twenty years, every time she came running into the store.

Mrs. Phạm sank into the chair, allowing her knees to give out. All the tension that she'd been storing—from hiding her health problems and her family drama, to the psychic's prediction in Kauai, to being worried about her daughter, Joyce—suddenly released itself from her.

"Yes," she sighed. "Still in New York, doing *who* knows *what* out there. She hasn't returned any of my calls. For all I know, she could be dead."

"Ah, you know how children are when they grow up!" He waved his hand, dismissing her worries. "They don't want anything to do with us old folk. Go enjoy your life! You should travel, see the seven wonders of the world!"

Mrs. Phạm harrumphed. "You *know* I don't like airplanes. That recycled air is bad for my weak lungs."

"Well, what about just local travel? Go on a road trip? Explore the parts of California you haven't seen before!"

"You *know* my lower back can't be in a car for more than an hour."

"What about . . . ah, well . . ." His voice trailed off, smile glitching. "Anyways, what troubles you, Chị? Is it Joyce again?" He put on his spectacles and took out her big file: the amalgamated history of Mrs. Phạm's hypochondria and idiosyncrasies. The folder was bursting at the spine, its frayed edges trying their best to hold together a splintered relationship between a mother and daughter.

"I've been having chest pain," she replied. "It rolls, like waves, over and over again, crashing against me."

"Show me where."

Mrs. Phạm pointed at the areas in her chest, describing the times in which the pain would surface and how long they lasted for. The old man scratched his head, and his face grew serious. "Chị, this is very troubling," he said. "This could affect your heart long term if you are not careful. Anytime there is pain near your heart, you must protect your most important organ at all costs. This pain is getting closer, breaching it, climbing the wall." He took out a new sheet of paper, and put it on top of her big file and began writing large urgent scribbles.

Mrs. Phạm gasped, and she clutched her fake Louis bag to her chest. "Trời ơi! I'm not *dying*, am I?" She began to bawl. "I'm too young to die! *Damn that psychic!*" She immediately thought of Joyce, as she always did. She knew she had to do whatever it took to live. She was all Joyce had left, even if their relationship was hanging on by a thread. Was she the one who was meant to die in Auntie Hứa's prediction?

"I believe your yin and yang are imbalanced. Your current worries and stresses in your family life are causing these pains. If you don't fix them soon, it could drive you to an early grave."

"How do I fix it then?" she exclaimed. "I'll pay whatever price is needed! I'll pay double! Triple! Just fix me, thầy!"

"Follow me."

They went back out to the front. He grabbed a little sack and walked around the store, stopping in front of certain barrels to scoop out a spoonful from each one, and then he'd move on to the next barrel. Mrs. Phạm shuffled behind him, moaning and complaining, moaning and complaining some more, filling his ear about all the trouble her sisters had been causing her recently. But most of all, she complained about Mai and how bitter her older sister had become.

After they completed a full circle around the store, they went back up to the counter, and the old man took out a mortar and pestle and crushed all the herbs together. He began to wax poetic about how the body always breaks down as all things tend to do with age. Mrs. Phạm was barely listening to him, too engrossed in her hatred of Mai. She talked over him as she always did.

The old man's gray eyes glistened as he began slowly turning all the herbs into a fine powder. "The first to go are always the bones—"

"—she was *always* the stubborn one—"

"—then the sinew—"

"—thinks her daughters are better than mine—"

"—then your spirit—"

"—and now she's putting *me* into an *early* grave—"

"—and as your soul reincarnates—"

"—everyone blames Mai for breaking up the family, she should have just welcomed Kim and her daughters—"

"Ah! Here we go, Chị," he interrupted as he poured the fine powder into an old glass jar and sealed it shut. "Boil a spoonful every morning when you wake up, and one before bed for the next month. This *should* help."

Mrs. Phạm thanked him and quickly took out wads of cash, wrapped in an old red rubber band, still complaining loudly about Mai and how she ruined everything by not simply accepting their half sister and half nieces when Kim Lương showed up on their front steps, twenty-some-odd years ago. The old man tried his best to hide his exasperation. Like everyone else in Little Saigon, he was sick of hearing about the Dương family drama. Surely, these women should have gotten over it by now? He turned around, and headed toward the northwest corner of his shop. This area was darker and dustier, and wrapped in a strange, shimmering mist that could be missed if you blinked too fast.

Mrs. Phạm stopped talking, and her eyes curiously followed the old herbalist around the shop. *How strange.* She'd been inside this shop so many times; she knew every nook, cranny, inch, and price tag of every barrel. Yet that corner seemed to have appeared out of nowhere, despite the cobwebs.

Like the rest of the shop, this corner was stacked with items and jars on every shelf, from floor to ceiling. Even the cracks between the jars had something stuffed inside. The old man rolled out a wooden ladder and climbed to the upper middle rack, blindly pushing and searching with his fingers. He reached deeper and deeper until his whole arm had disappeared into the shelf. Mrs. Phạm thought he was going to fall in. He finally gasped victoriously. He retrieved a small wooden box with dark red engravings. Despite every item in that corner being buried under dust, the box remained untouched by time. He carefully descended the ladder and brought it to the counter. He opened it in front of Mrs. Phạm, and took out a small glass vial of liquid.

"For your sister Mai. It might help."

Mrs. Phạm cocked her head, staring at it suspiciously. "What is it for?" She lowered her voice so no one else in the store could hear her, suddenly worried about how all her complaining was coming across. "Thầy, I'm not trying to *poison* her, you know. I was just *complaining* about her. You know how sisters are. I'm not looking for a . . . *permanent* solution, you know what I mean?"

"Trong tình yêu đích thực không có niềm kiêu hãnh," he said to her. "In true love there is no pride. Thích Nhất Hạnh."

Mrs. Phạm curiously stared at the little glass vial in her hand as she tilted it up, allowing the sun to flow through. "How will this help Mai? What's in it?"

He gave her a little wink. "Ancient Chinese Secret."

"Seriously?" Mrs. Phạm wrinkled her nose.

"No, I'm kidding. Just slip it into her coffee the next time you see her, and allow it to work its magic. Your own pain will only be cured if her internal pain is cured, as will the rest of your family."

"How much?"

"No charge."

"*Why?* You've never given me anything free the entire time we've known each other."

"Let's just say that we've all been cheering on the Dương women for a while. Consider it a gift from the spirits. There is only one cure for curses in this world, and I've been saving this vial for a long time. It's time it gets put to use. The world needs more of it."

Mrs. Phạm stared at him like he had just spoken in Mandarin to her. But she was never one to turn down any free items, discounts, or sales, so she didn't question him. She tucked the vial and her new herbs into her fake Louis and snapped it shut.

"Oh, and Chị?" the herbalist said. "Save a drop. Just a smidge."

Her ears perked up. "Who else would it be for?"

He gave her a tiny smile. "You'll know when the time comes. A small drop is all that is needed."

She slowly backed out of the store, staring at the old apothecarist, chalking up his strange behavior to him being secretly in love with her all these years. *Who could blame him?*

9

Thảo Nguyễn

THẢO NGUYỄN MISSED HER flight back to Los Angeles on purpose.

She sent an email to her investors immediately, saying that she'll take the meeting over video instead of being there in person. She claimed there was an emergency at the factory that needed her presence; she needed to stay behind in Sài Gòn. The truth was that she wasn't ready to face the reality waiting for her in California: her family. Her mother cried on the phone when Thảo called her to tell her that she wouldn't be coming home after all. In a bloodcurdling wail, she repeatedly asked how on *earth* could Thảo miss her flight. She should have known better when it came to Sài Gòn traffic and she should have headed to Tân Sơn Nhất International Airport hours early, *especially* for an international flight.

Thảo sighed and set the phone down on her bathroom countertop. She switched the call to speakerphone. Her mother's voice rang out, lecturing her over and over again. Thảo was used to it by now, being the youngest of three. She'd heard it all. She began drawing in her lip liner, then carefully applied a dark, sexy red stain. Her open suitcase lay empty, reflecting itself back in the mirror, reminding her of her calculated move. Her mother grew exponentially furious over the phone at how flippant Thảo was acting. Thảo, in a monotone voice, told her to stop worrying so much, as she began drawing in a sleek, black cat eye.

"Why do you love Vietnam so much? We escaped the war so we'd never have to go back there, and now you've bought a second home over there, *and* moved all your business operations over there. Are you insane?" Her mother's voice breaking the sound barrier over the phone. "What are you *doing* over there all the time?"

"I need to be closer to the seamstresses, pay them an ethical wage, watch over operations personally," Thảo explained, for the millionth time. She knew her mother would call again in a few days, asking the same questions, expecting a different set of answers, but feigning the same skepticism. Thảo pursed her lips in the mirror, making sure that her lipstick matched the rest of her outfit, a dark red, off-the-shoulder bodycon dress that exposed the kind of collarbones that rendered men unintelligent.

"Just because you have a Vietnamese face, doesn't mean you're one of them," her mother said.

"Yes, Mẹ," Thủy said.

"You have an American mind-set."

"Yes, Mẹ."

"Don't do drugs. Watch for pickpockets."

"Yes, Mẹ."

"Don't party so much!"

"Yes, Mẹ."

"Don't drink too much; you're going to get wrinkles."

"Yes, Mẹ."

"You will *never* be one of them."

"Yes, Mẹ."

Thảo finished her eyebrows and did her best to assuage her mother. She knew the right words to work her magic, which was to tell anything *but* the truth. Her mother hadn't been back to Sài Gòn in over three decades, so she wouldn't believe Thảo if she told her how energizing it was. That the new generation had modernized it while keeping certain traditions alive. Sài Gòn had evolved into a hub of tech, literature, music, and international businesses. Expats flooded the city, attempting to cash in on the Sài Gòn revival. This opulence and decadence was only known to those who knew how to navigate the twenty-four districts, unlike the white men who only wanted to pass through Bùi Viện Street trying to fill their time with women and watered-down alcohol.

"Listen, I have to go, Mẹ," Thảo said. "There's a work meeting I have to get to."

"Okay, con," her mother said, defeat in her voice. They both knew it was a lie; the time difference spoke for itself. "It's been a year since you've been home. Will you come back soon?"

Thảo stared at the clock, realizing that she was late. She said the same thing every time her mother asked this question. "Yes, Mẹ."

Her mother knew it was another lie, but she didn't want to break the fantasy for the rare chance that Thảo really meant it this time. "Okay, con, be safe."

Thảo did a last-minute touch-up, grabbed her purse, slipped on some strappy kitten heels, did a quick mirror fit check, and roughly let loose some of the pink balayage wisps she recently dyed to frame her face. She pulled her off-the-shoulder dress an inch lower, exposing her sleeve tattoo on the left arm. Then she took out her phone, pulled up the Grab app, and requested a motorbike to take her to District 1.

She walked outside to meet her driver, a young guy with slicked-back hair. The humidity hit her like a brick oven, but she was used to the weather in south Vietnam by now. In fact, her body had adapted so well to it, her hair began to shine brighter, and her skin became naturally dewy. It was almost as if her Vietnamese body, born on American soil, was genetically meant to be in this weather. When the Grab bike arrived, the driver handed her a helmet and she politely turned it down. She didn't want to mess up her hair or her outfit, either. She'd take her chances, whatever they were.

As she wrapped her hand around the waist of her driver, he expertly wove their way through the organized chaos. The feeling of being surrounded by the thousands of motorbikes that boxed them in was still thrilling to her, even after all these years of coming and going from Sài Gòn. Some motorists came so close to her that she could see the crow's feet lining their eyes. The men would flirtatiously smile back, while the fashionable women would stare at her, calling her a Việt kiều in their mind. Even though Thảo looked Vietnamese, they could instantly tell that she wasn't one of them, that she hadn't been raised here. It was just as her mother warned her.

The wind blew through Thảo's hair, and she arched her back and laughed as her driver sped up. She felt so connected, being in the middle of thousands and thousands of strange faces, all weaving around her, heading god knows where at this hour. She just felt alive, something she hadn't really felt before moving here.

The motorbike stopped in front of a lively bar in District 1, overcrowded with an international and chic crowd. Sweaty, drunk tourists spilled out into the streets, while bored Vietnamese workers followed them out, tired of taking care of them, but they persisted through the late night, carrying buckets of beer in case they wanted to buy another one. Expats nonchalantly stepped over the drunk tourists, looking down on them, while ignoring the bar workers as they made their way into the bar. Young Vietnamese professionals lined the steps, smoking cigarettes, their ties loosened until the morning light came, reminding them to tighten it to continue the work grind again and again until the day they died.

Thảo stepped out, thanked the driver, smoothed out her minidress, and walked up the stairs. She could feel eyes on her as she dodged through the crowd. Different accents and languages floated around her. British, German, French, American, Australian, Chinese, Japanese, it went on and on. Some were tourists, others were repeat visitors, or weekend warriors, but mostly, this was an expat rooftop bar. Thảo knew this bar well and expertly made her way to the second set of stairs, hidden inside the kitchen, known only to locals or adventurous souls, and walked all the way up the winding narrow metal staircase.

The rooftop opened up before her. "OH MY GOD! Thảo! *Thảo!*" Thảo instantly recognized the screaming voice and turned to see her Vietnamese Australian coworker, Alexandria, come running up to her. Alexandria drunkenly embraced her. "I *knew* you were going to miss your flight. There was no way in hell you were going to go back to America now, especially given the climate, *just* for a meeting." She flagged down a server and requested two more shots. "Besides, why would you ever *voluntarily* want to go back there?"

Thảo laughed. "My mom lost her shit, though. It's been a year since we've seen each other. I swear she was going to have a heart attack over the phone. I eventually do need to go back home at some point. I have Asian-daughter guilt for being away from home for so long."

"The key word is 'eventually,'" Alexandria said as the shots came, and she handed one to Thảo. "You think I also don't have Asian-daughter guilt? We can't keep doing things for our mothers. We need to break out of these generational cycles and expectations and live for ourselves. *We* can't waste our twenties and good looks doing what our parents want, right? Think like a Vietnamese daughter, but execute like a westernized daughter." Thảo laughed at Alexandria's drunken TED Talk and clinked her glass with hers, and they both took down the shots with ease.

Behind Thảo, a group of girls squealed and flagged her down, telling her to join them. They were her tightest group of friends in Sài Gòn. For the most part, they all lived either in District 1 or District 2. It was a mix of Vietnamese American, Vietnamese Australian, a Vietnamese Canadian girl from Montreal, and a Vietnamese girl from Paris. The common denominators were obvious: all first-generation Vietnamese women of the diaspora, the youngest in their families, and all drawn to live in Sài Gòn trying to understand their roots. But most of all, they all wanted to go as far away as they possibly could from their families.

"Girl, we had bets going on whether or not you were going to miss your flight," Evelyn said.

"Pay up, Evelyn," Sarah exclaimed, holding out her hand. Evelyn groaned and begrudgingly threw crumpled wads of đồng at her.

"I thought you had a big meeting in Los Angeles you had to be there in person for? With the investors? To set up the warehouse or whatever it is you do?" Evelyn asked Thảo.

Thảo laughed it off. "It's the twenty-first century, isn't it? I can be physically in Vietnam and pop up halfway around the world in a little box to speak to people."

"That's my girl," Alexandria said. "Or should I say, that's my boss?"

"You can only be my employee if you actually show up to the office."

Behind the group of girls, a man cleared his throat and said Thảo's name in a deep, radio voice, with just a hint of a South African accent. The women rolled their eyes and begrudgingly parted the sea, making clearance for Thảo to walk toward him. As the smile on Thảo's face grew wider and wider, the faces of all her friends contorted with pure disgust. Sarah stuck her finger down her throat, pretending to vomit. Evelyn rolled her eyes so far back, they could have popped out of their sockets. And Alexandria made a gagging motion and quickly requested for more drinks to be delivered. "Of *course* you didn't miss your flight for us. It was for Mr. Mediocre himself," Alexandria said.

"You're always too kind to me, Alexandria. I know you *definitely* approve of me," the man said as he swooped Thảo up in his arms and spun her around. "Hi. Hey. Is it true? Did you miss your flight for me?"

Thảo shook her head, but her eyes deceived her. "Of course not, Jeff. Had a few business things to take care of here. It just so *happened* I was able to catch you on your last night here before you went off to Singapore for a few months. Pure coincidence is all."

Jeff flashed her an award-winning smile, and she melted. His smile looked just like his dating profile: genuine, authentic, and a little mischievous. Despite Alexandria looking at his dating profile and saying that his smile looked like it was full of red flags, STDs, and the markings of a serial gaslighter. Thảo didn't listen to her; she never listened to anyone who ever warned her of her terrible choice in men. Because she simply didn't want to hear it.

Thảo was starting to grow attached to him, and she never grew attached to anyone. Not in this climate, where cute foreigners, tourists, and expats flowed freely every night, like they were living in Roman times, a never-ending turnstile of hot men in a transient city. Meeting men was the easy part; falling in love was unheard of.

Jeff wrapped his muscular arms around her, and she pressed her body closer to his. His eyes darted down her dress, and she pressed her body even deeper, allowing him to see everything. She *wanted* him to have all of her, especially the parts that he couldn't see. For Thảo, it was easy to get naked with someone, but it was much harder being intimate. There was the "Asian-daughter lie" that she gave to her mother earlier, the "cool girl lie" she gave to Jeff just now, and the real lie that she told herself every day: that she was ready for a real relationship and to fall in love. But she was afraid to admit that she was scared. She was scared of Jeff, or any man, for only ever seeing her as someone to call when they were just "passing through Sài Gòn." She was tired of always being an afterthought, never a forethought.

Thảo felt her phone vibrate, and she briefly broke away from Jeff. She glanced at the screen only to see that it was from her distant cousin, Elaine Lâm. She read the clipped message on her home screen without expanding the message: hey girl, heard ur coming back soon? Before u leave Viet, need favor . . . She raised her eyebrow, annoyed that Elaine was interrupting her. Thảo attempted to hide the message from Jeff, swiping the notification away quickly. Her mood turned sour. *Why was her family so embarrassing?* They treated Thảo like a drug mule, asking her for favors all the time, shepherding things back and forth from Vietnam to the States. Last time it was smuggling American cash to other relatives and friends who lived in Vietnam, or requesting she bring back dried goods or illegal plants. Thảo hated that her family was like this, just so . . . *unrefined.*

"Everything okay?" Jeff asked.

Thảo looked up and planted a cheerful smile on her face. "All good, just a work thing." It was another one of her white lies, a lie to make her life back home more palatable.

Familial responsibilities like this is why she kept staying away. Why couldn't her older sisters, Priscilla and Thủy, deal with this for her? Just because they barely spoke to each other didn't mean she should be the one to handle shit like this. She flicked her phone on silent, and grabbed Jeff's hand to pull him to the ledge of the rooftop so that they could people-watch from high up in their perch. She needed a distraction. Now.

Jeff flagged a waiter to order drinks for them. She stared at his rugged profile and she squeezed his ass playfully. "You're going to break my heart one day, aren't you?" she asked him.

He looked down at her and laughed. "Come on, that only works if people love each other. We're just having fun, right?" He winked at her.

Thảo felt herself freeze up and opened her mouth to protest, but she felt her phone vibrate again in her pocket, and she knew it was another message from Elaine or her mother or *somebody* from her family. She swallowed her words and flashed him that *cool girl* smile again and gave a weak laugh. "Right."

Now he squeezed *her* bottom and kissed her forehead. Behind him, she could see all her girlfriends mouthing at her to cut him out of her life. Alexandria turned her fingers into a pair of scissors and began snipping at the air. Thảo flipped them all off and mouthed at them to shut up. She focused on the cute guy in front of her who didn't want any of the things she wanted, but she forced herself to believe that he could change for her, one day. It was another "Thảo lie," but this time she gave it to herself, because he provided a good enough distraction from the fact that she was lonely in a city of nine million people.

10

Mrs. Khuyến Lâm

MRS. KHUYẾN LÂM ARRIVED AT the temple an hour early to avoid the crowd.

She liked to appear early, especially before her two daughters, Elaine and Christine. They always came to the temple with fifty pounds of makeup on, eyelashes heavier than brick, cat eyes sharper than a machete. As much as she loved them, she needed silence for this. She came to kneel before her ancestors and ask for guidance. Because whatever was infecting the women in their family was dangerously close to spreading to her daughters.

Mrs. Lâm was the only one in that temple, and that usually indicated desperation. She took off her shoes before entering the golden arches of the temple, grabbed a floor pillow that was stacked in the corner, and headed to the front. She stopped before a fifty-foot golden Buddha statue that towered over her 4'11" frame. She tipped her head back to gaze up at the statue's abhaya hand gesture, which symbolized fearlessness after reaching enlightenment.

As Mrs. Lâm fell down on her knees and began to chant, asking the Buddha to help guide her, she dug deep within her soul. She prayed, asking to help her find a way to allow forgiveness into her family. She wondered if there would ever be a day where everyone could forgive each other, before another decade passed them by. She asked if every mistake that had led them to this moment could be washed away. Mrs. Lâm was not one to beg or accept beggars back into her life, and yet here she was, begging Buddha for answers, wondering how to fix her broken heart that had seemingly outlasted her broken family by a millennium.

· · ·

After the morning's session ended at the temple, Mrs. Lâm and her daughters headed to their flagship nail salon that they owned. Mrs. Lâm forced her daughters, Elaine and Christine, to carry in the Costco-size supplies from the car, while she sat in a massage chair, setting it on the highest pressure, and kicked off her shoes, drained from all the family drama.

"*Christ*, what are in these boxes? They're so heavy!" Christine cried out. "I'm going to chip an acrylic. Can't we get one of the guys to carry them in? Like, I thought I was going to do more of the paperwork around here today, not so much *manual* labor!"

"I'm sorry, do you see *men* around here? If you do, please direct me to them. I haven't had sex in months," Elaine snapped as she rolled her eyes at her younger sister. "Stop complaining. You're in a *nail salon*, it's the emergency room for broken nails. I think you'll survive if you chip a nail."

Mrs. Lâm called out from the chair: "Both of you need to stop talking and hurry up. I need you to make another run for supplies for the coffee shop after this." Even Elaine cursed at her mother's endless requests. Mrs. Lâm had been making her girls work the nail salon and coffee shop since they'd been cut from her umbilical cords. She was used to ordering them around, both as a mother and as their boss. Mrs. Lâm would balk at all the social workers who would come sniffing around in their early years, saying that her girls weren't allowed to work, citing something called "child labor laws" and that she was in "violation" of them. Americans were so soft and doughy, like the inside of a bánh cam.

No wonder they didn't win the war, Mrs. Lâm would think to herself every time the social workers backed down.

Mrs. Lâm closed her eyes and allowed herself to take in her kingdom, one arm over her head, while her other hand instinctively went up to her earlobe, to tug on her jade hoop earrings, a tic she had whenever she was lost in thought. Her thriving businesses were her oasis, far removed from any family drama except from her nuclear family. She couldn't help but rerun the scene of Mai leaving them like that, with so much pain in her eyes. She'd seen that pain in her sister's eyes over and over again throughout the years, and yet, Mrs. Lâm always stayed silent. The day their mother forced Mai to get married. The day their mother forced Mai to give up her ownership over the Santa Ana home. The day their mother chose her first daughter, Kim, over all of them. Each time, Mrs. Lâm had left her sister to fend for herself. The guilt began seeping in her body. She knew that she'd never really been there for her older sister. Mrs. Lâm tried to shake the guilt from her. *What was there to do?* There was nothing she *could* do. The women in her family were born stubborn and would die stubborn. She needed to focus on running a healthy and thriving business for her own daughters' survival.

Her nail salon was crowded with customers, a mix of English and Vietnamese filled the air, and her eardrums fluttered like a fly on the wall, trying to catch any gossip that she could, in either language. Girlfriends sat side by side, drinking champagne with one hand, while their other hand was being tended to by their Vietnamese nail technicians.

"David *still* watches through all of my Instagram stories. Every. Single. One. *All*. The. *Way*. To. *The*. End."

"Girl, he's *obsessed* with you. Lock your doors."

"It's the Gemini in him."

"*Jesus fucking Christ*. I didn't know you dated a Gemini."

"You know me, I love toxic energy."

When Mrs. Lâm grew tired of their humdrum white-people problems, she switched over to the technicians for the real gossip. "I was at T&K Market the other day, and this poor, old woman collapsed on the floor," Vân said in Vietnamese. She shouted it from table one to Ngọc, who was working at table two. "Also, look at this woman's jewelry! How much do you think her necklace alone costs? How do you think she got it?"

Ngọc quickly glanced at the customer, a gorgeous, young blonde whose neck and ears were dripping with diamonds, and she cackled loudly. She responded back in Vietnamese to Vân. "The necklace? At least a few thousand. *At least*. Also, she didn't come in with a ring around her finger, so you know she's got some rich man buying her gifts in exchange for *you know what*. He also paid for her breasts, look at *them*. The earrings are fake though; you can tell when it catches the light. Fake, fake, *fake*! She's *clearly* not doing a good job giving him what he wants."

It was Vân's turn to cackle loudly. "You're terrible. Not like you can do a better job. You probably haven't been with a man since you left Vietnam. The most they'll give you is a pat on the back, if you're lucky. Have you ever even *been* in love?"

Ngọc sputtered. "I've been with *plenty* of men here. All *types* of men. And they'd be *lucky* to have a woman like me on their arm. Besides, only stupid people fall in love. I'm far too beautiful and smart to ever do that. Look at your blond customer; she's smart, too. Just take the diamonds—nothing else. Get assets and move on."

"Those men should be worried if you're hanging on their arms, probably pickpocketing their watches and wallets. That's the only way you'll be getting anything from them," Vân retorted. All the Vietnamese nail technicians who manned tables three through ten howled with laughter. Each took their turn to roast Ngọc, while all their white customers kept trying to talk over their laughter, to their white friends, pretending that the women in front of them, massaging their hands, didn't exist. As if they were nothing more than the help.

Mrs. Lâm chuckled quietly in her massage chair, her eyes still closed. She loved the women she employed. When the Dương women parted ways a decade ago, Mrs. Lâm sought sisterhood in other ways, as all wolves that break away from their pack do. These women had become more of a family to her than her own family, even though all the women were nhiều chuyện. A bunch of busybodies.

"—the old woman had this big mole on the right side of her cheek. I only noticed it because I was admiring the jade Buddha necklace she wore around her neck. I've never seen that color jade before, a strange, ombré color of dark purple that faded into a dark green. And I thought, what a unique necklace to match such a unique face—" Mrs. Lâm caught a snippet of Vân's description of the old woman who fell at T&K Food Market.

Mrs. Lâm's eyes shot open, and she sprung out of her massage chair. She bolted to Vân's table quickly, nearly knocking over the blonde with the fake earrings along the way. "Describe that woman again. Don't leave out any detail, even if you think it's minor. *I need every detail.* From her hair to her shoes, NOW," Mrs. Lâm instructed Vân, like a drill sergeant aggressively pushing for results from their reports.

Startled, Vân almost ruined the custom Swarovski nail art she was working on. She stammered, complaining that Mrs. Lâm was going to make her start over. Mrs. Lâm's eyes bulged out of her sockets, and she barked at Vân to get over it and to speak faster. Vân's voice was irritated as she repeated the description: mole on right cheek. Jade Buddha necklace. Purple hues that cut diagonally across but turned into an inky, dark green color. Spectacles that hung low above her nose. A purple matching silk set with a white knitted vest over the blouse.

And of course, a fake Louis Vuitton tote bag that hung casually off her arm—a signature Dương style.

Mrs. Lâm almost fainted at the description and grabbed onto Vân to steady herself. "Was she alone? Was she okay? Did an ambulance come? Speak faster, for *Buddha's sake*, Vân!"

"Trời ơi, you look like a rabid animal! I don't know!" Vân cried out in exasperation, and tried to swat her arm away. But Mrs. Lâm's acrylic nails were sharper than any knife as they dug even deeper into Vân's arm. "Everyone tried to help! But the man that was with her only spoke Mandarin, so I don't know what happened to her after the ambulance took her."

Mrs. Lâm removed her nails and collapsed in the chair next to Vân. "That woman you saw falling at the market, she's my mother." She burst into tears, remembering the reunion a month ago. She had left wondering if that was the last time she would see her mother for another ten years. The guilt crept up instantaneously, overwhelming her from all angles. She never stood up for her older sister, and now she felt guilty for not standing up for her mother the last time they were all together. *Was it too late?*

Vân gasped. "The woman who collapsed was your *mother*?"

Mrs. Lâm could barely nod her head before she picked up her phone to call her sisters, her hands trembling. Her mother had been a widow twice over. For her entire life, grief had followed her, like a black crow that remembers every debt that needs to be paid off, and can categorize every face as friend or foe. Her mother was like that. Yes or no. Immediate forgiveness or eternal grudge. In or out. Mrs. Lý Minh Dương of Cần Thơ, from south Vietnam, who now resided in Garden Grove, Orange County, at the youthful age of eighty-eight, had never strayed from any resolute decision she ever made. She didn't believe in regrets or dwelling in the past. And now Mrs. Lâm needed to do the same. She forgave Mai on the spot.

Mrs. Lâm sat there waiting for one of her sisters to pick up her call. She wondered if her prayers had been answered this morning from the temple. If the Dương women were graced by the Buddha with the ability to heal as a family before it was too late. *Was it too late?* Mrs. Lâm was not worried about her mother leaving this life with a mountain of regrets, because it was always the living who had them, never the dead.

She watched Elaine and Christine, who were still moving heavy boxes to and from the parking lot to the store, and she felt more guilt seeping over her. She wondered if she'd been too hard on them, and if they resented her or not. She insisted that her daughters never leave the Orange County bubble; she needed them close to her. Unlike her sisters, whose daughters were scattered in all corners of the world, Mrs. Lâm refused to let her daughters go more than a few miles from her. Because she was secretly afraid that if she were to ever collapse one day, alone at a supermarket, that not even her daughters would come to her aid.

THE FUNERAL

THE FUNERAL

II

Mrs. Lý Minh Dương and Her *Four* Daughters

MRS. LÝ MINH DƯƠNG HAD seen her death coming.

In fact, she saw it all. She saw the thousand lifetimes she had lived before, and she saw the thousands more waiting for her in every reincarnation. In her last moments on earth, Mrs. Dương touched her neck, where her jade Buddha necklace had resided for over seventy years. As soon as she felt the coolness of the stone, she remembered the day her mother had passed on the necklace to her, and she knew it was time.

Her mother had lain on a mat, bundled up in layers of linen despite the raging heat outside. A young Lý was tending to her dying mother, dabbing cold water on her forehead with a wet rag, trying her best to keep her stable. Lý forced herself to put on a brave face, knowing that death was close, but she struggled to offer the right comforting words since they hadn't spoken in months.

Ever since Lý turned down the hand of a young man her mother had attempted to match her with, a hairline fracture had penetrated their relationship. As Lý moved the cloth down to her mother's neck, her hand accidentally grazed the jade necklace, and she flinched, feeling the coolness against her skin. She'd always been wary of the necklace only because it was rather unusual; it wasn't like the common jade jewelry that the other woman wore in the village. It was a dark, rich purple jade that quietly bled into a dark green. Normally, it was the other way around.

Lý wrung out more water from the cloth and quietly pressed it against her mother's delicate frame, avoiding the necklace. She didn't have the strength to meet her mother's hooded eyes. Because she wasn't ready to let go yet, despite all the ugly words that had been exchanged months prior.

"This necklace belonged to your great-great-grandmother, Oanh Dương," her mother said in a raspy voice, breaking the silence.

"Wasn't she the one responsible for the curse on this family?" Lý asked. "Why would you wear such a cursed object around your neck? Don't we already have enough bad luck following the women in this family?"

They finally made eye contact. Her mother's eyes bored into Lý, and this time, she was looking at her differently, possibly seeing her for who she was for the first time in her life. Before, the only looks they could give each other were disappointment and scowls.

Her mother didn't respond. Instead, she attempted to sit up, her lungs struggling from the sheer physicality of such a simple act. Despite Lý's protests to lie down, she managed to get herself in an upright position. She took off the jade necklace and wrapped it in Lý's hands, her heavy breathing a reminder of the limited time they had together.

"Was I a disappointment, Mẹ?" Lý asked quietly, unsure what to do with the necklace. It just lay there, waiting for her to accept it and give it a new home for a new generation.

Her mother's eyes began to flicker, fading in and out. She fought to stay present. She managed to close Lý's fist around the necklace, her hand lingering. "No, Lý, I am the one who is a disappointment. I should have done more as your mother, instead of blaming you for things that were out of your control. One day, Lý, you will be a mother, and you will know what sacrifice means. I *know* you will be a better mother than I ever was."

Lý didn't remember much of what happened after. She just remembered the wind that day, how it felt against her puffy cheeks as she wept against her mother's lifeless body. It had been another unremarkable, sticky, summer evening in the southernmost tip of Vietnam, and the wind never traveled this far down the coast because it often got tired before it could ever reach it. But this time, the wind made the taxing journey south, braving the humidity, just for Lý. It came to help dry her tears.

War had just broken out between the north and the south, there were rumors of the United States intervening, and her father was gone. She was unsure which side he was fighting for, or if he was even alive, because she couldn't remember if the north or the south were for or against communism, and which side was right and which side wasn't. All she knew was that imperialism was bad, but isn't that what both sides were fighting against? But she didn't care about any of it anymore because she had just become an orphan. She didn't have to pick a side because she had nobody to fight for.

She mourned her mother's passing near the bank of the Mekong Delta. Even though no branches seemed to sway when she walked past them, her newfound friend, the amiable wind, seemed to follow her wherever she went, forming a cocoon around her, helping calm her. It reminded her of when her mother would slip her a chili pepper to chew on the most blistering of days, cooling her from the inside out. She slipped on her mother's necklace and felt a different kind of coolness from the stone against her hot skin.

She wasn't afraid of the necklace anymore, even if it was a peculiar shade of jade. As the sun slipped past her, disappearing for the night, she could feel the necklace settling in, becoming comfortable with its new home.

Later that night, when they buried her mother, she wrapped her hand around the jade necklace, and realized that her biggest fear in life was not the impending loneliness, or trying to make a living for herself. Nor was it about the war. Her biggest fear was that her mother was wrong about her. *Could* she be prepared for the kind of sacrifice that came along with being a mother?

She didn't have an answer for this question for the span of her life, up until the moment she knew when it was her time to go. Mrs. Lý Minh Dương's own psychic, an old Vietnamese woman who was once famous at the temples in Hội An, had told her that this was the year her body would be unable to process food properly. That she'd slowly stop eating one day, and very soon after, her body would surrender itself entirely. After forty-nine days, her soul would ascend, and she would experience motherhood all over again in her next life, and all the heartbreak that comes along with it.

When Mrs. Dương heard her fortune, she felt a deep satisfaction because she wouldn't have it any other way. She didn't want to experience another lifetime without being a mother. Her mother had been right about her; she had been a better mother than she had. Because the type of sacrifice that came with a mother's heartbeat was gut-wrenching, and she was prepared to give up her life, over and over and over again, because it had been worth it in the end.

Mrs. Dương died alone in a hospital bed at Fountain Valley Hospital.

It was the same hospital where six of her granddaughters were born. Unlike their births, her death was greeted without much fanfare, aside from the beeping EKG heart monitor as her company. Her daughters weren't by her side, and her boyfriend, Bao, had gone home earlier to try to get some sleep. But she didn't want to wait or hold on anymore. Her work was done here. She knew she hadn't been a perfect mother, but she had done the best she could. And she was finally okay letting go, after holding it all in for so, so long.

The last memory Mrs. Dương took with her before she departed this world was the night her firstborn daughter, Kim, showed up outside that crooked blue house in Santa Ana, with two suitcases in tow, holding the hands of two little girls. Kim had come back from the dead. Before the rift happened between all her daughters, before the anger and resentment, there was that one sliver of peace and wonderment of what would happen next. The moment was buoyant, and life had finally aligned for a group of cursed, heartbroken women.

It was Mrs. Dương's last happy memory because that was the only time where *all* four of her daughters and *all* eight of her granddaughters were gathered under one roof, safe from the outside world. The house had done its job, and so had Mrs. Dương.

· · ·

Excuses came pouring in from all corners of the world.

Priscilla Nguyễn sent flowers from Seattle and had Grace, her assistant, pass along a note that she was unable to come down for the funeral because she had to prepare for a Series B round of funding, and that her presence wouldn't be missed since she didn't *really* know her grandmother that well. They hadn't spoken in a decade. Thủy Nguyễn couldn't make it because a celebrity client had an inflammation breakout that she needed help with before her big movie began filming; it was the actress's only shot at an Oscar nomination. But she would stop by the temple over the weekend. Thảo Nguyễn sent flowers from Sài Gòn, texting that it was too expensive for her to come home at the last minute, but that she was thinking of everyone, and this was all followed by a bunch of sad emojis. Joyce Phạm sent flowers from New York City, saying that she had run out of paid time off, but that she was sorry and she wished she had known her grandmother better. Elaine and Christine Lâm dropped off food at the temple for the memorial, but they didn't stay long, either, as they both hadn't spent much time with their grandmother, and they needed to run the nail salon and the coffee shop while their mother was helping with the funeral arrangements. Lily Lương, also in Seattle for graduate school and an internship at Priscilla's company, had sent flowers as well, and expressed sadness because her grandmother had helped raise her, but she had just started her internship and didn't have that much time to take a leave of absence, but maybe one day she'd meet the rest of her half cousins and half aunties. It just wouldn't be today. And as usual, Lily's younger sister, Rosie, was off smoking weed somewhere, unbothered by all of this, because in her mind, death was just another destination in the journey, *you know?*

All eight grandchildren wouldn't be attending the funeral, despite all of them being the last thought their grandmother had. But she already knew they wouldn't come.

Mrs. Lý Minh Dương had left *very* clear instructions on how she wanted her funeral to be, and if they strayed from *one* detail, her spirit would know. She wrote down what type of food to serve, which photo to use, what outfit she wanted to be buried in, and even which of her favorite monks from her favorite temple was to preside over her funeral. Then she left a map of where all her gold bars, jewelry, and cash were hidden in the house, along with a will, requesting that *all* her daughters be present when the will was read out loud. And she meant *all* her daughters, having circled it several times for extra emphasis in her letter.

All four of them. No exceptions.

Mrs. Mai Nguyễn, Mrs. Minh Phạm, and Mrs. Khuyến Lâm arrived at the temple separately. As soon as the Dương sisters spotted each other, they immediately shifted their eyes and pretended that they didn't see each other. Each one of them promised themselves that they would not be the first to crack.

She thinks **I'm** *going to apologize* **first**? Mrs. Lâm angrily raised an eyebrow when she passed by Mai.

Mai **always** *wins.* **Every** *fight,* Mrs. Phạm grumbled to herself. *Not this time.*

I'm **sick** *of always sacrificing for this family.* Mrs. Nguyễn scowled at her sisters from across the room. *They never appreciate me. I'm the oldest, I made the most sacrifices.*

It's **always** *Mai's fault.* Mrs. Lâm closed her eyes, still full of regret for the last reunion. *Our mother passed away alone and scared.*

This is Mai's fault, Mrs. Phạm thought bitterly. *It's always her fault.*

The temple was packed to the brim. Mrs. Dương's presence in the little village of Little Saigon did not go unnoticed. She had been a formidable woman, fearless until the very end. She helped out where she could and generously redistributed her wealth. As the ceremony began, an elderly woman in her sixties approached the microphone stand. She also bore a birthmark on her right cheek, the same one as Mrs. Dương had.

Mai gasped and gripped her chair.

"Kính thưa quý gia đình và bạn bè gần xa," she said, greeting everyone and asking them all to take their seats. "My name is Kim. Kim Lương. I am Lý Minh Dương's firstborn daughter. Thank you all for coming today. My mother was an incredible woman, silent and humble in her bravery. She loved her community and her family fiercely, until the very end."

It had been ten years since Mai saw her half sister, Kim. This was the woman she'd been competing with the last twenty years, ever since she came back from the dead. The woman who took the little blue house in Santa Ana away from her. As she watched Kim talk about their mother, and all the memories they had together in the past decade, Mai's anger was replaced with grief. These were time and memories that Mai could never get back. She glanced down at her own wrinkled hands, wondering if it was too late with her own daughters as well. Daughters who didn't call her back, or come down to see her in her moment of grief. She was unsure if their relationship was irreparable or not. She'd been focused on the wrong things, meddling in all the wrong things. *The funeral, the pregnancy, the wedding, the grandson.* She's been focused on the wrong predictions. Because maybe Auntie Hứa was only right about one thing.

Maybe this was the year Mai really could lose everything.

$\cdots$

During the burial, they placed a bowl of rice, paper money, Mrs. Dương's reading glasses, and several weeks' worth of newspapers on top of her coffin so that she'd have some entertainment on her journey to the next life.

After the funeral, the family gathered back at the temple to assemble her altar for the next forty-nine days. Mai lit incense, Minh scooped out a fresh bowl of rice and veggies, and Khuyến arranged some fruits and snacks. And finally, Kim joined them to place a black-and-white photo of their mother at the center of the altar. A younger Mrs. Dương wore her signature jade Buddha necklace. Her eyes were less wrinkled, and her áo dài clung to her youthful body, which accentuated all her subtle curves. In this photo, capturing a long-forgotten moment, Mrs. Dương didn't look like a survivor, a dutiful wife, or a mother. She looked like a woman.

None of the four sisters spoke as they worked quietly and efficiently on their mother's altar. They fussed over it, down to the placement, making sure that it followed feng shui protocols. Their grief manifested into productivity: They set out to ensure there was enough food and paper money to last the week, until someone could replace the food the following week, and the next week, and the next, until their mother's soul completed the journey to her next reincarnation after forty-nine days. Mai slapped Khuyến's hand aside as she rearranged things. Khuyến responded by shoving Mai away from her area, and accidentally knocking Minh over. Kim tried to help Minh back up, but then Mai slapped *her* hand away *again*. Minh was after all *her* sister, and *not* Kim's. *Then* Khuyến jabbed a finger in Mai's face, and alas, all hell broke loose in front of their mother's altar, as both women refused to speak first, but resorted to slapstick ruses to communicate their feelings. Once again, everyone in Little Saigon began to take bets on who would win.

Because everyone knew that the Dương sisters were cursed.

Meanwhile, the black-and-white photo of Mrs. Lý Minh Dương watched all four of her daughters attempting to fight through their emotions. She sighed, impatiently waiting for them to finish, waiting for one of them to invite her ancestral spirit into their home. Even though she had four daughters and only sons were allowed to invite their ancestors home by tradition, Mrs. Dương assumed her daughters had learned at least *one* thing from her, and that they had enough foresight and Viet hustle to find a way to go *around* the damn curse.

12

Mai, Minh, Khuyến, and, Yes, Kim

MR. BÙI, THE ESTATE LAWYER, cleared his throat, and pushed his glasses up the low bridge of his nose. His wrinkled forehead matched his wrinkled clothes as he brought the will closer to his face, trying to make out Mrs. Dương's faded scribbles and her most recent ones. His eyesight and memory had been failing him more than usual, and lately, his own mortality had begun scaring him, especially when so many of his elderly clients were suddenly passing away. It made him contemplate his own will, which, ironically, he had been putting off for ages due to his own superstitions.

Mrs. Dương's will had been steadfast throughout the years. Nothing more than minor changes here and there. Only when her brood of granddaughters did something rather exceptional would she reach out to Mr. Bùi to tweak the will.

She had allocated gold bars for Lily when she got into her PhD program; jewelry pieces for Priscilla after she received her MBA; and a book of her favorite Buddhist quotes for Joyce, because, well, she *could* use the guidance. Elaine got her furs; it seemed appropriate for her *aesthetic*. Thủy inherited her library collection, while Thảo got a random grab bag of gold bars, books, and jewelry, because she was a mystery to her. Rosie and Christine each got a small pile of cash and prepaid tutor lessons to help with their terrible Vietnamese language skills.

Mrs. Dương, of course, had seasonal favorites to match her capricious moods, not-so-secretly pitting each granddaughter against the other—like a horse race, each horse moving up a level depending on who reached out to her the most. But during the estrangement, the race became void as a majority of her granddaughters stopped reaching out to her. Whether they did it out of respect for their mothers or they were forced to, she couldn't tell. Meanwhile, the will remained untouched, gathering dust for ten years, until a month ago, out of the blue, Mrs. Dương called Mr. Bùi to her home to make a *few* adjustments.

Mrs. Dương had expressed that her last will and testament be read at the little blue house in Santa Ana, where her firstborn daughter, Kim Lương, still resided. She said that if *all* four of her daughters were not gathered there, then no one was to get anything, and her wealth would be redistributed among charities in Little Saigon.

After the burial, all four sisters gathered reluctantly at the house, still a bit battered and bruised after the fight at the temple. Their fake Louis bags were neatly lined up on the living room coffee table. Mrs. Khuyến Lâm and Mrs. Kim Lương were both hunched forward, sitting as far away as possible from each other without falling off the couch. Mrs. Minh Phạm was busy rustling in the kitchen. The sound of clinking glasses echoed through the house.

Mrs. Mai Nguyễn walked around the house, as all the memories that she'd tried to erase flooded back. This house that had once belonged to her, where her children had grown up, was unrecognizable as her half sister's home now. Kim was a stranger to her, and so was this home. Mai felt her age pressing against her knees as she toured the living room, and saw the corner where Priscilla took her first steps, the bathroom where Thủy often went to hide from the rest of the family and read her books, and the garage where Thảo played make-believe with her stuffed animals role-playing as international spies. When she turned the corner, she saw the downstairs bedroom nearest to the staircase, and her eyes began to well, remembering the room where her three daughters, herself, and her husband shared the same bed for years. Most nights, Mai and Thanh slept on the floor, while her daughters took the bed. As she moved past the kitchen, she could see the old looming orange tree in the backyard, peeking at her through the window. The tree had stood the test of time, unlike their family. Mai lingered, afraid of the memories that came with an orange tree in Orange County. Flashes of her three daughters and her nieces seeking shelter under it, covering their ears from all the yelling coming from inside the house. Mai swallowed and looked away. It finally hit her how far they'd come. It had been a simple yet chaotic life back then, but at least they were all together. Now she wasn't even sure if everyone was as happy now as they were back then.

Minh came out of the kitchen, carrying a tray of trà tắc, looking jittery. Nobody saw her slip an *almost* empty vial back into her purse—a vial with only one drop left in it. She walked around and passed a glass of iced kumquat tea to the estate lawyer, then passed one to each of her sisters. When she stopped in front of Mai, she handed the biggest glass to her, and stared at her intensely, not moving until Mai got annoyed.

"Why are you hovering, Minh?" Mai hissed. "Go sit down."

"It's *really* hot outside," Minh said. "You should drink all of this. *All of it.* In one gulp. It'll help you cool down."

"Why do you suddenly care about my health?" Mai scoffed, sitting down. "What do you want? A parade for making us drinks? Money? A new husband?"

"I'm not moving until you drink this tea."

"For the love of Buddha, drink the damn tea!" Khuyến growled at her two sisters, breaking her silence. "Otherwise we'll be here longer than an American occupation!"

"I'm not *thirsty*! Why are you being so weird!"

The three sisters broke out in another fight as both Kim and Mr. Bùi watched, horrified. Kim attempted to shrink herself as her three half sisters began to claw over each other. Her face grew redder and redder as the shouting around her escalated, until her usual composed temperament cracked.

"JUST DRINK IT!" Kim shouted. "No wonder you all put Mẹ into an early grave! She had to die to escape all of you and get some peace!"

The room was instantly silenced. Mai opened her mouth to snap back at her, but something in her stopped. *What really was there left to say?* Minh watched with wonderment as Mai swallowed her fighting words, picked up the glass, and began drinking it. Minh reached out and tipped the glass further up, forcing Mai to finish the whole glass. She shot Minh a dirty look above the glass but kept drinking until the tea was gone.

Mai's nose wrinkled, and she curiously peered into the empty glass, wondering if Minh's cooking skills had gotten worse. Minh breathed a sigh of relief and finally took her place on the couch next to her sisters.

"Thank you all for coming," Mr. Bùi said cautiously. His hands gripped the glass, unsteadily bringing the iced kumquat tea to his lips, afraid to witness another squabble break out among the women. "I am here to read the last will and testament of Mrs. Lý Minh Dương." He plopped a tin box onto his lap, and pulled out a stack of letters, an assortment of trinkets, gold bars, and jewelry.

"To all my daughters, I've left a letter to each of you, explaining how much you meant to me. Even when you thought I couldn't see you, I want you to know that I always did. A mother *sees* everything," he continued, his voice becoming a mouthpiece for Mrs. Dương's spirit. He coughed and strained his eyes again to continue. "I also have written a letter to my first great-grandchild, whom I know will be born this year. I know that I will not be alive to witness their birth, but I already feel their presence. They're waiting to open their eyes to this world as I close mine—"

Minh, Khuyến, and Mai quickly glanced at each other and gasped.

"How did she know—?" Minh whispered.

"—trời ơi, is *everyone* seeing this psychic in Kauai?" Khuyến moaned.

"—I've never been able to physically or verbally express my love in the way you all needed me to," the lawyer continued. "But that didn't mean that I didn't love you all deeply. Even when your backs turned against me, I still kept loving you all from afar."

The lawyer got up and passed a letter to each woman. When he returned to the front of the living room, he continued reading Mrs. Dương's letter. "The jade Buddha necklace that has been passed down from generation to generation, starting with Oanh Dương, is ready to be passed down once again. Traditionally, I should pass it on to my firstborn daughter, but I've made too many mistakes between Mai and Kim, and consider them *both* my firstborn. I've addressed the daughter who shall receive the necklace in a letter. You will know who it is when you read your own."

All four sisters gripped their letters, trying their best to hold back their tears.

"They say that the firstborn daughter is the hardest to raise. I was lucky to have *two* firstborn daughters. I've spent the last twenty years trying to make it up to Kim for abandoning her back in Vietnam, and now I'm finally able to spend the next twenty years of Mai's life making it up to her, for forcing her to give up the house that you're all currently sitting in."

Mr. Bùi stopped reading and rummaged through the tin box until he pulled out a set of keys. He walked over to Mai and handed it to her. A confused Mai looked at the keys, then at her sisters.

"I've been instructed to stop reading the will here," Mr. Bùi announced. "I will finish the second half at the next location Mrs. Dương requested we move to. I'll drive everyone to the next destination, so if you can all please gather your belongings . . ."

Confused, the sisters retrieved their fake Louis and asked the lawyer where the next destination was. They all assumed it'd be back at their mother's favorite temple, but instead he gave them an address that was all the way across town. The sisters groaned about the traffic.

"That's so far!" Khuyến moaned. "Only white people go over there!"

"I *never* go to that side of town," Minh said, confused. "How does Mẹ even know it exists?"

Keys still in hand, Mai didn't say anything. She then looked up and met Kim's eyes, and this time there was no animosity, regret, or resentment between them. They both knew what their mother had done for them because only firstborn daughters could understand the shared responsibility of being a second mother to the rest of the family.

In her final moments as a mother, Mrs. Dương had made sure that the past had been taken care of, as well as the future. She finally fixed her one regret and created generational wealth for her daughters and her granddaughters so they never had to rely on a man for anything ever again.

• • •

The winding, cobbled road made Mr. Bùi's creaky Toyota rattle the women up, down, and sideways as they clutched their purses and grabbed on to whatever they could to steady themselves, including each other. An endless stream of complaints came out of the four sisters simultaneously.

"—this neighborhood is *full* of money and—"

"—they can't have proper streets to drive on—"

"—where are all the taxes going—"

"—rich people pay so much to look poor—"

"—where *are* all the taxes going?!—"

"—this is *exactly* why everything should be paid in all cash—"

Mr. Bùi gripped the wheel tighter, praying to the Buddha that he could go home soon to have dinner with his wife of sixty years. He pressed his foot down on the pedal as he battled a steep hill. A view slowly emerged as the car haphazardly careened its way around the bend. The sisters gasped when they saw the majesty of the Pacific Ocean herself materialize. It had been a long time since they saw the water. Though they'd been in California for almost forty years, they rarely ever went to the beach. They never felt comfortable being on these shores. The water reminded them too much of what life could have been like had they never left their coasts near the South China sea.

The lawyer drove through the neighborhood, past mansions, bungalows, craftsmans, and modern renovated townhomes. The only common denominator was that all houses overlooked the vast, mysterious ocean. Though the women saw no connection between this ocean and the ocean they had grown up with, they acknowledged that even waves on the other side of the world would eventually find their way here. Just like they did.

Mr. Bùi parked under an old sycamore tree and ushered the women out of the car. He then led them toward the smallest house on the block, which looked untouched by time except for the fading green front door. The door looked like it had welcomed friends more than strangers over the years. He coughed and motioned for Mai to open the door. Right, the keys.

"Welcome home, daughter," he said as he unfolded Mrs. Dương's letter to finish reading. "All I've ever wanted was for you to be safe. At the time, safe meant to get married and have a home. Protection against society and protection against the wind, the two things that women needed to survive. When Kim came back into our lives, I had nothing to give to her at that time, so I had to give her and my two granddaughters protection from the wind. I hope you find peace at your age, in a small house by the water that has four walls and a roof. And one day, you can pass this home to your daughters to keep them safe."

He looked up from the letter and saw a trembling Mai. Behind her, all her sisters were sobbing quietly, slowly inching their way toward each other. Uncomfortable, he shifted his weight and avoided eye contact, and kept reading. He wasn't used to seeing Vietnamese women show vulnerability. It was rather unnerving.

"As for the house in Santa Ana, I hope you can all understand why I gave the house to Kim. I thought I had lost her in the war, but when she showed up on our front steps twenty years ago, I knew that even ghosts and spirits would always need a place to come home to. I hope you can all forgive me one day, and invite my spirit to come into your home every once in a while. We've spent the last decade apart; I hope to make up for lost time in the future. Your mother, always, even when you didn't want me to be."

The lawyer paused. Much to his surprise, he saw that all four Dương sisters were now holding hands. He blinked a few times, unsure if his eyesight was failing him again. Without proof, no one in Little Saigon would ever believe him if he recounted this moment. Especially if he were to say that the Dương women had finally made up, finally giving some relief to the village who had no choice but to hear about the family drama for years.

Mai wiped her tears. She put the key into the lock, opened up the perennial green door, and stepped over the entrance and into possibility.

. . .

Days after, Mai felt very strange.

At first she thought she just wasn't hungry, then she thought maybe she was *too* hungry. Not since menopause did she experience such fluctuation. Her mood swings and her body weren't aligned. She whipped out her old bamboo fan, a relic from those days, to fan herself at night in front of the TV, watching her soaps, hoping to bring some balance back between her yin and yang.

Mai was empty inside. Everywhere she went, and even when she slept, she carried the keys to the house with the green door in her pocket. There was nothing she wanted to ask the woman in Kauai anymore, because what came after death? What could Auntie Hứa say that could help her overcome her staggering grief? None of her predictions could have ever prepared her for the kind of pain swallowing her whole.

Unlike her mother who left the world at peace, Mai was full of regrets. Regrets about the last ten years, the last twenty years, and regrets about her daughters.

Was it too late to fix her relationship with her daughters?

For forty-nine days, Mai sat in the parking lot at the temple—inside her car, for hours and hours. From 6:00 a.m. till 8:00 p.m., from the moment the place opened and closed, she waited, taking a few breaks throughout to pray at her mother's altar, and pick at some food the monks would bring out to her.

She didn't know who to call. Not her daughters, not her ex-husband (not that she could ever rely on him anyways). Everyone seemed to have abandoned her or was simply *too busy*. She went to the temple every day to distract herself by cleaning her mother's altar. Routine became her companion. Grief was funny in that way. At 5:00 a.m. on the dot, she'd wake up and say her prayers for an hour. Then she'd drive to the temple, park under the big eucalyptus trees, and she would cry some more. At least she wasn't crying in her empty home; she was crying in an empty parking lot. She was full of unanswered questions that only a mother had answers for, and she longed for a ghost that was not of this world anymore. She felt small, nothing more than a forgotten soul living on a pale blue dot. So, for two weeks, after the funeral and after the will was read, she was utterly alone.

Until one day, the third sister, Mrs. Lâm, opened the passenger door, climbed in quietly, and held her hand as she cried. Mrs. Lâm did it again the next day, then the next. Soon, Mrs. Phạm came and crawled into the back seat. And the three of them sat together in that car in silence, allowing Mai to cry. Then one day, out of the blue, Mrs. Lương opened the other back door and joined them. For once, no one argued, bragged, boasted, or exaggerated. Not over money, not over property, not over whose daughter was more successful, and especially not over who was to blame for causing the family estrangement in the first place.

Mrs. Nguyễn cried buckets for forty-nine days, until her mother completed her journey into her next body, and she didn't feel so alone anymore.

13

Elaine Lâm

A SLIGHTLY HUNGOVER ELAINE Lâm walked into the dimly lit coffee shop and breezed past all the Vietnamese girls wearing bikinis, who were walking around in six-inch heels, holding trays upon trays of coffee and boba tea orders. A group on their break were casually leaning over the counter, gossiping and complaining about their love lives and the horrors of online dating. She nonchalantly walked past tables full of ogling boys pretending to be men, and men pretending to be boys, and a table packed with curious tourists debating if it would be insulting to *not* look the women in the eyes. She continued to be undeterred by the half-naked women moonlighting as baristas, like they were caricatures inside a Bukowski novel—or any other novel written by a white man determined to figure out what makes women *women*. The Vietnamese bikini coffee shop that Elaine managed had a sentient neon pink sign that flashed *Girls! Girls! Girls!* over the counter. But she had become immune to it all because to her, it was just another ordinary Monday morning in Little Saigon.

"Where the *hell* have you been?" Christine, her younger sister, whined when Elaine burst into the back room and removed her sunglasses. Her sister's voice was extra irritating this morning. "I've been stuck here since seven a.m.! Old Man Chu is literally slobbering in the corner *again*. I am *not* going out there and cleaning up his shit like some underpaid caretaker. The man should be in a nursing home, watching Fox News or whatever, but instead he's always in here, open till close, sipping the same damn coffee cup, like some cheapskate, and eye-fucking all the girls and leaving *no* tips. Also, don't dicks stop working after forty? Like why even *bother* at his age?"

Elaine's migraine took a beating every time Christine's voice raised an octave. Rolling her eyes, she removed her rabbit fur vest and unhooked her fake Gucci waist bag to hang up on the coat rack. Her waist-length black hair cascaded down like a sleek waterfall, and her thick thighs felt watery from the six tequila shots she took last night. She had no idea why she drank so much at Sunday night poker. She was pushing thirty and was the only unmarried one of her friend group, and yet she still pretended like her body was forever frozen at twenty-one.

"Christ, calm down. I'm here now, you can dip out in a bit. Just make sure you do a last check around the main floor before leaving. Is Mẹ coming in today?"

Christine shrugged, her eyes glued to her phone. "I don't know, I think she's still busy with, like, the funeral, burial *stuff*, or whatever. She's always at the temple now, doing those weird Buddhist rites." Her acrylics made *tap tap tap* noises on her phone screen as she scrolled through her feed, sending off "hearts" and "likes" into the ether. She looked up, quizzically. "Oh *my* god, *dude*, when our mother dies, would *we* have to do all those rites for her?"

Elaine threw a towel at her face. "Don't say things like that out loud." She chastised her in a way that only older sisters could.

"Would you *stop*?" Christine cried out, throwing the towel back at her. She smoothed her blond balayage bangs. "I *just* did my makeup!"

"What'd you do last night? You didn't come home till late," Elaine asked suspiciously, leaning against the counter. "You better be careful about your partying. At the rate you're going you're going to end up like one of those sad Asian girls that just end up sucking Kevin Nguyễn–type dicks forever."

"Like *you're* not already one of those sad Asian girls? You can't even bag yourself a Kevin Nguyễn if you tried. Why do you care anyways? I was just smoking weed with Rosie and that whole group," Christine said, a casual boredom in her voice, her Orange County accent coming out in full force. "It's *not* a big deal."

"I still think it's weird that you smoke weed with our *half cousin* when you barely talk to our *full* cousins," Elaine said. "I thought all the aunties hated that side. Aren't we forbidden to talk to our half aunt?"

Christine shrugged. "Family feuds are for boomers. That stuff is *so* not conducive to what the rave movement is about anyways. Besides, I think Mẹ is talking to the aunties again after the funeral. Also our other cousins are pretentious as shit and think they're better than us—why would I even want to talk to them anyways?"

"You know what, you're right, they love to pretend they're not Vietnamese," Elaine agreed, ready to talk shit about her cousins at any hour. "Fucking Thảo won't even respond back to my text about helping me find a woman for the arranged—"

The back-room door suddenly burst open, and in walked a furious Jacqueline Hồ. Her heels angrily clacked against the cement floor. One wrong move from her and her bikini bottom that precariously covered her bits would have been prone to a wardrobe malfunction. Jacqueline's sleeve tattoos blurred together under the cackling fluorescent light, and she raised an angry finger and jabbed at Elaine's direction.

"Old Man Chu needs to go, or I go," Jacqueline declared. She was covered in coffee stains. "He *threw* iced coffee at me because he wanted my nipples to get hard! How many times is he going to keep doing this to me? Until the man keels over in his own urine or chokes on a boba? Why do you keep allowing him to come back here? It's demoralizing!"

Christine looked up from her phone and flashed Elaine a look. "I *told* you so, Elaine. The man has *no* respect for any of these women. He just crawls in here, expecting to be transported back to wartime Vietnam, expecting women to do whatever the hell he wants. It's gross as shit."

"Oh *Jesus Christ*," Elaine muttered, her headache near splitting now. Jacqueline's shrill voice pierced her ear. "Sorry girl, I'll take care of it. Just another Monday morning, right?"

"You said that *last* Monday morning, Elaine. This isn't a goddamn strip club and we are not making small talk at the office water cooler. I don't exactly do this shit for fun, I do it to pay for law school. *Now, do something about him.*" Jacqueline slammed her heels on the ground.

"I *know* we're not a fucking strip club. Let me go out and talk to him."

"I better get a bigger cut in tips this morning—"

Elaine let out an exasperated cry, threw her hands in the air in defeat, and brushed past Jacqueline. Behind her, she could hear both Christine and Jacqueline yell *finally!* Elaine went to the main floor, and walked up to Old Man Chu. She bowed and greeted him in Vietnamese, as it was expected of her to greet her elders with respect, even though the man was creepier than a dark alleyway at night.

She picked up a napkin to wipe the drool from his mouth. "I think it's time you head home. I'll call your caretaker to come pick you up."

He waved her off and dodged the napkin. He muttered to Elaine to bring Jacqueline back out, and pointed at his empty glass. He asked for a glass of Heineken, and Elaine gave her best customer-service smile, the same smile she'd been using since she was six years old, working at the nail salons with her mother.

"Xin lỗi, Chú," Elaine apologized and flashed him the smile again, like she had fish hooks on each side of her mouth. It never hurts to get the most tips out of any man, *especially* ones who were at death's door. "You've been a loyal customer for over six years, you know the rules. We *don't* serve alcohol here. We only serve *coffee*. How about I get you a cà phê sữa đá? But you have to promise not to harass Jacqueline again, okay? And *please*, tip her well this time." Old Man Chu slobbered some more, gave her a stink eye, and eventually took out his wallet. Satisfied, Elaine motioned toward another bikini barista to replace his coffee.

She sighed and slinked down into a chair. She was getting too old for this. How long could she keep being an ABG in the OC for? She thought about how differently her life could have turned out, had she just finished college and read more books. She could have been like one of her snobby cousins who worked in tech, medicine, or started their own businesses. Maybe she could have *been* something more. Elaine grew envious of another life as she scanned the dark coffee shop, watching bored women dangle their bodies over tables or drape themselves in velvet chairs, vaping while on their phones.

Maybe this was all there was.

A chuckle came from the corner, and she turned her head to see another one of her repeat customers eyeing her from the back table. Once their eyes met, she tried to stifle a laugh. A smile instantly crossed her face. She got up and headed toward the corner table. She didn't know names; she only knew faces. And she knew this face *particularly* well. His slicked, jet black hair, crisp white button-down shirt, and his gleaming gold Rolex was comforting to her and a warm welcome on a Monday morning. He was at least consistent, a rare attribute in the men she usually pursued. Elaine had a crush—more than a crush. She especially would never admit it to Christine, who would make fun of her till the day she died, cackling in her face that this man was the embodiment of an Asian fuckboy and a basic Kevin Nguyễn-type.

"Back again so soon, Chow Mo-wan?" she asked, sliding into the booth next to him. She decided to nickname him after the character in *In the Mood for Love* because he looked a lot like a young Tony Leung. And a young Tony Leung was *everything*.

The man almost spat out his coffee as he laughed. "You need to stop calling me that."

"Well, you're never going to tell me your real name so . . ."

"You're right about that."

"Who are you here for this morning? Jacqueline? Sylvia? Tammy? Pick your poison. You've memorized everyone's schedule by now."

He shrugged. "Doesn't matter to me, I really just am here for the coffee."

"You know, you should think about seeing a therapist. You might have mommy issues."

The man chuckled. "I don't need a therapist to tell me that I have commitment issues."

"Then go to a Starbucks."

The man lifted his coffee cup to toast Elaine. "I prefer to support small businesses in my community."

"Idiot." She clucked her tongue at him, but she wore a small smile. She hated that she loved unattainable men. It was purely the chase for her. Elaine's phone vibrated, and she pulled it out to see a text message from her cousin, Thảo, who was currently living in Sài Gòn. Thảo was notoriously difficult to get in touch with. She had no active social media accounts and wasn't in consistent touch with anyone in the family—including her own sisters. Her response time varied depending on her partying schedule.

sorry, can't help.

Also, I don't do things like that anyways.

seems illegal . . . ?

Elaine scowled. Oh, how she *hated* the Nguyễn women, all three of them. Priscilla, Thủy, and Thảo. She saw them all as white-chasers who conveniently forgot about their roots. It was a far cry from when they all lived together in that little house in Santa Ana, packed in like sardines. She rolled her eyes and muttered *bitch* under her breath, loud enough for the man next to her to hear.

Of *course* it's illegal, it usually is. Thảo pretended that she was above their hustle, above all of this *jungle* Asian nonsense, because *she went to school in Boston.* But somewhere, secretly, Elaine still kept hope that she would remember how they all used to huddle under the orange tree in Santa Ana, dreaming about a better life together. They all made the pact that they wouldn't be like their mothers when they grew up. This generation, it would be different.

Now she was the one left behind, the only one still working the family businesses and doing back-alley favors and deals for those in Little Saigon.

"Something the matter?" the man asked her. His eyes curiously examined everything on her face—from her false eyelashes to the dark shade of red lipstick from the celebrity makeup line she sported. Elaine felt her cheeks flush ever so slightly, but she played it cool. Like she always did when it came to handsome, unattainable men.

"Sorry, Vietnamese things, you know how it is. My uptight, pompous cousin thinks she's too good to help out on a favor."

"Well, what's the issue? Maybe I can help."

Elaine laughed. "I can't tell you, it's a stupid favor for my mother."

"I know a thing or two about stupid favors for Asian mothers."

"All right, fine. I need a woman—" Elaine began.

"—don't we all—" he interrupted.

"—I *need* a woman who is willing to marry this guy that's coming from Vietnam. He'll be here within the month. He's an uncle of a close family friend. One of my mother's *other* line of businesses that's off the books. I thought my cousin could help by talking to some people we know in Vietnam who have single aunties over here, who need the cash," Elaine said, raising an eyebrow at him, as if expecting him to understand where she was going with this. "You know, I need a *woman*."

"I see," the man said as he leaned back in the booth. He was quiet for a moment and Elaine could tell he was combing through the Rolodex in his mind. It oddly turned her on, watching him try to help the village out. She hadn't met a useful man in years, especially not the Kevin Nguyễn–types from San Jose. These types of deadbeat men reminded her of her father's generation, and every other man she'd witnessed growing up, where they'd punt everything to the women in the family to "take care of" while they drank their beers, smoked their cigarettes, and came into coffee shops like the ones she owned.

"What's his age?" he asked.

"Roughly late sixties, maybe early seventies."

"How much in exchange and for how long?"

"The family is willing to pay fifty thousand dollars for a legal marriage of five years."

"Seems a bit low for five years."

"That's all they have. Ten thousand dollars for each year. They've been trying to get him into America for a long time; this is the last shot they have."

"Any preference? Chinese? Vietnamese? Korean? Cambodian?"

Elaine shook her head. "Has to be Vietnamese, you know, to pass the tests. A language barrier wouldn't be a good look to prove that 'they're in love.'"

The man scratched his head and laughed. "As fate would have it, I actually might know a woman. This woman I've been kind of seeing, her mother sounds like a real divorced nutcase. Sounds like she could use the money, and the distraction, too. She'd probably love the money aspect more."

Elaine tried to hide her grimace at the mention of him seeing someone. "Oh! I didn't realize you had a girlfriend. Does she know of your . . . taste in *coffee*?"

He shrugged. "I wouldn't call her my girlfriend. It's not serious. You know me, it's *never* serious. She is nice, though, a good distraction from it all. Being a functioning adult." He reached into his pockets, dug out his wallet, pulled out his business card, and slipped it across the table to Elaine. "Now you finally get to know my real name. And it's *not* Chow Mo-wan, sorry to disappoint. Call me and let's set them up. Do I get a cut in this deal?"

"The only cut you'll get is free coffee," Elaine laughed. She picked up the business card and caressed his name under the dim light, running her finger over it again and again. "It's nice to finally meet you, Daniel Lê."

14

Christine Lâm and Rosie Lương

CHRISTINE LÂM DREAMT ABOUT putting everything she owned into her beat-up hatchback Toyota and driving all the way up the coast. She used to turn her car onto the ramp heading toward I-5 North, but would exit the minute she hit the Los Angeles County line, because she knew her mother would never allow her to leave Orange County.

She had the same car for nearly a decade, after her mother had forced her to buy a practical car, convinced of the longevity of anything made by the Japanese. Her mother would say anyone who placed their faith in anything made by the Vietnamese was a fool, as Christine would look down at her own Vietnamese hands, whose nails were elongated by black acrylics. She wondered if she'd ever be good at anything—aside from being the daughter of a woman who owned a chain of nail salons and questionable bikini coffee shops.

After Christine left the coffee shop that her sister, Elaine, managed, she hit up her half cousin, Rosie Lương, to see what she was up to, and if she'd be down to smoke a joint near the Santa Ana River. Christine had an affinity for rivers. It was profoundly comforting to know you have no agency in where the stream carried you—that there were truly things out of your control. She knew what it was like to be forever trapped in your own reality and have no say in how to alter it. Her phone lit up, and she saw that Rosie hit her back with a text that said fuck ya, need to escape. My mom is on my shit again.

Christine did a U-turn and headed to Santa Ana, which was in the opposite direction. Despite the estrangement and the feud between their mothers, the two half cousins were actually friends. They were the youngest in their families, and that meant nobody paid them any attention or cared about their opinion, which was the only loophole they could find in an otherwise very controlled existence.

As Christine passed through Bolsa Avenue, familiar Vietnamese cultural touches that almost every home donned followed her in the rearview mirror, and it felt suffocating, seeing it day in and day out. Each home had their standard Foo dogs, dragons, or stone Buddha statues staring out, hidden among bushes of basil plants and lime trees. Among the seemingly unified neighborhood, where Vietnamese families had resettled after the war, the dichotomy between bitterness and pride showed itself.

One home she passed had the old Vietnamese flag next to the American flag, loudly flying in the wind. Christine had seen this flag throughout her childhood, littered throughout lackadaisical graffiti across Little Saigon by spirited young teens, or painted on the walls of old-school phở shops that had been around since the seventies. The yellow background with three red stripes, each symbolizing the north, central, and south parts of Vietnam, was a constant reminder of the reason she had been born in America instead of Vietnam.

On the other side of the street, a warring home had the new flag of Vietnam waving back angrily. A red background with a yellow star in the middle, which represented the socialist republic. Even as Christine drove past the two homes, she didn't feel anything about either of them, because she knew it didn't matter what she thought. It only mattered when some white guy pontificated about why America lost the Vietnam War in the opinion section of some fancy newspaper. She was tired of hearing about it from them, her parents, and every opinionated elderly person on her block. She just wanted to smoke weed and figure out her life.

As soon as Christine pulled into Rosie's cul-de-sac, she drove to the end of the street and parked in front of a blue, crooked house and sent her an arrival text. Rosie came running out of the home and climbed into the passenger seat, immediately pulling down the side mirror flap, and began applying her lipstick. She fluffed her hair out and pried away the purple highlights stuck to her lip gloss.

"Sup boo, how are you?" Rosie asked, sucking through her teeth as she carefully applied a new coat of gloss over the lipstick. "How was work?"

"Same old shit," Christine said. "Same shit every day in this shit place."

"Jesus, sorry I asked. *What's up* with your attitude today?"

"Sorry. Just sick of Orange County sometimes."

"Who isn't? I get so jealous of my sister. Living in Seattle, traveling the world, doing research for her PhD program. I'm the dumb one who couldn't escape," Rosie said as she smacked her lips loudly several times, ensuring the gloss was evenly distributed. "But then, I think about what a little robot she is, clacking away at her keyboard, and I'm like *nah, fuck that.*"

"At least your mother encourages you to leave. My mother would have her claws in me if I even tried to move a few feet away from her," Christine said as she handed Rosie a joint. "I can't even move to Los Angeles. Los Angeles! That shit is only an *hour* away and yet it's further away than Paris to me."

"Shit's always greener on the other side." Rosie inhaled deeply, coughing sporadically on the exhale. "Trust me, all these other try-hards in our family getting their PhDs, running start-ups, going to med school, graduating college at nineteen, or that one cousin who thinks she's international now or some shit cause she lives in Sài Gòn—that shit is all social media fake and just a distraction from their real problems. Do you think any of the women in our family are actually *happy*? Look at the *disarray*. No one talks to each other, they all blame my mother, my mother blames all of them, and honestly, no one actually gets what they want at the end of the day. All they do is blame some family curse, but the only curse I see here is self-inflicted. Because everyone keeps making the same *damn* mistakes, over and over again."

"Goddamn girl," Christine whistled. "That was heavy. Since when did you become Asian Oprah?"

Rosie shrugged. "The key is to stop giving a fuck because nothing ever changes, so why bother?"

Christine didn't say anything. She just cranked up the stereo, rolled down her windows, and began blasting music as they cruised toward the Santa Ana River. The two laughing Buddha bobbleheads stuck on her dashboard, which her mother had given her for protection when she first got the car, began shaking their golden heads, side to side, up and down, seemingly laughing in her face. Christine ignored the Buddhas and pretended that she was the main character in her own story, because that was the only way she could get through the stifling days.

• • •

Rosie stuck her head out the car window as her half cousin Christine drove down the 405. Rosie, like a dog desperate to feel the rush of wind against her cheeks, stuck her head even further out despite the annoyed honks from the surrounding cars. She loved feeling the opposite of something; it fueled her rebellious nature. She was the daughter her mother couldn't control or figure out.

The sun hit her face at the right moment, and she soaked it in as much as she could before she reluctantly brought her head back inside the car. Christine passed her the joint as she swerved the car, trying to find the right song to play. Rosie took another hit, trying to erase the fight she had with her mother right before she got picked up. Her mother's bitterness flowed through her, and she closed her eyes, allowing her mother's ugly words to rear again.

"You waste your time chasing boys who don't want you," her mother said, lecturing her as she followed Rosie around, who was rushing to get ready, and trying on several different outfits. "Can't you be more like your sister, Lily?"

"Why would I *want* to become her? Lily doesn't even know how to *feel* or *notice* anything around her!" Rosie yelled back. "She literally doesn't even know what's going on half the time!"

"At least she's doing something with her life! You're not going to amount to anything if you sit around all day, smoking weed with your deadbeat friends!"

"Don't project your shit onto me. I know you got some heavy family drama going on or whatever, but it's *not* my fault you were the most gossiped about woman in Little Saigon and all those aunties hated your ass for years. Don't pretend you're all *kumbaya* now just because Bà died and now you're pretending to be a martyr and everything is *fine* with the aunties."

Her mother threw her hands up and called her a đĩ and con quỷ for wearing her makeup and hair like that. "You're breaking my heart, Rosie," her mother pleaded with her. She gestured wildly toward everything in the home, at everything inside Rosie's room and at her outfit. "All of this? All that you see in this house that has kept you warm for twenty-one years? All of that drama and fighting? I did it for you. To house you and your sister. We had *nothing* back then. We came here with *nothing*. Of course I took this damn house back then, and I'd do it all over again, too. I went through all that pain and loss to make sure your life could be together in the future."

"My life *is* together," Rosie screamed. "Just because it's not *your* idea of what a life is, doesn't mean it's not a good life."

"What are you going to do to make money? Become a hooker? Sell drugs?"

Rosie stared at her mother like she had lost her mind. She didn't say anything back. Her phone vibrated. Christine had arrived. "Forget it. You think *I'm* always the dramatic one? Look in the mirror. You think some wood, nails, and concrete makes this place a home? No, Mẹ, you got us a prison cell." She turned and ran out of the house, slamming the door behind her.

When the weed finally hit her, Rosie opened her eyes back up. Her mother's words evaporated instantly, and she smiled. "Why don't we move to Los Angeles, together?" Rosie asked.

Christine laughed. "Yeah right, our mothers would kill us."

"Seriously, why not? We both have money saved up. We can get a cute apartment together, figure out what we want to do with our lives. Get some plants, vintage furniture, maybe even a goddamn cat. You know, like how the white girls do it."

Christine grew quiet. "You're serious?"

"Why not? We can finally be two little fishes in a big ass pond. Let's get the *fuck* out of Little Saigon."

A smile broke out on Christine's face as the idea began to take root in her mind, even though she knew that realistically neither of them would move. It was still nice to pretend. "Fuck it, I'm in, let's do it." She honked several times, and the two girls screamed in the car. As they hit a red light, the car next to them rolled down their window, and a white guy with dreadlocks yelled out, "Ni hao, ladies!"

Christine and Rosie turned toward him, and in sync they showed him their middle fingers. "It's chào, bitch, *not* ni hao!" The minute the light turned green, Christine floored it. The two girls cackled loudly, and Rosie stuck her head out the window again and blew out more smoke.

THE PREGNANCY

15

Priscilla Nguyễn

BREACHES ARE SLOW, STEADY, and the effects won't be felt until long after the culprit is gone. A good breach comes in undetected, slowly stealing data from under your nose. You'd never see it coming, not until it's laughing in your face.

Maggie Chen was a good breach. She came in sneakily, deliberate, and carried a virus that would infect Priscilla's mind and slowly corrupt her system. Priscilla kept up the charade for as long as possible with Mark. It had been months since she discovered those texts from Maggie Chen on his phone. Ironically, she was terrified every day that Mark would know she saw them. She talked back less and apologized more, hoping that he would wake up one day and remember the way he used to look at her. And maybe, just *maybe*, she could salvage this.

Priscilla surprised Mark by taking him to her favorite hole-in-the-wall Vietnamese restaurant on Jackson Street. She pasted on a fake chipper smile, hoping to trick Mark into thinking she was still cool, spontaneous, and *exuberant*. As soon as they entered the restaurant, the hostess smiled at her, and much to Mark's surprise, Priscilla spoke to the woman in Vietnamese and asked for a table for two.

"You rarely speak Vietnamese," he said, raising an eyebrow. "Trying to impress me?"

Priscilla gave off a fake laugh, and she used the moment to test the waters between them. She dipped a toe in. "Just trying to brush up on it, I don't want to lose it. Wouldn't you want to teach our kids how to speak Vietnamese?"

Mark didn't confirm anything. Instead, he ordered a Bia Saigon for himself, and Priscilla quickly asked for one as well, even though she hated beer. Mark crossed his arms, leaned forward on the table, and stared at the television in the corner, which was blaring Vietnamese music videos.

"God, I love Vietnam. There is *nothing* more freeing than being on the back of a motorbike, traveling up and down the coast. You remember that story of when I almost died?" Mark said.

Priscilla nodded. Mark pulled back his sleeve and showed her the same scar on his elbow that she'd seen at every dinner party, where he would tell the same story about how he almost got thrown off his motorbike in central Vietnam.

"You know, I don't know why everyone loves the south so much, I actually prefer the north," Mark said. "So many secret alleyways that line the Old Quarter in Hà Nội. You've never been to the north, right?"

Priscilla gritted her teeth. "I've only ever been to the south. You know that already, sweetie."

"You're missing out, Pris. You *need* to go back. See it through my eyes."

Priscilla saw another opening, and this time, allowed herself to step into the water. "You're going back to China soon, aren't you? For work?"

Mark's eyes lit up. "Yes, I can't wait. Maybe I'll make a pit stop somewhere. It's been a while since I've been in southeast Asia. You *know* how much that place means to me. I really found myself there."

Priscilla paused; the water felt a little cool but it wasn't uninviting. Now that she was standing in shallow water, she felt confident to take another full step into deeper territory. "*Wellll* . . . maybe I can join you for part of your work trip? You can go to Beijing for work, and I'll head to Hong Kong for fun. We can meet in Vietnam? I can finally put my language skills to good use and you can show me the north."

Mark opened his mouth and closed it. Priscilla could see a thought bubble with ellipses hanging above his head. He started to say something, but then the waitress came back out, placing two beers in front of them. Mark turned away from Priscilla, and asked the waitress which part of Vietnam she was from. Priscilla braced herself for another long conversation with another Asian waitress.

The woman told him she was from the north, and Mark was delighted. He gave Priscilla an *I told you so* look and launched into a conversation about how special the north was. Mark plunged into a deep soliloquy about how striking Hạ Long Bay is seeing it for the first time—how the branches from banyan trees would dangle several feet from the ground, lining the alleyways that surrounded the coffee shops; and how his favorite activity was people-watching on red plastic stools. Priscilla's face grew a deep red as she felt herself being left further and further out of the conversation. She instantly regretted speaking Vietnamese earlier; the rare occasion that she spoke it, it always backfired.

The waitress pulled up a chair at Mark's behest, and she laughed at his story about how he managed to skirt the infamous midnight curfew by knowing which bars to hide out in. The conversation turned political as they talked about how corrupt certain parts of the north still were, how business owners would line the pockets of local police, and how—because of that—Chicken Feet Street was still a raucous party at 1:00 a.m. Priscilla quietly sipped on her beer, wondering if she should talk about her experience going back as a Vietnamese American woman, but nobody gave her an opening, so she retreated into herself. Yet Priscilla kept waiting.

Waiting and waiting—like a good dog.

She was waiting for Mark to remember. To remember the reason they were each other's emergency contacts, to remember why they had spent Christmas alone that one year instead of with their families, to remember why she held his hand after his sister was taken to the emergency room after a car accident, and to remember why he held hers whenever she cried about her mother.

. . .

Breaches happen because of human error. This particular breach happened at two in the morning. Priscilla was startled awake by the buzzing sound of Mark's phone next to her head. They were both naked and sticky in bed after sex. Mark had fallen asleep with his arm wrapped around her waist, and left his phone peeking out from under his pillow. She grumped an annoyance at him and reached for his phone to silence it. That's when she saw a string of messages from Maggie.

can we stay at the same hotel for the china trip?

Everyone is like soooo coupled up.

Bringing their partner for a WORK TRIP?! Who does that?!

Glad you're not boring like everyone else and have a gf

lets get drunk :) wanna go with me to singapore after?

or vietnam?? :)

Maggie had no idea who Priscilla was and this revelation gutted, haunted, crushed her. Maggie didn't even know she *existed*. But Maggie had existed in

Priscilla's mind for months. In fact, she had built her up and up and up as the *perfect* Asian woman. Younger, uncomplicated, free. Priscilla had done everything she could to become a better version of Maggie for Mark, and the girl didn't even know who she *fucking* was.

This was the precise moment Priscilla snapped.

All Priscilla could remember from that night was the banshee scream that erupted from her. Her Southern California Asian accent came out in full force. It was the type of screaming she remembered her mother doing to her father for years. It was the type of screaming that was reminiscent of her mother's warning shrieks to "never marry a Vietnamese man" because they were ngu dốt. It was the type of screaming that caused ten-year-old Priscilla to cover her ears and desperately wish they were Japanese or Chinese instead of being Vietnamese. The *normal* Asians.

"Do you have feelings for Maggie?" Priscilla paced back and forth, still naked, tearing her thick, black hair out. Tears streamed down her face.

"Jesus, NO. Of course not. Can you please stop being so insecure and jealous?" Mark said, staring at the clock, watching it turn 4:00 a.m. He groaned and slammed a pillow into his face, his post-coital shrunken dick shriveling in the moonlight. "I have a big presentation in the morning to prepare for the China trip. I cannot believe you're doing this to me right now."

"Show me your phone. I want to see every conversation you two have had."

"No. You're supposed to trust me."

"I *do* trust you. Just show me your phone. You can look at mine all you want."

"You know, Priscilla, my Thai ex-girlfriend never talked back to me like you do."

"Well, why didn't you fucking get married to her instead?"

"Because I didn't want to pay the goddamn sin sod, okay? That shit is so archaic."

"What the *hell* is a sin sod?" Priscilla shouted, so confused. "I'm not *fucking* Thai! You can't just throw words out like that for no reason and expect me to know!"

"It's like their version of a Thai dowry! I don't know the rules!" Mark yelled back, running his hands through his hair. "The groom has to give the family of the bride money or *something*. I don't fucking know!"

Priscilla stopped in her tracks and stared at Mark like he was a stranger. *Who was the man she'd been with the past three years?* Her voice shook. "You're telling me that you were with your Thai girlfriend for *three* years, but you didn't want to marry her because of a *dowry*?"

"*Why* are we talking about this now? Who the *fuck* cares?" Mark yelled, throwing his hands in the air. "That was a lifetime ago! I was *young*. We've all moved on from it."

"Do you not realize how problematic everything you just said was? You led that girl on for years. Just like how you're leading me on right now." Priscilla was incredulous as she tried her best to hold back her tears and keep a steady poker face. The breach had finally reached her heart and she was malfunctioning. "What happened to the man I fell in love with and who fell in love with me? I thought we *knew* each other. You're the only person who I can turn to. *You're* my family, Mark. I have no one left."

Mark began breathing heavily and hyperventilating. "I thought I was capable of being that person for you, Priscilla, but clearly I am not. You made me be your boyfriend *and* your best friend *and* your mother *and* your father *and* your sisters—*every fucking person* in this goddamn world. Who can live up to that kind of expectation? I am not your whole universe, Priscilla. No one can be that for you."

Priscilla faltered. It was as if Mark had slapped her across the face. She knew she should have taken a step back at this point, taken a breather, gone on a walk, and cooled off but she was tired of retreating. She'd been retreating her entire life.

"Go *on* then: Fucking leave. Find yourself another Asian girlfriend, like you always do! I'm just one in billions of Asian women out there!" She launched a pillow at his face.

"*Goddamnit,* Priscilla. You make everything so fucking difficult. Who the hell would ever want to be chained to *you*, your *family* shitshow, and your insane *mother*? Who would *willingly* ever marry into that?" Mark grabbed the pillow she had just thrown at him and his phone. He shoved past her, and slammed the bedroom door, throwing one last expletive at her before the door drowned out his voice. She could hear his muffled yelling from the living room. "Fuck this, Priscilla. I don't need this from you or anyone. I'll get my things tomorrow, then I'm off to Asia for work. We're done here."

Priscilla stopped dead in her tracks, unable to breathe. How could she let herself go off like that? She'd been so careful, calculated in not pissing Mark off ever since she found out about Maggie. Now she was alone in her bedroom at 4:00 a.m., and Mark wasn't ever going to come back to the room, to hug her, kiss her, say sorry, or say the words she wanted to hear in that moment: "I love you, I'm willing to do whatever it takes to make this work." She sank to the floor, naked and sobbing, wondering why she just couldn't *shut the fuck up* when she saw those messages. She hated it when her mother would yell at her father, and here she was, becoming the one thing she had worked her whole life not to become.

Maggie Chen was never the breach. It was always Priscilla.

Mark loved Asian women. If only she could have loved herself just as much.

Maybe if she did, she wouldn't have found herself one night—brokenhearted and alone in a half-empty apartment—re-downloading Tinder and mindlessly swiping from profile to profile, wondering if she was too broken and tired to swipe left on all the white men or if she simply was too lonely not to. So she swiped right on every profile, no matter who it was. It was all just a numbers game anyway. She kept swiping right on all the engineers who worked at Amazon; all the biotech people; all the recent transplants from San Francisco who came to join the latest start-up or become a director at a Big Tech; all the amateur rock climbers; all the new PhD candidates who flocked to the city. She swiped right on all of them. She kept going and going, hearing the chime of "It's a match!" go off, using it as a Band-Aid. The more she heard it go off, one after the other, a series of notifications filling her inbox, the more she got off on it. She answered all the messages, one by one, hoping to find someone, *anyone*, who could help her break the curse.

. . .

Priscilla's frontal lobe kicked in, and it didn't allow her to wallow for too long. She set out to optimize her chances at finding a life partner immediately after the breakup. She lined men up every night of the week, scheduling some nights back-to-back. For the more questionable ones, she did a series of video chats to screen them. Maximum results with minimum efforts. She realized if she followed a strict, rotational method, with a high turnover rate, she would increase her odds of finding love.

But after three dates, she began to see a pattern with the single men in Seattle. The data was all there. Men who questioned her credentials. Men who felt threatened and insecure with her career. Men who dangled the promise of marriage and children one day, but didn't actually mean it. Men who were obsessed with their package. Not *that* kind of package—their *total compensation* tech package, which included base salary and the number of stocks they were given. Men who paraded around as *nice guys* but secretly harbored incel thoughts. Priscilla's thoughts took a dark turn as she kept rehashing Mark, Maggie Chen, and everything that had led her to this moment. She was spiraling, and she wasn't sure how to pull herself out of it. But she continued to go on dates, and woke up next to strangers every morning because she was too afraid to go back to an empty apartment.

"Are you okay . . . ?" Lily Lương asked Priscilla tentatively one morning, when she saw Priscilla stumble into the office's shared kitchen, sunglasses on and wearing a wrinkled shirt. Lily looked like she'd come straight off a morning workout; her skin was glowing and her hair was pulled back in a sleek high ponytail.

Priscilla looked around to see who was speaking to her. When she saw it was her half cousin, also the intern, she flinched from how healthy Lily appeared in comparison to her, and she vacillated between being awkward or professional.

"Hey, Lily," she said, clearing her throat and putting on a serious voice. "How are you settling in? How's your internship going? How's your research project going?"

Lily also straightened herself and matched Priscilla's professionalism. "It's great so far, just experimenting with a new data model this week, hoping for some good results."

"Great, great . . ." Priscilla trailed off, trying to find some commonality with her estranged half cousin. "Did you end up going to the funeral? For Bà Ngoại?"

Lily shook her head. "I should have, but I was too busy here and to be honest, I stopped talking to her a while ago since I moved up here for my PhD program. My mother was pretty upset I didn't make the effort. Did you go? Did you know her well?"

Priscilla had an image of her grandmother covering her ears when she was young while her parents were fighting in the kitchen. She had rocked her back and forth, trying her best to distract her.

"No," she said, her smile thinning with regret. "I didn't go. I was also pretty busy." Their only commonality, it seemed, was that they were both terrible first-born daughters.

"Was your mother also upset that you didn't show up?"

Priscilla quickly grabbed a bagel from the counter and held it up to her face. "Sorry, lots of meetings today! Let's chat later, okay? Keep up the great work. Great having you here." She quickly retreated into the privacy of her executive office, grateful that she had banned an open-floor office plan when she first started her company.

The last thing Priscilla needed to admit was that on top of the breakup, on top of her securing $15 million in VC funding for the latest round, on top of regularly stalking Maggie Chen's social media, on top of all the marathon dating she'd been doing, she never actually returned her mother's call all those months ago.

• • •

Priscilla woke up one day and realized that she was late. Very, *very* late.

She threw off her duvet, ran out the door in her bedroom slippers, and sprinted to the nearest drugstore. Priscilla looked rabid as she grabbed a pregnancy test from the counter and quickly went back home. She rushed into the bathroom and administered the test. Waiting for the results, she slowly sank down to the floor and rocked back and forth, saying a prayer for the first time since she was forced to go to a Buddhist camp as a kid. There was no such thing as God, Buddha, or whatever was out there, but in this moment, it didn't hurt to believe—just a little.

When she finally had the courage to look up, she saw two little lines appear and she burst into tears. She reached for her phone and scrolled through, wondering who was her emergency contact now. She instinctively scrolled to Mark's number, which was next to her mother's number. She kept pulling the screen indecisively up and down, before scrolling to her sister, Thủy, but something was holding her back. She then scrolled to her youngest sister, Thảo, but she wasn't there for long before she scrolled back up to Mark's number.

She stared and stared at his number, willing it to ring. Her eyes kept darting *back* to her mother's number. She never thought she'd ever need her mother again, especially not after their fight last year. But at this moment, she didn't need an ex-boyfriend; she needed her mother. Her hand hovered over the call button, shaking, wondering what was scarier: pregnancy, motherhood, or speaking to her mother.

Priscilla caressed her stomach, wondering if she was prepared to make the kinds of sacrifices needed to go through with this, and if she'd be different than her mother. She looked down at the little stick in her hand and decided she was done running away from the kind of woman she had dreamt of becoming her whole life, because now she had to be better for whoever was growing inside of her. She hit the dial button.

The first ring had barely finished when her mother picked up. Priscilla's eyes welled up and she tried to keep her voice calm, but she broke out into tears instantly after hearing her mother's voice after more than a year of silence.

"Mẹ? Are you there?" She tried her best not to cry over the phone.

"Con, is everything okay?" Mai Nguyễn asked, her voice frantic with concern, as if the year of silence between the two never happened. "What's wrong? What do you need? Are you okay?"

No, I'm not okay. Can I please come home? I need you.

That was what Priscilla wanted to say. She felt it on the tip of her tongue. Like a plane waiting for the clear to finally descend, the words circled above her. From all corners of the world and across time and space, ghosts, spirits, witches, and her ancestors waited with bated breath for Priscilla to finally open up to her mother. They waited and waited for their union to be fixed, because they'd also carried regrets from their own fractured relationships with their mothers. But just like last time, Priscilla swallowed her words. She couldn't break the barrier. Not this time. Whether it was pride or fear, she didn't know what was stopping her. Just like how she spoke to Lily earlier, she retained the same professionalism with her mother.

Priscilla cleared her throat, kept an even tone in her voice, and wiped the tears from her eyes.

"Yes, Mẹ, everything's fine. Just calling about some paperwork."

16

Lily Lương

LILY LƯƠNG SPENT HER entire life chasing third chances.

Her mother, Mrs. Kim Lương, however, was convinced in the power of *second* chances, believing that they were karmic rewards from your previous life. Her mother had often said that the most pivotal moment in her life was when a house deed was serendipitously signed in Santa Ana. Once it went on public record, it revealed a signature that belonged to a Mrs. Lý Minh Dương, which triggered the private investigator who Mrs. Lương had hired. A second chance had unfolded. Her mother waited years to take that chance, saving every scrap for a one-way ticket to America, and she followed the trail to California, to an address that led them to a crooked blue house in Santa Ana and into the arms of a mother she thought had been lost forever.

But Lily knew that second chances were only there to fix mistakes made from the first go-around. It was shortsighted. The real magic was in the third chance, otherwise known as the third design system. It was the chance to get everything right from both the first and second attempt. The third design system had the best chance for true success.

When Lily was asked if she wanted to go to Hong Kong by herself for a last-minute research trip, she said yes right away. Priscilla had unexpectedly taken a long leave of absence, and then the principal engineer went on maternity leave, leaving the spot open. The request trickled all the way down the company until it landed on the intern's desk. Lily recognized the pattern of three in this request, and that the universe was aligning for her.

Because she knew that Peter, her first real relationship, was still in Hong Kong.

She'd been unable to solve the mathematical proof for the *what-if* between them for years. Their first attempt failed, their second attempt failed, and now she had a shot at a third chance. This time, it *could* be successful. It *could* be different. Lily had hope.

. . .

After some research on which neighborhood to stay in, Lily booked an Airbnb at the very top of 100 Queen's Road Central, the last stop off the half-mile Central Mid-level Escalator running right through the bustling Central District in Hong Kong, hidden between beautiful alleyways with overgrown, cascading vines.

The Central Mid-level Escalator was known for being the longest outside escalator system in the world—a surreal, dystopian ride crammed with locals, expats, and finance guys in Armani suits yelling into their phones; Filipina nannies running errands for wealthy Hong Kongese families; and tourists with their long range DSLRs. No matter their economic status, they would all ride side by side, up and down, past modern shops nestled next to more traditional mom-and-pop stalls. A mix of old and new, young and old, rich and poor. Modern boba lattes selling next to stalls hawking herbal teas in paper cups. The cheapest Michelin restaurants next to the most expensive Michelin restaurants. Riding the escalators was like watching a moving, living documentary about Hong Kong culture. It was a thrilling spectacle and testament of Hong Kongese resilience in the modern age, and Lily couldn't wait to witness it with Peter.

The romantic in Lily envisioned that their reunion would be as grandiose as red carpet premieres, kissing in the rain, running through an airport terminal. Because third chances deserved that.

As soon as Lily stepped onto the tarmac, she choked on the tangible mugginess. She wasn't used to this weather anymore since she left Vietnam as a very small child. But it wasn't the weather that she needed to get used to again; it was the fact that nobody had batted an eye at her the whole trip. She received no double takes, no eye lingering a bit longer on her features, nobody asking her *where are you from?* Or *are you Japanese?* Or the staple ni hao thrown at her. She was invisible. For once in her life, she blended in. The peace was resoundingly profound.

Once she walked out the terminal gate, she heard her name being called, and she looked up excitedly to see Peter run toward her, his brunette hair perfectly coiffed for the occasion, and his brown eyes beaming. He looked more at ease in

Hong Kong than Lily had ever seen before. Especially since she knew he often wrestled with his Chinese identity compared to his white side. Peter looked heart-breakingly handsome, and Lily felt herself melting as he scooped her up into his arms and swung her around. Her insecurities quickly escalated, along with her anxiety, as she remembered all the times he'd broken her heart. He was so worldly, and Lily felt sheltered and ignorant in comparison.

"It's so good to see you," he said as he buried his face into Lily's hair. He gave her the kind of comforting hug that only two people with a labyrinth of a past can do.

"I'm sorry, I bet I smell like an old sock," Lily groaned and laughed nervously as she attempted to smooth the wrinkles in her clothes out. "The flight was brutal. It's wild to be back in Asia again, but even more wild to see you again."

"At least you're a very cute smelly sock," he laughed. "I cannot *wait* to show you around Hong Kong." Peter grabbed her bags from her as he confidently led them to the MTR to take it back to the city. He lightly joked that she had packed an entire department store for just a week's work trip. With his free hand, he reached behind her neck, twisting the ends of her hair with his fingers, just like he used to, and Lily shivered at his touch. His hand dropped from her neck and found her hand, and he held it all the way through the metro station. She did her best not to react to it. Internally, she was screaming with joy.

This wasn't just *her* third chance. It was theirs.

Lily was in awe. After the initial culture shock she felt at the airport wore off, she couldn't *not* soak it all up. So this is Hong Kong. This was what Peter was so obsessed with, the reason why their second chance had crumbled. He had chosen Hong Kong instead of her. It was wonderful, mysterious, and chaotic—and an intense sensory overload. Lily started taking photos and selfies of everything inside the MTR, the underground metro city of Hong Kong that seemed to be the city's secret Atlantis. She began to imagine what her life would have been like had she followed Peter to Hong Kong instead of going into her PhD program.

She thought of her mother as she wandered through the MTR. Lily's mother had refused to talk about all the years she spent orphaned in Vietnam, thinking she'd been purposely abandoned, too afraid to move forward on her own and spending every waking moment believing she wasn't worthy of her mother's love.

"You can't rely on anyone else for your own happiness, Lily," her mother used to say to her. "You need to find it for yourself, because anyone can leave at any given moment, even the ones you think will never hurt you."

Lily snuck a glance at Peter. Doubt began to creep in as she wondered if she could ever rely on him to not leave her again. But she dismissed it.

Everything about Hong Kong was a juxtaposition, the retro soft colors next to modern vibrant colors. The women were elegant and gorgeous, and the men, rugged and painfully handsome. She was in awe of the thriving shops, restaurants, and bars inside a metro station. Peter was amused by Lily's innocence and commented on it several times, as her bright eyes widened to a new city in a new part of the world.

After an hour traveling through the MTR to get to the Central Mid-level Escalator, Lily's doe-eyes hadn't relented but she could feel Peter's excitement begin to wane.

"Is something wrong?" Lily asked. "Is it weird to see me here? It's weird, isn't it. I'm going to say it's weird. Or am I being an annoying tourist—"

Peter touched her knee reassuringly and shushed her. "*Stop*. Everything's fine. I'm just tired. I stayed up late to finish this work thing. I really am glad to see you, Lils. What are the chances you get sent here for work?"

"I think it's a sign."

The next stop was theirs. He tapped her knee gently, indicating that it was time to get off, and automatically grabbed her two suitcases to carry for her. He made a joke that suddenly her packing habits weren't as cute as they'd been an hour ago. Lily flinched a bit, remembering that Peter's jokes always had a kernel of judgment to them, and she remembered how they stopped being funny one day and began to hurt. She brushed it off and tried to grab a suitcase to help, but he protested and insisted on carrying them both still. As they exited the station, Lily's eyes brightened as she soaked it all in again. She whipped her phone out, ready to take a bunch of photos that would just end up crowding her cloud storage and she'd never look at again.

As they strolled through the aboveground walkway, they rounded the corner and Lily gasped, not from the spectacle of the city, but from the chaotic scene they stumbled upon. Her ears picked up a chorus of Tagalog being spoken all at once, as if each voice was fighting to tell *their* version, *their* side of the story, *their* gossip. For miles and miles, all throughout the rest of the footbridge, there were Filipina women—a crowd of young and old, all gathered in small groups, sitting on folded cardboard to cover the ground, nestled next to the railings, squeezed along the sides so they wouldn't disrupt the footpath. They were all laughing, napping, knitting, chatting, drinking tea, and eating food from Tupperware containers. Locals didn't bat an eye at the scene as they walked through. Only the other tourists, like Lily, were staring, wondering why all these Filipina women were here.

"What are they doing? Are they homeless?" Lily asked. "They don't look homeless."

Peter shrugged. "I don't know. It's normally on Sundays when you see them gathered like this, and they kind of hang out all day."

"You aren't *at all* curious why all these women are just sitting around in the middle of the day, crowding the pathway? They look like they're waiting for something. But what?" The researcher in her kicked into high gear.

Peter didn't respond; he just silently led the way to the Central Mid-level Escalator. Lily couldn't stop talking about the Filipina women the whole way there. Peter still didn't say a word. Once they reached the bottom of the escalators, Lily turned to look at Peter, her face full of childlike glee, and switched topics.

"Surprise! Our Airbnb is located at the top of these escalators. I did so much research and I thought it would be cute for us to go up and down them all weekend. It's one of the longest outdoor escalators in the world. Almost three thousand feet up, can you believe it? I know you live over in Kowloon, but it's kind of nice to play tourist for a weekend, right?"

Lily paused as she realized that Peter's face was unreadable. A myriad of thoughts bubbled up. Was she lame? Did Peter actually not want to be here? Was he just here because he was too polite to say no? Is this too touristy?

But Peter's face broke out in a laugh, and Lily allowed herself to relax. She recognized the tone of his laughter and she studied his face, remembering every fold and freckle that dotted his cheekbones. Lily could make a map of the world from them.

Suddenly Peter stopped laughing. His face went from amused to miffed and she knew him well enough to know when he was trying to bite his tongue. He simply raised his finger and pointed up. Lily followed where he was pointing, and craned her neck all the way up, her hand shielding her face from the hot sun.

"Lils, I think the escalators are out of order. The sign says it's under construction all week," he raised an eyebrow at her. "Basically the entire time you're here."

A horde of tourists next to them had also discovered the problem at the same time, and grumbles filled the air. Complaints upon complaints about how they were going to get all the way to the top in this morbid heat. One woman began to fan herself with her gigantic paper map of the city and bemoaned about *why* their honeymoon was in Asia, of all the *darn* places in the world. Only the locals appeared nonplussed, and they simply walked up the immobile escalators or moved over to the concrete stairs on the right.

"Still think it's funny that I'm not a light packer?" Lily laughed nervously.

Peter just gave her a thin-lipped grin, picked up both her suitcases silently, and stepped on the first set of stairs. Lily, feeling the mood shift again, just like it did back on the subway, kept silent. By the time they reached the top of the Central Mid-level, they were both drenched in sweat. Peter had sweated through his breezy white shirt, and the veins in his arms stuck out, like raised typography on his skin. Lily's pristine airport outfit she had picked for their reunion was also soaked through. Their reunion embrace suddenly seemed like it was ten years ago. They were no longer in the mood to hold hands.

Peter set the luggage down on the pavement and was finally able to pull the handles out to use. He rolled them down the alleyway, slightly ahead of Lily, the luggage making a huge racket as it wobbled against the old cobblestoned street. They walked through the cascading, overgrown greenery that Lily saw in the Airbnb posting. She had specifically chosen the location because of how romantic and moody it felt, and she thought it would be the perfect setting to tell Peter that she still loved him. But now the vines looked more like the fake prison bars found at Disneyland that tourists pose behind for photos.

· · ·

After Lily's jet lag had worn off, and a long nap, they woke up in each other's arms and the tension seemed to have died down. Maybe the awkwardness came from being two years apart. They just needed to remember their rhythm again.

"So, what's on the schedule?" Peter teased. "I know you have a big list of places to hit the next few days before you *actually* have to do what you came here to do, which is work."

Lily laughed and gleefully whipped out her phone to show Peter a map of places she pinned. "I thought you'd never ask."

"You know how much I hate agendas, lists, any type of planning."

"Yes, but you remember how much I *love* that."

"Okay, okay! Hit me with the first thing on your list," he said, laughing.

Lily paused and grabbed his hand. "I know it's really *really* touristy, but I'd like to go see the Big Buddha statue."

Peter sucked in his breath and bit down on a closed fist. "Lils, *no*. I'm sorry, I'll do anything but do that. Do you know how many times I've gone to see that Buddha statue? Anytime a friend comes to visit or a family member—"

"—but I have a *really* good reason. My grandmother passed away a few months ago, and I didn't go to her funeral. I was hoping to light some incense and say a prayer for her."

Peter took Lily's hand and played with her fingers while she kept begging him to come. He sighed. "Sorry, Lils, I think I'm still just too tired from work, I don't want to bring that negative energy and bring you down. Can we meet up afterward? For dinner? I know you have a restaurant on that list of yours you probably want to try."

Lily looked taken aback. "Did I do something wrong?"

"No! *No.* Of course not. I'm just not a very *touristy* person. Even being near the escalators has been a lot for me today. Maybe it's best if we each do our own thing today, you know? You go pay your respects to your grandmother. I'll head to a nearby coffee shop and catch up on some work and wait for you to finish."

Lily didn't say anything back. What *could* she say? Her face burned red, and her mind went to a dark place. Thoughts from their last breakup ran through her mind. Would she ever be good enough for Peter?

She just simply agreed to Peter's plan and said that she'd text him when she was done at the Big Buddha.

After Lily finished getting ready, she headed out on her own for the day. She stood towering at the top of the Central Mid-level Escalator and looked at all the steps she had to take to reach the bottom. Regret began to fill her as she took her first step back down. She'd only just reached the top hours ago, and now she had to do this every single day this week. With each step she took, she went through their exchange over and over in her head. She wished her reaction had been cooler, something that made her come across as less meek. Lily was afraid that Peter still had the same impression of her as he did two years ago. That she was nothing more than a quiet, good Asian girl.

With each step down to the bottom of the escalators, all 782 steps, she thought about the man who was waiting at the very top. She didn't know which direction would lead her to what she wanted; she just kept heading toward the bottom, hoping it'd somehow get her to the top eventually.

17

Mai Dương

WHEN MRS. NGUYỄN GOT UP this morning, it was the first time in months that she finally felt hungry enough to eat a full meal. Grief came and went, but each day had become more manageable than the last. Routine helped somewhat, but it only became bearable when she finally heard from her daughter, Priscilla, after a year of not speaking to each other. Though it was just small talk, it gave her the energy to get up again. It reminded her to push through because there were still things left on this earth she needed to fix—starting with her relationships with her three daughters.

She boiled rice to make a quick congee and drizzled Maggi seasoning over it, sprinkling it with dried pork floss and scallions. Just like how her mother used to make it for her.

After breakfast, Mrs. Nguyễn stared at herself in the mirror, examining every new wrinkle. She pulled back her skin, and tried to imagine what she used to look like when it was taut. She rummaged through some old crusty makeup, wondering if she should bother with it. She hadn't worn makeup in years.

Would it even matter? It was just a meet-and-greet.

A rather strange opportunity had appeared before her recently, and she decided to take it. It was strange in the sense that it was offered to her, but the opportunity itself was very common in Little Saigon. It was good money, and maybe she could fix up some things at the house by the beach. She hadn't been back there since her mother's will was read as she still didn't know what to do with it.

She decided to put on a little blush and lipstick, just in case, and attached a brooch to her sweater, as per the instructions she was given. As she stared back at her reflection, Mrs. Nguyễn saw someone she hadn't seen in a long time. Though gravity had taken its course over the years, Mrs. Nguyễn saw Mai Dương in the mirror, not Mrs. Mai Nguyễn. It was a sight she welcomed, like reuniting with an old friend who had gone away for a long time.

Mai was given written instructions to head to the food courts on the third level at the Phước Lộc Thọ, the Asian Garden Mall, off Bolsa Avenue. She didn't know who had given her the instructions nor did she *want* to know. Just in case she was ever questioned by immigration and the IRS, she would be able to pass a lie detector test.

As she climbed the steps to the mall, she passed giant red paper lanterns hanging low from the ceiling; rows of empty jewelry shops manned by old, bored Vietnamese women, their heads propped up by their hands; children, clamoring and begging their parents to go inside the small shops stuffed to the brim with Japan-imported plushies and games. She walked past all of it and headed toward the tiny corner food stall and sat down at the table farthest away from the entrance. Just as the instructions said.

A tray of bánh bột lọc and an accompanying saucer of nước mắm appeared before her, along with a glass of cà phê sữa đá. Mai eyed her watch, then fixated her stare on the coffee, watching it slowly drip from the metal phin that hung over the glass. The man was already ten minutes late. Men are such loafs. Irritation crept in. Her ex-husband was *always* late, too. The fact that it was a *business* meeting made this stranger's tardiness even more rude. Nothing had changed in her sixty-plus years of existence. Men were still men.

She dipped the glutinous dumpling into the fish sauce and popped it into her mouth, chewing slowly. Without realizing it, in between bites, she was twisting her jade bracelet, suddenly having second thoughts about this type of transaction. Fifty grand *was* a lot of money, and with her savviness, she could make it stretch for a long time. She thought about taking all three of her daughters to Hawaii on a family vacation so they could spend time together and try to salvage their relationship. If they were willing to try.

But to go through *another* marriage, even if it was just on paper . . .

"Chào Cô," a soft voice. A man walked around her, pulled out a chair, and sat down across from her. The first thing Mai noticed about him was his eyes, and it caught her off guard. They were a light brown color that had a sheen around the irises. She'd never seen eyes like that before. The second thing she noticed was that he immediately took off his newsboy cap and placed it on the table. She be-grudgingly grunted in approval at the respect he showed her. Though basic table manners were *nothing* to pray to Buddha or her ancestors about. He flagged the waitress down and ordered a cà phê đá, before staring deep into her eyes, unnerving her, holding her gaze with confidence and grace. Mai felt uneasy, the way his eyes bore into hers, taking her all in. It was as if he could really see her.

"Cảm ơn Cô đã gặp tôi," he greeted in gratitude. He extended his hand out to her. "My name is Anh Lê. What is your name?" He flashed her a smile. It was the type that radiated off his entire body, and she could feel the halo effect engulf her, luring her into his light. She twirled her jade bracelet, faster and faster, because for whatever reason, the man before her made her nervous. Except, she couldn't recognize this type of nervousness. She'd never felt it before in her entire life. She felt warm inside, as if she were about to enter an inviting, safe cabin after having trekked for so long alone, tired and hungry. Something shifted in her, and Mai recognized that she was, well . . . *attracted* to this man.

Suddenly, Mai choked on her dumpling, having been swept up in the mo-ment. She embarrassingly attempted to dry heave remnants stuck to the back of her throat. Anh immediately jumped up from his chair and sprung into action. Flagging down the waitress for a glass of water, he then wrapped his arms around her and began to do the Heimlich maneuver on her.

"Are you okay?" He watched her spit out the dumpling and gag out the shrimp carcass. He patiently rubbed her back, waiting for her to recover; constantly check-ing in and asking her if she needed anything else. His tenderness both touched Mai and made her uncomfortable. She hadn't had anyone care for her like this since she was a child.

Mai took a large swig from the water that the waitress handed to her. She stared at Anh, suddenly blanking on everything. She blanked on the original purpose of this meeting. She blanked on Auntie Hứa's predictions, her mother, her sisters, her daughters, losing her mother, the funeral. *One funeral, one marriage, one pregnancy. One grandson.* She was no longer plagued by the fact that her three selfish, thankless daughters barely called her, even when she was grieving. She simply forgot about it all because it morphed into white noise. Because at this moment, nothing really mattered, except for who was in front of her.

"My name is Mai. Mai Dương," she said softly, shaking his extended hand. The moment their hands touched, she had flashes of a young Mai—barefoot, running through the park back in Cần Thơ, laughing with her two sisters as they carried baskets of fruit, fresh shrimp, and pork belly home to their parents. Their mother was going to make bánh xèo, her favorite dish, for her birthday dinner.

Mai was still holding on to the man's hand, her jade bracelet grazing against his wrist, unable to let go. She stayed there for as long as possible because she was afraid that if she ever let go, she'd never get back those memories of who she once was. It had been so long since she'd seen the face of that little girl. The strange part of it all was that the man didn't want to let go, either.

And so, on the third floor of the food court at the Asian Garden Mall in Little Saigon, Orange County, two Vietnamese souls, who had been wandering the earth alone for quite some time, found each other under the most suspect of circumstances. Because it would seem that love was attainable for survivors after all.

· · ·

Something happens when a spark ignites. It sets off a chain reaction, inviting the universe to keep going, *no matter what.* Because life was always meant to unfold organically. Especially when the universe colludes with other spiritual forces at play; that's when it collides.

The moment Mai Dương fell in love with Anh Lê was when the curse began to slowly reverse. Somewhere on the island of Kauai, off the Kuhio Highway, a strange, petite, Vietnamese woman's ears perked up when she heard the fireworks go off. She wore a smirk, knowing that it was just a matter of time before everything else fell into place for Mai's daughters as well. At the exact same moment, somewhere in the little village of Little Saigon, an herbalist's glasses fell off his face from the shock of the impact as he, too, felt the same fireworks explode. His face broke out into a smile, realizing that the vial he had given to Mrs. Phạm had been released back into the world. He had been saving that vial for decades because he was waiting to bestow it to a woman who needed to believe again. On the ancestral altar of Mai's home, had anyone been home at the moment, they would have *sworn* that they saw the black-and-white photos of *all* the Dương women—going back generations—*smiling.*

Mai and Anh talked for hours. He even bought her a small plushie from one of those small shops she had angrily brushed past earlier. Mai's cheeks glowed, and she felt young again; even her body felt spry. She was finally living out her teenage fantasies, with a cute boy on her arm as they walked through the mall together. They walked past a boba shop and saw all the young lovers in front of the shop, cuddling with each other and taking selfies. Anh turned to Mai and playfully poked her. "Think we can do a better job?"

Mai blushed. "What do you mean?"

"Let's take a photo together. I want to send it to my daughters."

"Will . . . will your daughters be happy to see me in it? Me, with *you*?"

He laughed and he gingerly put his arm around Mai. "All my daughters want for me is to be happy, so yes, of course they will be happy if I am happy. They wanted me to join them in America when my wife passed away years ago, but marriage was the only way they could legally bring me over. Serendipitously finding love through this was the miracle I didn't know I needed." He took out his phone and turned it around so that the camera was physically facing them. He was unsure how to use the selfie angle, and Mai didn't know how to, either, so they decided to blindly press the button from the other side until they got it right.

"Một hai ba!" Anh counted before taking the photo. Mai held up her plushie and Anh threw up the peace sign. After a few failed blind attempts, Anh was able to finally capture a photo of them . . . even though it was a *bit* out of frame. He looked at Mai and cupped her face, his crinkled eyes full of love. "It has been a long time since I have felt like this. I finally feel cured of my grief."

Anh then put his arm around hers and they continued strolling through the mall, stopping in front of every food stall. Mai was absolutely delighted, especially when they split a bánh patê sô together. She'd always wanted to split the savory pastry with someone, since she never actually wanted a whole one. They kept walking until they reached the row of empty jewelry shops.

"I have three daughters. One in Seattle, one in Los Angeles, and one in Sài Gòn," Mai said, suddenly forgetting how angry she was at all her daughters for abandoning her. She felt her sly smile return, ready to brag about them. "One is a CEO, one is a dermatologist for JOHN CHO! And one is running her own fashion line."

"Beautiful *and* smart? I can see where they all got it from."

"Oh, stop it, Anh!" She giggled as she slapped his arm, and she leaned in close to him, nuzzling his nose. To the younger passersby who only cared about getting the game they wanted, it was gross to see two old people in love. But to the other forgotten, elderly folk, who sat waiting for their grandchildren on nearby benches to finish their arcade games, they couldn't help but smile as they all remembered how it felt to fall in love once upon a time.

Mai did not see Vivi Phạm, the infamous gossip queen of Little Saigon, on the other side of the walkway, staring incredulously in their direction for several minutes. Vivi dropped all her shopping bags. She couldn't *believe* her eyes! Was that *Mai? Mai Nguyễn?* On a *date?* With a *man?* Vivi quickly pulled out her phone and called Annie Lau, who then called Mrs. Đào. They all asked for pics or else it didn't happen. So Vivi followed Mai and Anh discreetly around the mall, trying to get in a few good angles. Obviously, *only* angles of Mai's bad side.

Anh and Mai strolled down the long walkway of empty shops, casually peeking at the jewelry egregiously displayed behind smudged windows. Beyond the jewelry you could see all the old women with their bare feet propped up on the counter. Some were knitting, some were napping, some were chewing on chả giò, while others were peeling fruit and watching their Chinese soaps on the shared big TV screen that hung precariously on loose twine from the ceiling. Anh stopped in front of one window and stared at the rows and rows of engagement rings reflecting back at him, *daring* him to do it. A small mischievous smile began forming.

"Let's go inside," he said. "Just for fun."

Mai felt like a million bucks as she held his hand tighter. Her ex-husband had *never* once taken her jewelry shopping, even just to browse. In fact, she couldn't even remember if they ever held hands in public. She pushed her fake Louis bag higher up her arm, and walked into the jewelry shop confidently. Had you walked past these two lovebirds, you'd never have suspected that they'd only met hours ago. They looked like they had never left each other's side for centuries.

Around the corner, Vivi Phạm had lost her damn mind. She quickly texted Annie and Mrs. Đào, giving them live updates. A flurry of messages began brewing between the three gossipers.

They're going into a jewelry store together!!!!

You don't think they're going ring shopping?

Mai would never get married again. She doesn't believe in it.

Do you think he's rich?

No, he was wearing a newsboy cap.

What does that mean?

Means he's a cheap son of a bitch.

I'm jealous. My husband hasn't bought me new jewelry in years.

So take my husband, he has a gambling problem.

Vivi Phạm kept watch like a hawk, going back and forth before the window, desperately trying to catch what jewelry Mai was trying on, but both of their backs were turned toward her. Was she trying on rings? Necklaces? Jade bracelets? *What was it????*

Inside the shop, love was brewing.

Even the old women, who all jumped up immediately when two customers finally walked into their shop, could spot their love. They'd been selling and appraising jewelry for so long, they could tell you when love was fake, and when it was real. These two souls before them had never dreamt that romantic love could happen at their age, in their lifetime, within this cosmos. The type of love blossoming right now was the very thing that they'd been taught was unattainable. It wasn't pragmatic for people like them because they needed to worry about men with guns, picking a side in the war, putting food on the table, finding work, providing for their children, and figuring out how to survive in a foreign country. These things always came first. Now, they were a living testament that their mothers, fathers, grandmothers, and grandfathers were all wrong, especially when Anh put a ring on Mai's finger and asked her to marry him in front of these old women, who had turned their attention away from their Chinese soap to watch the one in front of them instead.

18

Joyce Phạm

JOYCE PHẠM WAS OBSESSED with finding her perfect Korean husband.

In her twenties, she buried herself in Korean dramas, finding relief in the male love interests who were so romantic and ethereal, and defied toxic masculinity. Her disillusionment for real life grew as she binged and binged on these perfect men who existed within the confines of fiction. Because it distracted her from the things that made her sad; it was better than any medication she'd ever been put on. Soon Joyce was able to speak more conversational Korean than Vietnamese, which both annoyed *and* worried her mother. Her mother was constantly hovering, wondering why Joyce was the way she was.

Mrs. Phạm often called her đặc biệt. Joyce was *special.*

But finding the perfect Korean man in New York City for the past five years had proven to be more taxing than expected. The city was littered with noncommittal men, all of whom found it just as easy to order sex at four in the morning as it was to order dumplings. Joyce was lonely. It wasn't the typical loneliness that came with single life; it was a deep, aching loneliness where nothing seemed to satisfy her. Joyce tried every dating app possible, including the Christian Korean one before she got kicked out when they discovered she was a fraud.

Joyce had gone on a few dates, a bit excited and hopeful each time, but she could tell that toward the end of the night, both parties were equally disappointed in each other. They were always put off that she knew more about Korean culture than they did. Joyce came off as one of *those* Asian women. The men would try their best to laugh it off and politely end the night, despite how often they checked the time on their phone, hoping for a miracle emergency to save them from the date from hell.

"I feel like you're more Korean than I am."

"I barely speak Korean."

"Actually, I'm vegan."

"I was adopted, so I don't know much."

"I've been to Korea once or twice. Yeah, it was cool I guess. Mostly visited family."

"I don't like it *too* spicy. I know, weird, right?"

"Most of my girlfriends have been white, actually."

One night, Joyce was getting ready for another date. She was feeling rather defeated, more so than usual. She swiped on some mascara, managed to wrestle her thick black hair into a low ponytail, and wore all black out of sheer laziness. She tucked rogue hair strands behind her ear and she stared at her reflection in the mirror, trying to pump herself up for yet another date. But her mind was crowded by negative thoughts. *Was she really this abnormal?*

Her phone went off and she looked down to see her mother calling. Joyce let it ring through. She wasn't in the mood to talk to her mother because she was tired of lying. She systematically tossed out all the herbs her mother would send her, and would go on autopilot with the lies. She'd thank her for them, say she drank them all, and that it was helping her feel better. She would continue the lie and say she didn't feel as tired anymore, that she wasn't sleeping all day, and that she wasn't crying as much as she used to. But most of all, she was tired of her mother telling her to live in reality, when reality had never been kind to her.

. . .

Liam had a deep, Midwestern voice.

It was the kind of voice that was soothing to hear over the radio, and comforting enough to fall asleep to. His palms were rough, having grown up in a blue collar, immigrant Korean family, deep in the woods of Michigan. He spent the winters learning to chop wood and had his first cigarette at the age of eleven. They were the only Korean family for miles and miles and, at one point growing up, Liam even began to question if he was actually Korean or not. They were six thousand miles away from Korea, two hours from the nearest Asian supermarket, and their very white neighbors never knew what to say to them, except for Ni hao or Arigato.

The first thing Joyce said to Liam when she saw him outside of the restaurant was, "You don't seem very Korean." He had on a casual button-down with a heavy black winter coat. His hair had speckles of gray and was slightly wet, like he had randomly run water through it five minutes ago to give it some life, hoping to revive a dead plant.

Joyce immediately kicked herself for saying it out loud.

"Let me guess, you're one of those California Asians that think the only Asians that exist in America live on the West Coast," he said, rolling his eyes. He took out a cigarette and lit it up. It was the dead of winter in New York City, and Joyce couldn't help but see how cold his hands were, but he suffered through, just to get a few drags in. He pointedly looked Joyce up and down. "Yep, you look like a Southern California Asian to me." Then he winked at her to let her know he was messing with her.

Joyce, a bit taken aback by how brusque Liam was, wondered if she should end the date before it began. But as her stomach cried out in hunger, she realized she had nothing but half a bottle of wine in her fridge, and she'd rather just get through the dinner, split the check, and finish watching the Joseon historical period show she was bingeing. She suddenly felt old, missed her warm bed and her small apartment in Bushwick.

"That stuff can kill you, you know," Joyce said, watching Liam finish his cigarette and stub it out in the ashtray. Her eyes crinkled in judgment. She was half–grossed out and half-intrigued by how indifferent and yet *different* Liam was. Mostly, more grossed out. "Isn't smoking more of an early 2000s thing than a 'now' thing?"

"I'm counting on it killing me. And smoking only went out of style in America, not the rest of the world." He held open the door. "Shall we?"

When Joyce walked past Liam, she smelled the tobacco on him, and she almost gagged, feeling her throat close up. The thought of kissing a smoker made her want to become a born-again virgin and run straight back to the comfort of her shows. Once they sat down, they immediately began to bicker. The argument started off small, as most wildfires do.

"Want to share?" Liam asked, barely glancing up from his menu. "I'm not really into veggies though, never eat them, but feel free to get some for yourself. Just don't let them touch my fork."

"You . . . *never* eat veggies?" Joyce repeated slowly, confused.

Liam shrugged. "I mean, I'll pick at some if they're in front of me."

"What does that mean? You just supplement your nutrients with nicotine?" Joyce asked, her disgust growing more palpable by the second.

Liam laughed, a deep, genuine laugh that came from his belly. "I see we have a live one here, folks." He flagged down the waiter and gestured for some beer and soju for the table.

Joyce was instantly annoyed and eyed the clock on her phone, wondering how much longer she would have to suffer through this. She was a five-minute woman; that's all the time she needed on dates to be able to tell if it was going to work or not. And they usually never worked out.

"So, what do you do?" Liam asked, as he thumbed through the menu.

"I preserve art," Joyce responded quickly, attempting to usher the conversation along so she could get home faster. "So, should we get the japchae, soondubu, short ribs, and the seafood pancake? Don't worry, I'll get the salad for myself. I promise not to let the greens touch your precious plate. And if it's too much, I'll pay for it and take it home as leftovers." Efficient and to the point.

Liam raised his eyebrows, and a smirk appeared on his face. "Think we can finish all that? That sort of implies it's going to be a long dinner?"

Joyce looked taken aback. "What did you think we were going to do here? Chew on tobacco all night?"

Liam shrugged. "Just start off with a few drinks? If we decide we like each other, then we'll order some food?"

"But you're the one that suggested we share plates!" Joyce said defensively, her face getting heated.

"Sure, but I meant *small plates*. It's par for the course when drinking soju. I wasn't talking about ordering a buffet."

Joyce's face burned a deep red and she hissed at him. "I'm *aware* it's best to have small plates of food when drinking. I'm well versed in Korean drinking culture, thanks very much."

"Whoa there," Liam said. "Didn't think I was speaking to the leader of the BTS ARMY." He laughed at his stupid joke, and Joyce grew more annoyed by the second.

The waiter interrupted the tense moment and put down two beers and a bottle of soju and two shot glasses. "Ready to order any food?"

Liam rattled off some small plates for them to share. "Leave the menu, we might order some food later."

Joyce turned to look at the waiter and spoke in fluent Korean. "Yes, if I happen to pass the litmus test in order to get to round two."

The waiter laughed and responded back in Korean. "First date, I see."

Liam raised his eyebrows at Joyce. "You speak Korean?"

"Not fluently, just third-grade level."

"You're not one of those girls obsessed with Korean culture or Korean men, right?"

Joyce stammered. "*God, no.* Course not. Those girls are like horse girls. *Super weird.*" She averted her eyes.

Liam poured them both shots of soju. "Cheers? I think?"

Joyce clinked glasses with Liam and took it all in one shot. She slyly eyed her phone again to check the time. "So, what do you do?" Joyce asked, feeling the soju burn her throat, attempting to change the topic.

"Graphic designer." Liam poured a second shot. "But after tonight? I'll probably have to become a firefighter."

"Why a firefighter?"

"Because I'd need to be able to put out the fires you start with the lasers coming out of your eyes." Liam chortled. Joyce stared, wondering if he was being serious, and she was about to argue back when she suddenly found herself laughing at his comment.

"There we go. See? This isn't so bad, right?" Liam smiled at her. "A Midwestern Korean guy and a SoCal Vietnamese girl, breaking bread like this? Maybe there is hope for world peace after all."

Joyce laughed again, thinking how absurd Liam was. His voice really was very soothing. But she couldn't tell if it was the soju that was talking or her.

An hour went by and soon plates of food arrived at their table. They ended up sharing, and Liam even grabbed some of Joyce's salad. Joyce took note of this. He was malleable, easy-going, and it was obvious his dry humor stemmed from his Midwestern roots and East Coast upbringing. They talked about everything: their relationship with their parents, living in New York City, their favorite haunts, hobbies, and weird quirks. Joyce loosened up more and more, as the liquid courage softened her up. They went through a third bottle of soju, and she was beginning to feel comfortable, comfortable enough to maybe even be herself for once.

"So, why are you single?" Joyce asked Liam. Her cheeks flushed red from the soju.

"Ah, the fateful question. The 'damned if I am and damned if I'm not' question," Liam said as he wiped his mouth with a napkin. "To be honest, I think I'm too blunt for my own good, and a lot of women that I've dated say it's not what they expected in a Korean guy."

"You are pretty blunt," Joyce said. "It was a bit jarring at first."

"I mean, I'm not gonna be one of those guys in a Korean drama that would live and die for the girl, you know what I mean?" Liam said as he took a bite of japchae, and chewed with his mouth open.

Joyce looked at Liam with sudden suspicion, and she put her chopsticks down. "What's wrong with that? Do you even watch Korean dramas?"

"Eh, I watched a few growing up, but to me they're no better than Disney movies. It just sells a lie and raises expectations, when life, romance, and relationships aren't like that at all." Liam said.

"Well, maybe you're just not Korean enough," Joyce snapped. She felt the soju bubbling up. She squirmed in her chair, immediately regretting what she had said. The mood changed instantly.

Joyce could visibly see the walls going up on both sides; they retreated into their respective shells. She kicked herself for ruining the progress being made between them. It had been the type of progress she hadn't seen in a long time, the kind that gave her a little bit of hope. They were two strangers who had both walked in hoping that maybe, just maybe, they were a step closer to not waking up so lonely the next morning. And now they were two strangers readying themselves for battle.

Liam stared at Joyce intensely. His fingers began tearing apart the paper wrapper around his beer bottle until it was a wet crumple on the table.

"*Goddamn*," Liam said. He picked up his beer and chugged from it. He spoke carefully, enunciating each word, as if he'd been prepared for this speech his entire life. "You're clearly looking for a very specific type of Korean man. The kind that doesn't exist, and if he does, he sounds pretty basic to me. Stick to your dramas if you want to live in your fantasy world. Call me if you ever want to live in reality. And by the way? You're not that special." With that, Liam finished his beer, got up from the table, and put on his coat. He looked at her one last time before he turned and left the restaurant, leaving the tab behind for Joyce. Joyce sat dumbstruck, staring at all the uneaten food before her, wondering how the date had ended so horribly.

When she got back home to her apartment in Bushwick later that night, Joyce felt Liam's words still haunting her. She'd been in a daze the whole subway ride back, echoing his words over and over. Joyce poured herself a glass of wine and turned on Netflix, resuming the last episode of the K-drama she was bingeing. But Liam's last words clung to her skin. *You're not special.* So did her mother's words. *Joyce is đặc biệt.* Joyce is *special.*

Joyce didn't know who to believe anymore. She just knew that she'd been living with this *thing* inside of her for as long as she was sentient. This disease inside of her had become her roommate, crowding her mind.

After her third glass of wine, Joyce angrily shut off her TV. It irked her how much she let him get to her. But she still went to bed that night thinking of Liam and how calming his voice was.

The following few days, Joyce began obsessively checking her phone more than usual, checking to see if Liam had logged back into his dating profile. The more Joyce tried to convince herself that Liam was an asshole, the more she poked holes in her own psyche. Liam was a smoker, clearly out of shape, had no style— also, she was pretty sure he was an alcoholic, based on the amount he consumed in one sitting. There were a lot of red flags, but not the kind of red flags she was used to seeing or picking up on. They seemed to fight over every little thing: what to order, politics, the weather. On paper, it made no sense; in person, it was absolutely ridiculous. But it had been a long time since anyone's voice made her want to stay a little longer and listen.

She was curious about Liam, someone far from the realm of what she thought she wanted. She was particularly curious to know what living in reality would be like for a bit. She thought of her own mother, who had always been too afraid to live life to the fullest, yet would ironically tell Joyce to stop living in fake worlds—when fake worlds were safer than this world. Joyce wondered if Liam was just as tired as she was, and if he ever thought about forming his own island. Just as she was picking up the phone to call Liam out of curiosity, a text from her mother came through, asking her to return home immediately for an emergency.

19

Mrs. Minh Phạm and Mrs. Khuyến Lâm

MRS. PHẠM BEGAN THE PROCESS of finalizing her last will and testament. She tried not to panic, but she *did*, and sent a text to her daughter, telling her that she needed to come home immediately. The sharp pain in her chest would come and go, though it was never consistent; it never seemed to fade, either, which only exacerbated her fear even more. Whatever was in her had become parasitic, and she knew it would eventually rot her from the inside out.

Ever since the funeral, Mrs. Phạm was convinced she was the next to go. Mai's psychic in Kauai had gotten it all wrong. There would, in fact, be *two* deaths this year. Seeing her mother's face so still, so eerily quiet, with no blood running through her body, lying in her casket, Mrs. Phạm blacked out. She wasn't ready to face her own mortality as she grieved the loss of her mother. She began to see spirits around her, informing her that she would be joining them soon.

Mrs. Phạm burst through the door of the apothecary and headed to the back room, knocking over anachronistic jars containing questionable remedies along the way. Protests and curses from the elderly workers in the shop rang out, telling her to shut the damn door because she was letting the air-conditioning out. She blew past the beaded curtains and went right up to her herbalist, slammed down the satchel he had given her on her last visit, and began complaining that the medicine he had concocted for her wasn't working.

"My chest pains haven't gone away!" Mrs. Phạm exclaimed. "In fact, it's gotten worse."

He pretended to be puzzled because he knew better than to tell her the truth. Everyone in Little Saigon sensed the Dương' family curse beginning to reverse itself; the universe was shifting—they could feel it under their feet. He knew what was really ailing her. Grief had taken over her reality, and she was living in a different world altogether. No medicine in this physical world would be able to cure her of her sadness.

"Is it still in the chest area?" he asked gently as he peered at her over his spectacles.

"Trời ơi, yes," Mrs. Phạm moaned. She paced up and down his office. "I feel as if I am at death's door."

The old herbalist nodded and continued the charade. He grabbed random ingredients to throw into his mortar and began to grind them in front of her. He explained that he would make a stronger remedy. But really he was making her something to try to calm her heart. It wasn't a cure, but perhaps it could help. He gave her instructions to drink it every night for the next month. Mrs. Phạm eagerly grabbed the little leather sack from him and thanked him.

"Just remember that there is nothing in this world that can cure you of the pain you are feeling," he told her. "All you can do is manage it, as time goes on."

Mrs. Phạm nodded, but she took his words literally, as if he was telling her that there was no chance for her to recover from this. She took it as a sign for her to get her affairs in order. When she turned her back to leave, the herbalist called out to her. "Chị, you still have that vial I gave you? You have one drop left?"

She turned back around and nodded. "Yes, I kept one drop left like you said. I just don't know when I'm supposed to use it or who to use it on."

The old herbalist gave her a small smile and pushed his sliding glasses back up the bridge of his nose. "Like I said Chị, you will know when the time is right."

• • •

When she got home, Mrs. Phạm kicked off her shoes at the entryway, climbed into her comforting silk slippers, and shuffled past her husband, who was passed out in his armchair, covered in Vietnamese newspapers, snoring loudly. She threw him a dirty look as she headed straight to the fridge and took out a plate of leftovers of mì xào gà and popped the noodles into the microwave. She then went to the pantry, ripped a hefty chunk off a fresh baguette, and put it in the toaster oven. As soon as both the microwave and the toaster *dinged*, she grabbed the hot plates, and plopped down in her corner with a bottle of Maggi seasoning and poured it all over. She tucked into her meal, and immediately felt comforted. It was the kind of comfort she hadn't gotten from anyone in her life. Not from her husband, her sisters, her daughter, or any medicinal herbs or tea. She inhaled her plate, absentmindedly piling and grabbing more snacks within reach of her, and eating them in between bites of her noodles.

Mrs. Phạm knew that she wasn't okay, not externally or internally, because nobody ever checked in on the middle child. She ate her sorrows away, as she'd been doing for the last ten years. Alone, in her corner of her kitchen, where nobody ever disturbed her, all she wanted was for her husband to ask her what he could do for her, for her daughter to call her every once in a while, and for the grief that she felt in her heart over her mother's passing to simply *go away*. So she ate, and ate, until she felt full—even if it was temporary.

. . .

Later that night, Mrs. Phạm began collecting all the gold bars, cash, and jewelry that she had squirreled away in linings, crevices, and cracks throughout the years, hidden far from the eyes of her scheming husband, and far away from the hands of grubby American banking institutions, and away from the pestilent, watchful eyes of the IRS. She gathered what tangible fortunes she could and locked it all away in a secure metal box under her bed.

Once all the artifacts were squared away, she sat down to write a letter addressed to her daughter, Joyce Phạm, with the key to the box taped to it, along with a separate set of instructions on how she wanted her funeral to run. In the letter, she detailed which photo to use, which outfit she wanted to be buried in, and which of her jade and gold jewelry she wanted to wear in the afterlife. Just like how her mother left them instructions. And for *god's* sake, she underlined this part several times, to *please* ensure that her funeral was *her* day, and not let Mai be the *center* of attention for *once*. And, finally, to make sure that Khuyến doesn't drink too much.

While the instructions were strict, the letter itself was harder for her to express. Con gái Mẹ, she started to write. This was the only chance she had to finally express all the feelings she could not put into words for her only child. Whether it was in Vietnamese or in English, the language did not matter, because during the entirety of their relationship, she'd been unable to use her tongue to tell Joyce that she was proud of her. She knew how difficult it was for Joyce to get out of bed every day, but she still kept going. Mrs. Phạm knew

Joyce had inherited the disease from her, but it manifested itself in other patterns. She sat down at her old wooden desk, began tugging on her jade necklace pendant, as she ruminated on what she wanted to say. The Vietnamese words slowly came to her.

We are both growing older, but we are not growing together. My hair turns whiter while yours becomes stronger, thicker. Because I wasn't able to have more children, you had to carry all my worries, my love, my meddling, my anger, my resentment, but most of all, you carried my sorrow on your shoulders, and that is the greatest burden to bear. But it came at a great cost to you. You retreated inward. I watched you become less vocal, and let life carry you along, instead of demanding what you want. I never believed there was a curse in the family, because I had you. Con, I know that you wake up sad every day. I also am rất rầu

Mrs. Phạm sat back and hovered her pen over the last word. Something inside of her stopped her from finishing the sentence. They'd never spoken about the darkness that they both had inside of them. Mrs. Phạm knew what it was called in English, but she'd always been too afraid to say it out loud.

Her eyes darted to her purse in the corner, where, tucked in the back pocket, was the last droplet of whatever was inside the vial that her herbalist had given her. Thoughts swirled around her as to what could possibly be in the vial. She put the pen down and folded up the unfinished letter. Before she left this earth, she was going to help Joyce one last time.

· · ·

Mrs. Lâm avoided T&K Market for months. She kept having nightmares of her mother falling over and over at the Asian supermarket, with no one around to help her. Over time, her mother's face in her dreams melded into her sisters' faces and soon her own face.

Her grief had heightened her controlling nature. Her iron grip around her nail salons, her coffee shops, and her daughters' activities around the house grew even tighter. She made Elaine and Christine get groceries for her, and forced them to follow her around, each one taking on a strict schedule to make sure she wasn't alone for very long. She didn't know how Mai and Minh were surviving without their daughters who were so far away from them during this delicate time.

"Where do you think *you're* going?" she asked Elaine one night, when she saw Elaine draw on eyeliner and curl her lashes. "It's ten p.m. on a Thursday."

Elaine turned away from the mirror, arched a perfectly threaded eyebrow, and stared at her mother, slightly bewildered. "I'm almost thirty years old and still live at home—let me *live*, woman!"

"Let *you* live? I *gave* you life! Who is going to stay home with me tonight?" Mrs. Lâm bemoaned. "You're not going anywhere!"

Elaine inhaled sharply, and she tried to remain calm. "Christine will come back soon. Don't worry, Mẹ."

"Well, she's not here right now! And you're about to leave!" Mrs. Lâm could feel her anxiety bubbling up. "What if something happens to me?" She absent-mindedly began tugging on her jade hoop earrings as she paced back and forth, up and down the hallway.

Elaine put down her mascara. She went outside the bathroom, and grabbed her mother by the shoulders, shaking her a little. "Mẹ! Everything will be okay! Just relax! Try to enjoy yourself, you have the whole house to yourself. Go watch your shows, drink some wine!"

Mrs. Lâm threw Elaine's arms off of her. "That sounds like my worst nightmare. Don't you dare tell me to relax. What's the point of having daughters if they don't take care of me in my old age!"

"There is *nothing* fragile about you, Mẹ. Don't pretend. We deserve one night off; we've been your chaperone for months. We also have lives, you know." Elaine sighed. "Why don't you go on vacation somewhere? What about Hawaii?"

Mrs. Lâm glowered at her. "Don't you *dare* mention Hawaii." Mai's psychic's predictions ran through her, and she couldn't help but feel frightened by Auntie Hứa's power. *What will happen next? The pregnancy? The wedding?* She looked her eldest daughter up and down as she took in her makeup and outfit, and her voice quickly changed into judgment as she assessed that perhaps it could be *her* daughter who would be getting married. "Who are you getting dolled up for anyways?"

"I don't dress up for men. I dress up for myself."

"Well, why don't you start dressing to find a husband then?" Mrs. Lâm snapped at her. "We need extra security around here!"

Elaine threw her hands in the air, her frustration filling the space between her and her mother. "I'm leaving now. I'll be back later—*don't* wait up." She grabbed her purse, went to the entranceway to put on her heels while Mrs. Lâm protested behind her, following as closely as she could, desperate to be near a warm body. She argued for Elaine to stay back, that she couldn't be left alone in her time of crisis. She pleaded and pleaded, but Elaine quickly strapped on her heels, shrugged on her leather jacket, gave her mother an exasperated look, and walked out the door, leaving Mrs. Lâm alone for the first time in months. The sound of the heels clacking against the pavement went further and further away until she could no longer hear Elaine.

Silence soon surrounded Mrs. Lâm as she stood frozen in the entranceway. She began to wring her hands together, her breath was uneven, and then she was absentmindedly tugging on her jade earrings. She eyed the clock and decided she couldn't be home alone in case something happened, so she reluctantly grabbed her car keys off the hook and headed to her car. She sat behind the wheel, debating between going to her blood sisters or the new sisters she had formed for herself the past decade of estrangement. She decided to go to the sisters who were more concerned about her future and less about her past.

. . .

Mrs. Lâm turned the key and walked into the salon. The familiar smell of acetone hit her immediately; the stench had been festering all night in this stuffy place after hours. She was used to the smell by now, after having worked her way up from a nail technician to owning several salons. She suspected if she were exposed to acetone poisoning, she would be immune to it. The salon was pitch black and almost silent, save for the sound of soft repeat thudding coming from the back. She knew the women were awake, and were trying to fix the television static. She shuffled to the back room, following a footpath lit by the moon coming in through the windows.

She didn't knock or announce herself; she just burst through the door, nearly crashing into a propped-up television perched precariously on a broken TV tray.

"Khuyến!" A horde of women shouted in unison, irritated. "Be careful!"

"—our *one* source of entertainment—"

"—thinks she can just barge in—"

"—can't even have a moment of peace—"

Vân gestured for Mrs. Lâm to move out of the way, as she was blocking the television. Ngọc then told her to move *the other way* because she was now blocking *her* view. Mrs. Lâm weaved her way through five women, huddled around on floor mats in pajamas, and eventually found a spot to squeeze herself into. Someone handed her a basket of rambutans and she plucked one, peeling it and squinting at the television.

"Why are you all watching the news?" Mrs. Lâm asked, her mouth full as she slowly chewed her away around the seed inside the fruit. Everyone turned to *shush* her and Ngọc turned the volume up. All the women fell silent as they watched live footage of riots and protests.

"America is terrifying, isn't it?" Vân said, her eyes glued to the screen, as she blindly looked for the fruit basket. All the women in the room agreed. "Why are Americans so passive? Just overthrow the president. Drag him through the streets, make an example out of him. You know, the old-school way."

"Much more effective," Ngọc agreed.

"*Effective?*" Quyên laughed brusquely. "They'll just replace him with another dictator. A dime a dozen."

"Can't be Black in America. Can't be Asian. What can you be here anyways?"

"You can be free."

All the women laughed loudly at the notion, and someone threw a rambutan at the woman who said that.

"I don't know why I left Vietnam, it's much safer over there than here," Quyên sighed loudly as she took a swig from her beer. "I'm sleeping on the floor inside a nail salon. This isn't the freedom I imagined it would be."

"Trời ơi, you think the cops in Vietnam are better than the ones here? You're delusional. The cops over there would extort you for money," Ngọc scoffed loudly.

"And you think the cops won't kill you here?" Quyên laughed as she pointed at the screen.

"At least there's a community in Vietnam and we speak the language, not like here. Everyone here is just out for themselves! Don't be such an imperialist lover."

"Enjoy capitalism while you can. You think you'd have a nail salon back in Vietnam? Go back if you want to suffer in communism. I like California *much* better."

"Oh shut up, Vân! Don't be so brainwashed by war propaganda!"

"*Don't tell me to shut up, Ngọc!*" Quyên stood up and threw her empty beer bottle on the ground. "My family suffered through war atrocities—"

"—you think you're the only one?!" The women broke out into another fight as they tried to outtalk the other. Mrs. Lâm didn't say anything; she just sat there silently, thankful that she at least had two homes to turn to now when she had none for a very long time.

20

Thủy Nguyễn

THỦY BLAMED EVERYONE BUT herself. She blamed her mother especially. It'd been months since she'd faced her mother in person. Aside from food drop-offs on her mother's front porch, she'd been unable to break out of the double life she'd been living. Andy grew more and more suspicious of her every day, especially when she made an excuse to not show up to her grandmother's funeral. But he never pushed or questioned her because that wasn't who he was.

Thủy couldn't show up to the funeral out of deep shame. She barely recognized who she was when she looked in the mirror. Her life had become wayward ever since Daniel came into it by way of her mother's meddling. She spent nights trying to justify what she was doing. Thủy wasn't doing *anything* wrong, *wrong*, right? They hadn't done anything physical; they were still just *chatting*.

Thủy snuck out to meet Daniel at their usual spot. She'd been doing it once a week, seeing him at the park bench that overlooked Echo Park Lake—the same spot as the night they had met. As Thủy sat waiting, her guilt weighed heavy on her heart. She hadn't been sleeping well, and clumps of hair had begun falling out whenever she showered. Andy had doubled down on taking care of her, waiting hand and foot, bringing her hot tea or wine whenever he deemed appropriate. It made her feel worse. He would repeatedly blame her behavior on her grandmother's recent passing, her fallout with her mother, and her estranged sisters as the cause for her growing distance. Thủy never corrected him, and allowed her fucked-up family narrative to cover her indiscretion.

Thủy's vision suddenly went out as warm, familiar hands covered her eyes. She laughed and looked up to see Daniel's face. He reached down and pinched her nose and she gave him a small smile in return. It reminded her of when Andy would pinch her nose, and she flinched, remembering how she reacted back then. There was no going back now.

"Hi." Her voice turned soft as she transformed into a different Thủy altogether. A more playful, confident Thủy, without any of the complications that came with the old Thủy.

"Hi yourself," he responded back as he slid in next to her, and intertwined his hand with hers. They hadn't done anything physical beyond holding hands. It was the type of wholesome affair that belonged on *Sesame Street*. Thủy just couldn't bring herself to go to the next level—not when she still had Andy in the back of her mind. "Ready?"

"Where are we going?" Thủy asked. "You're always so mysterious each time we go out."

Daniel shrugged. "I can't reveal all my cards right away, can I?" He reached forward to tuck a stray hair behind her ear, and she stiffened. He flashed an annoyed look but quickly recovered.

"Sorry, *sorry*, I've just been feeling so guilty," Thủy said. "I still haven't figured out yet what *we* are, and I know it's not fair to you or Andy."

Daniel looked away from her and stared down at the view of downtown Los Angeles. The skyline backlit his face, and Thủy couldn't help but melt when she saw his profile glow in the night. Daniel didn't say anything; he just got up, took her hand, and gestured for her to follow him.

"No worries. We're on your time, not mine. I'm in no rush. Not like either of us are running down an aisle anytime soon, right?" he said, flashing her one of his smiles to assuage the tension. "In the meantime, want to go have fun?"

Thủy blanched at his marriage comment, unsure if she should see it as more negative or positive. It's not like she ever wanted to get married, anyways. Right? She masked it by putting on her new Thủy persona. "Always."

They walked to his car, and Daniel opened up the passenger door for her. As Thủy climbed into the leather seat, she couldn't help but notice all the little superficial things that Daniel had in comparison to Andy. She'd never cared before about how much Andy made, but as she got older, her mother's platitudes began rearing their ugly heads and filled her ear. She was haunted by flashbacks of when they were young, inside that house in Santa Ana, crammed with two other Vietnamese families and five other Vietnamese girls. *Never marry a poor man*, her mother had screamed at her repeatedly throughout the years. She never wanted to end up like her mother, and her mother never wanted her to end up like her, either.

"You okay?" Daniel turned to her as he climbed into the driver's seat.

"More than okay."

He started the car and began to drive up Sunset. Thủy felt relaxed and taken care of. Daniel reached around to the back seat and pulled up a bouquet of peonies, and handed it to Thủy. "I almost forgot. You mentioned that peonies were your favorite, right?"

Thủy took the bouquet and gave a shaky smile. She didn't want to tell him that peonies weren't her favorite, because she didn't want to ruin the moment. Andy would never have gotten her peonies; he'd have gotten her wildflowers from the farmers' market, like he'd done every Sunday morning for the past three years. She could have sworn that she and Daniel never talked about what her favorite flowers were before, so she wasn't sure why he assumed peonies were her favorite.

"You remembered!" she exclaimed, maybe a little *too* loudly as she ignored the nagging voice in the back of her head. "They're gorgeous, thank you."

Daniel shot her a smile, and turned his head to the side. *That smile. That damned smile.* He drove all the way up Sunset until he exited off Vermont. Thủy immediately knew where they were going.

"Isn't it closed? It's past ten p.m."

"Don't worry, I know a guy."

Thủy felt those butterflies go off in her again, and she accepted whatever was going to happen next. She held on to the bouquet of peonies and brought it up to her nose, and inhaled deeply. It had such a distinct smell, like it belonged in one of those manicured rooms in design magazines that were often on display in the waiting room at her office. Maybe she *could* be the type of woman who likes peonies? Peonies were feminine and sexy. Wildflowers suddenly seemed sophomoric. Thủy settled deeper into her seat, allowing herself to feel like a *woman* around Daniel. Not like a woman of color, a quiet Asian woman, a dutiful daughter, or a model minority. But a desired woman who just wanted a man to look at her the way he did.

. . .

At the top of Griffith Observatory, Daniel wrapped his arm around Thủy from behind and he leaned into her. They gazed at the view overlooking the entire city, watching the lights blanket it entirely. "You sure have a signature move, don't you?" Thủy teased him. "You love bringing women to see views at night."

"Hey, it's worked for me so far!" Daniel said. "Why break something that isn't broken?"

"Just *how* many women have you brought up here?"

"None of them mattered as much as you."

Thủy rolled her eyes and punched his arm.

"I'm serious! You make me want to give up my selfish ways," he whispered in her ear.

Thủy laughed so hard she almost choked. "Daniel, please, you *really* don't have to pull out all these recycled lines on me. I wasn't born yesterday."

"Sorry, I . . . I just meant . . ." His cheeks turned red. "It's hard for me to explain, I've just never really been a *commitment* kind of guy. It's scary for me to reach that stage. One person for the rest of your life seems a bit over the top, you know?"

Thủy grew silent and she turned around until they were face-to-face. "I guess I'm afraid of commitment, too."

"Yeah," Daniel laughed, a bit too loudly. "I picked up on that kinda quick. I think you're more of a commitment-phobe than I am."

Thủy cocked her head slightly to the side. "What do you mean by *that*?"

Daniel hesitated, pulled away from her, and awkwardly put his hands into his pockets. "I mean, come on, Thủy, do you really need me to spell it out for you? You sneak out once a week and we drive around all night, doing random shit. We barely hold hands. It just seems like you're trying to figure out how to politely blow up your life without hurting that other guy. You're clearly running from commitment or *something*. It's not really my place to call you out but someone has to because even I'm starting to feel bad for that guy—whatever his name is."

Thủy's lips thinned at the mention of Andy. A swirl of shame and guilt creeped up around her as she was violently pulled back to reality. *Why am I here?* She turned back around and pretended to be engrossed in the view. A shiver came over her suddenly. She forgot how cold Los Angeles could turn at night, slowly morphing into a man-made desert at sunset. Tonight was especially cold, as she sensed the ocean's atmosphere drifting further and further inland. But she'd forgotten a lot of things the past few months. She'd forgotten what she was like before, she'd forgotten how to be a better partner, a good daughter, and she had especially forgotten the promise she made to herself when she was young.

"His name is Andy," she said quietly to herself.

. . .

Later that night, around two in the morning, Daniel drove back to their bench on the Eastside. The drive was slightly tense, but he still held her hand the whole time. As soon as he spotted her car, he drove up next to it, and lifted her hand to his mouth to kiss it. "I'll see you again next week? Same time?"

Thủy nodded, but she wasn't sure what she was agreeing to. She left the car and as she watched Daniel drive off, a million thoughts ran through her mind, trying to pinpoint what Daniel had said earlier. What exactly *was* she running from?

Thủy sighed and slowly turned around to open her car door. In the distance, she spotted a shadow approaching her car, and when she squinted, she saw Andy staring straight at her, with the look of someone whose heart had just erupted.

. . .

Andy and Thủy didn't talk for days.

Andy had locked himself up in the shared office, refusing to come out. He would purposely wait for Thủy to leave for work before he emerged. On the sixth day of silence, when Thủy came home from work, she saw him sitting on their couch, with his packed bags surrounding him. He looked disheveled, and his eyes were bloodshot.

"Do you love him?" Andy asked, his tone low.

"No! Absolutely not," Thủy exclaimed, bleary-eyed, as she stood in the archway, afraid to come too close to him in case she spooked him. "All we did was *talk*. You have to believe me. He's just an escape, Andy. We just go on stupid long drives every week. He's a distraction, nothing more."

"Every *week*?!" Andy's jaw dropped. "You saw him every week? So go to fucking therapy then if all you want to do is talk."

"It's not that simple, Andy."

"Explain it to me like I'm an idiot. That's what you clearly see me as anyways."

"You're not an idiot!"

"Fucking *explain*, Thủy. How could you do this to me? To *us*?"

"I'm sorry, Andy." She realized just how confused she was as well. "It just *happened*. I didn't know how to stop it."

"This isn't like you at all."

Thủy felt that deep in her gut. "*Why?* Because I'm Thủy Nguyễn? Just another goody-two-shoes Asian woman?"

Andy stared at her incredulously, as if he was staring into the face of a stranger. "No, Thủy, because you're not a cheater. You're not your father."

Thủy felt like he had metaphorically smacked her in the face with that line. *There it was*. The cold, hard truth. She'd done everything in her power to not end up like her mother, but she wound up ending up like her father.

Andy stood there, dumbfounded, digging at his hair. "I asked you to let me in, Thủy. Why didn't you?"

"I'm afraid," she whispered. Her sadness overwhelmed her as she realized how everyone around her could see how fucked-up she was. But she couldn't see a damn thing. "You and I, we're not cut from the same cloth, okay? You're stable internally *and* externally. I just *appear* stable. At the core of it, we're different. We grew up differently. There are just some things that are hard for me to talk about."

"So you blew us up? For some Asian fuckboy with a gallon of hair gel and a BMW who patrols Koreatown in fake Ray-Bans? Because me and him are two *entirely* different people. We're not even in the same damn universe."

"I know that!" Thủy cried out. She couldn't explain to Andy that she wanted to *try* to be a peony kind of woman instead of wildflowers. She knew she would sound crazy if she said it out loud. Because being a peony woman offered the kind of life that was less complicated.

"I wanted to marry you, Thủy," he said, exasperated, as he stood up and grabbed his bags. "I was willing to do anything to make it work. I'm an idiot. You're a walking red flag. In fact you've told me repeatedly throughout the years that you were on the fence about marriage and kids. I should have listened, but I kept ignoring it, hoping you'd change your mind one day."

"I'm sorry, Andy," Thủy's voice grew quieter. "I never deserved you. I've always known that."

Andy just stared off, and she knew he was trying his best not to cry more. She knew him so well. Andy had always been an open book, ready and willing to be read.

"I hope he treats you well," Andy said finally. "And I hope you let him in—or anyone in. Your mother, your sisters, whoever. Because it sure must be damn lonely being you."

Thủy opened her mouth to stop him from leaving, but nothing came out. She just watched him head toward the door. He turned around and stared at her one last time, sadness etched across his face. But there was another look there that Thủy hadn't seen before: It was the look of the last person in this world who believed in her, finally giving up on her.

"You're right about one thing, Thủy: You don't deserve me," he said. "For the record, we didn't have to get married. I knew what your triggers were. I *know* how you grew up. I will probably never understand what it was like for you, but I knew. I was more than okay just growing old in this house together—baking bread, being whatever you needed me to be, and taking it day by day. All I ever wanted was for you to *just* talk to me."

The moment Andy walked out the door, leaving Thủy in silence, she felt all the emotions escape her—everything that she had tucked away in her mind palace; all her issues and repressions she'd pressed down and down and down over the years, like an overstuffed suitcase, hoping it would fit. That was when Thủy was finally able to blame herself and only herself.

She regretted everything. She sat down on the couch and cried.

Hours later, her phone vibrated, and she looked down, hoping it was Andy. To her surprise, it was a text from her older sister, Priscilla, whom she hadn't spoken to in over a year, telling her that she was coming back home with some news.

21

Thảo Nguyễn

THẢO HADN'T BEEN GHOSTED. It was worse: She had been breadcrumbed. She still took every crumb and scrap Jeff gave her, hoping for a bigger one next time. She followed the bleak trail for months while he was in Singapore, not realizing that it was heading off a cliff. There was the occasional text here and there, a random shirtless selfie at midnight, and an accidental FaceTime while he was on a jog. Eventually the trail went cold and Jeff stopped texting. She stalked his Instagram every hour, watching stories of him partying at Clarke Quay, a different girl on his arm every night. Despite the mounting evidence of his indifference, she kept waiting and waiting by her phone, like a Victorian woman waiting by the window for her lover to return from war—hoping that, one day, Jeff would miss her.

She knew it was in vain. Nobody ever missed Thảo because she had purposely designed her life to appear like she never needed to be wanted or missed. It had been months since Thảo missed her flight back to Los Angeles. Had she been on that flight, she'd have been able to attend her grandmother's funeral; she could have been there for her mother in her time of grief, and reconnected with everyone she had cut off. Sài Gòn had been her escape, a chance to reinvent herself. But now it had turned into regret. Her mother was right: She was more American than Vietnamese. And her American side meant being selfish whenever she needed to be.

But when she chose it, she wasn't prepared for everyone moving on without her. Thảo carried on, hoping Jeff would realize what a mistake he had made. Because she was desperate for anyone out there to miss her.

"Just *forget* him, Thảo, he's *so* basic," Alexandria said. "Do you know how many mediocre dicks there are in the sea? Let me give you a hint: A LOT! There's a *reason* why the ocean is losing oxygen; it'd rather die out than choke on any more mediocre dick." She lit up a cigarette on Thảo's ground patio in her home in District 2, and blew out a long smoke. They were wading their feet in the mini pool, their white button-ups opened all the way, exposing their bikinis. They sipped on nước mía that they had spiked with vodka. Alexandria adjusted her straw hat and playfully shoved Thảo, attempting to jerk her out of her bad mood.

Thảo groaned and splashed Alexandria with water while chugging her sugarcane drink, waiting for the alcohol to kick in. She looked up at the blue sky, past all the cascading vines that littered her back patio. "I feel like a fool, Alex. I thought he loved me. I really did think he wanted to settle down in Sài Gòn with me. I even thought that *maybe* I'd take him back for Lunar New Year this year and introduce him to my family. And I've *never* introduced any man to my family before."

"*Love?*" Alexandria howled, almost choking on her drink. "The man has a tribal tattoo and works in *social media marketing*. He doesn't *love* you, he just doesn't have much of a life back home. The man is a ten in Asia and a four back in South Africa. Let that sink in for a moment. Don't let the first man you introduce to your mom be a gutter bum."

"Right, *you're right*. The man is scum. Gum on the bottom of my shoe," Thảo said, listlessly, not really believing it. "I'm just tired of the lifestyle here. No one is *serious*."

"Hun, that's the beauty of it. You have your fun here, and be serious when you go back home. Just no more subway rats, okay?"

"Right, right. No more sewer rats." Thảo side-eyed her phone screen, hoping for a miracle, hoping to see it suddenly light up with a message from Jeff, telling her how she's the only woman in the world for him. But all she saw was an empty screen. Nothing from Jeff, her mother, her sisters, or anyone from back home. It was as if everyone had erased her from their mind. She knew it was her fault, too. She'd pretended she was too busy for anyone, and the irony was now everyone was too busy for her.

"Okay, that's it! You're far too young, beautiful, and successful to be waiting around for someone named *Jeff* to call you back. We're going back out again tonight. You want a white guy with a tribal tattoo? No problem. Every single backpacker here is *that* guy."

Thảo groaned. "I wouldn't mind staying in for once. I haven't sat on my couch and watched TV in so long. Doesn't that sound kinda nice?"

"I said *we* are *going* out." Alexandria stood up, and grabbed Thảo by the shoulders and forced her to get up. "Get up, bitch. Staying in is for the dead and for those who don't know how to properly put on fake lashes."

· · ·

One of the girls put her finger in the air and motioned for another round from the server. The music was unusually loud; Thảo couldn't hear a thing. She just sat moping, slumped over in the corner, sipping on her drink, watching all the drunk tourists and expats stumble around the rooftop. This was a scene she once thrived on, but it was depressing to watch tonight. From the corner, Thảo tracked a group of guys staring at them. It was hard not to miss them; they were staring like they were circling the watering hole, waiting to pounce—like they were in a *National Geographic* documentary.

"Look at how *thirsty* they look," Evelyn said with a bored drawl as all the girls noticed the guys. They all tilted their heads sideways, staring at the men staring at them, assessing them. "Any bets on where they're from?"

"Easy. Brits. Londoners in fintech. Trying to invest in the next big start-up here. Give me something harder," Sarah said as she tapped an acrylic nail against her empty glass. The mood was lethargic, and everyone in the group could feel it.

"Okay, what about those guys over there?"

"*Easy*. They're trying to launch a streetwear line. It'll go bankrupt in a month."

"British men are the worst. Constant horndogs," Alexandria interrupted. She lit up a cigarette. "They all have yellow fever. You can see it in their eyes. Looking for their next Cho Chang to ride."

"Ew, Alex," Evelyn said. "You have the worst mouth."

"Well, it's true, isn't it? Would you rather I lie?" Alex said, throwing her hands in the air, accidentally ashing the group of tourists behind her with her cigarette. They yelled at her to watch it, but she ignored them. "I bet they don't even realize that *Cho Chang* is NOT a real Asian name."

"The woman speaks FACTS, ladies. Brits *love* Asian pussy," Sarah said. "Colonizing is their blood sport."

All the girls grudgingly admitted it was true, and took a deep drink. The mood wasn't as lively among the group of girls as it usually was. Their usual spot was overrun with tourists tonight, which meant that the secret was out on this particular rooftop bar, and they had to find the next secret spot that only catered to expats.

"I think one of the guys literally just wiped the drool from his mouth, staring at us," Thảo said in disgust as she sank deeper into her lounge chair. She felt homesick for the first time in a year. The feeling was foreign to her, more foreign than the makeshift city around her, which she called home.

"A true Neanderthal," Evelyn commented.

Thảo grabbed a cigarette from Alexandria's pack, and headed off to the side of the rooftop, to look out at the view. She was hoping that when she saw the crowd below, and the packed rooftops of nearby bars, it would cheer her up. Just as she was about to light her cigarette, one of the British guys, who had been watching them from the corner, immediately popped up next to her and extended a lighter under her cigarette.

"I got ya, pretty bird," he said. She gave a forced smile, thanked him, and inched a bit backward. But like all men who had a few drinks in them, and didn't know the first thing about consent, he moved closer.

"So, are you a local or from elsewhere?" Closer and closer. His breath reeked of alcohol, and his eyes roamed over Thảo's body. "I just moved here a month ago. It's wild here, man, *wild*. Absolutely chaos, but I love it. Nothing like London. Asian girls here are *fuckin'* gorgeous. Stunning. Absolutely stunning."

Thảo didn't say anything; she just kept walking backward every time he inched closer. She blew smoke into his face, hoping he'd take the hint. The man's voice began to fade as her eyes began to wander over to the rooftop bar next door, looking for a distraction to save her. She suddenly felt eyes on her, and shivered. This was a different kind of stare; it electrified her, inside and out. She combed the crowd until she saw the one salmon swimming against the current. His eyes were heavy on her, as if she were the only person left in a city of nine million. He had a calmness about him, despite being in the middle of a crowded dance floor. The attraction was palpable, especially in the sticky air where lust danced on skin. An attraction that could only come from two international people so far from home, on a sweaty, humid spring night on a rooftop bar in Sài Gòn. He seemed older, someone in his late thirties, but that didn't bother her so much. What did age matter for a night? Her mind wandered briefly to what Jeff was up to in Singapore right now, and if he was thinking about her. She knew that he wasn't. And right now, there was a guy who thought she was attractive standing across the rooftop bar from her.

She was done waiting for people to miss her first.

The guy across the way pointed at the guy next to her, who was still talking. He rolled his eyes and motioned for her to ditch him. She laughed heartily and pointed at her drink. *Need more to get through this shit.* He mouthed a solution— *Stay there—*

"—oh! Sorry!" The guy next to Thảo loudly slapped his forehead. "Bollocks, apologies. Keep forgetting I'm not in London anymore. No wonder you're not responding to me. Ni hao . . . ?" At those words, Thảo whipped back to reality, turned around, stubbed her cigarette out, and flicked the butt into the man's face, leaving a black smudge on his right cheek.

"I'm *not* Chinese, motherfucker." She looked him dead in his shocked, vacant, drunk eyes. With that, she turned back around to look for the rooftop guy, but he'd already disappeared into the crowd.

"Are you putting the 'ho' in Hồ Chí Minh City tonight—?" Alexandria said, sauntering over. She took one look at the guy next to Thảo, whose mouth was still ajar, and shooed him away with a flick of her hand. He turned and stumbled away, stunned, and went to try his luck with another group of Asian women in a different corner. Alexandria followed Thảo's eyes back to the rooftop next door, as she searched for the guy who disappeared. "Window shopping?"

Thảo sighed and gave up. "He *was* so cute, Alex. But there's a plethora of cute guys here, but none of them are Jeff. I still can't get over him."

Alexandria groaned. "*Why* are you doing this to yourself right now? You're the CEO of your own company, you went to Harvard, *why* are you pining for *Jeff* of all people?"

Thảo threw her hands in the air. "I don't know, Alex! I don't need a pep talk right now, okay? I *know* I have a lot going for me. But I'm . . . I'm fucking lonely." She lit up another cigarette and took a long drag. "There. I admitted it."

Alexandria didn't react; she just simply agreed. "Everyone's lonely in Neverland. Even wild animals need rules."

Thảo quickly stole a glance across at the other rooftop. Still not there. She was disappointed, but she knew better than to expect fleeting glances like that to last long in Sài Gòn. Moments like that were a dime a dozen here. Everyone was attractive, successful, and looking for company for the night.

"He'll be back. If not, there'll be another soon," Alexandria said. "Horny expats here are like STDs; they're the gift that keeps giving." They both laughed when they were interrupted by a voice behind them.

"But hopefully it's a good gift?"

Thảo turned around. It was the guy from the rooftop next door, standing right behind her, with a hopeful look on his face. She detected a slight British accent, and she wasn't surprised. Asia was full of British men roaming the expat scene, like the asshole from before. Her body soon became like water, adjusting to the heat of the moment. She felt that same electricity from earlier pulse through her, which confirmed what she already knew—this was *something* at first sight. Alexandria whistled and mouthed *I told you so* and slipped away, but not before she threw an approving wink at Thảo.

"I love presents in general," she said, giving a perfect flirty smile that she had trained herself with after learning how to navigate the hookup culture here. "What took you so long? You could have saved me from earlier, you know." Her phone vibrated, and she looked down to see that her oldest sister, Priscilla, had messaged her. She was taken aback, as Priscilla hadn't spoken to anyone in their family for a full year—not since Priscilla and her mother had fallen out. Just as she was about to read the message, the guy interrupted her thoughts.

"Will you forgive me for my tardiness? I had to battle past some people vomiting on the sidewalk to get to you," he said, flagging down a server to get them drinks. "I haven't seen anyone projectile vomit like that since my uni days, and us Brits know how to handle our liquor."

"Well, British people are the Americans of Europe, so not sure you should be proud of that," Thảo said in a deadpan voice, flipping her hair to one side to expose her shoulders more. "So, what are you doing in Sài Gòn? Business or *pleasure*?" She flipped her hair to the other side. Her body immediately went on autopilot as she began to reel him in. He laughed, and she could feel the heat coming off him. *He wanted her.*

"Originally business. I was in China for work months ago, but I sort of quit my job in the middle of the trip. I went through a rather nasty breakup back in Seattle, was sick of my job, and decided to keep going for as long as possible," he said. "I've been in Vietnam for over a month now. Was in Hà Nội last week. The north is incredible."

As the drinks arrived, he handed her a cocktail, turned his profile to face the crowd below them, and sipped on his drink. The glow of the neon lights from the surrounding rooftop bars illuminated his face even more, and Thảo continued to absorb that electric pulse from earlier. She prayed there was something deeper beyond an objectively good-looking face. She wanted something more than another man trying to find himself in Asia.

"Nasty breakup, huh?" Thảo asked. "You're doing this trip solo then?"

He laughed. "Don't worry, it's been half a year since the breakup. I'm over it now. And yes, I was traveling with someone for a bit, a coworker. She was supposed to go with me to Vietnam after China, but we didn't end well so we parted ways."

"Oh that's a shame for her, but I guess a win for me." Thảo looked him up and down, assessing him, and leaned in closer to study his face. He had deep-set brown eyes, and there were touches of silver in his hair, but there was a softness to him that made her curious.

"First time in Sài Gòn or . . . ? Because you seem a bit *too* comfortable being in Asia. You're not like one of those white guys obsessed with southeast Asia, right?"

He almost spat out his drink from laughter. "God, no! I'm not *obsessed*. I did live in Bangkok for a few years after uni, though, some of the best years of my life. And yes, I've been to Vietnam a few times before."

Thảo raised an eyebrow. "Yeah, but you're not one of those white guys who *only* dates Asian girls, right?"

He took a large sip. "I mean, *no*. I don't *just* exclusively seek Asian women. I just *happen* to be around Asian women all the time. I work in tech, and would travel to China a lot for work. It comes with the territory that I meet a lot of Asian women."

"Hmm, okay," Thảo said. Her analysis of him was almost complete. She decided not to think too hard about it and pressed her toned body harder against the metal railing. At this slight movement, he gave her a hungry look, and she knew she got him. Behind her, her friends loudly whooped and cat-called; the music disappeared completely; the scooter bikes zipped along the city; but all she could see was a warm body in front of her who wasn't running away.

"What happens now?" he asked her quietly, leaning in.

Thảo looked deep into his eyes and the deeper she looked, she began to see a kaleidoscope of the life she wanted. It didn't necessarily have to be with *this* guy, it could have been with anyone. He just happened to be there at the right time, the right place, and he came *right* after Jeff. She imagined herself finally bringing home a guy and introducing him to her parents. She saw herself married, in a house with a white picket fence, with a big, cozy family of her own. The bigger the family she had, the more people she would have to miss her. She'd never be alone.

She decided right then and there to start inching toward making this her reality. This guy didn't seem like he'd run for the hills; in fact he looked like he wanted all the things she wanted.

"We're going back to my place," she said, grabbing his collar. "Right now."

22

Priscilla, Thủy, and Thảo Nguyễn

THẢO HEARD THE NEWS from her oldest sister, Priscilla. Priscilla had heard from Thủy who heard from Auntie Phạm and Auntie Lâm. They had FaceTimed Thủy when she was at work in her dermatologist clinic in Beverly Hills. When Thủy picked up, they immediately began barking orders at her to go run errands on their behalf, demanding she drive them everywhere to get "all the essentials." Telling her they hated driving in Los Angeles. Asking her why she was a degenerate daughter for not helping her mother out during her most special time.

Thủy snuck into her back office for privacy, and closed the door on her celebrity clients, who heard a mixture of Vietnamese and English being shouted at her through her phone. The repeat line everyone kept hearing was *bad daughter*. It was a cacophony of insults, compliments about her glowing skin, and questions—mostly asking if John Cho was there right now, and if he was, could she *please* turn the screen around. Thủy, trying to decipher the words of two aunties whom she hadn't spoken with in a decade, was utterly confused.

"Xin lỗi, Dì." Thủy apologized to her aunties as she sat down in her chair. "But *what* the *hell* are you *both* talking about?"

"The wedding, con, the wedding!" They shrieked.

"*What* wedding?" Thủy raised her voice incredulously.

"—can't believe you don't know—"

"—typical of your mother to never say anything—"

"—she always was the dramatic one—"

"—at *her* age—"

"—suddenly she's *so* positive about life—"

"—was *still* grieving last month—"

"—STOP!" Thủy shouted, trying to redirect her aunties back to the main topic. She shook the phone out of frustration.

"Con, your mother is getting married next month!" they finally said at the same time. "You need to help her plan the wedding! You need to *attend* the wedding; *everyone* needs to attend! This wedding will be our family reunion, our first in over ten years—"

"—still can't believe *she* found love—"

"—thinks she's better than us now—"

"Who is she getting married to?!"

"His name is Anh—" Auntie Lâm started.

"—very handsome—" interrupted Auntie Phạm.

"—has money—"

"—she *really* does think she's better than us now doesn't she?"

"—the new house—"

"—the new *man*—"

Thủy stared at her phone in disbelief, watching her two aunties, whom she barely recognized anymore, arguing about where to get the flower arrangements for the wedding, and whether or not Auntie Lâm could steal some from that fancy restaurant next to her nail salon, who always tossed them out at the end of the day—*what a waste.*

"Do Priscilla and Thảo know?" she asked, still dumbfounded.

"Con, you need to tell them. They're both hard to get ahold of."

"—and you know, considering how your mother and Priscilla left things a year ago—"

"—everyone heard about their nasty fight—"

"—both *so* stubborn—"

"Why didn't she tell us herself?" Thủy finally said quietly.

Auntie Lâm and Auntie Phạm stared at each other for a while and it was as if they had a whole conversation with just their eyes alone.

"One day, con, you will know what it's like to lose your mother. Especially when you become a mother yourself," Auntie Lâm finally said.

"The hardest wounds to heal are with your own daughters," Auntie Phạm chimed in.

With that, they hung up, and Thủy was left alone in her office, wondering if she really was a bad daughter for not knowing her own mother was getting married, or a bad person for allowing her fears to dictate her life. Thủy sat there for a long time. Why did she spend most of her adult years running away when her mother had been strong enough to stay? She allowed her mind to wander toward Andy, just for a moment, even though she'd done her best to compartmentalize him. She knew he was better off without her, but she couldn't help but latch on, wondering what it would have been like had she just been strong enough to stay.

. . .

All three Nguyễn sisters were suddenly in a group chat. It had been a year since they were active with one another. Despite the sudden ice break, they still had a stiffness in their interaction, each one unwilling to reveal more than they could emotionally give. The three infamous sisters had always circled each other, hoping someone else would break first. Over time, budding competition and general sisterly annoyances had escalated among each other, preventing them from seeing the other as more friend than foe.

Thảo: who tf is she marrying????

Thủy: idk, all i know is his name is Anh

Thủy: i haven't spoken to her in months

Thủy: been going through some personal stuff

Thảo: same

Priscilla: same . . .

Thủy: are you both able to come next month?

Thảo: ya, i'll buy my ticket soon

Priscilla: yes, i'll come

Thảo: kk, well i'll see you all in cali then. i might be bringing a date

Priscilla: really? Who? you never bring anyone home

Thảo: someone i'm getting serious with, haven't asked him yet

Thủy: i guess i'll bring a date too?

Priscilla: andy? i always liked that guy

Thủy: i'll explain later

Not one sister bothered to ask follow-up questions. Because while they were innately curious about each other, they had tunnel vision about their own lives, each one stuck in a cyclone of their own negative thoughts, fears, and emotions. Each terrified that they would regress back to what their lives had been like living in that blue house back in Santa Ana. Had they had the foresight to look beyond what was in front of them, they could have realized that they were all trying to reach the same goal through different paths: ensuring that this generation, this time, things would be different.

. . .

Priscilla had an inkling of the father's identity. She wasn't entirely positive, but statistically it made sense, and she was never one to argue against numbers. Upon hearing that her mother was getting married again, something inside of her stirred. She debated dialing his number and working up the courage to tell him that she was pregnant, that she was keeping the baby and that she was well past the point of no return. Priscilla had crunched several scenarios of his potential reaction and in the end, calculated that it was best that he didn't know.

One day, she'd tell him. It just wouldn't be today.

Priscilla went into the office to get some things before making the drive down to California. She decided to make a whole road trip of it, take her time, and see the West Coast in its entirety. She'd never had the time to do that before, so she considered it her solo babymoon.

Back in the office, what was once the place where she'd thrown her whole identity behind—countless late nights coding, putting together presentation decks, and crying alone in her office after her breakup with Mark—was now just simply a place with four concrete walls and a bunch of tacky motivational posters that littered the hallways. The wheel had kept turning even while she was away, and she had finally learned how to let go.

As she walked the hallways, she passed posters that talked about disrupting the world, machine learning analytics for the cloud, and innovating for the greater good. Priscilla stared at the empty hallway leading to her office, wondering how the hell she became entrenched in this superficial world for so long. She rubbed her growing belly and began the long march to her office. She didn't want to be a disrupter; she just wanted a quiet life that she could be proud of one day.

"Priscilla?" A familiar voice behind her spoke out.

Priscilla turned around and saw her half cousin, Lily, holding a box of her things. Lily gasped when she saw Priscilla's stomach, but she held her tongue, and didn't comment on it.

"Lily!" Priscilla said warmly. Lily looked rather surprised at Priscilla's welcoming reaction. Priscilla gave her a quick embrace while Lily's arms, after dropping her belongings, awkwardly hovered over Priscilla. "What are you doing back here?"

"I got a return offer and I accepted," she said. "Just bringing some stuff in to make my desk situation more cozy."

"I heard you did great work during the summer," Priscilla said. "Especially the research you did in Hong Kong. Are you excited to be back here full time?"

There was the faintest hesitation as Lily answered *yes*, she was excited to be back. But Priscilla picked up on it because she could feel the seismic ripple effect of that hesitation. Because a long time ago, she had the same feeling about what to do with her life.

"Are you heading to California next month for the reunion?" Priscilla asked, switching topics to give her a reprieve.

Lily gave Priscilla an odd look. Her eyes briefly flickered down toward Priscilla's belly before politely returning her gaze. "Yes, I'm flying down. Crazy how the aunties mended the burned bridge after all these years. I guess I'll see you down there?"

Priscilla nodded and they parted ways, each going the opposite way as they had always been taught to. But this time, something stopped Priscilla in her tracks, and she turned back around. "Hey, Lily?"

Lily turned and gave her a quizzical look.

"Don't settle for the first thing that comes your way," Priscilla said, making the first effort to extend an olive branch to the side of the family she was once asked to shun. "You might not see it now, but something better will come along. It always does. It's okay to go into the unknown for a while, maybe even forever."

• • •

After her half cousin retreated to her office, Lily looked down at the box in her arms. It contained framed photos, a mug that said "World's Most Mediocre Coder," stacks of notepads, a mechanical keyboard, a desk humidifier, and her favorite green tea. On top of the stack was a framed photo of Lily standing alone in front of the Big Buddha statue during her summer trip to Hong Kong. She had asked a stranger to take a photo of her that day because she had no one else to take it for her. Her eyes lingered on the photo a little longer, taking in what Priscilla had said. And she began walking. She walked past the office kitchen, past the bathrooms, and past her empty desk that had been assigned to her. She kept heading in a direction she'd never once considered before.

. . .

Thảo was running a million miles a minute in every direction.

She'd bought a plane ticket to Los Angeles, and had thrown a random scoop of clothes in the direction of her suitcase and all over her bed, hoping for a miracle that it would somehow pack itself. She was attempting to wrap up some work when the doorbell rang, and she dashed to grab it, still in her robe, her wet hair wrapped in a towel.

Alexandria stood at the door, and she held up a six pack of Bia Saigon, her sunglasses covering half her face. "I've come to help."

"Don't lie."

"Okay, I've come to drink beer while I watch you pack."

"There we go." Thảo opened the door wider, bowed, and allowed Alexandria to step through.

"Where's Mr. Darcy? Where's the little *bugger* hiding?" Alexandria asked in a horrible fake British accent as she peered over her sunglasses. "Have you secured your place as mistress of Pemberley?"

Thảo lightly smacked her behind her head. "Very funny. He left this morning. He's gone back to his place for the weekend."

"Nice to see you finally surfaced for air. It's been a hot minute. Wasn't sure if I should have sent search and rescue."

Thảo's face turned red. "I'm *trying* to make it official between us. Things are going really well. I'm thinking of inviting him back to California with me for my mother's wedding."

Alexandria whistled. "That's a *big* fucking *step*. You really like this guy, don't you?"

Thảo flinched, slightly offended by how judgmental Alexandra was being. "He's the first guy I've met here who is not afraid of commitment. In fact, he's staying longer in Vietnam. For *me*. Isn't that romantic?"

"Sounds more intense than romantic to me."

"Maybe I need someone who wants me like that. I need to stop chasing and *be* chased."

"Maybe," Alexandria said as the sound of a beer can opening rang out. "Or maybe he's love-bombing you."

"I think I've dated enough douchebags to recognize red flags by now."

Alexandria laughed as she took a swig of beer and plopped down on Thảo's bed, on top of the pile of messy, unfolded clothes. "Sure, whatever you say. I was always a Mr. Bingley stan anyways."

Thảo quietly grabbed clothes underneath Alexandria and began to fold them, trying her best not to be annoyed at Alexandria's pessimism. She folded a pair of jeans, folded some cardigans, and folded the dress she would be wearing to the wedding. Finally, she snapped and threw down the dress. "Just say it. You don't think I should invite him to the wedding."

"It's your life, Thảo," Alexandria said with a shrug. She removed her sunglasses. "Just make sure you're doing it for the right reasons, and not because you *think* you should be settling down, getting married, and having a traditional life."

"What makes you think I want that life?"

"Most lonely people want that life."

When Alexandria left a few hours later, Thảo was even more confused than ever. If her mother could find love again, surely she could, too? Thảo reached into her pocket, pulled out her phone, and opened up the group text with her sisters. She felt compelled to ask if she should bring this guy home, hoping they could provide the kind of advice that only older sisters would have the answers for. But as she reread their group chat, she realized how they acted more like coworkers or acquaintances than sisters, and she realized how right Alexandria was.

Even if it was for the wrong reasons, it would still bring her one step closer to what she really wanted. So, Thảo texted him and asked if he'd come home with her.

23

The Dương, Nguyễn, Phạm, Lâm, and Lương

THE AUNTIES HAD BEEN working round the clock to make sure the wedding was a success. It was their chance at redemption, to prove to their mother's spirit that order could be restored among the Dương women and their offspring—between all four sisters and all eight granddaughters. It was a chance to correct all the wrongs from the past.

Auntie Phạm summoned her daughter, Joyce, to come home from New York City. Auntie Lâm put Elaine and Christine to work, to help plan out the rehearsal dinner. Auntie Lương lectured her daughters, Lily and Rosie, to be on their best behavior, because as the former outcasts of the family, they had the most to prove *and* to lose.

For Mai Dương, this was her chance to repair her relationship with her daughters.

There was little time to prepare for the sudden descent of generations of Dương, Nguyễn, Phạm, Lâm, and Lương women.

Priscilla Nguyễn was slowly making her way down the coast from Seattle and had finally crossed the border from Oregon into northern California. Thảo Nguyễn had just landed at LAX on her flight from Tân Sơn Nhất International Airport. Joyce flew out from JFK, despite not wanting to—she barely knew Aunt Mai anyway. But her mother's ominous message that she had something important to tell her made Joyce nervous. Lily Lương hopped on a flight from Seattle into John Wayne Airport, and got picked up by her younger sister, Rosie.

The state of the women was all up in the air, especially after the year they've had. But no one—perhaps not even Auntie Hứa—could have predicted what happened next.

• • •

Thủy pulled up to her late grandmother's driveway. The family reunion was to be held there as everyone felt it would be appropriate. Thủy hadn't been to her grandmother's house in a decade, not since the estrangement began. She turned and squeezed Daniel's hand. He sat in the passenger seat, his hair slicked back in his usual style, his crisp white button-up evenly tucked into his slim-fitted slacks.

"Thanks for coming with me to this," she said. "I really appreciate it."

"Of course. I can't have you face your family alone." He returned the squeeze, then he ran his hand through her hair. "It sounded like it's going to be intense. A reunion after ten years of not speaking? Sounds like something straight out of a movie."

"The women in my family love to be dramatic," Thủy said, nervously laughing. She cleared her throat and prepared herself to ask the question she'd been dreading on their drive over. "Hey, how should I introduce you to everyone?" Ever since Andy moved out a month ago, Daniel kept avoiding the topic every time she brought it up.

"Let's just say we are *really* good friends for now," he said. "I'd rather not complicate things, especially since you have *so* much going on."

"Right. Makes sense," Thủy said, trying to cover up her confusion.

Daniel checked his reflection in the car mirror, and grabbed the bouquet of peonies from the back seat. "Ready?"

Thủy gave him a half nod and they both left the car and headed toward the house, passing the gigantic stone Foo guard dogs. Thủy did a double take. She could have sworn that one of the dogs bared its teeth at Daniel as they walked by. As they entered the garden, Thủy spotted Priscilla pacing in the garden, her back toward Thủy. She felt a strange flood of sentimentality go through her as she realized she hadn't seen her older sister in almost two years.

"Priscilla!" Thủy called out. "Why didn't you call me when you arrived?"

Priscilla froze.

As she slowly turned around, Thủy gasped. "Actually, I had to drive down." She caressed her stomach. "Given the circumstances."

"Oh my *god*!" Thủy cried out and took a step back, like Priscilla was infected. She was unsure if she should run toward or away from her. "You're *pregnant*? Why didn't you tell me!" After she recovered from the initial shock, she moved forward and put her hand over her older sister's stomach. "Is it Mark's?" she whispered, just in case her mother was within earshot.

Priscilla had beads of sweat running down her face. Though she was in her midthirties, even she didn't have the balls to walk into that house with no ring on her finger and present a pregnant belly to her fiscally conservative mother. "Well, that's the problem. I'm not a hundred percent positive that I *know* who the father is. I don't want to tell that person yet based on an assumption." She let out a faint chuckle and threw her hands in the air, as if she were a circus performer finishing an act to an unamused audience. "Surprise?"

Thủy looked Priscilla up and down. She couldn't help but start laughing. Her older sister was a *mess*. Perfect Priscilla. The crown jewel in her mother's possession. The perfect Vietnamese daughter—the oldest daughter, a double bachelor's from UCLA and an MBA from Wharton, the one who made her first million at the age of twenty-five and was CEO of her own company—was pregnant and had no idea who the father was. Thủy started laughing and doubled over.

"If you walk in there looking like that, I think our mother might actually pass away on the spot when she sees you," Thủy said, wiping tears away. "Here, take my ring and pretend that you and Mark are engaged at least."

"Okay, you're right," Priscilla said, putting the ring over her engagement finger. She looked up and finally noticed Daniel standing behind Thủy. "Who the hell are you? You're not Andy."

Thủy felt her cheeks flush. "Andy and I broke up. This is Daniel. He's my . . . *friend*."

Daniel stuck his hand out toward Priscilla, and she shook it cautiously. "You must be a very *supportive* friend," she said.

"You could say that." Daniel said, flashing her a megawatt smile, which made Priscilla almost roll her eyes. She could sniff guys like Daniel out a mile away. What the hell was Thủy doing with a guy like him? She *liked* Andy. *Everyone* liked Andy. Well, aside from their mother . . . but for the *most* part, everyone liked Andy! What was her sister doing with some smooth-talking Kevin Nguyễn–type with slicked-back hair and a gold Rolex? This wasn't Thủy at all.

"Listen, I don't care who you are. Just keep your *damn* mouth shut and play along," Priscilla said, jabbing a finger toward Daniel, her pregnancy out in full force. "We just need to get through the next few days without my mother losing her shit over me."

Daniel raised his hands placatingly, pretended to zip his lips, and nodded.

Approaching footsteps could be heard from behind them, and the Lâm sisters soon appeared. In the daylight, Elaine's and Christine's lashes were heavier than usual, their outfits matched their acrylic nails, and their blond highlights appeared even brighter in the California sun. Their heels *clicked* and *clacked* against the stone pathway. Each Lâm girl carried flowers, fruit, and bags of home-cooked Vietnamese food.

"Oh god," Thủy whispered to Priscilla. "Are we really doing this reunion?"

"Be nice," Priscilla whispered back. "You don't get to pick your family."

"No, but you *can* pick your sense of fashion."

Elaine and Christine Lâm soon stood in front of the two Nguyễn sisters, awkwardly hovering, their arms weighed down by all the fruit. The tension was palpable between the two sets of sisters, their disdain for the others' lifestyles shone through.

"Well! If it isn't the Nguyễns! Though, it seems like we might be missing one," Elaine said, a tangible fakeness in her voice, as she peered around, pretending to look for Thảo. "Last time we were all together like this was when Thủy was puking her guts out from food poisoning after eating too many jellies at that old house. Remember that? We were all *babies*."

As Thủy opened her mouth to defend herself she saw Elaine's face contort from contempt to confusion. "Daniel? What are *you* doing here?"

Elaine, Christine, Thủy, and Priscilla all stared at Daniel's handsome face, which seemed thrown off its normal game. "How . . . how are you related to Thủy?" he asked. Panic set on his face.

"We're cousins," Elaine said slowly, enunciating each word like it was a question, as if she wasn't sure how to explain it. "How do *you* know her?"

"We're together," Thủy said defiantly, breaking protocol, and grabbed his arm. "Now, hold on . . ."

"*Together?*" Elaine's stare ricocheted between Thủy and Daniel. "So, that's why you never called me back after our first date? Why did you act so fucking romantic then? Sneaking us into the Griffith Observatory after hours?"

"Are *you* kidding *me*?" Thủy said. Her face heated up as she turned toward Daniel. "You took *her* to the same spot you took me?"

Priscilla's hormones began flaring up, standing under the hot sun; her ankles felt ten times more swollen than usual, and her lower back was screaming in pain. She just wanted to sit down somewhere, anywhere. "Don't *mess* with my sister like that. Either commit or don't."

Elaine snorted and bowled over with laughter. Then she dropped her bags and rolled up her sleeves. "I *knew* it. Daniel Lê, you are the biggest fuckboy in Orange County. You can't even commit to a pair of socks."

"I *trusted* you!" Thủy shoved Daniel and he stumbled back. The peonies in his hand went flying across the yard.

"*Peonies?*" Elaine shrieked. "*PEONIES?!* You *know* those are *my* favorite!"

Thủy slowly turned toward Daniel, a flurry of emotions went through her mind as she realized she'd never once told Daniel what her favorite flowers were. The final emotion that went through her mind was regret. She couldn't breathe anymore.

Daniel began sweating as he tried to piece all the connections together. "Wait, wait, *wait*. If you two are *cousins*, and you're all here for a reunion for Thủy's mother's wedding rehearsal—"

The iron front door suddenly cracked open to reveal Thảo, the youngest Nguyễn sister, whom no one had seen in a year, not since she moved to Sài Gòn. "—would you all keep it down? I can hear you yelling from the living room—oh my god, Pris? Are you . . . *pregnant?*"

"Look, if anyone asks, it's Mark's baby, got it?" Priscilla said despondently as she began walking toward the house and up the steps, away from the drama with Daniel. "I'll explain later. Right now, I just need to sit down; my ankles are about to give out. It's good to see you, Thảo, even if you *do* think you're better than all of us." She was at the front steps, shaded from the hot sun, when she stopped dead in her tracks.

Behind Thảo, the door had widened to reveal a white man with flecks of gray in his hair. "Mark?" Priscilla whispered. She tried to shield her belly with her hands, in a poor attempt to cover up her pregnancy. "What the hell are you doing here?"

"Wait, *your* Mark?" Thủy asked, and she looked at Thảo. "What's Mark doing here?"

"What do you mean by 'your' Mark?" Thảo said slowly, coming down the steps and standing in front of her two sisters.

"Why is fucking Mark here? Why is he with *you*?" Priscilla asked, her voice rising. Thủy saw the heat rising off of her, and for a split second, Thủy had to decide between saving her oldest sister or her youngest sister. She did some quick calculations and decided that Thảo would need the most help. At least until Priscilla calmed down. Priscilla had inherited their mother's ill temper, and had a penchant for throwing objects across a room. Coupled with her hormone flare-ups, the middle sister was worried that the oldest might actually commit a crime in front of a *lot* of witnesses.

"Mark is my boyfriend," Thảo said, still looking confused. "We met at a rooftop bar in Sài Gòn not too long ago. He was visiting Asia for work, and made a stop in Sài Gòn, and well, he just stayed. *For me.*" She went, grabbed Mark's hand, and pulled him to join the group. Thảo was beaming. "You know me, I *never* bring guys home, but this—this is the *real* thing."

Mark still hadn't said anything; his whole body was shaking, and beads of sweat had begun dropping off his pale face.

"Pris . . ." he started. He wiggled his hand out of Thảo's and pointed at Priscilla's stomach, his finger shaking uncontrollably. "Is . . . is that mine? I just heard you *say* it's mine."

• • •

In the distance, Christine Lâm lit up a joint, inhaled deeply, and passed it off to her half cousin, Rosie Lương. "Girl, this shit is *messy*." She stared at all the adults in the middle of the front yard, whose arguing had escalated to the point of no return.

"Who are we rooting for again?" Rosie said, taking a drag.

"Honestly, I can't tell," Christine said, squinting her eyes, trying to make out who was who. "I think we're supposed to be *against* the British white dude."

"I mean, isn't that a given?"

Two groups had split off to deal with their indistinguishable messes. In one corner, Daniel, Elaine, and Thủy were arguing. In the other corner, Priscilla, Mark, and Thảo were yelling. Nobody had seen Joyce walk in with her date, Liam. Upon seeing several groups of people shouting, Liam slowly backed away, and went to join Christine and Rosie in the corner to smoke a cigarette.

"Okay if I hide out here with you two?" Liam asked. "I'm not trying to get involved with, well, with whatever is going on over *there*."

Rosie and Christine looked him up and down, their eyes judging his hair all the way down to his shoes. "Sure," Christine said. "Just give us a cigarette."

Liam raised an eyebrow. "Are you two old enough to smoke?"

"Don't be racist and just give us one," Rosie said.

"She means two. Give us two," Christine piped up.

"Whoa, how was *that* racist—" Liam began, but when he saw their pointed look, he grumbled about how much he hated Southern California Asians and handed over two cigarettes.

. . .

"What the *hell* is going on here!" Joyce wailed as she tried to break up the fights, going between the two groups, unsure *who* to help and *how* to help. Daniel was using Thủy as a shield against Elaine, who was trying to claw him, while the shield herself was bawling, blaming Daniel for ruining her life. Meanwhile, Mark was getting verbally eviscerated by Thảo while following Priscilla around, begging to know if he was the father.

But because it was just Joyce, everyone ignored her.

"Incestuous bastard!" Priscilla shouted at Mark.

"I had no idea she was your little sister, Pris! Trust me. This is the *last* thing I ever wanted. Do you think I *wanted* to run into you like this?" Mark pleaded. "Why didn't you tell me you were pregnant? *Is the baby mine??*"

"You go to *those* coffee shops? You're disgusting!" Thủy could be heard crying at Daniel. "I can't believe I ever fell for you!"

"Don't talk about my business like that, you pretentious, uptight, Beverly Hills ho!" Elaine snapped at Thủy. "You're not even *from* Los Angeles! You're from fucking Garden Grove!"

. . .

Liam, Christine Lâm, and Rosie Lương were now very invested in the fight, and had moved on to sharing a spliff among the three of them. They had settled into a rhythm, each one taking on the role of lead commentator, narrating the action to ensure nothing was missed. They watched everything unfurl before them, like they were watching the series finale of a show. Liam took a big inhale and attempted to map out who was who.

He used the spliff as a pointer. "So, you're telling me that *that* chick—Priscilla, right? And *that* pasty bro, Mark, were together for three years? But now Mark is dating Priscilla's *little* sister, Thảo? And Priscilla is *possibly* pregnant with his kid?"

Rosie accepted the spliff that he handed over. She inhaled deeply, blew it out, and passed it over to Christine. "Yeah, pretty much."

"Damn." Liam shook his head and whistled. "I almost didn't come on this trip, but I am *so* glad I did. Okay, so, for the other group, it looks like *that* chick—Thủy, right?—She broke up with her longtime boyfriend to pursue *that* guy, Daniel, but Daniel has commitment issues, and it seems like the other chick, Elaine, is in love with him, or they went on some date together? And Thủy and Elaine are *cousins*?"

Christine took a long drag. "Yep, you got it. You only hit the first generation's drama, though. You haven't seen the mothers' drama yet. Welcome to the family."

"Whoa, hold on, don't welcome me just yet. I'm just the date to the wedding. *We* just met," Liam said as he jerked his head toward Joyce, who was still feeling helpless in the middle of it. "Low-key, I think she just likes me cause I'm Korean."

"Yeah, sounds about right," Rosie and Christine said at the same time. "Don't get too comfortable."

"What the hell is happening here?" Lily Lương said, aghast at the scene before her when she arrived. "I thought I was supposed to prepare for a wedding, not a UFC fighting match."

"*Shh*, come over here, you're blocking our view." Christine waved at Lily to join them in the corner. "We'll fill you in."

"Maybe you should pay more attention to the outside world, rather than the code in your head, sis," Rosie said to her older sister, Lily.

Priscilla's, Thủy's, and Thảo's voices soon hit ear-splitting levels, and the whole neighborhood could hear them now. The Chinese neighbors who lived across the way all sat on their front porch, sipping on tea, watching silently, craning their necks. In an adrenaline rush, Priscilla picked up a potted plant and threw it at Mark, sending it crashing against the side of the house when he ducked.

Upon impact, their mother, Mai Dương, ran out of the house, yelling at them to keep it down in Vietnamese. A mishmash of screams and wild Vietnamese were being thrown in the mix as Auntie Lâm, Auntie Phạm, and Auntie Lương all ran out to see what all the commotion was about.

When Mai saw Priscilla and her belly, she dropped to her knees and began to thank Auntie Hứa for her prediction.

Priscilla waddled toward her mother, mistaking her for having fainted and screamed for help.

Auntie Lâm, Auntie Phạm, and Auntie Lương all shook their heads.

"*Tsk tsk,* all this shouting and yelling is *not* the answer," Auntie Lâm said.

"They're acting like heathens, like cave women!" Auntie Phạm agreed.

"The younger generation just doesn't know how to behave," Auntie Lương added.

"*Grandson?*" Priscilla could be heard in the distance arguing with her mother. "What the hell are you talking about?"

"WHO IS THE FATHER!" Mai's voice echoed.

The confusion was infectious and soon bled into both generations. Mothers began yelling at their daughters to stop yelling, daughters yelled at their mothers, sisters yelled at each other, cousins yelled at cousins, half cousins yelled at cousins. Just like when they all lived together, back at that home in Santa Ana: three Vietnamese families and six little girls all under one roof, trying to survive day by day.

"This might be a bad time, but technically does this mean you two kind of slept together? 'Cause y'all fucked the same guy?" Liam asked, pointing at Priscilla and Thảo. "Is that weirdly incestuous? 'Cause you're sisters? Or does that logic cancel each other out? Do you know what I mean? *Or* does that mean you're a throuple?"

Joyce turned around and slapped the back of his head. "Shut up, Liam! Not now!"

"What are you talking about? What sister is fucking what sister? My daughters are *fucking*?" Mai screamed. She pointed an accusatory finger at Mark. "Nobody should be fucking anyone. Especially on a day like today. *Today is my day, remember? It's supposed to be a happy day!*" She groaned and grabbed on to a banister, sliding down the steps.

Anh Lê suddenly came running out of the house, and headed straight to Mai to try to calm her down, but it was too late. Mai's vein on the side of her neck had made an appearance.

"You," she breathed, her finger still pointing toward Mark, who had been poorly seeking refuge in the corner of the garden, trying to make himself disappear into a hedge. "You may be the father, but you are not welcomed." Everyone in the universe could feel Mai placing a curse on Mark.

What happened next was the stuff that would go down as legend for all ensuing reunions for the three generations of Dươngs, Nguyễns, Phạms, Lâms, and Lươngs and all their unwitting romantic partners.

Because out of nowhere, poor, sweet Andy had emerged, let out a warrior cry, and charged toward Mark's back. He had mistaken Mark as the man who ripped Thủy and him apart, the man who ruined the best relationship he had ever had. He ran like he was running with the bulls, and charged full force, straight into Mark, tackling him to the ground, calling Mark a home-wrecker and— "*Stay the hell away from Thủy!*"

All the women screamed at the impact, and Thủy circled the two men who were rolling on the ground wrestling, and shoving their palms into each other's faces. Thủy was yelling at the top of her lungs, and Mark screamed at Andy, telling him that he didn't know who the *hell* Thủy was. Andy became even more confused when Christine, Rosie, Priscilla, and Thảo kept yelling and encouraging Andy to keep beating up Mark, and that he deserved it.

"You got the wrong guy, mate!" Mark begged, gasping for air as his hands tried to push Andy off him. "Please!"

"Hit him harder!" Christine called out.

"We demand reparations, colonizer!" Rosie chimed in.

Andy stopped hitting Mark and rolled over on the grass. He propped himself up on his elbows, and apologized to Mark. "Sorry, man, you looked Asian from behind. I wasn't wearing my glasses. Safety reasons, you know." He paused to breathe, cleared his throat, then imitated a deep masculine voice. "Where the *fuck* is Daniel Lê?"

Mark groaned as he clutched his stomach. "No worries." He pointed in Daniel's direction; the guy who had been trying to quietly sneak out during the commotion. "I think that's the one you're looking for."

Everyone in the garden turned their attention away from Mark toward Daniel.

"I know that young man!" Anh Lê said, beaming. "He was my contact for helping me set up my arranged marriage with Mai!"

"Oh!" Mai smiled warmly. "Come inside, *come inside*, we owe you so much gratitude for setting us up."

"*Me!*" Thủy cried out, her annoyance reverberated throughout the neighborhood. "That's the man *you* set *me* up with!"

Mai squinted her eyes at Daniel, as did Mrs. Lâm, as did Mrs. Phạm. They hovered their hands above their heads to shield the sun out of their eyes.

"Oh *yes,* I remember now. That was so long ago! Very wealthy man," Mrs. Lâm nodded approvingly. "So handsome." All the aunties nodded in agreement and murmured how handsome and wealthy Daniel was and what a good choice he would be for Thủy.

"Can't expect us to keep track of *everything*—" Mrs. Phạm said, huffing.

"—so much has happened in the past year," Mrs. Lương agreed, as she placed her hand over Mrs. Phạm's arm.

"Wait a minute," Andy said to Mai. "*You* set Thủy up with *him*? You told me you wanted me to be your son-in-law! You invited me here to help me get Thủy back!"

"What?" Thủy glanced between Andy and her mother.

"I mean, Andy *does* only make sixty thousand dollars a year—" Mrs. Phạm whispered.

"—it's hard to support a family of four on that salary—" Mrs. Lâm agreed.

"—*and* to pay California double income tax—" Mrs. Phạm said solemnly.

"—I'd honestly just pick Daniel at this point—" Mrs. Lâm said.

"—trời ơi, *only* sixty thousand dollars a year?" Mrs. Lương whispered.

Daniel ran his hand through his hair and winked at all the aunties, and they all suddenly felt flushed.

Andy turned toward Thủy, his face pleading with her silently. Thủy stared right back at Andy, feeling a familiar pull. All Thủy wanted was to have fresh wildflowers on her dining table from the farmers' market again. Thủy took the first step toward Andy, and just as she was about to proclaim her love for him in front of three generations of Dương women, a bloodcurdling scream interrupted her. Rosie Lương and Christine Lâm ran forward, pushed Thủy aside, and began pelting both Daniel and Mark with fallen fruit from the garden. Thủy jumped back, shocked at her young cousins.

Christine hurled a grapefruit at Mark. "Go back to *England*, Charles!"

"Go back to *San Jose*, Kevin Nguyễn!" Rosie yelled at Daniel and threw lemons at him.

All the aunties couldn't help but feel pride as they watched the men try to take cover from the flying fruit.

"That's my youngest, Rosie," Mrs. Lương said. "She's a bit of a wild child, but I know she'll get there eventually."

"My Christine is a *freethinker*," Mrs. Lâm said, loudly interjecting. "Creative minds are the rarest. She will probably be *famous* one day."

Amid the chaos, noise, and fighting, something warm stirred inside Mrs. Phạm. The family was together again, after several decades apart, and she was grateful to be alive to see everyone's faces one last time. The women weren't perfect, but no Vietnamese woman was. Sometimes yelling and cutting fruit was all they knew when it came to expressing their love for each other. So, no longer able to hold back her secret, Mrs. Phạm cried out that she was dying, and everyone stopped fighting, a silence fell upon the garden, and Rosie and Christine dropped all their fruit to the ground.

24

Mrs. Phạm and Joyce Phạm

MRS. PHẠM SAT IN THE squeaky-clean waiting room, distracted by the intercom going off every five minutes. Her irrational fear of hospitals started flaring at the sound of doctors being called, patients being transferred, emergency code reds. She closed her eyes and tried to remove herself far away from it all, and she tried not to recall the last time she was inside a hospital, when she watched her father go in and never come back out. She tugged on her jade pendant necklace, hoping this would all end soon.

Joyce, still fuming, sat down next to her, and silently handed her an ice pack to help nurse the scratches on her arm. Earlier, Joyce had tried to convince her mother to go see a doctor right away, but she refused and said that she was *fine*. Joyce had to physically drag her mother, kicking and screaming, into the car.

Liam sat down uncomfortably next to Joyce, avoiding eye contact with Mrs. Phạm. He twiddled his thumbs. As he looked up, he saw a horde of Asian women staring at him. Mai Dương, Mrs. Lâm, Mrs. Lương, Priscilla, Thủy, Thảo, Elaine, Christine, Lily, and Rosie, all sat across the way, lined up, with their arms folded. Behind *them* sat Daniel, Mark, and Andy, all in the second row, all three slightly banged up.

"This is the worst second date of my life," Liam whispered to himself.

"Why do you keep doing this, Mẹ?" Joyce asked her mother, finally breaking the silence between them. "Why can't you just *simply* take better care of yourself?"

Mrs. Phạm grumped at her and didn't answer.

"Why do you always treat yourself like a victim?" Joyce's voice rose. "Why can't you go to a *modern doctor*, not some quack Vietnamese herbalist?" Her mother still didn't respond; she just kept staring straight ahead, waiting for Joyce's tantrum to subside, just like she always did when she was younger. "Why can't you get *real* proper care, a diagnosis from a professional?" Joyce was becoming more pissed off the more her mother refused to speak. "Maybe all this could have been prevented. What if we're too late? What if it's *cancer*?!"

Liam coughed and tried to interject. "Hey, let's all take a breather—"

Joyce brushed him off and powered through. "Why *won't* you *say* anything?"

Mrs. Phạm regretted saying anything earlier. She wished she could go to her grave silently without anyone causing a fuss—just like her mother had done.

Joyce soon grew hysterical and she choked back tears. Liam reached over and took her hand into his, trying to calm her down, tightening his hands over hers. Mrs. Phạm watched as Joyce's breathing steadied. Her eyebrows raised when she saw how quickly her daughter calmed down when their hands touched. *How interesting.*

"So, what do you do for work, Liam?" Mrs. Phạm asked curiously, finally saying something. She shifted in her seat and leaned across Joyce and closer into Liam, studying him.

"Oh, here we go! Now the woman speaks." Joyce turned to Liam. "Don't answer her."

Liam whipped his head between the dying elderly woman to the new girl he was dating, and he wasn't sure which one he was supposed to be more subservient to. "Uh, I'm a graphic designer."

"So, you're an artist?"

"I guess that's one way of describing it."

"How much do you make a year?"

"Mẹ, stop!"

"Graphic designers make good money now," Mai interjected from across the aisle. "They get to work in tech now, isn't that right, Priscilla?"

Priscilla nodded as she rubbed her pregnant belly. "It's not bad money, especially if you design apps."

"I design T-shirts," Liam added slowly, wincing as he prepared himself for the onslaught from the aunties *and* the first-generation Asian women across from him.

"Oh—"

"—trời ơi, he thinks he's Coco Chanel or something—"

"—why does *every* Korean man think he's—"

"—is there even money in T-shirts—"

"—I guess everyone needs T-shirts—"

"—Joyce *can't* marry a poor man—"

"—Joyce barely makes enough money to support *herself*—"

"—like *streetwear*?"

All the women began discussing the legitimacy of Joyce and Liam's relationship, and calculating their success rate. Priscilla even took out a notepad and began a projection chart.

"Mrs. Minh Phạm?" The doctor came into the waiting room, looking down at his clipboard.

When no one answered, the doctor looked up, only to find that the whole room fell silent. Joyce almost dropped her coffee on Liam's lap. An earthquake with a magnitude of 9.5 had rocked the room because every woman acknowledged that they were staring at the *most* handsome face they'd ever seen in their lives. The doctor looked like he had walked right out of a Korean drama set. His sharp jaw could cut glass, but his thin-framed Clark Kent glasses and perfectly coiffed bangs made him look like a soft boy character. A mix of sweet and sensitive, but with a bad boy streak hidden in him, waiting to be unleashed by the love of a good woman. He flashed them all a smile, and everyone felt a shiver go through them.

"*Fuck*," Liam said under his breath. "Now *that's* a handsome Korean guy."

"Oh *come on*," Daniel muttered in the corner, icing his cheek. "Give me a break. His watch is like twenty dollars."

"I mean, even *my* breath was taken away . . ." Mark said as he removed the bloody tissue from his nose and tossed it into a trash can.

Mrs. Phạm eyed the doctor up and down and gave a low whistle. "I would have come to the hospital earlier had I known *this* was an option."

All the women jumped up at once. Priscilla, Thủy, Thảo, Elaine, Christine, Lily, Rosie, Mai, Minh, Khuyến, and Kim began clamoring around him.

"Here! She's right *here*," Thảo said, putting her hand over Auntie Minh's back. "Come now, Auntie, let's get you *all* fixed up."

Priscilla brushed away her little sister's hand. "Back off. I got her, you *barely* know her."

"Don't worry about *her*. She's just trying to trap you into being her baby daddy," Elaine said as she bumped Priscilla out of the way. She extended her hand to the doctor. "I'm Elaine. Elaine Lâm." She shot him a sultry look, batting her heavy lashes at him.

Mai began pawing at the doctor's white coat. "Will my sister be okay? A handsome doctor such as yourself, you must be *very* talented. Have you met my daughter Thủy? She's John Cho's dermatologist."

Behind Mai, Andy threw his hands up in defeat. "I'm still *right* here, Mrs. Nguyễn! Hello? Remember me!"

"Andy, can we talk?" Thủy seized the moment, and grabbed on to Andy's arm. He took a step back and shook her arm off.

"I . . ." Andy's voice faltered. "I . . . wish your family nothing but the best." He turned around and awkwardly walked away, leaving Thủy crestfallen.

The Korean doctor held his hands up and laughed. He managed to stop the women from clamoring over him and kept them back. "Hold on, ladies, only one can go in with Mrs. Phạm at this time. Let's not overcrowd her. Or me, for that matter." Though he did give Elaine a wink, and she winked back, knowing that she had planted her flag.

"Let's go, Mẹ," Joyce said quietly. "I got you." She put her arm around her mother's shoulder, steering her as they followed the doctor down the hallway and into the examination room. Mrs. Phạm had fussed and fretted over Joyce her entire life, but little did she realize that Joyce had fussed and fretted over her, too—just in different ways.

. . .

After two hours of running tests and doing a complete body scan, Dr. Hak sat Joyce and her mother down. Joyce and her mother joined hands, like they used to do when she was a child and needed help crossing the street. Her mother would hold her hand everywhere, her grip tight on her, almost digging into her skin, terrified of something happening to Joyce.

He opened up his patient folder, scanned the results, and looked bemused at the both of them.

"What did your doctor say you had again, Mrs. Phạm?" he asked her as he scratched his chin.

"He's an herbalist. But none of the medicine he gave worked on me," she said, pulling out tissues from her fake Louis, ready for the news. "The pain would just hit me randomly throughout the day, and it never got better."

Dr. Hak was trying to hide his grin now. "Would you say the pain would hit you after you ate?"

Mrs. Phạm racked her brain. The dim sum restaurant with Mai, the lychee jellies she had outside the deli where she also met her sisters, and countless other times . . .

"Yes. Always after I ate," she said confidently.

"What does it all mean, Doctor?" Joyce whispered, holding on to her mother's hand even tighter. "Just tell us, we can handle it."

That was when Dr. Hak released his smile that he couldn't contain anymore. "Ma'am, you just have heartburn. I suggest you watch what you eat from now on. Nothing too greasy, less pâté, less pork belly, more greens, go easy on the fish sauce and soy sauce, and opt for condiments with less sodium. Go easy on the dessert, too."

"Jesus Christ, that's it?" Joyce exclaimed, releasing her mother's hand. "For the love of god, will you start going to see real doctors now? Your imagination runs wild every time you see that quack!"

Mrs. Phạm stared at Dr. Hak. She had blacked out the minute he told her no more pâté, pork belly, or fish sauce, and she looked at him as if the man had lost his mind. She dismissed his UCLA medical school training and scoffed in his face.

"*Over my dead body* am I giving up any of those things," she said, clutching her fake Louis bag close to her chest, as if her bag was an Asian supermarket that contained all the recipes and ingredients she loved.

· · ·

Back at her own house, Mrs. Phạm was bustling about making tea for Liam and Joyce and set out three cups. After everyone had parted ways at the hospital, Joyce and Liam had taken her home, and the car ride back was growing tense. When they arrived at the house, Mrs. Phạm couldn't help but eavesdrop, her ears pressed to the door while pretending to make noise in the kitchen.

"Look, maybe it's best I catch the next flight back to New York City," Liam said quietly. "I don't really feel like it's my place to be here right now."

Mrs. Phạm cracked open the door just a *little* to observe. It couldn't hurt to peek.

Joyce was pacing in the living room while chewing on her nails. Mrs. Phạm knew that it was a sign that she was nervous.

"I'm sorry if it's been really intense so far," Joyce said. "But really, this is it! No more intensity. It's just the wedding left and then we can head back."

"It's not that . . ." Liam's voice trailed off.

"What is it?"

"I just feel like these moments are usually reserved for a very serious partnership," Liam said finally, slumping back onto the couch. "And I'm not quite ready yet for this heaviness so early on. I don't know if I've ever really been ready."

Joyce stopped pacing, and stared out the window. Even from Mrs. Phạm's vantage point, her face looked defeated. "All right, fair enough. I can't force you to stay. I can't really force you to do anything."

Mrs. Phạm quietly closed the door, and sadness shrouded her. She knew that all Joyce ever wanted was to find love. She'd never been shy about it. Just like how Mrs. Phạm turned to food as a temporary cure, she knew Joyce turned to her Korean dramas to help mitigate her depression. Mrs. Phạm didn't have the cure for Joyce's depression, but maybe she could help with something else. She shuffled to the corner, grabbed her fake Louis bag, pulled out the vial with the last remaining droplet of the potion, and poured the last of it into Liam's teacup.

25

Mai, Priscilla, Thủy, and Thảo

MAI HAD CONVINCED HER three daughters to meet her at an address all the way across town. Despite the grumbles of traffic, braving the heat, and wondering how on earth their mother even knew of such an address, Priscilla, Thủy, and Thảo headed there around sunset, even though the unresolved anger between the sisters and their mother had worsened since the ill-fated reunion.

Thảo was the first to arrive. She parked her rental car and got out. Confusion swept across her face as she double-checked Google Maps to make sure she had gotten the address right. In front of her was a large, faded green door, taunting her to knock on it. Behind the house, the sound of the ocean waves crashing against the beach eclipsed the fighting seagulls circling in the air. Thảo took a deep breath and inhaled. It'd been years since she had been near the Pacific Ocean, and she was surprised by how much she missed California. Or rather, how much she missed home. Thảo walked up the brick pathway and hesitantly knocked on the door, and much to her surprise, her mother opened it.

"Welcome home!" Mai said cheerfully. Almost *too* cheerfully. She'd never said anything like that before. Thảo gave her a suspicious look and stepped through the threshold.

"Welcome . . . home?" Thảo repeated it back. She looked around to see an empty home with no furniture. "Mẹ, what are we doing here? Did you break in?" she whispered, as she walked through the living room, the clicks of her heels echoing throughout.

"Did you rob some unsuspecting white family?" Priscilla blurted out from behind. She walked in wearing a flowing white dress while caressing her belly, topped with an oversized sun hat. Priscilla and Thảo locked eyes and quickly looked away from each other; neither of them knew how to address their rather *sticky* entanglement. Priscilla lowered the sun hat to cover her eyes and she awkwardly pretended to look for something in her purse. Without ever admitting it, Liam's comment about both sisters' little . . . *blip* . . . with Mark had embarrassed them to their core.

There was a knock, and everyone turned to see Thủy hovering at the door, her hair piled up in a messy bun, with the same confused look on her face. Dark bags heavily drooped under her brown eyes. She looked like she hadn't slept in weeks. "Why do I feel like we're committing a crime just by being in this neighborhood? I don't think I've ever even *gone* to this neighborhood growing up."

"I'm sorry it's empty," Mai said. "I haven't stepped foot inside this home since your grandmother's funeral. I just didn't know what to do with it, especially at my age. What am I going to do with a big, empty house in a neighborhood that isn't Little Saigon?"

"What do you mean you haven't been here since the funeral?" Priscilla asked, her eyebrows raised suspiciously. "Whose home *is* this? I was joking about the robbery earlier, but now I'm afraid to know the truth."

"Mẹ, what's going on?" Thủy asked. "I thought you were getting married at the temple? Is this a rental?"

"Your grandmother left this home for me in her will." She turned around to face her three daughters. It was the first time she was alone with all three of them in one room since Priscilla and Mai's fight almost two years ago. "I don't know how she managed to afford this place; it's a mystery to me."

"Bà Ngoại bought this house?" Thảo gasped. Her eyes widened as she drank in the crown molding, the floor-to-ceiling windows, and the homey kitchen that was begging for a Vietnamese woman to simmer phở broth for hours. "How on earth could she have afforded this?"

"She must have saved every social security check for decades—" Priscilla gave a low whistle.

"—and somehow quadrupled it each time," Thủy said.

"Damn," Thảo muttered. "And I thought I knew how to hustle."

Mai ushered them to keep going to the back of the house, past the empty living room and out onto the wooden deck that looked out into the vast open water. The three sisters were dumbfounded as they kept walking through the house, their jaws dropping when they realized that the private view of the ocean forever belonged to their little family of women.

Mai gestured for her daughters to follow her out into the backyard. As soon as the Nguyễn sisters stepped outside, they gasped. The sound of the ocean had appeared distant from the front of the creaky bungalow, but behind the home, as soon as you stepped into the backyard, there was a massive view of the ocean, ready to greet them every day, for infinity. Red paper lanterns hung delicately from the trees, string lights formed a wall behind the veranda, and a paper heart cutout that spelled "MAI & ANH FOREVER" was draped across. Scattered mismatched patio chairs that had been borrowed for the wedding littered the deck.

All four women stared out at the view, taking it all in. The sun was starting to set behind the horizon as the last drops of golden hour skipped across the water.

"I finally figured out what to do with the house," Mai whispered, her voice full of conviction for the first time in her life. Thủy and Thảo tentatively sat, while Priscilla hovered behind them. Mai remained standing, the humble wedding decorations still behind her.

"I can only apologize in the only way I know how," Mai said wistfully. "And that is through actions."

Mai walked over to Thủy and gingerly took her hand in hers. She placed a small, black velvet box in Thủy's hand and curled her fist around it. Thủy curiously opened it and inside were two rings. One rusted golden band and one simple, modest ring with a tiny diamond on it.

"Aren't these your and Bố's wedding rings?" Thủy asked, confused. "Why are you giving them to me?"

"They're both fake," Mai said with an apologetic smile. "The diamond is cubic zirconia and the other isn't even gold, I think we spray painted it to make it look gold at the time. I was so embarrassed to be wearing fake rings. Your father never got me a real ring, even when we finally had money. Oh, how I *hated* how poor we were. It was shameful to me because I wanted to give you all the world, when I couldn't even have it myself."

Thủy stared at the little box in the palm of her hand, and tears began to well.

"Con, I spent years. *Years.* Trying to break you and Andy up," Mai said, cupping Thủy's chin. "Because I simply didn't want you to end up like how your father and I did. I thought you needed a man like Daniel—someone wealthy, with a fancy car, and a nice watch. But you weren't yourself when you were with him. Around Andy, you are calm, you are your true beautiful self. These rings symbolize something. Just because it was broken for me, doesn't mean it will be for you."

"You want me to marry Andy?" Thủy whispered.

"Yes, con. He's a good person," Mai said. "Much better than most people, especially me. You will be very happy."

Thủy turned her head away and tried not to let the tears overwhelm her. She closed her hands around the velvet box and tucked it safely into her purse. Her heart was full of thoughts about Andy. She hadn't seen him since their brief interaction at the hospital when he refused to speak to her. Her mind was convinced that he wouldn't ever forgive her. What were the chances that he was still in love with her after what she did to him? She placed the blame entirely on herself and only herself.

Mai turned toward Thảo. "My youngest child. So independent, free-spirited, and stubborn, but also my loneliest. You've been running for so long. I know you want to come home; you just don't know how to," she said. She pressed a set of keys into Thảo's hand. "I took the money that Anh was supposed to pay me to marry him, and I signed a one-year lease for you so you can have an office here. You can choose to use it if you want to move your business back here. I miss you, con. Come home. I want you here." Mai paused and looked at her other daughters. "*We* want you here."

Thảo stared at the keys in her hands, her mind churning. A year ago she'd have stormed out had her mother signed a lease without asking her permission. But now she was exhausted. Her mother had recognized her exhaustion in a way that only a mother could. Thảo just wanted to rest for a bit and not chase young nights in Sài Gòn that only made her older. She clamped her hands over the keys and nodded as she allowed herself to cry for the first time all year. She was more than ready to come home. She was ready to be wanted.

"Mẹ, you . . . you still kept the money that was meant for the arranged marriage?" Thảo asked, as tears brimmed in her eyes. "Even though you're marrying for love?"

Mai clucked her tongue, and lightly hit Thảo on the back of her head. "Have I taught none of my daughters anything? Marriage is a contract! With love *or* without love, get that money no matter what!"

"Hey!" Thảo exclaimed, spewing a series of profanities under her breath.

"Finally, my most stubborn daughter. My firstborn," Mai said as she turned to Priscilla. "Our relationship was always the most fractured one. I was scared when I had you, and that fear kept growing. You will soon experience that same fear. I put too much on you to be perfect, to be an example for your younger sisters. I'm sorry, Priscilla. I've never said those words to you before, but I *am* sorry."

Priscilla was silent. She held the same protective stance she had over her stomach since she walked in. She didn't know how to bend and accept her mother's apology because she wasn't sure if it was real or not.

Mai gave her a sad look. "I don't want to lose any more time between us, especially when my grandso—my *grandchild* is on the way." She pulled out a folder, removed a stack of papers, and handed it to Priscilla.

Priscilla reached out and opened it. Her eyes scanned the document, widening every second. She shook her head and pushed the papers back to her mother. "Mẹ, what are you doing? I don't want it. I don't need it. I don't need *this*."

"I know you don't *need* it, con," Mai said. "But I don't want to wait till I'm dead to pass it on. It will make me happy knowing you are close by, with my first grandchild safe and warm."

Priscilla pursed her lips. She stared at her mother, taking her in, trying to understand the woman before her. She tried to see her as not her mother, but as Mai Dương. Was this another one of her traps? Was she being sincere? Was the apology real? Mai Dương never apologized to anyone in her entire life. Behind Priscilla, the sun had finally set, and turned the lights off for the night. The only light that illuminated the backyard came from the string lights meant for the wedding ceremony. Priscilla looked out into the ocean, closed her eyes, and she finally allowed her mother's words to wash over her, like a gentle wave looking for a place to rest. Priscilla's shoulders softened, and the crease in her brows released. When Priscilla was finally able to let go of the past, everyone around her, and watching from above, was able to breathe a sigh of relief. The entire lineage of Dương—past, present, and future—was able to move on together. Because finally, a Vietnamese mother and daughter had met in the middle.

"Pris, what is it?" Thủy asked softly.

Priscilla began laughing. Her wheezing from the laughter loosened her hands around her belly. "She gave me the house. *This* house. I thought I'd never, *ever* move back to California."

Mai reached out for a hug and though Priscilla hesitated, she awkwardly went to her mother and reciprocated. The Nguyễn women weren't big huggers, not because they didn't want to—they never learned how to be. Priscilla eventually managed to relax, leaned in a bit more, and allowed herself to open up to her mother for the first time in her life. Her mother's jade bracelet touched the back of her neck and the stone felt cool against her skin.

That's when Priscilla knew the apology was real.

• • •

The next day, Anh went to Priscilla, Thủy, and Thảo to formally ask for their mother's hand in marriage. He took them out for coffee and boba, and the three women stared intensely at Anh, memorizing his newsboy cap, brown eyes, and crooked teeth, while sipping on their drinks. Anh looked nothing like their father and his disposition was also the complete opposite. Though they internally already approved of him, they still had doubts about men in general, given what they'd all gone through the past year.

"Why do you want to marry our mother?" Priscilla asked, her CEO skills came roaring in, as if she were interviewing him for a position at her start-up.

"Because she is selfless. She puts everyone first before her."

"What do you love most about our mother?" Thảo asked, her MBA kicking in, as she calculated Anh's ROI and whether or not he would be a good investment to make.

"Her humor." Anh laughed. "She's absolutely ridiculous. She makes me laugh all the time, even though I know it's not intentional."

"What's your skincare routine?" Thủy asked, because she was *just* a dermatologist.

"Your mother makes me wear sunscreen daily now," he said.

"Why do you want to get married?" Priscilla asked curiously.

Anh crinkled his eyes. "Because she deserves to rest, and I will love her for her. I will carry us the rest of the way from here."

Thủy immediately thought of Andy. Sweet Andy, who reminded her of Anh. Thủy hoped and hoped that Andy believed in second chances, just as much as her mother did. Thảo felt empty, having no one to think of, after a year of chasing shadows. All she saw was a faceless figure in front of her, and she hoped that that face would become clear one day. Finally, Priscilla touched her belly, because just as their mother had finally found her once-in-a-lifetime kind of love, so had she.

After all three checkpoints cleared, they realized that Anh and Mai were truly in love. And like any good Vietnamese daughter would do, they paid the bill and took their soon-to-be stepfather home to their mother.

THE WEDDING

26

The Wedding

FORMAL INVITES ARRIVED IN red envelopes with gold embossing. Informal invites arrived in the form of gossip. Mrs. Đào told Annie Lau, who told her best friend, who *then* told the gossip queen of Little Saigon, Vivi Phạm. Vivi Phạm spread the word at one of her infamous karaoke parties, where she made everyone at the party eat her special chả giò and get drunk off banana wine that she had brewed herself. Old Man Chu had choked on one of the egg rolls because he didn't chew properly, and was given the Heimlich maneuver. The first sentence out of his mouth when he recovered was "Where is Jacqueline Hồ?" Jacqueline, of course, was hiding in the corner, away from his vulturelike wrinkled hands. Anyway, not a soul could believe the gossip they had heard! Everyone raised their eyebrows and repeated the name to make sure they had heard correctly.

Mai Dương—not Mrs. Mai Nguyễn—*Mai Dương*, of Garden Grove, Orange County, age sixty-five, the oldest of three sisters, and mother to three daughters, was to be wed to Anh Lê, age sixty-five, of Cần Thơ, Vietnam, a widow, father to two daughters.

Everyone who is *anyone* was invited to their wedding. Their wedding reception was to be held at the most expensive seafood buffet, in their Podunk part of Orange County. The couple had met through rather suspect circumstances, but it wasn't the Vietnamese way to disclose any illegal back channels that could open their little community up for investigation—*especially* by immigration. So, they knew how to circle the gossip without getting caught. All the women scratched their heads and whispered behind their hands, wondering why Mai had gone back to her maiden name, and why she decided to marry again, after decrying marriage and Vietnamese men forever.

"It must be one of *those* marriages. She *does* live alone and she *does* love money," Mrs. Đào had whispered at the karaoke party. "I wonder how much she got out of it?"

"Well, it's certainly not for love. Who gets married for *love*?" Vivi whispered back, as she plied Mrs. Đào with more banana wine, trying to get *more* information out of *her*. "She must have gotten seventy thousand dollars out of the deal. *At least.* I suppose the man isn't *hideous*. They'll be stuck in that house for a bit, while immigration checks in on them. Might as well have something nice to look at every day. But you *know* it's fake, no such thing as love in a marriage."

"I don't know," Mrs. Đào whispered back. "I saw them holding hands at Mile Square Park the other day as they made a lap around. They were holding on to each other and smiling."

All of the gossipy women fell silent as they wondered what that would be like—to experience that kind of love. The kind of love where they didn't have to worry about putting food on the table, because love was enough to feed their hunger. It had been a long time since any one of those women were held in such a comforting embrace that, for once, they weren't jealous of Mai Dương. They were in fact, secretly, cheering her on.

"Do you think he has a brother?" Annie Lau asked wistfully as she stared at her passionless husband whom she'd been married to for over forty years. He was slumped over in the corner, already fast asleep, a half-eaten chả giò dangling from his mouth.

. . .

On the morning of the wedding of Mai Dương and Anh Lê, the whole family gathered at Kim Su Seafood Restaurant on the corner of Bolsa Avenue and Ward. In lieu of a formal tea ceremony where traditionally the groom would ask the bride's family for her hand in marriage, both sides of the wedding party decided to buck tradition and go for a hearty dim sum brunch at the same restaurant where Mai, Minh, and Khuyến had first reunited. The waitstaff was overly cautious about their return, and had armed themselves with several layers of clothing for extra padding, *just in case*, despite the 90-degree weather outside.

The bride and groom had opted out of tradition because they were both doing something for themselves for the first time in their lives, breaking what had been expected of them. They were finally marrying for love.

The family hadn't been together since the hospital, where everyone nervously sat waiting for Mrs. Minh Phạm's *proper* diagnosis. Once they realized it was just heartburn that had been plaguing her this whole time, the wedding planner informed the dim sum restaurant to keep all the greasier foods away from her plate and to provide a *special* menu instead. Fewer chicken feet, more gai lan, despite Mrs. Phạm's attempts to convince everyone that *she was fine*. But her protests fell on deaf ears, especially her daughter's. Joyce still hadn't forgiven her. Mrs. Phạm had officially been marked as the *most* dramatic of the Dương sisters, usurping Mai's seat.

The women began trickling in slowly. All the aunties wore matching áo dài and all the first-generation women wore a mix of traditional and modern outfits based on how they felt, because it was their right to be able to go back and forth and define their identity as they saw fit. Thủy walked in alone. Priscilla waddled in with Lily's help. Thảo also trickled in alone. Elaine walked in holding on to Dr. Hak's arm, showing him off like she had won the Westminster Dog Show. Christine and Rosie sauntered in, rather late, after smoking weed together in the parking lot. Joyce walked in with Liam, who looked very confused about what year it was and why he was still there. Somewhere above, Mrs. Lý Minh Dương was smiling, watching from afar, because she knew that the Dương women were close to the end of their dramatic saga.

Mai and Anh sat at the head of the table, next to her sisters, Kim, Minh, and Khuyến. As everyone began settling in and piled their plates high, there was a collective *smacking* in the air, and the dwindling conversation only meant that the food was to their liking. Everyone was enjoying themselves except Mrs. Phạm, who'd been stuck with piles of greens, because Vietnamese people didn't know how diets worked.

As Mai looked around the room, she couldn't believe the sight before her: peace among all the Nguyễn, Phạm, Lâm, Dương and Lương women. She squeezed Anh's hand and thought of her great-great-great-grandmother who had fled to Cambodia to run away with a man she'd fallen in love with, and Mai realized she would have done the exact same thing—because she was cut from the same cloth, just like every woman who crowded the dim sum restaurant.

● ● ●

Mai Dương stepped out in a cascading red áo dài with white silk pants, and wearing a khăn. The gold oval headpiece looked like a cosmic halo. Having the ocean as the backdrop set a rather opulent mood for the ceremony, especially for the small crowd of elderly Vietnamese folk who hadn't seen the ocean in years. Mai adjusted the bouquet in her hand nervously as she felt her jade brace-let brush against her other wrist, the coolness of the stone calming her down. She walked down a path covered in petals that led out to the veranda, and her gown flowed like a river behind her, hugging her curves. The crowd gasped at how strikingly she looked like her mother, the late Mrs. Lý Minh Dương. And it gently reminded everyone watching that, once upon a time, Mai Dương was a woman first.

Minh, Khuyến, and Kim stood at the front of the aisle, holding bouquets, along with Anh, who began tearing up. His two daughters flanked his side.

"Isn't that the gold khăn that belonged to Mẹ?" Khuyến whispered to Minh. "How did she get her hands on it?"

"I think she found it in the attic at Mẹ's house," Kim whispered back.

"I mean . . . she's not going to *keep* it, right?" Khuyến whispered back even louder, as Mai made her way down the aisle, with her three daughters walking beside her. "That headpiece should be passed around. What if Elaine wants to get married? Or Christine? She doesn't get to just *keep* things like that."

"You're right," Kim said. "What if Rosie and Lily want to wear it on *their* wedding day, too?"

"*Oh please*," Minh hissed loudly, as Mai shot them a dirty look from down the aisle. "We all know Joyce is getting married next. Do you see the way Liam looks at her?"

Kim and Khuyến stifled their laughs. "I know you love to ignore reality, but that man is counting down the days when he can go back to New York City and never be around us again. I've never seen a man pray harder for a natural disaster to miraculously happen."

"I wouldn't be so sure," Minh said, a devilish glint in her eye. "He stayed for the wedding, did he not?"

"We were taking bets on when he'd leave," Kim said, her tone full of curiosity. "I *am* surprised he stayed."

"What'd you do, handcuff him to the radiator?" Khuyến asked suspiciously.

"The man *chose* to attend the wedding of his own free will. Nobody *forced* the man to stay," Minh said, her voice slightly higher pitched than normal. "I suspect he'll be around awhile, perhaps maybe even forever."

"Please, who cares! Did you *see* the way Dr. Hak looked at Elaine? Elaine is definitely getting married next," Khuyến said with pride.

All the sisters reluctantly agreed that Dr. Hak was in love with Elaine. All the mothers were jealous that Elaine had bagged a doctor—and a handsome one at that!

"A doctor in the family! *Finally!*"

"You did well. You bested us all. Marrying your daughter off to a *doctor*."

Khuyến beamed. "Well, who can turn down Elaine's *beauty*? She got it from *me*. It is, after all, *my* genes."

"I mean, I did see Dr. Hak *look* at Joyce when they first met, but you know she was taken," Minh said.

"Oh *please*. Don't lie on a day like today. It'll ruin the setting."

When Mai finally arrived at the front, she turned to give Minh her bouquet and though she smiled through her teeth, her eyes were full of daggers as she told them politely and quietly, barely above a whisper, to all *shut* the *hell* up. She turned back toward Anh and instantly became demure again, a glow radiating off her. She was a woman in love after all; she was above pettiness . . . at least for a *little* bit in front of her soon-to-be husband.

The moment Anh and Mai locked eyes, even all the gossip queens of Little Saigon who witnessed that day could not deny their love for each other. It was truer than anything they'd seen in their lifetimes.

When the monk asked who represented Mai Dương, Priscilla, Thủy, and Thảo all bowed in unison behind their mother. Because despite the tumultuous relationship they all had with one another, between mother and daughters, sister and sister, the invisible filaments that bonded them was the same umbilical cord that kept the billions of stars together in the Milky Way.

. . .

The reception was boisterous, and in traditional Vietnamese Southern California fanfare, full of horrible karaoke, flowing cheap alcohol, and seven courses— including shark fin soup (though a few guests questioned if the shark fin was real or not because Mai was *notoriously* cheap). While someone's drunk uncle was screeching into the microphone, Mai and Anh walked hand in hand, visiting each table, collecting all the red envelopes full of money to start their new lives together, and they personally thanked each guest for coming.

All the drunk aunties, mothers, and queens of Little Saigon sat in a dark corner, gossiping about the women and their daughters, their sisters, their cousins, their daughters' dates, and of course, the bride herself. Even though the crowd couldn't see them, they could see all.

"This wedding is ostentatious. Mai is clearly just showing off."

"She rented a home by the *water*? *Just* for the ceremony?"

"Look at Thảo, her youngest daughter, she's not even wearing an áo dài for the reception."

"Does she hate being Vietnamese that much?"

"I thought she lived in Sài Gòn?"

"Doesn't make her more Vietnamese if she's wearing *that* dress."

"Look at Old Man Chu over there. He's about to choke on the cake; should we help him?"

"Leave him, it's his time to go on to the next life, anyway."

"Look at Thủy Nguyễn. Where is that *weak, poor* boyfriend of hers?"

"Oh, Andy? I heard they broke up. She cheated on him with someone richer."

"Good for her. Get that bag."

"Oh my god, is that John Cho over there?"

"Quick, hand me my lipstick."

"Why didn't Mai have more Vietnamese food options? Why are there so many American dishes here?"

"Are you surprised? Look at Mai's daughters. So Americanized. Probably eat cheeseburgers for dinner and hot dogs for breakfast."

"Why is Joyce Phạm dating a smoker?"

"That man looks like he's about to keel over any minute. I walked past him earlier and almost choked on the air around him."

"And the man is *Korean* no less. *Tsk tsk*."

"I think Elaine Lâm's date is Korean."

"That's okay, though, he's at least a *doctor*."

"And *look* at Priscilla, can you believe she's not married and about to have a child?"

"Mai must be so embarrassed. I wonder who the father is."

"I heard it was some British man."

"Of course she would be chasing a white man."

In the other corner, all the first-generation women sat clumped together, staring suspiciously back at the gossip queens of Little Saigon—the same women who had talked about them over the years, ever since they were born on American soil. They meddled in their lives, slyly asking who they were dating, where they were going for college, what score they got on their SAT, and how much they made a year.

"Do you think they're talking about us?" Lily asked, a hint of worry in her voice.

"Duh," Christine snorted. "You've just been too stuck in numbers and code your entire life to realize what's going on around you."

"Leave Lily alone, she's the most brilliant intern I've ever hired," Priscilla said, rubbing her belly, her ankles groaning under the crushing weight.

"Don't even get me started on *you*," Thảo snorted. "You two are definitely related, cut from the same cloth."

Priscilla shot her a death glare. "Technically, my head *is* up in the clouds. I *do* work for a cloud start-up where we do provisioning for the—"

Everyone groaned and cut her off. "Please, stop boring us with that."

"Oh my god, is that John Cho over there?" Christine whispered.

"Quick, hand me my lipstick," Rosie said.

"He's too old for you," Elaine said.

"Please, I can get *anyone*," Christine said as she applied lipstick. "Just watch me."

"Sorry, you misunderstood me, I said he's too *good* for you," Elaine said.

"*Shut up.*"

"Am I going to die alone?" Thảo asked over their voices, as she slumped over in her chair, watching her mother and her mother's new husband dance the night away.

"Don't be so defeatist. There's always Mark." Priscilla gave her a smirk.

"God, had I known he was your sloppy seconds, I'd never have touched him."

"Whatever, you brought him with you like a carry-on bag from Vietnam."

"At least I didn't go around post-breakup, ho-ing myself out to anyone on Tinder and getting knocked up because of him."

"Would you just shut the f—" Priscilla suddenly cried out and held on to her belly; she felt a deep pain inside of her. "Oh shit. *Fuck. Fuck.* I'm contracting. Shit the baby is coming early. *Shit. Fuck. Shit!*"

All the women jumped up at once. Not since they rushed Mrs. Phạm to the hospital did they spring so quickly into action. Efficiency ran through their veins, and everyone began doling out assignments, while the men uselessly stood to the side, looking utterly confused.

Mai shoved her new husband out of the way and ran toward her oldest daughter the moment she heard the commotion. Khuyến and Minh also jumped in, both crying out, "It's time! It's time!" They all said a prayer to Buddha, and thanked Auntie Hứa for her prediction because her predictions had all come to fruition so far. They had prayed and prayed for this moment, for this particular prediction to come true, because it could break the curse of their family's lineage. The birth of a grandson finally meant that the tides would turn for their family.

Everyone scrambled and made way for Priscilla. In her bridal gown, Mai mowed down people, pushing them out of the way as if they were bowling pins. She got to the front and yelled at the driver to open a door for her and yelled for Dr. Hak to follow them, just in case Priscilla gave birth in the car.

Mai screamed at the poor old Vietnamese driver to *drive faster* while Priscilla shrieked from the contractions. Thủy screamed at her mother to stop yelling and Dr. Hak calmly tried to get everyone to calm down, to not put more stress on Priscilla . . . only to be yelled at by everyone else in the car.

Once at the hospital, like a funeral procession, all the cars pulled up in a line, each car containing generations of Dươngs, Nguyễns, Phạms, Lâms, and Lươngs. All the aunties were eager to see if Auntie Hứa's final prediction had come true. Priscilla's new child would be definitive proof that Auntie Hứa was the real deal. That the strange, petite Vietnamese woman—who lived off the Kuhio Highway on the fourth-largest Hawaiian Island—had the kind of powers that could see into Asian souls and help guide them on this earth, and well into the next.

THE GRANDSON

27

Charlie Nguyễn

NO ONE WAS MORE of a wreck than Mai Dương. She paced back and forth in the waiting room. Her husband, Anh, tried to calm her down, but she swatted him away, relegating him to the corner. He sighed and grabbed a newspaper, ready to settle in for the night; he knew that their marriage had immediately begun and that there was no grace period. He intrinsically knew *to stay out of her way.* Meanwhile, Mrs. Phạm had to fan herself with a bamboo fan, to keep her anxiety at bay. This was her second visit to a hospital in a short amount of time, and the *smell* of it made her *gag.* She had to cover the smell up somehow. She got up and snuck off to the cafeteria to try to find something to comfort her—away from her daughter's prying eyes. Just *anything*! A steamed bun for Buddha's sake, a fresh-baked baguette, a soft spread of pâté . . . She was too stressed to handle this moment without carbs.

Mrs. Lâm went to find a quiet corner in the hospital to pray. She prayed for the coming of a healthy baby boy. She just *hated* that it would be Priscilla's son. Oh how she *despised* that it would be Mai's grandson and not hers. The first boy in the family should have belonged to Elaine. *Mai always got everything.* But she tried to push her thoughts aside and tried not to curse the spirit of Oanh Dương. Although Mrs. Lâm spent a majority of the time praying to Buddha for a safe delivery for Priscilla, she snuck in an *extra* prayer for Elaine to get knocked up by Dr. Hak and that she'd have *twin* boys. *Just* to upstage Mai by a little.

Thảo, Christine, Rosie, and Lily were sitting ducks in the waiting room. Their phones were out as they all mindlessly swiped left and right on Tinder. Every once in a while, a notification of a match went off, and the four of them compared notes. Joyce and Liam were quietly arguing in the corner, and bits and pieces of their conversation could be overheard. Liam kept wondering why he had no control of his thoughts and motor functions, while Joyce lectured him to stop smoking cigarettes.

As everyone was preoccupied, Thủy walked out alone to the parking lot to get fresh air. She'd been bombarding Andy all night with text messages, especially during the wedding reception. Copious texts of how much she missed him, that she wanted to talk, and how sorry she was. She had sent him another text an hour ago, that they were all at the hospital and that Priscilla was about to give birth any minute. She quickly followed up with another shameless text about the time they picked out baby names for their future kids, despite the continued silence.

Andy hadn't messaged her back once. Not since the reunion. Not since he went with them to the hospital for Auntie Phạm, then left quickly. It was excruciating.

Thủy found a small bench outside the hospital, and she sat down, exhausted. Watching the ambulances come and go, doctors sneaking a cigarette behind pillars, and nurses standing around in groups, taking a break between shifts. The stillness of the night compared to the chaos of a hospital drained Thủy. All she wanted was to bake banana bread with Andy, curl up with him, and binge Netflix.

"Is this seat taken?"

She recognized the wispy but commanding voice immediately and looked up. Andy. His messy black hair covered his eyes. Thủy could tell how nervous he was. One hand was inside his blazer pocket, while the other was straddling his messenger bag strap. He looked like he hadn't slept in days. *Sweet, Andy.*

Thủy could feel her tears forming the moment she saw his comforting face, and she quickly stood up, her hand covering her cheeks as she scanned his familiar body in surprise. Happiness flooded her. "You came."

"That's because I'm an idiot. Of course I was going to come. This is a big moment."

"You're not an idiot."

"I clearly am when it comes to you."

Thủy stepped closer toward Andy, and when he didn't react, she took another cautious step forward. "Does that mean there's still hope between us?"

Andy didn't say anything. He looked up at the sky and sighed heavily. He awkwardly ran a hand through his hair, tucking wild strays behind his ear. Thủy knew what this meant: Andy was ready to leave. Anytime he tucked his hair like that, at any party they had gone to, it meant Andy was ready to retreat home.

Thinking quickly, Thủy reached into her pocket and took out a tiny wildflower and passed it to Andy. "I saw this on my walk last week and thought of you. I pressed it to preserve it. I . . . I think a lot about how you'd grab the tiniest bouquet of wildflowers from the farmers' market every Sunday for me, and how I never appreciated it before. So, here. Take it, it's stupid."

Andy accepted the tiny blue flower, and their hands briefly touched. They both looked away, even though they felt it. That *tiny* little electric shock that proved that there was still a pulse between them. A surge of hope went through Thủy.

They both stared at the little flower. It was unassuming, quiet, and simple. It was Andy and Thủy in every way.

"How's Priscilla?" Andy asked, trying to change the topic, the flower awkwardly dangling from his hand.

"Andy, I have something to say—" Thủy started, her voice shaking.

"—*don't*, Thủy. There's nothing for you to say. I don't want to hear it. Let's not ruin the moment."

Thủy froze. The velvet box with the wedding rings weighed down her purse. She'd been carrying them with her every day since she got them, imagining the ten million ways she could ask Andy to marry her. But in every simulation, he had said no.

She just had to fucking *do* it.

"*Andy*," she said, more confidently, tracing his name, treasuring every syllable. *How many more moments would she have to be able to say his name out loud?* Still in her wedding attire, a pristine silk áo dài, in front of all the doctors, nurses, and patients at Fountain Valley Hospital—the same hospital where her grandmother passed away—Thủy did the bravest thing she had ever done in her life.

She got down on one knee.

"You told me once that all that you needed from me was possibility. I ruined an *infinite* amount of chances with you before they even began. I am sorry, Andy. Not just about Daniel, not just about my mother, but I'm sorry for taking you for granted, for not seeing *you*. I wasn't strong enough to not allow my past to dictate my future. I know it's not an excuse, but I was afraid." Thủy opened up the velvet box that contained her parents' rings, which stared up at Andy. Behind them, all the onlookers gasped, silently cheering them on. "I'm not afraid anymore."

No words. Andy just stood there, slumped over, always a bit disheveled like he'd woken up from a nap. But he looked perfect to Thủy.

"You don't have to say yes. All I need is possibility," Thủy whispered. "I promise never to squander chances with you ever again. I promise to take a leap of faith with each one. And I promise to ruin more moments if I'm lucky to have them. Will you marry me, Andy Dinh Tran?"

Andy exhaled, and he awkwardly shifted his stance. The silence had now stretched on for an uncomfortable period. Thủy's knee began shaking from being on the sidewalk for so long, and she realized that it was futile.

"Thủy . . ." Andy finally said, breaking the silence.

She knew it. Thủy tried her best to save face. She had always known Andy would never forgive her. She lowered her face toward the ground, breaking eye contact.

"God, sorry, I'm an idiot," Thủy said, fighting back tears. "I didn't mean to bombard you like this. I—"

Just as she looked up, she realized Andy had also kneeled down on one knee, and had opened his own velvet box facing her. In it was a diamond ring, an ostentatious type of engagement ring, that could only have been handpicked by Mai Dương.

As the two faced each other, both still kneeling, they began to laugh. Andy's shoulders shook with laughter as he stared at her. He stared at her the way he used to.

"My mother?" Thủy asked, smiling.

"Your mother."

Somewhere up there, her grandmother, Mrs. Lý Minh Dương, was watching, waiting, and smiling. So was her mother, and her mother's mother. And so was Oanh Dương, who according to legend, was the great-great-grandmother who had been the cause of the curse. The curse that seemed to have finally met its end. Because not only was a Nguyễn woman going to marry a good husband, but her husband would be able to invite them all home to their ancestral altar.

• • •

As soon as Thủy and Andy got back to the waiting room, holding hands, they were greeted with a chaotic scene before them. All the Dươngs, Nguyễns, Phạms, Lâms, and Lươngs were standing around and yelling.

"What the hell is going on, *now*?" Thủy cried out, exasperated, her happy moment ruined. "Why are the women in our family always getting into fights! I wasn't even gone for that long!"

All the women pointed in the same direction and she saw Mark, with his tail between his legs, carrying a bouquet of flowers in one hand and a stuffed animal in the other.

"Someone forgot it was trash day," Christine commented.

"His stench is killing people in this hospital," Rosie chimed in.

"Maybe he missed his flight back to England."

"Maybe he's been *excommunicated* from England!"

Mark nervously cleared his throat. "Look, I'm not here to cause trouble. I'm just here to do the right thing."

"And *what* exactly would that be?" Thảo asked. She jabbed a finger into his chest. She ripped the teddy bear from his arm and waved it around. "You potentially knock up my sister, and you conveniently leave out parts of your dating history. *Which* part are you trying to make right here?"

"If that kid is mine, I'm prepared to be the father."

All the women howled. They were all still in their wedding attire, and they couldn't help but bowl over from laughter at the thought of Mark being a good father.

"I'm serious!" Mark said, his voice turning dark. "I intend on helping raise the kid. Believe it or not, ever since I found out that kid could be mine, my perspective on life has changed. Especially—"

"Ugh, save your epiphany, William," Christine groaned. "Just go conquer a land or something."

"Should I tackle him again?" Andy asked.

"Why am I still here?" Liam said to himself as he stared at his hands. "I feel *so* funny. I want to go home. Please, let me go home."

Just then, Dr. Hak burst through the swinging doors in scrubs, smiling. Elaine shot up out of her chair, and her mother, Mrs. Lâm, quickly reached up and un-buttoned the top of Elaine's blouse to show off her curves. "Stop that, Mẹ!" Elaine exclaimed as she swatted her mother's hands away.

"Tell us, Doctor!" Mai went up to him, still in her wedding gown. "Is the baby healthy?"

"Charlie Nguyễn has just been delivered. A *very* healthy, beautiful baby. All ten toes, ten fingers. The mother is doing well, just recovering. You can go in and see Priscilla and the baby in a bit."

Mai cried out. "Charlie? Did you just say Charlie? Little *Charlie!*" She clapped her hands together, overwhelmed. "A baby boy! My grandson! It's a boy!" She looked at her sisters, and they all held each other, jumping up and down. They all wished their mother was alive to see this moment.

Little did they realize that their mother *was* there, watching from above, shaking her damn head.

"Charlie?" Mark gasped. He pronounced it carefully, pride filling him. "*Charlie! I have a son!*" He began to whoop loudly in the waiting room and pumped his fist in the air.

"Why does every white guy love to fist pump?" Christine whispered to Rosie.

"Oh my god, I think I just found Mark on Tinder," Rosie said. She snickered and held her phone up, confirming a photo of Mark throwing up a peace sign, on the back of a scooter in Vietnam. "You think he's into Asian women?"

Dr. Hak looked at the aunties and Mark in confusion. "The baby isn't a—"

The sound of popping champagne interrupted him as all the aunties gathered around, pouring some into red plastic cups, and toasting Auntie Hứa. The daughters, however, had heard what Dr. Hak said.

"Bless that witch's soul!" Mai cried, her cheeks flushed with pure ecstasy.

"Give me that woman's phone number," Mrs. Lâm yelled exuberantly. "I'm going to fire my psychic and go to her from now on. Which island is she on again?"

"A boy! *A boy!*" Mrs. Phạm whooped loudly, imitating Mark and fist pumping. "Finally, this family is saved! We're saved!"

All four sisters teared up, finally seeing the end of that dreaded curse that had followed each Dương woman to their grave and onto the next. In the corner, their daughters watched their mothers and Mark embrace each other and dance in a circle as they cheered on the birth of Charlie Nguyễn.

Dr. Hak walked over to the daughters, bewildered. "Shouldn't we say something?" Concern creased his perfect brows. "I don't think they heard me."

"Let's not burst their bubble just yet," Thủy said coyly. "I'd rather see the look on their faces after."

"I love seeing the look of pure disappointment on their faces," Christine said, glaring at them. "It's been a while since I messed up."

"She gave you that look yesterday," Elaine said to her sister.

All eight daughters agreed to keep quiet as they watched their mothers' faces light with the kind of euphoria none of them had ever experienced for themselves. After all, they were nothing more than just Vietnamese daughters.

. . .

Charlie Nguyễn was born with a divine mop of generous, sticky black hair that would eventually grow into jet black hair, thick as rope. The minute Priscilla saw the hair, she knew immediately. Because it was the type of hair that would be easily recognizable anywhere in the crowd. Not only was Charlie's hair Vietnamese, the baby had a birthmark on the right cheek, eerily similar to the one that Mrs. Lý Minh Dương had, once upon a time.

Charlie came out as a tiny bean, at a mere 5.5 pounds, and when Charlie was placed into Priscilla's arms, she found herself not caring anymore about all the earthly stresses that once plagued her. Because she had now entered a different realm altogether. Her life had reshaped into a different puzzle set, and now she needed to figure out how to piece it all together. But she had at least the corners done, because Charlie had centered her.

This time, this generation, it would be different.

"Are you ready to let them in?" Dr. Hak asked Priscilla gently. "I think there is quite the crowd outside, waiting to meet little Charlie. There is one particular Asian mother who is about to have a heart attack out there."

Priscilla found the strength to tear her eyes away from her baby, and she laughed, sniffling. "Send them in."

The minute Dr. Hak opened the floodgates, Mai and Mark were the first to rush in. Mark saw Priscilla holding on to the baby, and he dropped the bouquet of flowers and knelt down at her side. "Mark, what the hell are you—?"

"Marry me, Priscilla Nguyễn," he said as he took out a ring box and held it up in front of everyone. All the aunties gasped at the gigantic diamond that glistened back at them. Even they began to begrudgingly admit that the ring wasn't *that* bad. It had a good amount of karats. "I promise to be a good husband and an even better father."

"Look, Mark—"

"—I am so sorry for the way I behaved before—"

"Mark!"

"—I promise to make it up to you forever."

"MARK!" Everyone yelled behind him and he looked up.

"What?!"

"The baby isn't yours!" they all said, in various tones.

Mark almost dropped the ring box, and fell back on his hands. "How do you know? We didn't even do the DNA test."

Priscilla laughed and she carefully tilted the baby's head up. "We don't need a DNA test. She's got a head full of one hundred percent Vietnamese hair."

"But that doesn't prove—"

Behind Mark, all the aunties gasped. Mai rushed forward, practically stepping over Mark with her heels and hitting him over the head with her fake Louis bag. "*She?* Did you just say *she*?"

"Trời ơi," Mrs. Phạm gripped the bed railing, suddenly feeling the extra tiramisu cake she had snuck in earlier. "Why'd you name her Charlie then?"

Priscilla looked at her confused. "I wanted to give her a gender-neutral name."

Mark was still on the floor looking upset. "So, it's not mine . . . ?" he asked in a whiny voice. A faint Tinder notification went off in his phone just then, informing him of a match. Rosie stifled a laugh as she showed Christine that Mark had swiped right on Rosie earlier.

Mai clutched her heart and gestured for help from Anh, who quickly came to her aid. Dr. Hak shouted for water and a chair as everyone tried not to crowd Mai Dương.

"Mẹ!" Priscilla yelled from her bed, still holding on to little Charlie. "Are you okay? Somebody open a window!"

Chaos erupted as someone pulled out a bamboo fan and waved it furiously in front of Mai's face. Dr. Hak got a cold washcloth to put over her forehead and checked her pulse. Mai collapsed into a chair, as she realized the universe had played a cruel joke on her. Half-sentient, she began to cry out about the curse and about Auntie Hứa.

"Never mind, I don't want to go see this psychic," Mrs. Lâm whispered to Mrs. Phạm. "What a waste of money."

"The woman I go to is good," Mrs. Phạm reassured her. "She lives in Fountain Valley. Much closer. Why waste your money flying to Kauai every year?"

"What did she say this year would look like for you?"

"She said that this is the year that everything we ever wanted would come true."

"Do you think she was right?"

Mrs. Phạm looked around the room as half was taking care of Mai, while the other half was helping Priscilla and the baby. "Yes, I believe so," she said with a satisfied look, even as she could feel another heartburn coming on, punishing her for going off her diet earlier.

Mai finally recovered from the shock of it all, and she slowly got up from the chair, despite everyone protesting for her to remain seated. "Let me see my granddaughter," she kept insisting, her voice rising higher and higher, until everyone caved.

Anh and Dr. Hak both held on to Mai, and she managed to inch her way toward Priscilla. The moment she looked at her first grandchild, she knew her mother's spirit was nearby. Because above the little child's right cheek, there lay her mother's signature birthmark. Mai then looked at her oldest daughter's face, and saw how she looked at her baby. It was the same look that Mai had, nearly thirty-four years ago, when she held Priscilla for the first time. The same kind of hopeful love that only took root when you were staring into the eyes of your daughter. It was the kind of hopefulness that had the potential to break curses, despite being born in a world not built for Vietnamese women.

28

Christine Lâm and Rosie Lương

MONTHS LATER, CHRISTINE WAS scrolling through her phone while working her regular shift at her mother's nail salon. An old high school friend, Lisa, walked in, asking if she could get a free acrylic set today. Christine shrugged and said why not, and decided to join her. The two girls sat side by side, getting their nails done, gossiping about everybody in their lives. The nail technicians who ran Mrs. Lâm's shop listened in closely because they were always curious as to what the youngest Lâm girl was up to. They watched her hover aimlessly around the salon, day in, day out, eyes glued to her phone, always a *bit* out of it.

They would never say it out loud, but they felt sorry for her. Everyone seemed to have moved on with their lives, except for Christine.

Christine scrolled through Instagram with her free hand, while her other hand was being worked on. She stumbled upon a girl she knew from high school. Good, ol' gold standard, Rebecca. What a perfect Asian.

Christine scrolled through Rebecca's profile from the beginning, and watched as Rebecca went to med school, got engaged, and settled somewhere in the Bay Area working for the Chan Zuckerberg Initiative.

"Lisa, you remember Rebecca from high school? Look at this photo of her trying on her wedding dresses," Christine said, showing it to Lisa. Lisa was busy adjusting the back massager in her chair to get it to the right speed. She couldn't help but feel a tinge of jealousy as she watched Rebecca escape the fate of being just another Asian girl from Southern California.

"Didn't she end up with some white dude?" Lisa asked, barely glancing at the photo, as she blew on her nails to get them to dry faster.

"No. Indian. Doctor. Guess they met in med school?"

Lisa snickered. "Well, isn't she just the perfect Asian daughter? Whatever, who wants a life like hers anyways? She's like, not even that pretty, you know?"

"Yeah, right," Christine responded as she kept scrolling, watching all of Rebecca's friends and family heart, comment, and like all her posts, showing that they were rooting for her every step of the way. Christine sat there and kept scrolling, fully aware she had no idea what dreams of her own she wanted to achieve.

· · ·

As the sun set by the Santa Ana River, Christine and Rosie finished off the last of the joint between the two of them, and Christine flicked it into the water. Rosie coughed sporadically, slowly exhaling out the smoke from her lungs.

"Do you have any dreams?" Christine asked randomly.

Rosie shrugged. "Anything but work a nine-to-five? It'd be kinda cool to be an influencer."

"Are you serious?"

"Why not? It's an easy scam. I can hawk shit all day. I'm Vietnamese."

They both leaned back in a haze, their arms propping them up. On the other side of the river, they saw young kids tagging graffiti in the tunnel.

Rosie threw her empty boba cup at Christine. "What about you?"

"C'mon, you know this. You know I'd leave Orange County in a heartbeat," Christine said, trying to hide the irritation in her voice.

"Where would you go?"

"I dunno. New York? Shanghai? London? Fuck it, who cares. As long as it's not Costa Mesa, Santa Ana, Irvine, Anaheim, Long Beach, Fountain Valley—"

"—you mean to tell me that you don't want to be among the perfect Orange County Asians with their perfect Asian families—?"

They both looked at each other and screamed. "PERFECT NORMAL ASIANS!" And they slapped each other, screams echoing down the empty river dam. The young teens across the way shot them a dirty look. They were now higher than their mothers' expectations of them as the sun finally set behind them. It quickly grew dark. Their hands began tracing the constellations as time slowed down around them.

"How did we end up the black sheep of our families?" Christine said, after a long silence.

"Whatever, I like being a black sheep, at least I'm self-aware," Rosie said. She took out a cigarette. "Nothing matters. Everything is fake. 401(k)s, lashes, contouring, sneakerheads, those K-town boys up in Pacific Palisades, college degrees, six figures, marriage. It's all for show."

Christine lay back on the concrete and stared up at the night sky, the only sky she had known her whole life. As she looked up, seeing the same familiar stars staring back down at her, she laughed. "Remember when we talked about moving to Los Angeles? Can we please make a pact to move there one day? It sounds a hell of a lot easier than Shanghai."

"Sure, why not. Not like I have anything better to do."

They did their secret handshake and lay there silently, watching their predictable lives pass them by. They kept staring up at the sky, and accepted that they were nothing more than two Asian girls from Southern California.

. . .

Christine realized she hadn't spoken to Lisa, or any of her friends, in a while, but she didn't actually miss them that much. She went back to her natural hair color, removed all acrylics from her nails, stopped wearing heavy foundation, and began to look for part-time jobs in Los Angeles so she could attend a certificate program at UCLA. Maybe it really was time to leave the Orange County bubble, start small. Her mother took notice of her transformation and was immediately suspicious.

Mrs. Lâm barged into her room one day. "Who are you dating?"

"Nobody, Mẹ. Just going for a different look."

"Well, why not? You're not getting any younger. Find a man. Your sister is dating a doctor now; you should do the same."

Christine snapped. "I'd rather die alone than be miserable in a marriage like all the women in our family have been."

Her mom didn't say anything back immediately. She just stared at her youngest daughter, wondering what the hell had gotten into her lately. "Okay, just eat more. You look frail. There's cut fruit in the fridge." And she closed her bedroom door, puzzled by the change.

The next day, Christine sent a text to Rosie. remember that day by the river when we talked about moving to LA? u still up for that?

She saw Rosie type, delete, type, and finally she sent a text, after what seemed like an eternity. when are we going, b?

pick u up in 5.

guess her age at all. But she was surprised by how petite the woman was in stature. The legend seemed taller than the woman herself.

"Come in," the witch said kindly. "You must be tired. Come, rest your feet."

Oanh was taken aback by how gentle the woman seemed. She was nothing like how the midwife or how the stories described her. Even the young guide wasn't sure how to describe the woman. He preferred not to meddle in such affairs of the universe; after all, he was just a simple man. He had inherited this job from his father, and his father taught him to never question the women who came to them.

Oanh followed the witch inside, and she gestured to the round wooden table on the floor. Oanh immediately sat down, seeking comfort next to the fire. Behind the witch, the beaded curtain parted, and out stepped a little man, similar in stature to the witch, carrying a tray of tea. He wore a wool hat, and he had the kindest eyes she'd seen in a long time.

"I've made you a special herbal blend. It should help warm you up faster, after braving the cold." He handed her a warm cup. "The mountains are especially harsh this time of the year."

Oanh thanked the man as she eagerly drank it, allowing the liquid to pour into her like a sun's embrace on a summer day in her village. She immediately felt heat flow through her, all the way down to her toes. The witch introduced the man as her husband, and encouraged Oanh to drink all of it. "He's an herbalist; he heals invisible scars. Though I personally think he's a bit of a quack."

Her husband grunted at her and shot her an annoyed look.

Oanh quickly downed the rest of the tea, and thanked the couple for their generosity. As she felt her body relax, Oanh gathered the courage to ask the witch the one question that she had traveled so far for.

"I came to ask you for a favor," Oanh began, nerves lining her voice. "I came to ask you to reverse the curse you placed on my family. My ex-mother-in-law, Lan Hoàng, had visited you a long time ago when I left her son for another man."

The witch stared at Oanh, and began absentmindedly rubbing her chin. "I remember this woman. Nasty little temper. Crooked face. Horrid breath. I put on quite the little show for her." The witch laughed at the memory and turned to her husband. "Remember when I told her you were smashing a snake for its heart?"

Her husband bellowed with laughter. "The *look* on that woman's face!"

"What have you brought me in exchange?" the witch said to Oanh, her laughter subsiding.

Oanh reached up and removed the jade Buddha necklace from her neck, and passed it toward the woman. It was a strange piece of jade, light purple, but in a certain light, you could see it turn into dark green at different points.

"All I have is this." She slid the necklace across the table. "My most prized possession, though, is back home. My family. My husband and my three daughters. Please, do not harm them. I am prepared to give up my life in order for my daughters not to be cursed."

The witch held up the jade necklace to the light, and she inspected it carefully. Then she inspected Oanh. The mole that sat on her right cheekbone, her thick black hair, and eyes just like her daughters' eyes. And the witch laughed. How she laughed and laughed, as she allowed time to pass through her and she saw the future lineage to come.

"Do not be so dramatic, dear," she said finally, returning the necklace to Oanh. "Pass this necklace on to your oldest daughter, and when your oldest daughter is of age, the necklace will help her bear the children she wants. She will continue passing down the necklace, throughout the generations, and the necklace will always reveal their real desires in their children."

The witch peered at Oanh and leaned in closer. "In your heart, you knew that you always wanted daughters, did you not?"

Oanh looked quite shocked. Suddenly she began laughing, too, and through her laughter, happy tears fell. "I did. I wanted daughters more than anything; I just was never allowed to wish for it out loud. But my firstborn was a son and he passed away in a miscarriage. Was that your doing?"

"Chị, I do not meddle. I only help the universe along, helping it unfold exactly as it was always meant to."

"Is my son okay? Is he happy in the afterlife?"

The witch took Oanh's hand in hers and patted it comfortingly. "He is waiting for you, whenever you are ready to join him, but it is not your time yet. It will not be your time for a long time. You will know it is time to go when the sky turns red and you can hear the sound of your third grandchild coming, waiting for you to leave so she can take your place. That grandchild will grow up and give birth to another daughter. She will then grow up to give birth to three daughters, and one of those daughters will give birth to three more daughters. You will see your son in another lifetime. Do not worry."

Oanh burst into tears, as she remembered her firstborn who never came to be. "But how will I be able to visit my ancestral altar when I pass, Cô? Only sons are allowed to invite spirits into their homes. So many daughters!"

"You will have to wait a long time," the witch said regretfully. "All your future daughters and their daughters will be scattered, beyond this country, and beyond the country they resettle in. It will take a few generations, but one day, all will be right again. When they all find their way back home, that is when you will be able to come home as well. But you will have to be patient and watch from above. That is the *real* curse."

"Cảm ơn ạ." She smiled through her tears and thanked the witch. She carefully took the jade Buddha necklace from the table, and put it back around her neck. She thanked the witch profusely and bowed at her. "Cô, what is your name?"

The witch smiled at her, offering the strangest smile Oanh had ever seen in her lifetime.

"My name is Linh Hứa. But you may call me Auntie Hứa."

30

Mothers and Daughters

MRS. LÂM KNEW THIS DAY would come eventually. She'd done her best to keep her daughters as close to her as possible. Her claws had been practically digging into them since they were cut from her. But then came the time when even she had to acknowledge that she had to let them go.

"You know, Khuyến, you should have let them leave your nest years ago," Mai said to her as they sat folding clothes at Khuyến's house and organizing boxes for Christine's move to Los Angeles and for Elaine to move in with Dr. Hak.

"And what? And have my daughters turn out spoiled like yours? Your girls were scattered all over the world, and never once did they call you. Not for years!" Khuyến snapped back as she began to slowly pack all the clothes into boxes, her heart feeling heavy.

"Your daughters can't be your whole world, you know," Mai said as she sat on the edge of the bed, and patted her sister's hand. "You need to live for yourself. Have you considered meditation?"

Khuyến scoffed. "Don't pretend to suddenly be so *wise*. After all, you were the one who visited the same psychic for over ten years, fretting over your daughters, trying to predetermine every single move they would make."

"And look how they turned out! Financially stable, full of accolades, and all in healthy relationships!" Mai waved her off. "For Buddha's sake, one of them is even *John Cho's* dermatologist!"

"Trời ơi!" Mrs. Phạm walked into the room and gestured toward Mai. "This woman suddenly has amnesia over everything that happened the past year. Now she thinks she's so wise just because she's in love, has a grandchild now, and fixed her relationship with her daughters."

"Being a *grandmother* changes things, you know." Mai sniffed. "I'm more relaxed now. Now I can just have fun, enjoy my life as a grandmother instead of as a mother."

Mrs. Lâm's hands began to shake and she gave up folding, throwing the blouse haphazardly into the box. She quickly turned her head to hide her tears from her sisters. Both her sisters sprang up and ran toward Khuyến. She was never quick to cry.

"What's wrong?" Mrs. Phạm said. "Trời ơi! You're acting as if Christine is going to India! She's just going to Los Angeles. That's barely an hour's drive. Call an Uber, that's what the kids are all doing now. Splurge a little, have someone drive you instead."

"Terrible traffic, the five all the way up," Mai agreed. "Thankfully, Anh *loves* to drive. So all I get to do is be a passenger."

Mrs. Phạm rolled her eyes. "Yeah yeah, we get it. Your husband is *amazing*."

Mrs. Lâm couldn't stop herself. She finally allowed the floodgates to open, unleashing everything inside her.

"Come now," Mrs. Phạm said gingerly. She rubbed Khuyến's back. "This is all good! Enjoy an empty house, enjoy the silence! *And* who knows, maybe Dr. Hak will propose this year. You could have your first grandchild soon enough!"

Mrs. Lâm bawled and bawled. Minh and Mai stared at each other, concerned, wondering how to comfort Khuyến, who was always so tough and never asked for help. She was, after all, the youngest child, the one whose words could cut through glass. The military tank.

"What's wrong, Khuyến?" Mai asked gently.

Mrs. Lâm hiccupped, and soon she was able to calm down. "I won't have Christine working for free for me anymore," the youngest managed to say. "I'm going to have to hire someone and *pay taxes*."

Minh and Mai nodded empathetically, and they clicked their tongue, knowing how difficult that would be. The IRS was worse to them than immigration and TSA combined. They kept patting Khuyến's back, trying to comfort her and to get her to look at the bright side of things.

"Stupid girl," Mrs. Lâm sniffed as she held Christine's sweater, which had the words *sugar baby* embroidered over it, and caressed it. "I could never control her. So stubborn."

"Well, she's just like her mother," Minh said.

"I know someone who can take care of your tax *problem*," Mai said confidently.

Both Khuyến and Minh looked at Mai and cringed.

"I don't think either of us are going to use any of the people you go to."

"We'll stick with our own connections."

• • •

Everyone in Little Saigon knew the Dương women were dramatic, emotional, loud, and always entangled as someone's inamorata or *something else.* Nevertheless, their saga had provided the little urban village with enough entertainment to last for decades. In fact, it reminded them all of being back in Vietnam, where everyone was always in each other's business, where the gossip was more reliable than the papers.

Mrs. Mai Dương walked into the coffee shop in a pair of new kitten heels and her staple fake Louis Vuitton bag hanging casually off her arm. On her other arm was her husband, Anh Lê. It had been a year since they got married. A year since her mother passed away, and a year since her granddaughter was born. *One marriage, one funeral, one pregnancy.* A box of Lysol wipes stuck out from her purse flap and she took one out and immediately began wiping down all the tables at Elaine's new coffee shop, which was currently being renovated. (Not that kind of coffee, the *other* kind of coffee shop. A *Vietnamese* kind of coffee shop.) She stared in disgust at the dim lights, the metal pole that was smack dab in the middle—so odd for a coffee shop—and the peeling wallpaper that seemed stuck in the seventies. Mrs. Dương wasn't stupid though; she knew what that pole meant. She'd seen photos *and* movies before.

"Odd event venue for a baby's first birthday party." Her nose wrinkled at the faint smell of cheap latex and ceiling mold that had been painted over as an attempt to cover it up. She slapped Anh's hand away from resting on the table. "Don't touch anything. I bet there's semen everywhere. You'll get cancer."

Anh shrugged. "It can't be all that bad. At least this place is friendly for the elderly."

"What do you mean?"

Her husband pointed at the metal pole. "Just in case we get tired crossing the room, we have a pole to lean on." Mrs. Dương opened her mouth to correct her husband, but then slowly closed it. She didn't want him to be a repeat customer around the seedier parts of Little Saigon—not like Old Man Chu and his gang.

Speaking of Old Man Chu, she heard a hacking behind them, and she turned around to see Old Man Chu choking on his bubble tea in the corner. "Yes, there is *definitely* semen everywhere," she muttered under her breath, and shuddered at the image of it all. Jacqueline Hồ walked past Old Man Chu, and he began to choke harder, begging her to put her arm around him and help him spit out the rogue boba lodged in his throat. But she rolled her eyes, and left him to fend for himself, muttering under her breath for a quick death.

"Trời ơi, don't be so picky," Mrs. Lâm said as she walked out and set out the food platters. "You're lucky Elaine owns this coffee shop so she can put on this event for *your* granddaughter. For *free.*"

"Yes, yes, my granddaughter is really lucky," Mrs. Mai Dương whispered, watching in horror as the baristas dressed up in bodycon dresses, with their bosoms hanging out, went around serving guests mini boba teas. If they bent any lower, they'd have matched the bulbous tapioca pearls. "Looks like a Vietnamese Hooters here."

"That's the idea, Auntie," Elaine said, placing her arm around her aunt and steering her toward the main area. "I'm thinking of franchising soon. What do you think? You want to invest? Take a bit of a cut?"

Mrs. Dương raised her eyebrows. She was never one to turn down a potential business venture. She wouldn't necessarily be the *main* pimp; that was work she disapproved of heavily. She had no *idea* how Khuyến could do it, day in and day out, operating on such loose morals. What would her next life be like? The karmic retribution would be deadly. *However,* being a side investor, the silent backer—but not the *main* pimp—was okay in her book. "Call me on Monday," she whispered to her niece as she grabbed a bubble tea off a passing tray, and walked over to join her sisters in the corner.

"Congratulations, Mai," Kim said as she scooted over. "I heard Andy and Thủy eloped." They turned to the corner to see Thủy and Andy slow-dancing by themselves, with nothing but love on their faces.

"Don't congratulate me just yet. Now I'm legally stuck with a poor son-in-law," Mai groaned. "Their family has no money. Just a bunch of social do-gooders who all work in *nonprofits.*"

All four sisters clucked their tongue, feeling sorry for Mai for getting stuck with such a poor son-in-law, forgetting the fact that just a year ago, Mai had welcomed Andy into their family with open arms.

Yes, it had been a full year.

They let the moment sink in. They all leaned back quietly, taking in the scene before them. Never in a million years would they have been able to envision the scene before them. The patched-up lines in their family cracks had allowed them to come back together again. Without realizing it, each sister—Kim, Mai, Minh, and Khuyến—were touching their various jade jewelry on their body, thumbing it to feel the coolness of the stone against them. At that moment, they all quietly thought of their mother, and their mother's mother, and eventually they thought about Oanh Dương, the woman responsible for the family's curse. Though they'd never admit it in public, they were all grateful for the curse. Because having Vietnamese daughters had saved them all in the end.

Priscilla was bouncing little Charlie on her hip. Thảo was laughing with a new mystery man she had brought as her date. Andy was holding Thủy from behind. Elaine was making use of the metal pole in front of Dr. Hak, wrapping her legs around it to do a full spin. Rosie and Christine looked bored as usual in the corner. Joyce and Liam were talking to Lily and her new boyfriend, James, a civil engineer, whom she had met on recent travels. These were the women of the Little Saigon diaspora, and though they had all gone their separate ways the past decade, they finally managed to find their way back home.

Soon the cake came out and everyone sang happy birthday for little Charlie Nguyễn whose eyes lit up, and she attempted to blow out the lone candle to much applause. Exclamations of how smart little Charlie was erupted as all the aunties barked out which college she should attend and which field she should go into. Priscilla chided them, telling them that Charlie would be able to pursue whatever she wanted. They all rolled their eyes and called her an *American* mother. Another argument began to break out among all the women . . .

Little Charlie's cake-covered, chubby hand reached up to touch her great-grandmother's jade Buddha necklace, which hung from her neck. It seemed comically large against the backdrop of her gentle collar.

Mrs. Lý Minh Dương had left her fourth and final letter addressed to her *great-granddaughter*, and she had gifted Charlie the jade Buddha necklace, the family heirloom. Because Mrs. Dương had gone to a different psychic who had *correctly* guessed the sex of Priscilla's baby.

Little Charlie thumbed the necklace. Mai took it as a sign. Though Mai was just a Vietnamese daughter, she said a silent prayer for her mother's spirit to come down and join them for the party. Even if all the tall tales and superstitions only allowed sons to invite their ancestral spirits, Mai thought that the universe could make a one-time exception today. Because among all these mothers, daughters, and sisters present, surely there was enough energy there to break tradition.

Mai would later swear that her jade bracelet turned hot for a second after she finished her prayer. So, she quickly touched her jade bracelet to make sure it was still cool, and that was when she knew it was all real. Everything in front of her was real.

Epilogue

17 years later . . .

PRISCILLA NGUYỄN SAT IN the monochromatic all-white waiting room with matching marbled floor tiling. It was her first time sitting there, and she was unsure how to digest the strange environment. She sighed heavily, her foot dangling nervously over her crossed leg. Her eyes began to wander, observing how packed the room was. Some visitors were loudly snoring in the corner, having waited since 5:00 a.m. for their turn to see the strange, petite Vietnamese woman who lived off the Kuhio Highway.

She tried not to think about everything that was waiting for her back home. Priscilla and her husband were in the middle of renovating their home, a small bungalow with a green door by the beach. Before she had left, she didn't tell her husband the real reason she was on the little island of Kauai. She didn't tell her husband, her sisters, or her stepfather, Anh. Because she wanted this time for herself. Because she was a mother full of unanswered questions.

Her phone went off, and she stared down to see that her oldest daughter, Charlie, had sent several texts.

i'm sorry for yelling last week.

i just don't want you meddling anymore.

i'm 18. i don't know what I'm doing with my life.

i'm not you.

Priscilla sighed. She wondered how she had turned into the type of mother she had set out to avoid becoming. Behind her, a couple in their twenties argued in French. She caught bits and pieces of their fight, having lived in Paris for a few years, after running another start-up there. It was also where her cofounder, Lily, lived with her husband, James. Lily was still running operations over there, and yes, she still had her head in code every day. Priscilla couldn't help but smile at the young couple arguing over the compromises of everyday life and accusing each other of not being capable of love. She caught the young girl telling her boyfriend that she was going to ask the Vietnamese woman if they were meant to end up together, and her boyfriend told her how stupid she was, to waste her money over a psychic, that psychics weren't real. At that age, Priscilla would have flown to Kauai to ask a psychic about a boy, too, had she known about this woman. But now at the age of fifty-three, she had different questions to ask, questions about a different type of love.

The young receptionist looked up from her table as the clock struck 10:00, and in a bored voice she called out Priscilla's name. The whole room erupted in groans as everyone began flooding the receptionist's desk, wondering when it would be *their* turn. They were all one-time visitors from all different corners of the world, and they came to see this woman out of morbid curiosity. Though they were all distracted by the bluest waters that they'd ever seen in their lifetime, waters that were marred by Chinese tour guides frantically waving their flags to guide sweaty tourists back to the bus or by the tacky wedding destination package holders who would crowd the beaches, replete with faux hula dances that were innocuous to the white gaze, but were insulting to the indigenous souls of the island.

"Is this woman even worth it?"

"약속이 있는 줄 알았는데!"

"Tôi đợi lâu lắm rồi!"

"¡Solo tengo una pregunta!"

However, the repeat customers—the mothers who would fly into Oahu to catch a connecting flight into Kauai—knew better than to be distracted by the clearest waters they would ever see in their lifetimes. Because they were impatient for the kind of answers that no amount of silent praying, meditation, or any amount of offering to Buddha could give them. The mothers came to ask the woman about their children's futures, their grandchildren's futures, and if their husbands would ever look at them one day in a different light. Most of all, they wanted to ask if they would ever find their own happiness—a life outside of their children—even though they were never taught to seek it for themselves. Because neither their own mother nor their mother's mother had ever found it.

But Mai Dương had found it. And Mrs. Lý Minh Dương. And Oanh Dương. And now it was Priscilla's turn to find it for herself.

Priscilla got up, put her shoes back on, smoothed out her floral sundress, and tossed her bag casually over her arm. She nervously began walking to the windowless back room. As she opened the door, she saw a Vietnamese woman whose age seemed to play a mind trick on her, and whose thick hair reminded Priscilla of her mother's hair, and her mother's mother's hair. Priscilla's mother had passed away a few years ago, and Priscilla was still grieving, unable to let go of their tumultuous relationship. The grief never seemed to go away entirely, no matter how hard Priscilla worked toward alleviating it.

When Priscilla walked in, she almost did a double take because she could have *sworn* she saw her mother's reflection staring back at her from a glass cabinet. But as she looked closer, she just saw her own face, fifty-three years old. It was the wrinkles that made her think she saw her mother. She shook her head and brushed it off.

Priscilla took a seat across from the woman and cleared her throat nervously, unsure if she should speak in English or Vietnamese. The strange Vietnamese woman pushed a box of tissues across the desk toward her and Priscilla couldn't help but laugh at the gesture.

"I don't think I need that," Priscilla said in English, laughing nervously.

"We'll see," the woman responded warmly in Vietnamese because she could recognize another Vietnamese woman before her, even if it was a different type of Vietnamese woman. "Is this your first time here?"

"Yes. My mother used to see you all the time, once a year, for almost ten years," Priscilla chuckled. "So strange, because you look my age. According to her, you'd be nearly a hundred years old now."

The woman didn't say a word; she just fanned out a deck of playing cards, not looking at it once, and she closed her eyes, allowing the warm, Hawaiian sun to engulf her. Once again, she gave permission to allow the currents to enter her. When she opened her eyes, she looked deep into Priscilla's. "What is it that you want to know, Chị?"

Priscilla paused, took a deep breath, and opened her mouth to ask the one question that had haunted her for the last eighteen years. The one question that she traveled almost three thousand miles for. The one that kept her up at all hours of the night, tossing and turning until the sun came up.

From one Vietnamese woman to another, Priscilla asked the woman if her daughters would . . .

Acknowledgments

I AM NOT THE same writer (or person) today as when I first started this book. Growth thankfully happened, but not without a lot of help from my village. I first have two very special women to thank for airlifting me out of the fog. This book belongs to us.

To my agent, Stephanie Kim, whom I refer to as my binky. You saw potential in the very first iteration of this manuscript. Writing has always been a lonely road for me, thank you for being the first rest stop along the way. Without your steadfast hand, I don't think I'd have continued on. I always wondered what it'd be like to have an agent, and I can't think of a better agent who shares my love of Korean dramas, makes reality TV references, and brainstorms with me all in the same phone call. Thank you for your unwavering support, advice, and humor. Can you believe this moment? I still can't. "We did it, Joe."

When Stephanie and I went on submission, my dream was to have a Vietnamese American editor acquire this, but I didn't think it was possible. What were the chances? When I had an opportunity to work with Loan Le, I knew we could open the door into our Vietnamese community in the way we wanted to. To my editor, Loan Le, you are the reason we made it to the finish line. Your notes from the very very very beginning till the end, saved this book. This book was fated to land on your proverbial desk, because you saw the vision in a way I couldn't. You allowed it to flourish, and in the end, we made a beautiful narrative of Vietnamese women simply being women, in all the raw, messy aspects we are allowed to be. From one Vietnamese woman to another, cảm ơn Chị.

I couldn't be more thrilled that my debut landed at Atria. The excitement and support behind this book have brought on waves of imposter syndrome. *This book?*

I kept asking myself. While I was over here doubting myself, the team channeled the hustle spirit of Mrs. Nguyễn to bring this book to fruition. To the art directors Min Choi and James Iacobelli and the cover artist, Sandra Chiu, who captured the women's emotions so well. When I first saw the cover, I cried because it made the book tangible. To Libby McGuire, Lindsay Sagnette, Dana Trocker, Maudee Genao, Gena Lanzi, Paige Lytle, Liz Byer, Lisa Nicholas, Anh-Thu Truong, and everyone else at Atria . . . you all have my lifelong gratitude.

I also could not imagine a better agency to help navigate this brave new world. To Katherine Curtis, Pouya Shahbazian, Victoria Hendersen, Veronica Grijalva, Meredith Barnes, and everyone else at New Leaf Literary, thank you all for believing.

Of course, I have many more women to thank in my decade-long pursuit of becoming an author. To Jes Vu, a new friend I've made along the way in my publishing journey, thank you for all you do for the Vietnamese community. (I will never forget the Heineken vs. Bia Saigon discourse.) To my meddling mother, to whom I dedicate this book, Kimberley Duong, who supported (and questioned) my writing pursuits. My mother has always been an eccentric; a secret academic who couldn't pursue higher things because she was born the only daughter in a family of sons. Of course, Vietnamese daughters have different obligations than sons . . . I wanted to write a story of redemption, a reminder that there is still time for anyone, even if the whole world is against you.

Family has always been a touchy subject for me. There are elements of truth in this book that were taken from my own life. I used to wave my hand in a dismissive way when someone would ask about my family in polite conversation. But estrangement is real, painful, and multiplies loneliness, especially for first generation kids navigating the diaspora on their own. Are we better today? I still don't have the answer to this, but I do thank my nuclear family, despite the cracks. Those cracks are the reason I became stronger.

To my chosen family in Seattle, to whom I confided my hopes and dreams for the last ten years: During the dark winter days, you were the family and life I made for myself. To Alex Sanchez, for yelling at me for a decade to pick up the pen and continue writing, and by extension, to the Sanchez family and CJ, for taking me in as their adopted daughter for the holidays, thank you. To my other chosen family in Hokkaido, Jun and Yukiko Matsuura, I still dream of Brendon. Brendon was the reason I wrote the original short story five years ago, because

I needed an outlet for my grief. Because what psychic can predict death? To all the deep friendships throughout the years, Cherlaine Ordona; Morgan Gilchrist; Keoni Becles-Dulay; Aubrey Jackson (who read the original short story and the full manuscript); my Viet sis, Max Lam (the real Mrs. Khuyến Lâm, thank you for letting me use your Vietnamese name)—my twenties wouldn't have been the same without you all. To my oldest friend, Catherine Tran, for always picking up the phone at the oddest hours of the night to listen to me cry about my latest heartbreak. To Cat's better half, Ron Deopante, for helping me move up and down the West Coast too many shameful times to count. To Vandy Ramadurai, mostly because she will kill me if she's not in this section. To Joyce Kim, for holding my hand throughout the edits and bringing my dog into my life. And of course, to my lifelong fellow writer and friend, Sarah David, I wish we could celebrate with a 40 oz on a rooftop somewhere and laugh about how our lives turned out. I miss you all very much. I am nostalgic for the past, but hopeful for the directions your lives are heading. One day, we will all converge again, and it will be beautiful.

This story took me five long years to finish. My rabbit, Nimbus 2000, sat at my feet while I wrote the beginning, and soon enough, a new addition joined our little family: my dog, Pili Huynh, who sat with me through the edits. This book was originally a product of grief and loneliness, and as the years unfolded, I began to see hope, just like the women do in my story.

Finally, to the strange, petite, Vietnamese psychic I saw in Hawaii all those years ago, who is probably winking at me right now . . . you were absolutely right. Life turned out well. Because this generation, this time, things will be different.

Thank you for reading all the way till the end. Until next time.

About the Author

CAROLYN HUYNH grew up in Orange County, California, not appreciating the weather enough. She has a BA in journalism from Seattle University and an MS in human-centered design from the University of Washington. The youngest daughter of Vietnamese refugees, she focuses her writing on her mother's tall tales and superstitions, the diaspora, and memory (both real and imaginary). She especially loves stories about messy Asian women who never learn from their mistakes. After living up and down the West Coast, she currently resides in Los Angeles with her rabbit and dog. She still doesn't appreciate the weather enough. When she's not writing, Carolyn daydreams about having iced coffee on a rooftop in Sài Gòn.